Anton

Library and Archives Canada Cataloguing in Publication

Eisler, Dale
Anton : a young boy, his friend & the Russian revolution / Dale Eisler.

ISBN 978-1-894431-46-0

I. Title.

PS8609.I75A77 2010   C813'.6   C2010-902929-1

Photo of boy on cover sourced from Germans From Russia Heritage Society
Additional cover images © www.istockphoto.com/Albert Campbell
WP Chambers/Павел Жовба/Andrea Gingerich
javarman3/Aleksandr Volodin

Layout and design: Heather Nickel

Printed and bound in Canada by Friesens Printers
on 100% recycled paper

June 2010
Second printing: December 2010

Your Nickel's Worth Publishing
Regina, SK.

www. yournickelsworth. com

Anton

a young boy, his friend & the
RUSSIAN REVOLUTION

DALE EISLER

E VERY FAMILY HAS A STORY. Mine is rooted in the distant past, in an era I can only imagine and never hope to fully understand. My family's story has always fascinated and, in some ways, haunted me. Not in a menacing way, but in the sense of needing to know it better. As if until I at least tried to explore it, I would never really come to terms with myself and my identity.

The story is about my mother's family during the six-year period of 1919-1925. It's set in a small town in the Black Sea region of southern Russia. My mother's family, like countless thousands of others, eventually fled the economic and religious persecution they faced and came to the New World of North America.

So, to some degree, I think you can say there is a universal dimension to it, a story that speaks to the core of North America's immigrant society. While the immigrant experience is diverse, there is a unifying thread of the search for a better life.

My mother sometimes spoke of her life in Russia as a young girl many decades earlier. Always, though, only in brief fragments because she would become too emotional to talk of it at length. These small glimpses left me intrigued by her family's untold story and feeling unfulfilled that I didn't know more about it.

I live with regret, knowing I never pursued the story the way I had intended, by speaking with my uncles and aunts about those years in Russia. It was always my hope to take the time to hear them tell it to me individually. But one by one they died, and other than brief reflections, I never explored their story with them in depth.

As I write this, my mother, the youngest of her siblings, is the last still alive. But she now lives out her life with her memory gone, her recollections of that time many, many years ago, lost forever. A time when revolution, civil war and cruelty shaped her young life and the lives of her brothers and sisters.

There have been diverse and unconnected moments, as well as periods in my life that helped crystallize the need for me to write this story.

One was more than 30 years ago. My wife Louise and I lived in Regina, Saskatchewan at the time and were visiting Saskatoon, where my uncle, Tony, lived. He offered to babysit our young daughter one evening while we went to a movie. When we returned, I remember Tony was showing our daughter, Paula, how to play table-top hockey in his basement rumpus room.

When my wife and daughter went upstairs to visit with my aunt, Madeleine, and I was alone with Tony, I asked him about what had happened that day in 1919 when his father—my grandfather—died. He began to tell me the story, but, like my mother, quickly broke into tears and couldn't continue. I felt guilty that my question caused him pain and never asked again.

Before his death, Tony lived in a Saskatoon nursing home and, sometimes, when I was in the city, I would stop and visit him. Each time his memory was more faded and eventually disappeared.

Another of these moments came at a family reunion more than 20 years ago. I was asked to say a few words and took the opportunity to speak very briefly about that day in 1919. Afterwards, many of my cousins told me that they, too, didn't know the story well and some had never heard it. They all felt they needed to know more.

The final motivation was more intensely personal and is harder to describe. It came from my granddaughters. They have psychologically and deeply connected me to my grandfather, who died almost a century ago. My grandfather was always a distant, mythical figure to me, more fictional than real. He died more than three decades before I was born and I never felt his emotional presence in my life. Until, that is, Madeline and Genevieve entered mine.

My own two granddaughters gave meaning to my unknown grandfather. As my emotional attachment to Madeline and Genevieve deepened and I understood the closeness of a grandparent to a grandchild, my grandfather suddenly became closer, more real and relevant, to me.

For the first time, I felt his presence in my life.

The story you are about to read is more fiction than history. But its essence is true, and that's what matters to me.

IF YOU'LL ALLOW ME a short personal aside, I want to thank a few people who have helped me with their advice, perspectives, opinions, encouragement and friendship.

One is Steven Hayward, author of two widely acclaimed novels, including his award-winning *The Secret Mitzvah of Lucio Burke*. A professor of English literature at Colorado College, Steven provided me with invaluable advice, guidance and insight into the contours of Anton's story. He is a great writer and novelist.

Also, my thanks to Harry Adams in Paignton, U.K.; David Lockhart in Ottawa, Ontario; John Rainford in Lyon, France; Colin Laughlan in Vancouver, British Columbia; as well as Joe and Janice Montano in Denver, Colorado. Each of them, in their own way, provided invaluable opinions and ideas as they read the manuscript in various stages of development. Such a widely dispersed, disconnected and disparate group proved to be the kind of focus group every writer needs. My thanks as well to Heather Nickel, whose editing and design were superb.

More than anything, writing this novel made me think about the meaning of friendship and why it matters to us all. So, in that context, I want to mention Peter Lloyd, Alan Darisse and John Barrett. They, along with David Lockhart and me, number ourselves as members of a self-styled "National Roundtable," a small informal, beer-drinking social circle going back to our days in Ottawa. We gathered regularly to debate and solve the great issues of our time. Although we have gone in different directions, our friendship endures as the NRT debates continue in cyberspace. And I also want to mention Derek Ferguson and Tom Townsend, whose friendship reaches back to our lives in Saskatchewan, as well as Jonathan Massey-Smith, Jodi Redmond, Greg Jack, Bob Quinn and Colin MacArthur, friends and colleagues in the truest sense. They and many others have all enriched my life.

My high school sweetheart and wife, Louise, offered love, patience, encouragement and insight as Anton's story was being written. She has a tender heart.

And finally, I want to thank my family. This story is for them.

Dale Eisler,
Denver, Colorado
April 2010

INTRODUCTION

O N JANUARY 9, 1792 in the Moldavian town of Jassy, a treaty was signed between the Russian and Ottoman Empires that brought an end to a savage conflict between Turkey and Russia that had raged throughout the previous five years.

The *Treaty of Jassy* came after the Russians won several pivotal battles, including clashes that gave it control of the lower Dniester and Danube rivers. Under terms of the treaty, Turkey ceded to Russia the entire western Ukrainian Black Sea coast, stretching from the Kerch Strait westward to the mouth of the Dniester River. It also officially transferred to Russia a region known as Yedisan, which Russia had annexed after the war between Russia and Turkey of 1768-1774. What was then Yedisan is today a region in southwest Ukraine that lies north of the Black Sea and between the Dniester and Dnieper rivers. These military conquests came under the reign of Sophia Augusta Frederica, better known as Catherine II, Empress of Russia, and more commonly referred to as Catherine the Great. She ruled from 1762-1796.

Catherine was installed as empress of all Russia in a military coup that replaced her husband Peter III barely six months after he had ascended to power. Peter was regarded as an eccentric, slightly simple and immature man, who wedded Catherine, his second cousin, in an arranged marriage. Both had lovers and Catherine, suspecting that Peter planned to divorce her to marry his mistress, plotted to overthrow her husband. Peter, foolishly, made the decision to vacation at Oranienbaum, the Russian royal retreat on the Gulf of Finland, while Catherine remained in St. Petersburg. On July 14, 1762, Peter was deposed and arrested by the imperial guard. Three days later, Peter was shot and killed while in custody. While there was no definitive evidence, many believe that Catherine had a hand in her husband's execution.

To say Catherine the Great was a woman of excessive ambition, ruthlessness and cunning clearly would be an understatement. Indeed, in the annals of history, she ranks as an iconic figure who, in many respects, was the architect of a Russian empire that more than three centuries later—even though its stature has diminished from the influence it wielded in the mid-20th century—still ranks as a world power. Her ambition was not unusual. Hers was a time when the widely held consensus was that strong powers must grow stronger at the expense of others. Catherine sought to acquire for Russia an influence in European affairs that would equal what Louis XIV had achieved for France almost a century before.

The expansion of Russian territory was very much an integral part of Catherine's ambition. Of German ancestry, she sought to build a greater Russia, one that would replace the Ottomans as the dominant empire straddling Europe and Asia Minor. Shortly after taking power, Catherine issued proclamations in 1762 and 1763 inviting Europeans—other than Jews—to settle and farm the Volga River region, with settlers from Germany her main targets of recruitment. Catherine believed the work ethic and determination of the Teutonic people would be well-suited to exploiting the agriculture potential of Russia's unsettled regions. Many thousands of Germans, lured by the promise of free farmland and assurances they could retain their language and culture, migrated and settled the Volga. In the immediate wake of the *Treaty of Jassy*, Catherine sought to consolidate Russia's hold and presence in the new region stretching north and west from the Black Sea. Towns of strategic importance were quickly created, such as Tiraspol in 1793 and Odessa in 1794. Odessa was of particular importance. Located on the shores of the Black Sea in Ukraine, Odessa was to become a key port for the expanding Russian empire.

The territory taken from Turkish domination included vast, fertile grasslands that throughout history had been largely the domain of nomadic groups. It was, in effect, virgin land, uninhabited and untouched by agriculture. For Catherine, the Great Steppes of Ukraine in southern Russia offered unlimited potential for cultivation and agriculture production. A particularly fertile territory lay between the Kutschurgan and Beresan regions northwest of Odessa. She called it "my dowry to the Russian empire."

Catherine did not live long enough to see the promise of the steppes realized. Its development fell to her grandson, Tsar Alexander I. Aware of Catherine's success luring Germans to the Volga, in 1804 Alexander issued a manifesto inviting people from across Europe, and Germans in particular, that set out incentives to settle and farm the steppes. These immigrants were offered the same rights and privileges that had been extended to the Volga Germans four decades earlier. But Alexander also took a more selective approach, seeking "only capable agriculturists and artisans." The hope was that these farmers and settlers would quickly transform the virgin steppes into productive agricultural farmland.

The March 1804 manifesto signed by Tsar Alexander set out clear and specific incentives to immigrants from other lands who would settle the steppes. Among the concessions: religious freedom; exemption from taxes for the first 10 years; exemption from military service; interest-free loans to be repaid within 20 years;

and, a grant of approximately 80-160 acres of productive farmland. Immigration agents were put in place and immigrants organized into groups of 20-30 families, each with a self-appointed assigned leader. A welfare committee for German colonists was established in Odessa that aided in the allocation of land and the establishment of German-speaking villages on the steppes in the region north and west of that city. During the wave of immigration from 1804-1825, the German immigrants were settled in "mother" and "daughter" colonies, each assigned to one of 10 enclaves, which had within them villages organized by religious affiliation, whether Roman Catholic, Lutheran or Mennonite.

By design, the German settlers were able to maintain their ethnic identities, language, values and religious customs in their new land. Like all immigrants, they were industrious, hard working and dedicated to achieving success in their adopted home of Russia. Indeed, their stubborn Germanic nature and tireless work ethic made them exactly the kind of people Catherine and Alexander believed were ideal for settling and farming the rich, fertile virgin steppes of Ukraine in south Russia. Within a generation, the German farming communities had become well established and prosperous; in no small measure because of the qualities the people brought to the development of an agriculture economy. But with their success came tension. They were seen as outsiders, intruders of a sort, and were never accepted as part of the larger Ukraine and Russian community. In fact, their success was resented by many, attributed to the special incentives of free land and loans that had lured them eastward from Germany to Ukraine.

To make matters worse, the Germans themselves did little to integrate into Russian society, or ingratiate themselves with neighbouring native Russians. Instead, they existed as tiny national communities, focused on themselves, their language, their Germanic culture, their religion and their economic success. Contact with surrounding non-Germanic communities was infrequent and when it did happen, it was, at best, an uneasy and forced civility.

For decades, the Germans' sense of their own superiority to the Russians was matched only by the resentment felt by the Russians towards the Germanic intruders. But for the most part, this tension fell short of manifesting itself in outright hostility. As long as the Germans kept mostly to themselves, living in their small communities, they were tolerated, if not accepted. And as long as speakers of Russian and Ukrainian did not try to interfere with them, the Germans in Russia were quite happy to live their lives separate and apart.

But in the early years of the 20th century all that began to change. As German imperialism and military belligerence began to grow, unease between the Ukrainian and Russian people and the Germans in their midst grew as well. With the outbreak of the First World War, and Russia facing German-Austrian aggression because of Russia's support of Serbia following the assassination of the Austrian archduke in Sarajevo, the latent hostility many in Russia felt towards the Germans in their country became real, palpable and visible. The Great War, the overthrow of the Russian aristocracy, the violent Bolshevik revolution, civil war and famine conspired to create a culture of cruelty. The fact that more than a century had passed since the first German immigrants settled the steppes and that generations had lived peaceful, productive lives, keeping mostly to their ethnic enclaves, did not prevent the brutality that was to unfold and engulf Russia.

One such German enclave was called the Kutschurgan, named after a river of the same name. The mother colonies, or towns, in the region were Selz, Baden, Kandel, Elsass, Strassburg and Mannheim. It also included several small "daughter" colonies, or villages. One was named Fischer-Franzen.

This is the story of one boy who lived there. Some of it is true.

*The significance of friendship is that
it unites human hearts.*

CICERO

PROLOGUE

THERE IT WAS AGAIN.

He had come to expect it every night, just before he drifted off into a deep and vivid sleep.

It began ever so faintly, somewhere far off in the hazy distance.

Long ago—it was impossible for him to know how long—he had come to recognize the sound. Now he would lie in bed and wait for its return, a frightening ritual he did not understand. Each night was the same. At first he would wonder if he had heard it. Or was it his mind playing tricks on him? Then, for an instant he would hear it again. Or had he? What he thought he heard would always dissolve into a void of silence. Had it been only his imagination?

A few seconds later it would be back, this time faintly louder, more discernible and not quite completely fading away like before. Then back it came, louder still, only to fade again slightly. There was a cadence to it, a staccato-like rhythm that steadily grew stronger until it was almost more than he could bear. He wanted to scream out for it to stop, but his voice would not come. His mind would not let him and he could not force out the words that welled up inside.

Lying in bed, he had become a prisoner of his emotions, a

victim of his senses. His feelings and thoughts were locked inside, trapped by a mind that could no longer express what it had buried within. It took every ounce of energy to speak even a few jumbled words that made little sense to others, even though he knew his own thoughts. What made it worse was that his sense of hearing was painfully keen; as if to compensate for his loss of speech, it had become even sharper and more acute than he could ever remember, even as a young boy. So, as he heard the sound, his mind was filled with ideas that could never escape.

He didn't know how long it had been this way. Months, perhaps years. He had completely lost track of time. All he knew was that the sound stirred something deep inside him. It unleashed a panic that spread through him as it grew louder, until he was swallowed by a dark fear that he did not understand.

Then, both the sound and the fear would slowly fade into nothingness, retreating more quickly than it had grown to engulf him. Mercifully, the panic subsided as the sound drifted off into the distance, going back from where it came.

Sleep would always follow.

CHAPTER 1
The Kutschurgan, July 31, 1919

M Y NAME IS ANTON and I remember when my life began. I know that sounds crazy, and you probably won't believe me, which is why I've never told anyone before. But it's true. I swear. I really can remember the very moment my life began.

Not in the sense of when it actually started, like when I was born or anything outrageous like that. I don't remember that far back. Nobody does. Nobody, except maybe those people who insist they were abducted by aliens. And they don't even realize that what they're really remembering is when their life started. They think they were captured by Martians, or something, because they have this really frightening, weird memory of something happening to them.

Have you ever noticed how they all talk about the same thing? They see this bright light and then strange, scary faces of aliens from outer space. This might sound really far out, but I figure that's just them remembering their birth, which is locked deep in our subconscious. It's them emerging, head first, out of their mother's birth canal and into the bright lights of the delivery room, with doctors and nurses all wearing masks. I'd say that's enough to scare anyone and leave a deep imprint on your subconscious.

So in that sense, I guess, you could call me normal. At least, I don't think I was abducted by aliens.

In fact, as I think back on my life now, I don't remember much of anything from the first four years or so, which, I guess, isn't such a big deal. Nobody remembers much of anything before they were, I figure, about four. Unless, that is, they're lucky— which in this case means unlucky. And even then it's only a faint memory about someone, or something, or somewhere. For example, you might remember something bad, really bad, that happened. Like if someone close to you—maybe your grandpa or grandma, or worse, one of your parents, or brothers or sisters— died. That's the sort of thing you remember, even if you don't remember anything else about your life at that time and not much after until you get older and your brain's memory starts filling up with things.

For example, I know that's the case with Kaza. He was real little, only four—four years, two months and three days, to be exact—when the wagon tipped and squished his older brother Omar to death. Squished him like a bug. Kaza only talked to me once about his brother getting squished. And that was when he was six, going on seven.

We were alone, lying on our backs on the ground in my family's backyard looking at clouds on a hot, sunny, summer day. It was June 26, 1922, 1:42 in the afternoon, to be exact. We used to lie on our backs and look at the clouds a lot. It was kind of a ritual for Kaza and me. I liked looking at clouds because it made you think differently. And I know Kaza felt the same way, because we used to talk about it together. Everything changed when you were lying on your back looking at clouds. You had a completely different perspective because all you saw was the sky. It was like, all of a sudden, the world disappeared and all there was, was this big blue space with clouds floating through it. It always made me feel kind of strange to lie on my back and look up at the clouds. Not strange in a bad way. More in the sense of being small and insignificant. I guess you could say it made me think about God.

We were staring up at the clouds when Kaza said that one of the clouds looked like the wagon he and his brother were riding that day with their father when his brother got killed. He pointed to a cloud that I thought looked like a castle, or maybe even a church. But Kaza, he said it looked like the wagon that squished his brother. Kaza said something scared the two horses pulling the wagon. His dad said he thought it was a fox that ran out of the bushes in front of the wagon. The horses reared back and started galloping. The wagon flipped when the wheels bounced out of the ruts just as his dad was trying to get the horses under control while they were going around a sharp corner in the trail.

It was one of those wagons that made loud groaning sounds when it was moving. It had big wooden wheels with metal rims and big spokes. The wagon had thick, heavy wooden sides to hold hay bales. The thing Kaza told me he remembered the most was his brother's guts. "They wuh-were oozing out buh-between the buttons on his shur-shirt, and from his mouth—one of his eyes was even buh-bugged out," Kaza told me. Kaza said all he remembered was landing face down next to the road in thick grass. Just a few feet away was the overturned wagon, his brother lying on his back under its full weight. One of the heavy wooden boards meant to hold in the hay bales had pinned Omar across the stomach. "It wuh-was like he was kuh-cut in half. I kuh-couldn't see his legs, or anything. Just, luh-like, from his stuh-stomach to his huh-head."

After he said it, I didn't know what to say, so I stayed quiet and kept looking up at the cloud Kaza had said looked like the wagon that squished his brother to death. After a minute and 10 seconds I felt that I had to say something, so I said, "Do you miss your brother?" He said, "Suh-sometimes, sort of." I waited for a minute and then I said, "How does it make you feel?" He seemed to think about what I asked and didn't say anything for maybe 15 seconds. Then he said, "I-I, don't know. Mama says he's in huh-heaven." Kaza never, ever talked about it again. And I never asked again, even though over the years we talked about every-thing.

I'm telling you this story for two reasons.

First is because Kaza was my best friend, back when my life began. His real name was Kazamir, but everyone just called him Kaza for short. I'm pretty sure that Kaza's life began on the day his brother got squished by the wagon. I say that because he didn't remember anything about his life before that. And if you don't actually remember something, if you don't know it hap-pened or remember experiencing it, then it didn't happen. At least not in the sense that it's a part of your life that means any-thing. I figure things are only real in your life if you actually re-member them, otherwise it's someone else's memory, not yours, and that doesn't count.

The second reason I'm telling you about Kaza and his brother being squished is because it helps prove that I'm telling the truth about remembering when my life began. You see, I remember when Kaza's brother was killed because my life started exactly five days before Omar died. My life started when I was four years, five months and nine days old. It began on July 31, 1919, at 11:16 in the morning.

I know what you're thinking. You're wondering why I can say right to the day and minute when my life began, or when other things happened. Or how I know that Kaza and I were looking at clouds on June 26, 1922 at 1:42 in the afternoon. Or that I waited a minute and 10 seconds before I said something after

Kaza said the cloud looked like the wagon that squished his brother. Or that Kaza was four years, two months and three days old when his brother Omar died. I'm not making it up. I just know because I honestly feel like I remember to the minute. Maybe it's just my imagination, but it feels real and it's been that way my whole life. Don't ask me how I remember or why I remember things this way, I just do, and it's true.

WHEN MY LIFE BEGAN I was living in a place called Fischer-Franzen. It was a small village 52 kilometres northwest from the city of Odessa, which is on the Black Sea. Our village was in the Kutschurgan valley, and was part of a collection of ethnic German villages just north and slightly west of the towns of Selz, Strassburg, Baden, Kandel and Mannheim. Fischer-Franzen was what you call a "daughter" colony of Selz. What that means is our town was much smaller, more a collection of farmhouses, than a real town like Selz or Strassburg, which had stores and shops in the centre of town, with houses on streets that circled outwards from there. As you might expect, in our town we almost exclusively spoke German, although some people could talk Ukrainian or Russian. I know it's kind of strange, but now, as I think back on those days, my memory is in English. The reason, I guess, is because most of my life has been here in Canada, and even though I still speak German sometimes, I think in English.

Fischer-Franzen was on the west side of the Kutschurgan River, which today would put it in the region of Bessarabia in the country of Moldavia. As for Selz, Mannheim, Kandel and the other villages in the Kutschurgan Valley, they were on the east side of the river, which meant they were in Ukraine.

There was one road that ran through our village. And there were exactly 19 houses—13 on one side of the road and six on the other. On the side where there were only six houses, the yards were much smaller and the houses closer together. A wooden sidewalk ran down one side of the road, in front of the bigger houses, which was the side of the street our house was on. On the other side of the road there was no wooden sidewalk, only a dirt path. Nine of the houses, like ours, had three floors and were built from either stone or wood from trees that came from the Elsass forest, which was north of Mannheim. The four other houses had two floors. The other six across the road—like the house where Kaza lived—were much smaller, had only one floor and were small made from a mixture of brick and rough logs. All of the homes had something in front to mark their yards, either a row of bushes or stones stacked on top of each other to make a low barrier, which, by coincidence, came to the top of my head the day my life began. I was exactly 3', 1" tall when my life started.

Each front yard on our side had a walk made up of big, flat white stones laid down close together that led to the front steps of the house. And every yard of the larger, two and three-storey houses like ours had a flower garden and at least one tree. In the back, people who lived in the larger houses had big vegetable gardens, with at least two big trees—some of them apple, like in our backyard. Six of the backyards had a small house made of stone that for some reason, and I don't know why, was called the "summer kitchen," even though we used it all year round. The house where I lived with my parents and my nine brothers and sisters also had a barn, except we didn't call it a barn, where we kept our horses and the hay bales to feed them. Behind our yard was the cattle yard, which was a fenced in area of six acres. Beyond the cattle yard, the land sloped gently upwards for about 150 metres and then it was perfectly flat. The steppes, or prairies, reached all the way to the Karstal Hills, which were 23 kilometres in the distance. When I think of the steppes, the image I have is this panorama of land stretching into the shimmering distance under a hot summer sun. It was the rich soil of prairie land where we grew wheat, oats and corn in the fields and cattle grazed in the pasture. My mom said that my dad used to say that from up there "you could talk to God." I don't actually remember my dad saying that. But my mom told me, so I know it's true.

The region I lived in was called the Kutschurgan, named after the river that was only a kilometre and a half from our house and flowed southward, where it widened out and formed a *liman*, which is a lake. The river resumed at the south end of the liman and eventually emptied into the Black Sea. The Kutschurgan is a fairly wide, lazy river, its gentle banks lined with tall grass. There was a small stream called the Andrejaschevski that ran next to our village just behind the houses on our side of the road, a tributary that eventually made it to the Kutschurgan.

The "Andre," as Kaza and I called it, was where we'd go exploring when we were little. The Andre had crystal clear water and was only maybe 18 metres across at its widest point and no more than a metre and a half deep at its very deepest. It was perfect for Kaza and me to go wading. Even though our mothers told us to stay out of the water, we couldn't resist taking off our shoes and socks, rolling up our pant legs and wading in near the edge. Standing in the water near the shore we could see small trout swim by and sometimes a green mud turtle would stick its nose out of the water, take one look at us, and swim away into the reeds and disappear.

The water was cold on our feet, especially until the end of June. By then, the summer heat would warm the water to the point that we would take our clothes off and go swimming naked. Kaza was thinner and taller than me, even though I was three months older. I always envied Kaza when we went swimming in the summer because he had dark skin and never had to worry about getting a sunburn, like I did because my skin was so white. His mother was from Turkey and his dad was Bessarabian, born in Moldavia. Kaza had thick, curly black hair that seemed unaffected by water. It was like it was impossible to get Kaza's hair wet. We could go swimming in the Andre for hours, going under water, pretending we were deep sea shark hunters, and whenever Kaza's head came up from under the water his hair would look like it always did—a thicket of tight curls. I swear it was as if Kaza's hair repelled water. It would glisten in the sun and, after a minute or two, be bone dry. The best way to describe Kaza's hair is like those wire pot scrubbers my mom had hanging on the wall next to the sink in our summer kitchen. Mom used to say that when she needed a new pot scrubber, she would ask Kaza's mom to cut Kaza's hair and bring her the clippings so she could weave them into a pot scrubber. For years I believed her. But I know now she was only making a joke.

Today, this same region of what was then Russia is called Ukraine, which now is its own country, and Bessarabia, which is part of Moldavia. Almost all the people who lived in the region were farmers. They grew things like wheat, oats, barley and corn, and had animals like cows, pigs, goats and chickens. Some even had small vineyards on the slope that rose to the plains, where they grew grapes and made wine.

So, as I was saying, I don't actually remember anything before 11 o'clock in the morning on July 31, 1919. At least, not that I can say for sure, like I can for everything else afterwards. Sometimes, I think I remember something from just before that day, maybe one or two days before. But I can't be sure. For example, I have this faint recollection of sitting on my dad's knee in a room with a bunch of other men from town. They're all smoking, talking very loudly and seem upset about something. They are saying bad words. I seem to remember my dad saying in German, which, if you'll excuse the swear words means: "Fuck them, fuck the Bolsheviks. Goddammit, the bastards can kiss my ass." I can't be sure, but I think there were five or six men in the room, not counting my dad. At least that is what I think I remember. But like I said, I can't be sure. In fact, I don't even really remember my dad, other than what I am about to tell you.

The first thing I remember for sure about my life was standing next to my mother. She was crying. Not an out loud kind of crying, more a quiet sob, and you could see tears on her cheeks. It made me sad, so I started crying too. She picked me up and I wrapped my arms around her neck and buried my face in her shoulder and kept crying. I remember the smell of her dress like it was yesterday. We always washed our clothes in a large wooden tub in the backyard and used lye soap that smelled like lemon. Mom's dress smelled like lemon that morning.

It was a hot and humid day. We were standing in the shade under the big oak tree in our backyard when I started crying and she picked me up. Two of my brothers and sisters were there too. When my life began I had a baby sister, a younger brother, an older brother and six older sisters. Their names, from youngest to oldest, were Mary, Frank, Christina, Theresa, Emma, Rachel, Magdalena, Eva and John. I was born between Frank and Christina. When I started crying, Frank and Christina did too. My mom squatted down and my brother and sister started hugging my mother and me. I don't know where Theresa, Emma, Magdalena, Rachel, Eva and John were. But I know they weren't in the backyard with us when we were crying. I think Mary was inside the house sleeping or playing with Emma.

The next thing I remember was my dad coming out of the barn and walking towards us and thinking that my dad was really tall. But I know now that Dad was short and stocky, maybe five feet, eight inches and 200 pounds. He had smooth dark hair, a thick mustache that turned down his chin at the sides of his mouth, muscular strong arms and the thick hands of a farmer.

According to what Mom would tell us when she talked about Dad, he had clear blue eyes that seemed almost florescent the way they sparkled when he laughed, which he did a lot, especially when all of us—Mom, Dad and my brothers and sisters—sat around the kitchen and sang our favourite songs. Everyone's favourite was *"Freut Euch de Lebens,"* which in English means "Life Let Us Cherish." My favourite line from the song, which I remember to this day, is: "For he who honest lives, and true, and helps his poorer neighbours too, will shortly find that happiness, has come with him to dwell."

That day, I remember clearly he was wearing a sweat-stained, workshirt, a tattoo of a crucifix partially visible on his right bicep under his rolled-up sleeve. His coarse cotton pants were frayed short, showing thick, muscular, hairy calves. He was with another man I had never seen before and never saw again. The stranger had a thick black beard and hair that grew out of his ears. Long, greasy strands of black hair hung down to his shoulders. He wore a filthy white shirt, soiled by dirt and sweat. His rough hemp pants were held up by thick, black leather suspenders. His pant legs were tucked into high-top black boots that were laced only halfway to the top.

He spoke fast and was obviously upset. Spit sprayed from his mouth as he talked excitedly. But his eyes seemed somehow unreal. Like black stones. They were expressionless. He had dark pupils that matched his hair and beard. "They're all dead," I heard him say to my father as they walked towards us. "I saw them lying in the street, swollen and rotting in the sun. The flies were at them."

My father said nothing to him. He turned to my mother and spoke curtly.

"Take the kids and get into the house."

"What are you going to do?" Mom asked.

"Never mind. Just get inside the house. We don't even know if they're coming here. I think they might be heading to Mannheim. Keep the kids in the house until I tell you otherwise."

My mother rushed the three of us in the back door and up to our parents' second floor bedroom. She sat all of us on the floor, huddled between the bed and wall. "Keep quiet. Everything will be all right if you stay quiet. I promise"

I'm not exactly sure what happened next. The best way to describe my memory of it is a bit like watching a movie where some of the frames are missing. You see images, but some of them are disconnected and don't flow seamlessly one into the other.

There was the sound of horses' hooves on the wooden sidewalk that ran past our house and loud voices I could not understand. Then, I was peering out the front window through a crack in the drapes. I could see a man standing on our front walk and hear my mother's voice from somewhere below, which I imagined to be at the front door.

On the sidewalk and in the road were these strange men on horseback. I didn't count them at the time. But I can remember clearly. I can see them like I'm looking at them again, right now. There were eight of them. I remember being frightened and feeling a sick panic in my stomach. They looked fiercely intimidating. Unshaven, unkempt, rifles slung across their backs. They wore no uniforms. Each had a rifle in one hand, a pistol in a holster, belts with bullets slung across their chests and five of them had long knives sheathed on their hips.

"*Schergevitch*," one of them shouted. "Water, get us water. We need to drink."

I saw the man standing on the front walk—I thought it was my father—turn and walk towards the house and out of my sight.

Then I heard voices and footsteps downstairs, perhaps inside the house or on the front steps, I couldn't tell. A woman was crying and then the man, my father, returned to the front stone walk, carrying a pail of water and a ladle. The men had gotten off their horses and stood inside the front gate. My father handed one of them the pail of water and each took turns sipping water from the ladle.

The next thing I remember was two of the scary men grabbing my father by the arms and leading him to the road in front of our house. In my mind I have this clear picture of the man, my father, standing with his hands tied behind his back with a rope. Then, I heard footsteps from below again, faint at first, growing louder, the sound of heavy boots on wood. One of the men walked up to my dad from behind, took the pistol out of his belt and pointed it at the back of his head. Then I remember a loud, sharp exploding sound that made me put my hands over my ears, close my eyes and crouch face down on the floor.

I don't know how long I hunched down on the floor on my knees, with my hands over my ears and my face buried in my thighs. All I can say for sure is that the next thing I remember was the terrible sound of a woman shrieking, then wailing. I had never heard that kind of thing before, or since, and I have never been able to quite describe it. All I can say is that it was this forlorn mixture of fear, torment and anguish. So indescribable that the sound seemed almost inhuman, even alien. I couldn't see her, but somehow I was sure it was my mother. It made me feel panic and fear all at once, so afraid in the pit of my stomach that I became sick, right there in my parents' bedroom, all over my shirt and pants.

CHAPTER 2

S O THIS WAS MY LIFE, starting at the beginning. I know it to
be true. My dad's body, and the other dead men, were laying
in the street, face down in kind of a row, their heads pointing in
the same direction. There were 12 of them, including Dad. I remember peering down on the street from between the curtains
in my parents' bedroom window, my chin touching the sill, and
counting—one, two, three, four, five, six, seven, eight, nine, ten,
eleven, twelve—touching the window pane with my index finger
as I pointed at each body.

This is going to seem really weird, but actually I was disappointed there were only 12. That's because I could've counted
even higher. When my life began, I was able to count all the way
to seventeen, which was pretty impressive for a four-year-old, although sometimes I got confused with the numbers between 14
and 17. I was very proud of being able to count that high.

At first, I remember thinking the bad men were Gypsies. When
I say that, I don't mean at the time I literally thought they *were*
Gypsies. I was only four and didn't know who Gypsies were and
didn't really know anything about Gypsies until I was older. All I
know is that in the first few weeks after my life began I remember

seeing strange people coming through our town, people others referred to as Gypsies. They came like a small cavalcade, some riding on wagons, a few on horseback and many simply walking. I remember them stopping at our house and asking Mother for food. She gave them grapes, apples and bread, and they would leave without saying a word, not even thank you. To this day, I remember laying in bed at night and wondering why my mom gave food to the people who killed my father. It made me feel really afraid and gave me nightmares because I thought that if we didn't give them food they would kill my mom and me and my brothers and sisters.

It wasn't until much later that I realized it wasn't the Gypsies at all, but that different groups of men—members of the Bolshevik militia—were hunting down men like my father. They operated as teams, kind of coordinated hit squads, and planned their attacks for the same time in different towns. It was a Saturday when my dad died, and most of the men were at home with their families. They all got shot the same way—in the back of the head. I can't tell you exactly when I realized it was the Bolsheviks who killed my father, or who the Bolsheviks even were and what was going on in the Kutschurgan. Like with a lot of things, when it comes to understanding the world and your life, it happens gradually, bit by bit, over a longer period of time. When you're a little kid, knowledge and understanding is a process, not a kind of moment-in-time revelation.

That's the thing about telling you this story. Let me try to explain, because I think it's important.

If I knew then what I know now, I wouldn't have thought the things I once did. But I didn't, so I did. So as I talk to you and remember how my life began, it's as if there are two parts to me telling the story. One is the thoughts and feelings of a young, naive child, the other is me knowing now what I didn't know then. Does that make sense? I hope so.

Not everybody in Fischer-Franzen was a farmer, and the few who weren't lived on what my mother called "the other side." So you could say the road that ran through the village was a dividing line, a kind of invisible wall. It was a physical, psychological and social barrier separating Germans from Russians, Catholics from Cossacks, *kulaks* from peasants and, when my life began, Whites from Reds. But I didn't know any of that at the time. At first, I used to take my mother literally when she said something, which all little kids do because they don't understand nuance, things like figures of speech or hyperbole. So when Mom said "the other side," I took her to mean the other side, as in "the other side of the road." I didn't think anything of it, because it was true. Eventually, of course, I came to realize it meant much more than I'd thought.

Kaza and his family lived on the other side of the road and I remember Kaza used to tell me that his uncle, who lived in Tiraspol, called us Germans "the *Nushniks.*" It wasn't until much later, when I was six and more grown up, that I learned *Nushniks* was the Russian word for "shitheads." But I didn't care, because Kaza was my best friend and he never called me a *Nushnik.* Kaza wasn't like that. He didn't have a mean bone in his body.

There were lots of kids in our town. In fact, most families had at least four or five children, so I had plenty of friends. The Bengerts had 11 kids, including twins Heidi and Jacob who were only three days younger than me, and lived only two doors away. I played a lot with Heidi and Jacob, but Kaza was my very best friend. After they killed my father, I knew my mother would rather that I stopped being best friends with Kaza. She didn't tell me why, exactly. I knew it wasn't because she didn't like Kaza, or thought he had been a bad boy or was a bad influence on me, or anything like that. But I somehow I knew it had something to do with people she called "the Bolsheviks" and the people who lived on the other side of the road.

Like I said, our side of the Kutschurgan River was technically in Moldavia. The river, as is so often the case when it comes to geography, was a demarcation. But it didn't really matter. What's important to understand is that at the time the entire region was in a state of upheaval and uncertainty. We considered ourselves part of Ukraine in south Russia, but because Fischer-Franzen was on the west side of the Kutschurgan, we were technically on the eastern edges of Bessarabia. This was a region between Ukraine in south Russia and Romania that arced northwest from the Black Sea to the border with Moldavia, which at the time was a disputed part of Romania. Bessarabia, like much of the south Russian region, was what you might call an ethnic stew, populated by a mixture of south Slavic people such as Romanians, Bulgarians, Moldaves, Poles and Croats. Interspersed as well were German enclaves like Fischer-Franzen and some Jewish communities, although the Jewish towns tended to be more in the Ukraine part of south Russia.

The ancestors of the German-speaking people, like me and my family, had immigrated to Russia from the Rhineland of Germany beginning in the 19th century. My great-grandfather and grandmother were among the wave of German families who settled as farmers on the Steppes of Ukraine and the neighbouring region of Bessarabia. They came in 1815.

Of course, I didn't know any of this the day they killed my father. But I learned it slowly, in the weeks, months and years after. Gradually, I was able to piece together the reality of my life and eventually came to understand why the strange men had murdered my dad and the other men in town that day. That's the way you learn things when you're a little kid. Bit by bit, from different conversations you hear, things you see with your own eyes and what other people tell you.

I saw them kill my father with my own eyes. So that much I knew was true and no one had to tell me. What I didn't know was why. I learned that by listening, watching and remembering. And, like I said, for some reason I'm really good at remembering. Don't ask me why, because I don't know. All I can tell you is that beginning with the day they shot my father, I remember almost everything, sometimes down to the smallest detail. It might sound stupid, but it's true; like the exact time of day something happened or what someone was wearing, or if they parted their hair on the left or right side or not at all. Some people would say it's useless information. Who cares where someone parts their hair? It's trivial stuff that doesn't matter.

Except, of course, until it does.

Most of the other towns in the Kutschurgan were ethnically pure, so to speak. By that I mean they were either German or Ukrainian-Russian, and only a few had both living in the same town. So, in that sense, our town was different because we lived together—or at least across the road from one another. When I say "Russian," it includes lots of different ethnic groups that lived in Russia, like Ukrainians, Jews, Slavs, Cossacks, Moldaves and even Gypsies. But the truth was, they were not considered to be real Russians by the Russians themselves. They were outsiders.

Bessarabia was unique. It had a diverse mixture of ethnic groups, each with its own language, culture and religion. It was an amalgam of displaced or nomadic people, disconnected from each other and their homelands. But Black Sea Germans were different. They might have lived in Russia for generations, like my ancestors, but they were never considered true Russian citizens and never would be. They were foreigners who didn't really belong and it didn't matter how long they lived in Russia. Which,

I guess, sort of explains why Kaza's neighbour used to call us *Nushniks*.

The other thing that made us different was religion.

At the south end of our town was a big Roman Catholic church. It was situated at the spot where the road turned sharply to the right, then left and continued south to Strassburg, which was nine kilometres away along the Kutschurgan. The church was called St. Joseph's. It had a high steeple with a cross on top, a steep copper tin roof that had turned green from oxidizing in the sun. There were 14 stained-glass windows, seven on each side of the church—one for each Station of the Cross—and a big white statue in the front yard of the Virgin Mary holding the baby Jesus. In the back of the church was St. Joseph's cemetery, where people from Fischer-Franzen were buried, except for my father and the 11 other men who were shot the day my life began—they were buried in secret graves in the fields behind our house. At one point, I know there were 126 graves in the church cemetery because I counted them years later when I was eight. In the middle of the cemetery was a large wooden cross and a plaque with the words from Psalm 126: "Those who sow in tears will reap with songs of joy." I remember thinking that there could only be 126 graves because of Psalm 126.

One of those who lived on the other side of the road was Yuri Podnovestov. I never did see Yuri and his family in church and later I learned it was because he was a Jew. He, his wife and five kids lived above what was a small hardware store where he sold tools, pieces of lumber and small farm implements like pick axes, saws, hammers, twine, nails and things like that. But he would also do special orders for people who wanted bigger items that had to be brought in from Tiraspol by wagonload. One of the things Yuri could special order was on display in the yard in front of his store. It was a large dual steel plow with thick carved wooden handles and a shiny leather harness for the plough horse. Podnovestov was also the town carpenter, which meant he served as the local undertaker because he knew how to build caskets out of the scrap wood he couldn't sell.

After the bad men killed my father and the other men in our town, they went to see Yuri Podnovestov and told him the bodies were not to be buried in the cemetery. I know this because I was there when Yuri was talking to my older brother John later in the day. John was 19 years old and had been working in the field threshing hay with a team of horses when the Bolsheviks came and murdered our father and the other men. He didn't know anything about it until my older sister Christina, terrified and crying, ran out the back of the house and into the field for almost three kilometres to find him. I still remember Christina was wearing a blue and white dress that day, with red trim on the hem and a red bow on the back of the waist and a white bow in her long dark hair. She wore it to the 9 o'clock Saturday morning mass and was planning to go to her friend Andrea Marquart's 11th birthday party.

Sometimes I get scared by how clearly I remember things. It's not like having a picture in my mind, even a clear one, when I recall something that happened in the past. It's more like when I think of something, it's actually happening for real. Like I'm experiencing it again. That's the way it is when I remember seeing John, like it's happening and I'm there.

Most people would describe John as short and stocky. In that sense he was the mirror image of our father, except with our mother's thick curly hair. He had broad shoulders, a thick neck, big chest, heavy arms, meaty hands and short powerful legs. He was wearing rough overalls, a workshirt that was soaked in sweat, dirty, low-cut leather boots with metal clamps at the ankle and a weathered leather hat that had a silver metal rim on the peak.

He looked like he hadn't shaved for days and, when I saw him, he had our dad's double-barreled single shot musket slung over his shoulder by its leather strap.

John and Yuri were standing at the bottom of the three steps at our back door. I watched and listened to them through the screen door and I'm pretty sure they didn't know I was there. They were too intense to notice me, and besides, I know John wouldn't have used the bad words he did if he knew I was listening.

"What in God's name can I do?" Yuri was saying. "They told me not to touch the bodies. Said they are to rot in the sun. 'Let the dogs, crows and coyotes eat them or we'll come back for you,' they said. John, I believe them. They're ruthless. They'll be back. I fucking know it."

For a moment, maybe 15 seconds, John said nothing. His face, tanned from hours working in the fields, was strangely pale. He hands and shoulders shook like he was cold. But it was 28 degrees Centigrade outside, and I remember thinking *John must be getting sick*. Of course, I realize now he was shaking from something else, which I can only guess now was a mixture of cold fear, boiling anger and a sickening dread.

Then John spewed out his anger. "Fucking cocksuckers. The fucking, Commie swine bastards. I want them back. I'll kill the Bolshevik fuckers. I'll rip their fucking hearts out with my fucking bare hands."

Yuri didn't say a word.

"Which direction did they go? When?"

"They headed east. About an hour ago. I dunno, maybe they're headed to Strassburg or Selz, maybe Mannheim. What can we do?"

"What about Mathias?"

"He's dead too."

Mathias was Mathias Fischer, the town's mayor, whose great-grandfather founded the town. Mom says he was also my dad's best friend. When I heard my brother John mention his name, a memory of sitting on my dad's knee a few days earlier, when he was meeting with other men, grew sharper in my mind. I remembered clearly the man I now believe was Mathias Fischer was also there. We were in the church basement. And with my dad and Mathias were all the other men were from our side of the street, except for Yuri, who was also there. I remember they were talking about "the revolution," the Communists and the Bolsheviks. They were scared about what might happen to them and their families and were trying to figure out what to do. I remember my dad saying he wasn't afraid, which made me feel good.

John came up the steps and into the house, pulling open the screen door.

"Anton, we have to get Mama and your brothers and sisters. Come with me."

I followed him to the living room. I got scared when I saw Mother curled up in a chair, her legs pulled up beneath her and her head buried in her arms, sobbing quietly. I started crying too. All my brothers and sisters—Magdalena, Rachel, Eva, Emma, Theresa, Frank, Christina and Mary—were crying and huddled around my mother. I noticed she was wearing different clothes from when the bad men first came to our house and I saw the side of Emma's face was red and swollen. She was clutching her blouse with both hands crossed on her chest like she was afraid it would fall open.

John had tears running down his cheeks as he leaned down to hug Mother and stroke her hair. When he reached over to Emma and pulled her close, she began to sob uncontrollably.

No one said a word. We just cried. I know I cried because my mom was crying and felt afraid because I knew something terrible had happened to my family.

After two or three minutes of silence, broken by our sobs, John finally spoke quietly to my mother. His voice was calm, dispassionate, his words matter-of-fact, cold.

"We will bury Father. Then I will hunt down the murderers."

Mom said nothing and did not raise her head.

My dad's body lay in the street for hours, as did the bodies of the 11 others executed that day. I could see them from the window in my parents' room when I peeked through the crack in the drapes. I was just tall enough when I stood on my tiptoes to peer over the sill and could see my dad laying face down on the dirt road, his legs pointing towards our house. The corpses were all near each other, in a row on the road in front of our house, all of them on our side of the road. Dogs came by occasionally to sniff the bodies. Crows were already gathering, sitting on fenceposts and rooftops. I remember wondering why only the men on our side of the road were killed. I know it sounds stupid, knowing what I know now, but at the time it didn't seem fair to me.

At nightfall, under the cover of darkness, John, my mother, Eva, Rachel and Magdalena went outside. Emma was too upset to go with them. She stayed in her bedroom, in bed under the covers, completely silent. Her faced was still swollen and the redness on her cheek had turned into a bruise the colour of grapes. Instead of going with Mom and my sisters, Christina and Theresa stayed back and sat on the bed next to Emma, and with a damp cloth stroked Emma's hair crusted with dried black blood, sticking to the side of her swollen face. I watched from the front window and then through the screen door at the back as the others quietly wrapped a white sheet around Father's stiff body and carried him quietly behind the house, through the backyard, past the summer kitchen, up the gentle slope to the fallow field where their shadowy figures disappeared into the dusk of nightfall. I stayed home with my brother and sisters. They came back three hours and 10 minutes later, when I was in bed and still awake in the bedroom I shared with Frank and our baby sister, Mary. When I heard them I went downstairs to the kitchen. John and mother were sitting alone at the table.

When John saw me, and before I had a chance to say a word, he said very quietly: "Daddy's with God now, Anton, but everything will be all right." He kissed my cheek. "You go back to bed." I noticed that both his and Mom's hands looked like mine when I played in the dirt, their fingernails black from soil and their hair matted by sweat against their foreheads. Mother stared down at the table, never raised her head and didn't say a word. It was not like her not to kiss me goodnight. It made me feel sad.

Even though I knew everything wasn't all right, I didn't think that John was lying to me or anything like that. I might have only been almost four-and-a-half but I understood he was just trying to make me feel better and not be afraid. But I *was* afraid and couldn't help it. In fact, when I went back to bed, I couldn't stop shivering even though I was under the covers and it was still very warm in the room after such a hot and humid day.

IT WAS KAZA who told me about Mother and Emma. At first I didn't know what he meant and, actually, he didn't know either when he told me.

The day after Father died, Kaza came to my house. It was the afternoon and we went into the backyard to lay on our backs and look at clouds. As it turned out, it was a perfect day for cloud- watching. Hot, humid, sunny, breezy; ideal conditions for cumulus clouds. In case you aren't into cloud-watching, cumulus clouds are the best; cumulonimbus, to be precise. They're the most common; big and fluffy, like monster cotton balls floating across the sky. Better yet, they come in different shapes and sizes, so your imagination can run wild.

Looking at clouds was exactly what I needed the day after Father was murdered.

We always tried to lie head-to-head in opposite directions, Kaza and me, when we cloud-watched. That way you got to experience more of what was in the sky from a different perspective. What I saw, Kaza saw upside down and vice versa. So if I saw a cloud that looked like, let's say, a hippopotamus, upside down it might have looked totally different for Kaza, like maybe a steamship. It's amazing how perspective changes things, which is what cloud-watching taught me and Kaza.

"Sorry about your da-dad," Kaza said.

"Uh, thanks," I said.

"My dad says your muh-mom and Emma were raped by the bad men yes-yesterduh-day."

"Is that bad?" I asked.

"Uh-huh. I think it means they wuh-were really muh-mean to them."

"Oh."

I thought about that for a minute. I remembered Emma's swollen, bruised face, her torn blouse, the sound of heavy footsteps and my mom wailing when I hid in my parents' bedroom after I saw them shoot my father.

"Look at that cloud, Kaza," I said, pointing directly above. "It looks like a bear. See the legs and the paws?"

"Hmmm. That's funny. You know, tuh-to me it doesn't luh-look like anything. Just a cloud."

That's the thing I remember best about the day after they killed my father: the blue sky and the clouds. They were beautiful. So pure white, so puffy, so soft. It made me feel like I was floating up from the ground towards them, not even part of my body, as I stared at the sky. We must have laid on our backs looking at clouds for more than an hour. It helped make me forget and to feel better, at least for a little while. I even forgot what Kaza said about what had happened to Mom and Emma, until I overheard John that night.

It was dark and I had already gone to bed when I heard voices in the backyard. I looked out from our bedroom window and could see John carrying a kerosene lamp, walking with other men into our summer kitchen. Frankie and Mary were sleeping. My mother always kept the door to our bedroom open just a little bit, which was just enough for me to slip through without having to move the door, and that was good because the hinges creaked when you moved the door slowly. So I quietly went downstairs, stepping on the outside edges of the staircase by walking bowlegged so the stairs wouldn't creak. I went down the hallway, past the kitchen, through the screen door and out into the backyard. I walked up close to the window of the summer kitchen, where I could see a faint glow from the lamp. I took an empty apple box crate from against the wall and quietly moved it under the window, and listened. Standing on my toes, I could see John and eight other men. They were John's friends, men the same age as him and sons of the other men in our town who had been killed by the scary men who had come on horseback.

There were crickets chirping in the summer night, so it was hard to hear what they were saying. My heart was pounding and echoing in my head, so I even had to hold my breath to hear better. Luckily they were just on the other side of the wall. Then John moved, his back was right next to the window, blocking my view. He was wearing a black and red checkered shirt I had never seen before. I could only make out some of what they were saying. They were talking about going after "the fucking Bolsheviks." I didn't know what "fucking" meant but I did know it was a bad word.

I heard John clearly say: "They'll be back. We need to be ready.

There's a place near Stepanowka where we can surprise them. Swarm them. Kill them before they can react."

At that time, I had never heard of Stepanowka and wondered if it was the name of a person who lived by the road. But I found out later that it was a small German farming colony of maybe six or seven families halfway to Strassburg.

I couldn't make out much of what else was said because often they were talking all at once, sometimes shouting and arguing. But what I could tell is that they didn't all agree what to do. Some of them thought John's idea was a good one. Some of the others said it was too dangerous, that even if they killed the Bolsheviks, there would be more who would come and hunt them down and maybe kill more of their families and burn down more houses in Fischer-Franzen, like the two that burned the day before and were still smoldering. Hearing them argue made me feel afraid and I began to shiver, so much that the apple crate I was standing on began to wobble. So, I slowly climbed down and quietly went back into the house to bed. But I couldn't sleep and didn't finally doze off until there was already light in the sky.

As it turned out, I never saw John again, at least not alive.

The next morning when I went down to breakfast and sat at the table with Mom and my brothers and sisters, John wasn't there. No one asked about him or mentioned his name and I didn't say anything because I thought maybe he was out in the field threshing hay or doing chores like watering the horses, or feeding coal to the pigs. Now that Dad was gone to heaven, someone had to do the extra work, so I just figured John was busy.

Later that day, at 3:15 in the afternoon, a band of 15 strangers—I know because I counted them—rode into town on horseback. The one at the front was leading an old plough horse, pulling a flatbed wagon filled with men piled in a heap. At first I thought they were sleeping.

It so happened that Kaza and I were sitting on our front steps when we saw them coming down the road just after they passed the church. We ran to hide behind the trunk of the big maple tree in our front yard and, as I squatted to peer through an open space in the hedge, I could see the men stop not 25 metres down the road. They got off their horses and began lifting the sleeping men from the wagon, piling them one on top of the other in a pile in the middle of the road. I counted eight and wondered why they didn't wake up.

Then one of them took a can with a long spout from the wagon and poured something all over the pile of bodies. There was a soft breeze blowing towards us and I could smell kerosene, like what we used in our lamps and lanterns in the house. Then the man threw the empty can aside, pulled something from his pocket and suddenly the pile of bodies erupted into bright flames.

"Burn, you German scum!" he snarled, spitting into the flames.

As the fire burned, I could see the arm of one of the bodies jut stiffly out from the pile. It was covered by a black and red check- ered shirt, just like one John had worn the night before. Instantly I understood. John was dead. He and his friends had gone to find the men who murdered their fathers, to ambush them. But something had gone terribly wrong.

Suddenly, overwhelmed by the fear quivering in my stomach, I ran into the house, down the hallway, through the kitchen, out the back door, past the cattleyard, into the fields. I didn't stop running until I got to the cornfield and then hid, huddled on the ground amid the high stalks of corn until it got dark. I can't tell you exactly how long I hid in the cornfield, but it seemed like a long time. I didn't move until I heard my sister Magdalena's voice calling my name in the far-off distance.

"Anton! Please, Anton! Where are you? Anton, please come. Please!"

CHAPTER 3

"**M**Y DEAR FRIENDS. We are united today by unspeakable grief. We come together with pain beyond the capacity of words to express, sorrow so deep it overwhelms our ability to face the future, and anger so powerful it reaches deep into the core of our very being to darken our souls.

"I stand before you with trepidation, feeling inadequate and vulnerable. As a priest and a disciple of Jesus Christ, the father of our parish family, the one whose calling it is to help guide each of you through your spiritual life, to make sense of our temporal selves in the grand design of our Father, I can only confess my own doubts.

"Like Thomas in the Gospel of John, who doubted the resurrected Christ, I too must stand before the Lord our Father and express my doubts. How can I—or any of us enduring this deep, dark time, swallowed by the enormity of our grief and consumed by our thirst for revenge—not doubt the existence of a kind and loving Lord Jesus? How can we not question our faith? How can we not lash out in anger at God? How can we not feel betrayed by the trust we put in Him? How can we not feel abandoned by Jesus? How can this be part of the plan of a gentle and loving Father?"

It was hot in the church, the air heavy and still. The bright, late-morning sunlight streamed in through the stained glass window at the front of the church, casting its warm glow on Father Frederich who, instead of standing behind the pulpit on the right side of the sanctuary, today stood directly in front of the altar, facing the congregation. He was illuminated by the focused rays of sunlight, which came through the large window with an image of the ascension of the risen Christ looking down on an adoring faithful. The small church was filled beyond its capacity of 170; those unable to find room in the wooden pews stood at the back. People had come from other towns, like Strassburg, Selz and Mannheim; people I hadn't seen before.

As always, my family sat in the third pew from the front on the righthand side of the aisle facing the altar. Before my dad was murdered, he would sit next to the aisle and Mom would sit at the other end with us kids in between. We always sat according to age, from oldest to youngest starting next to my dad, which meant that Mary, our baby sister, was closest to Mom. I was kind of in the middle, but closer to Mom than Dad. John, being the oldest, would sit next to Dad, with Eva next to him and so on. Now that both Dad and John were dead, everything was reversed. Mom sat next to the aisle and Eva was at the far end.

Like most kids my age, I didn't usually listen to Father Frederich's sermons. Mostly I would daydream. I especially liked to look at the arched ceiling of the church and imagine swinging on the ornate lanterns, from one to another, that hung from the ceiling on long gold chains. I could imagine leaping from the railing of the choir loft at the back of the church onto the first hanging lantern, the momentum of the jump making the lantern swing just far enough that I could reach the next, let go of the first lantern, swing to the next and so on. The problem was always the last lantern. It hung directly above the altar rail and, as hard as I tried to imagine, I couldn't see how I'd get off the last one because it was too far from the altar for me to swing enough distance to grab the big crucifix and shimmy down. The only way would be to go back the way I came and swing from one to another—like Tarzan from a hanging vine—until I got back to the choir loft.

But that day I didn't daydream about swinging from the lanterns that hung from the ceiling. I couldn't help but listen to Father Frederich's sermon. Six wooden caskets were lined up at the front of the church, and my brother John was in the third one from the right. I knew that because when we walked into the church behind the caskets and got to the front of the sanctuary, Mother leaned down on his casket, laid her head on it like it was a pillow and wept, for her lost son, and a husband whose body now lay hidden in a field. We stood on either side of her, all holding hands, crying. I touched the casket. It felt rough and smelled of pine.

I, too, was trying to understand the sadness, fear and anxiety I felt. Why my father and brother were dead, why our family had to suffer this way. Mostly, I wanted somehow to help my mother. To help her stop crying, to make her happy again, to make my brother and sisters feel better, to make our family whole, to erase the last four days.

"It is in times like these that our faith is tested; our belief in the resurrected Lord at its weakest, our ability to make sense of the teachings of Jesus—or to even believe in God—the most difficult. Indeed, for some it will be impossible.

"Like you, I am struggling with the same doubts, the same anguish, the same anger and bitterness that come with a feeling of being abandoned by our God. Like Jesus on the cross, we cannot help but ask, 'My God, my God, why have You forsaken me?'

"Somehow, I must, we all must, reach deep within ourselves, and seek the comfort of our faith. We must not seek to understand, but to believe, to believe that the test of faith we face, the unremitting and overpowering grief we feel, the bitterness of the hatred that wells from within, is to teach us that, just as Jesus suffered for us, so too shall we suffer. That in suffering comes our personal challenge. And if we meet the challenge, if we overcome our anger and bitterness, if in our overwhelming grief comes acceptance of the Lord, that there is a greater destiny for all than what we experience here on earth. That if we meet the challenge He has put before us, we will find redemption. As Jesus said to the doubting Thomas: 'I am the way and the truth and the life. He whosoever liveth and believeth in me, shall never die.'"

That was the first time I'd heard that, the bit about never dying if you believed in Jesus. For some reason it made me think, even though I was only four-and-a-half, about what it meant. It actually made me feel not so sad about what had happened to my dad and brother. I figured that if I went to church, which was where God lived, I never had to worry about dying. And because Dad always went to church, he was all right, even though I saw what happened to him. So I began to think that he must now be living at the back of the church with God.

Directly behind Father Frederich was a huge cross on a pedestal above the altar. It had a larger-than-life Jesus hanging from it. His skin was porcelain white, contrasting the red blood that dripped down his face from a crown of thorns and the blood that came from his hands and feet, which had been nailed to the cross. Blood also gushed from his side, pierced by a lance. I always wondered about Jesus on the cross, and as the priest talked about suffering, I began to understand, or at least I thought I did.

The next afternoon, Kaza came over to look at clouds with me. It's always best to look at clouds in the afternoon. There are usually more of them. They sort of stack up more, and tend to come in bigger and different shapes and sizes.

As we lay on our backs, head-to-head, gazing at the sky, I felt the inevitable relief that comes with looking at clouds. Like I said before, you feel detached from the earth, like you're floating in space, suddenly disconnected from reality, when you look at clouds.

For me, escape was important, if only for a few brief moments. That's because the night before, Rachel had come into the bedroom I shared with Frank and Mary. My bed was next to the door, which was always left slightly ajar so we could find our way to the outhouse in the night if we needed. Frank and Mary were sound asleep, but I couldn't sleep. I felt too afraid, too upset about what had happened and what might happen to me and my family. I wasn't exactly crying, more just sniffling, trying not to cry out loud. But my big sister Rachel, who was 16, heard me when she walked by, came in and sat on the side of my bed. I remember thinking how beautiful she looked. Rachel had long, smooth, dark hair that fell past her shoulders and seemed to glisten in the sunlight when she was outside. She took my hand in hers. Her hand felt warm and smooth and grown up.

"Anton, *Herzchen*, try not to cry. I know you're sad about Papa and John. We all are. But they're with God now and someday we'll all be together again. Don't worry, I promise. And besides, you're the big brother now. We need you to be strong. Mama needs you to be a big boy who's not afraid. Your other brother and your sisters need you to be strong, Anton. All right?"

"All right," I said, between muffled sobs.

Rachel kissed my forehead and left.

As I lay looking at clouds with Kaza, I couldn't help thinking about what Rachel had said. Now that Dad and John were with Jesus, I was the big brother. That made me feel strange; I can't quite explain it. There isn't one word that captures the feeling; proud, afraid, anxious, upset. But more than all those things, I felt determined. Determined about what, I couldn't say, exactly.

Just determined to be a big brother for Mom and everyone else in our family.

Looking at clouds with Kaza made my mind drift. For a few minutes, all my worries vanished and I felt myself floating with the clouds, like ships on a beautiful azure blue sea. Suddenly, I felt confident and determined, not afraid at all, like a big brother should.

"Kaza, you know something?" I asked.

"What?"

"I'm the big brother in our family now."

"Uh-huh."

IT WOULD BE MANY YEARS before I knew the meaning of the words "war communism." Not that it matters, but I can't tell you when exactly. Let's just say when I was much older and wiser, like I am now, and leave it at that. But for the purposes of my story, it's important that I explain. Important because it helps make sense of what was happening when you look back at those days. For some people—you know, academics, historians and the like—there is still this kind of romanticism about the Russian Revolution. They look at it in the context of world history, this pivotal time that reshaped the world and its politics for much of the 20th century. Which, of course, it did. But, of course, they were untouched by it in any real or meaningful way. For them it's an academic exercise, an abstraction they use to validate their beliefs. I hate that about academics. For example, I remember one time after I retired, going to a public lecture on the Russian Revolution by this professor at the university with a Scottish accent who, apparently, was some big expert on Russia. He talked about things like "historical materialism" and the "alienation of labour" and "false consciousness," as if it was all so profound. They think they're smart, but, if you ask me, they're actually pretty clueless because they're so completely detached from the real world. None of them actually *lived* through it. What they totally miss is the truth of those days. They never really consider the unspeakable suffering of innocent people, the horrors inflicted on a nation—all in the name of communist revolution. I might have ended up being just a simple farmer with only a Grade 8 education and not the most educated person. But when I got older, and especially after I retired, I read a lot about the Russian Revolution and I'm smart enough to know that blind ideology, of whatever sort, does that to people. And often the ones with the most closed minds are academics who think they know everything, even though they don't.

Eventually, I learned "war communism" was what they called the period from 1918-1921, when the Bolshevik government of Vladimir Lenin implemented its collectivist economic policies. Without getting into great detail, the objective was simple—and brutal: the state would take control of all economic production and distribution. The Bolsheviks said these policies were necessary to deal with the aftermath of the First World War and the civil war that raged between the Reds and the Whites, between the communists and those loyal to the former tsar, between the revolutionaries and the reactionaries. To put it bluntly, Russia was in economic and social chaos. A drastic situation required drastic measures, ergo war communism, which affected every aspect of economic life. All farmers were forced to surrender, at prices fixed by the government, their excess production, which was defined as everything they produced beyond what they needed to feed their immediate families. The system was initially enforced for the first few years by "special detachments" of workers and peasants, namely those who were loyal to the Bolsheviks. But, eventually, the seizure of farm production was taken over by the security police, who had unchallenged power to confiscate what *they* determined to be "excess."

Meantime, industrial production and distribution was also taken over by the state. Nationalized industries were managed by *glavki*, which were controlled by the Supreme Economic Council. Labourers with skills were conscripted into labour armies under the control of special soviets. Banks were nationalized, inflation ran wild. Before long, people began starving to death by the millions.

I know this now because I've lived a long life and long ago was old enough to understand what I didn't understand in those days when I was so young. When you actually live through something and see things with your own eyes and learn from listening, you quickly begin to understand things differently. My family lived through it and saw what happened. The truth was something I learned gradually and came to understand slowly the reasons for things when I was still a very young boy. But that's what happens when you're the big brother and you have to grow up fast.

That's what happened to me.

Things in Fischer-Franzen became very different after they killed my father, the other men, and John and his friends. The people on "the other side," as mother used to call them, took control. In a way, that wasn't surprising because the only men left in our town came from the other side. I took my mom literally —which you tend to do when you're a real little kid—when she said "the other side," thinking she meant the other side of the road. Of course, I know now "the other side" meant much more than I thought at the time. I learned that on the day my father died, only one of the men who lived on the other side was killed too. His name was Martin Usselmann. Unlike my dad and the others, who were shot in front of their homes, the Bolsheviks went into Martin Usselmann's house and shot him as he sat at his kitchen table with his wife.

"They said he was a collaborator with the Whites and the German tsarists. That's why they shot him," Michael Brossart told me one day, weeks after my father and John were killed.

It was a cool day in autumn, the leaves were turning colours and I was sitting on the front step, watching things when Michael saw me and came over to talk. His dad had been murdered too, but unlike me, even though he was 11 and much older, Michael wasn't the big brother of his family. He had a big brother named Thomas who was 14.

"What you doing, Anton?" Michael asked.

"Nothing. Just watching."

"Watching what?"

"Everything."

"What ya mean, everything?"

"I dunno. Just stuff. Mostly watching for the bad guys."

Ever since I became the big brother in our family, I'd decided that I had to be on the lookout for my mom and brother and sisters. So I was always watching for bad people, like the ones who came that day in the summer. Our front steps were a good place to be on the lookout. I could see to both ends of the road in our town, and even further, though on the south side, the road made a turn in front of the church and you lost sight of it for a bit, but it came back into view beyond the church as it went up a gentle hill. At the other end, to the north, I could see two kilometres outside town before the road disappeared into a thicket of trees. So, if I watched out and saw them coming, I could warn Mom and everyone else and we could hide in the cornfield like I did that day when Magdalena came to find me. She didn't really find me, you know. I was totally invisible. That's because when you lay down in a cornfield between the stalks of corn, it's really dark because the sun can't get through. I just gave myself up when I heard her calling me, which is something I would never do if the Bolsheviks were looking for me and I was hiding in the cornfield.

"You can stay on the lookout, Anton, but I don't think the Bolsheviks are going to come back," Michael Brossart said.

"Yuri said they would," I answered, remembering what I'd overheard him telling John. "Yuri told my brother John, 'They'll be back. I fucking know it,'" I said, repeating Yuri's words.

"Anton, you shouldn't use swear words," Michael said. "There's no reason for them to come back. They killed everyone they wanted to and the only men left here are their friends." Then he told me about Martin Usselmann being a collaborator.

"What's a calabrator?" I asked.

"It's when you have good guys and bad guys, and one of the bad guys is really a good guy, but he keeps it a secret and pretends to be a bad guy, but he's really trying to help the good guys."

"Oh. A bad guy who really isn't."

"Right."

So I thought about that for a moment. It made me believe that now there were no more good guys left in our town. Unless there was still a calabrator pretending to be a bad guy, who was really a good guy. I wondered if Yuri Podnovestov was a good calabrator because he had tried to help John. But then I wondered if he was only pretending and was really a bad calabrator. Just thinking about it made me feel mixed up and afraid. Even though I didn't know, deep down inside I realized I couldn't trust anyone except my mother, sisters and brother. And Kaza.

WHEN I THINK OF IT NOW, it's pretty hard to imagine a more tragic and hopeless place on earth. You might think that's an overstatement, but in the summer of 1919 the Kutschurgan and Bessarabia were convulsing with anger, reeling with pain. It was expressed in many ways: bitter ethnic divisions; extreme and conflicting nationalisms; religious tensions; deep cleavages drawn on political, economic, religious and linguistic lines—all subsumed in a civil war spawned by the Bolshevik revolution. Much, if not all, of it was the product of a tortured history.

Don't get me wrong. I don't know this because I'm some brainy historian with a bunch of fancy letters after my name. I know it because I once looked it up in the *Encyclopedia Britannica* and wrote a paper on Bessarabia called "The Trials and Tribulations of Bessarabia" for my eighth grade history class. For some reason it has always stayed with me, maybe because I got an A for the paper, which was the only A I ever got in all eight grades I went to school. I quit school after Grade 8 because I wanted to start working and earn money, which I did, as a farmhand.

The history of Bessarabia goes like this. Geography had made Bessarabia strategically important to the rise and fall of dynasties and failed attempts at empires throughout the centuries. As the gateway between the Danube Valley and Russia, Bessarabia was a natural east-west corridor for invading armies between Europe and Asia. Virtually all the empires at one point or another laid claim to Bessarabia. The Greeks had control as far back as the 7th century BC, and later it was part of the Roman Empire. Down through the ages it was claimed by Huns, Svars and Magyars, before it was seized by Cumans and Mongols, then the Turks and the Crimean Tatars. In the 16th century it became known as Bessarabia, but, like an orphan, no one knows with certainty where the name came from. Most people think it was derived from *Bassarab*, the name of the Walachian princely family. Eventually, the region including Bessarabia became known as Moldavia, until Bessarabia was ceded to Russia after the Russian-Turkish wars that ended with the *Treaty of Bucharest* in 1812. Then, after the Crimean War, the southern half of Bessarabia was given back to Moldavia, only to be returned to Russia by the Congress of Berlin in 1878 after the Romanian war of independence.

The final twist came in 1917 when the anti-Soviet national council of Bessarabia declared it an autonomous republic and then, a year later, renounced all links to Russia and considered itself an independent Moldavian republic. Within two years it reverted to become fully a part of Romania, a move that was validated by the *Treaty of Versailles* in 1919 that redrew the map of central and eastern Europe and the Middle East in the aftermath of the First World War. The Bolshevik government in Moscow did not acknowledge the secession of Bessarabia to either Moldavia or Romania. So, as always, Bessarabia was treated as someone's chattel. It never rose to the level of nation state, but existed throughout history as a region, a kind of accident of geography that fell short of reaching the moral threshold of self-determination. Without a common culture, religion or language—a place where the ebbs and flows of history brought occupying powers, forced migrations and settlements from other parts of Europe and Asia—Bessarabia was never able to find its identity, define its nationalism or claim its destiny.

In a very real way, situated as it was on the edge of Bessarabia, Fischer-Franzen was itself a tiny reflection of the conflicts at the core of the wider region. The town was also known by its Russian name of Novo-Sewitzski and the Romanians named it Covasna. The Ukrainians called it Dubasari. Today, it is known as Novoye. During my childhood, in that one small town of less than 150 people and its immediate vicinity, people spoke German, Romanian, Russian, Ukrainian, Hebrew and Greek. Like Bessarabia itself, it was a rural community divided by language, class, culture, religion and, in 1919, politics.

As a human endeavour, like most people I have learned through the course of my life that politics is one of the great forces of both good and evil. It can be the means to achievement, a vehicle that raises individuals to a higher purpose than their own self-interest. Or it can be the refuge of demagogues who debase the individual by appealing to instincts that instill alienation, prejudice, division, envy and anger, that corrupt the human spirit. Growing up in the Kutschurgan, it was impossible not to be confronted by the brutal truths of politics. As a child, I didn't know what politics was, or what the word even meant. In fact, no one that I can recall ever actually used the word. But still, I discovered that what I learned as an adult about the politics prevalent in my youth filled me with a strange blend of fear and fascination. The conflict between the individual and the collective, between the rights of the individual and the communal needs of society, which is at the core of all politics, is something that I came gradually to recognize as a young boy, if not fully understand. The same feelings about politics have stayed with me my entire life.

You learn about things, whether it's people or politics, by observing and listening, by watching what others do and say. It was my mother who taught me how to learn. "Anton," she said. "No one ever learned anything with their mouth. You learn through your ears and your eyes. You will come to understand in life that the silent ones are the smart ones." That sounded like good advice to me, so from that day to this, I have tried to do what my mother said—watch, listen and say little.

Over the months since "the days of the Bolsheviks," as Mother referred to the time when Father and John died, things changed in our town. Not only were many of the men gone, but something even more fundamental had changed.

The best way to describe it is a feeling. I felt afraid, and so did my mother and sisters and brother. Mother never really talked about being afraid, but you could sense it. The closest she ever came to actually saying it was one time around the dinner table.

It was November 20th, 1919 which Mom told us was Dad's birthday. She asked us all to hold hands as we sat at the table so we could say a prayer for him and John.

"Dear Father in heaven," Mother said. At first I thought she was talking to Dad, but then realized she was speaking to God. "Please bless and be merciful to Father and John. Watch over them and take them into Your care. Forgive them their sins and let them share in the joys of heaven.

"Dear Father in heaven, thank You for your many blessings. Please watch over and protect our family from all harm. Give us the strength to do Your will on earth, to follow Your example, to forgive those who have done us harm, help those in their time of need. Bless my children, may they have a life safe and secure in the comfort of Your loving arms and warm embrace."

Actually, hearing Mother ask God to "protect our family from all harm" made me feel scared. If we needed God to protect us, then, I figured, there was reason to be afraid.

I remember one early evening in late winter the year after Father was murdered, with snow still on the ground in our front yard, I was sitting on the front steps, on the lookout. Being on the lookout had become a ritual for me. It wasn't just something specific I did, like sitting on the front steps. It was more just the way I became. The need to watch what was happening around me, what people were saying, how they were behaving, who was associating with whom, was what I did. I guess you could say it became something of an obsession. It also helped me to learn and understand people, the way they thought and why they acted the way they did. One of my favourite lookout positions was my mother's bedroom. It was on the second floor above the front door and had a curved bay window. That meant I could stand at either end, out of sight, and look out the far end of the window in the opposite direction. The line of sight to the west was unobstructed and it was possible to see all the way to the church at one end of the road. The other direction wasn't as good because the Hermann house three doors down had a big fir tree that blocked part of the view. There was something soothing about being alone in my mother's bedroom. I think it was the quiet and a sense of calm it gave me, a kind of extension of my mother herself.

Over the months there were two things I noticed. One was how I felt about Fischer-Franzen and how, like I said, it had changed since the "days of the Bolsheviks." The other was what I saw and heard.

Feelings are never easy to describe, but let me try. I felt that the town was different. It's hard to explain. But the best way to put it is that the men from the "other side" never did seem that upset about what had happened to my father, John and the others. Only a few of them came to the funeral we had for John and his friends. I knew instinctively as a child that ours was a divided town, a place divided emotionally, psychologically and economically. It didn't make sense to me because I could see what it did to my mother and sisters and brother. Mother didn't talk very much anymore. She always seemed sad, lost in her thoughts. Every night, my mother would sit in the rocking chair in her bedroom and rock. The curved wooden rocker rolling back and forth against the hardwood floor made a kind of rough, rumbling sound of wood against wood, interspersed with the squeaking of the hardwood floor from the swaying weight of the rocker. I could hear the sound from my bedroom down the hall. It became a nightly ritual. When I went to bed, I would slowly fall asleep to the rhythmic sound of my mother rocking in time with the faint ticking of the old clock on the mantel I could hear from downstairs.

CHAPTER 4

THEY MET every Monday and Thursday. In the evenings, at Alexandre Yulinov's, in a small log workshed behind the farmhouse. There were five of them. Always the same five, always all five and always for 90 minutes. And the agenda for the meeting was always the same: recitation of an excerpt from Lenin's revolutionary dogma, review of collectivization progress, report on subversive activities and individuals, and other business.

Other than Yulinov, who was clearly the leader, this particular soviet included Sergei Popov, Petr Smenev, Andrew Kurbesky and Leonev Kuzma. Their ages spanned five decades, their personalities as diverse as their ages. What they shared was a passion for their Russian heritage. Smenev, the youngest at 27, was the most volatile and hyper. Kuzma, the oldest at 63, the most intense, his language profane, his personality dark and brooding. Popov, 36, was quiet, almost withdrawn, while 51-year-old Kurbesky was a nervous wreck and a dreadful alcoholic.

Yulinov, 45, was, in many ways, a combination of the other four. He was the smartest, physically intimidating at 6 feet, three inches tall and 225 pounds, a passionate and fiery orator, and susceptible to mood swings that made him unpredictable. Quiet and serene one moment, he would be loud and aggressive the next, his anger boiling quickly into physical aggression. Each of his traits was amplified by alcohol. The truth was the other four members of the Andrejaschevski soviet respected Yulinov because of his intellect, but they feared him physically even more. Intelligence and intimidation, brain and brawn, can cast a powerful spell.

On this night, the soviet was meeting for only one reason—to discuss the impending visit of Lev Davidovich Bronstein, better known as Leon Trotsky, and the elimination of the remnants of the German resistance. But, as always, Yulinov, ever a disciple of the dogma, always a proponent of discipline, insisted that the full agenda be followed. The men sat around a rectangular table, with Yulinov at one end and two of the others on each side. The lantern in the middle of the table cast an orange glow, making their faces seem almost luminous. One look at the seating arrangement and it was obvious who was in charge. Yulinov opened with Lenin's dictum. Each of the men joined hands and stared intently straight ahead, speaking forcefully, in staccato-like fashion, and in complete unison:

Revolutions are the feast-days of oppressed classes.
If we, the oppressed, do not rise up,
if we do not strive to gain a knowledge of weapons,
to be drilled in the use of weapons,
if we do not possess weapons,
an oppressed class deserves only to be oppressed,
maltreated and regarded as slaves.

The recitation was a reminder, a call to revolutionary arms and an exhortation to the downtrodden to rise up.

It was vintage Lenin.

The review of collectivization was led by Kuzma, a heavyset

man with thick forearms, powerful hands, long white hair and a curious, full beard that, unlike his hair, was almost completely jet black. Kuzma had been the soviet's deputy responsible for collectivization for the past two years, ever since the region had been secured by the Bolsheviks with a brutal suppression that led to a mass execution of the Whites.

He was a good choice. His age and the fact he was born and lived his entire life in the Selz district meant that he was well known and gave him credibility. Serious to the point of being dour and overly intense, Kuzma was a man impossible to like and easy to fear. A constantly grave demeanour gave Kuzma a flat personality, as if he had no emotional range beyond melancholy and anger. There was a constant sense of his dark side lurking, but never quite emerging into the open. Except, that is, on one occasion that had become legendary throughout the district. When he was 17 years old, Kuzma had killed a Russian man twice his age, in a fight that erupted over a packet of cigarettes. The two had come to blows when the Russian, a tax collector from Saratov, accused Kuzma of stealing cigarettes from a pouch in his knapsack when he set it down to get a drink of water from the cistern in the middle of Selz's town square. The Russian called Kuzma "a fucking lying Ukrainian cocksucker" and slapped Kuzma across his face.

The teenager reacted instantaneously, and lethally, delivering a full force kick to the Russian's testicles. As the Russian fell, clutching his groin, his face contorted in pain, Kuzma knocked him onto his back with a fierce mule kick to the face, the bottom of his heavy boot crushing the bridge of the man's nose, his face erupting as if Kuzma had stomped on a blood-filled balloon. In virtually the same motion, Kuzma dropped to his knees on the man's chest and snapped the Russian's neck with a swift stranglehold. It was a brutal and chilling assault, ending in execution.

From start to finish it lasted perhaps 20 seconds and gave Kuzma the menacing aura of a cold-blooded man perpetually on the edge of violence. He received no punishment, beyond being ordered to keep the peace for a year, because his actions were deemed to be self-defence and the death unintentional in spite of the viciousness of Kuzma's overreaction. But from that point on, Kuzma was someone who commanded respect because people feared his dark side.

"Progress continues, but more work needs to be done," said Kuzma, which is how he always opened the report on collectivization. "We have now fully established eight *kolkhozy* and three *sovkhozy*, which means we are nearing our objective as set out by Comrade Orlensky." The goal had been to create 12 collective farms, or *kolkhozy*, and six state farms, known as *sovkhozy*. Since the summer of 1919, much of the agriculture production in the Kutschurgan had been transformed from individual farms, mostly owned and controlled by German *kulaks* and their families, to collectives. Those who had not willingly embraced the revolution and agreed to work on the collective farms were either driven from the land and exiled to do industrial labour, or executed.

The Andrejaschevski soviet had been officially formed 21 months earlier, but it had been operating as an underground cell for almost four years, as part of the local resistance against the anti-communist Romanians, Bessarabians, tsarist White Russians and German *kulaks* during the civil war. There were 30 others from the district associated with the soviet, but Yulinov was its leader, designated by the Saratov regional soviet, which took its orders directly from Moscow. Yulinov, like all heads of soviets, was selected based on two factors: his clear and unequivocal commitment to the revolution as demonstrated by his actions and the purity of his ideological thoughts.

He was a good choice. His intimidating physical presence, powerful personality, passion and intellect gave him the very attributes for leadership in the revolution. But more importantly, Yulinov had exactly the right kind of commitment to the Communist revolutionary cause—one that came with a sense of grievance and corresponding entitlement.

An ethnic Russian born into a peasant family near Sverdlovsk in the Urals east of Moscow, Yulinov's family had lived an itinerant life from the time Alex was a young child. The family moved at least once a year as his father, Vladimir, sought work as a farm labourer from spring to fall, and doing whatever other piecework he could find during the winter months. Vladimir Yulinov was himself the child of a peasant labourer. Although he never had more than two or three years of formal education, he developed intensely political views that he openly and forcefully shared with his wife, seven children and anyone else he encountered. It was a bitterness rooted in the frustration, deprivation, grinding poverty and sense of servitude that dominated his family's life. His entire life, Vladimir Yulinov saw himself as a victim, powerless to better his lot. He was trapped in poverty because, as a landless peasant in a system where land ownership was the determination of wealth, class and social status, he was forever condemned to subservience. He carried a powerful resentment with him to the very end, when, at 48, he died of a heart attack. Three months earlier, Vladimir Yulinov had brought his family to the Kutschurgan, where he found work baling hay for a German farmer. It happened on a sweltering summer day. Yulinov was carrying a 100-kilo hay bale on his back, the sixth of the day, up a slope to a waiting wagon and team of horses. Steps from the wagon, Yulinov suddenly groaned loudly and fell face first to the ground. Under the weight of the hay bale, his body hit the ground with a sickening thud and sharp cracking sound as his ribs snapped. Yulinov, blood oozing from his nose and mouth, was dead within seconds.

So Alexandre Yulinov's revolutionary zeal was in his genes. He learned it at his father's knee, quite literally. In fact, Alexandre often described how his father, sitting next to the campfire as the family trekked in search of work, would gather his wife and children around to talk about the meaning of justice. He would recite what his father had said about the system he believed was fundamentally unfair, controlled by a minority who exploited the underprivileged like himself and his family.

"There are two kinds of people in the world: the rich and powerful who control the land, and the masses of poor peasants and those living in squalor in the cities whose lives are at the disposal of the rich. The poor own nothing, not even their own labour. Not even their lives. They are the playthings of the rich."

This sense of injustice was something Alexandre Yulinov had come to accept as absolute truth. His father's death, labouring under the wealthy German landowners who farmed the steppes, was, for Yulinov—only 12 when his father died—the ultimate indignity.

Like his father, Yulinov had never risen beyond a similar peasant life of working for others—except for one small difference. Yulinov was at least able to avoid the itinerant life of his childhood into which his father had been forced. After his father died, Yulinov's mother kept her family in the Kutschurgan region of Bessarabia and Ukraine, doing domestic work for the German landowners. Finally, the family settled in the town of Selz, where Alexander Yulinov married, built a small, modest, two-bedroom home, raised four children and worked in the fields. He also used his skills as a carpenter to do work for the wealthiest of the landed class, whose large homes provided a steady diet of work for someone with Yulinov's talents and sheer physical strength.

Anyone who met Yulinov couldn't help but be impressed by his physical presence and his crystal clear, piecing blue eyes. He had broad, athletic shoulders, muscular arms and huge hands with knuckles gnarled from years of hard labour. The middle two fingers on his left hand were missing, victims of a hatchet blow that had sliced them off to leave only stumps when he was splitting logs for winter fuel. His head was shaved bald, making his appearance even more intimidating, contrasted as it was by the dark moustache that turned down and extended to the bottom of his chin on each side of his mouth. He projected a cold sternness.

"Comrade Popov, what can you report on subversive activities?" Yulinov asked, knowing exactly what was to be reported.

"Comrade, we have maintained our surveillance. Since I last reported, we can confirm that Hermann is continuing his anti-revolutionary activities, associating on almost a daily basis with the small group of anti-revolution sympathizers and reactionary *kulaks* and, in particular, the tsarist toadies.

"He has been seen meeting with and talking to those known openly to be enemies of the revolution, in particular those we believe are engaged in planning counter-revolutionary activities. Hermann is often seen visiting the home of Longinus Meier, where a group of four meet regularly. He does this in the most brazen fashion, making no attempt to disguise his activities. I have confronted him about this on at least five occasions and each time he claims he is acting on collectivization efforts and carrying out the work of our soviet."

"How do you know he's not telling the truth?" asked Yulinov. "Is he not chief of collectivization for Fisher-Franzen?"

"He is. But the fact is the little prick shows little interest in it. He is responsible for the collectivization of all 16 farms that were owned by the German *kulaks*. Yet other than the widow Meier, he seldom visits the others to ensure they're meeting their production quotas. Other than Meier, I have noticed or been told that on occasion he has also been seen going to or coming from the Schergevitch home."

"The pig. The fucker is likely servicing the women. You know, there's lots of lonely women in that town," Smenev interjected.

"Shut the fuck up," Yulinov snapped. "Let Sergei talk."

"But what is most disturbing, Comrade Yulinov, is the on-going activities and associations involving Frederich. It is most bizarre."

"How so?"

"Hermann and the others have been seen late in the dark of night—I'm talking midnight or later—emerging from the rear basement entrance of the rectory. What reason have they to be visiting with the priest at that hour? I don't think they're praying the fucking rosary."

"Maybe they're drinking vodka and mixing it with—what do they call it?—holy water," Yulinov joked, which helped put Popov at ease.

"We all know Frederich is a subversive and bourgeois lover," Popov said. "Sure, he wears his holy clothes and preaches forgiveness and love from the pulpit, but in private I know he's urging the *kulaks* to resist the revolution at every turn. There are many who believe he remains in contact with the anti-Bolsheviks, associates of Deniken, Kornilov and Alekseev. I tell you, Frederich can't be trusted. I'm fucking positive he's passing information, scheming and planning with the Whites. Our informant is certain."

Yulinov didn't reply. He stared intently at Popov, thinking about what he had just heard. The others knew better than to interrupt the sudden silence and waited for Yulinov to say something.

After more than a minute, Yulinov finally asked, coldly: "Have we planted the information with the *kulaks* about Trotsky's visit?"

"Yes. He told them," Popov replied.

"And?"

"We're told they are planning an ambush and a public execution."

"Are you confident that our intelligence is solid?" Yulinov asked.

Popov seemed uneasy with the question. "I am, sir," he replied. He knew everything hinged on the reliability of the information they had on what the Germans were planning. The stakes were immeasurably high. Without absolute certainty that they knew what the enemy was planning, the whole strategy could end up a disaster and Trotsky put in peril.

"Well, you better be more than confident. You better be totally fucking *certain* we can trust what we've been told," Yulinov said.

There was a long awkward silence as Yulinov stared at Popov.

Smenev shifted nervously in his chair, crossing and uncrossing his legs, while the others sat motionless, waiting for Yulinov to speak again.

"What does Kozokoff say?" Yulinov finally asked.

Kozokoff was Viacheslav Kozokoff, the soviet's Bessarabian connection. He lived on the other side of the Dniester, near Krasna, and was key in providing on-the-ground intelligence. Kozokoff was truly remarkable, and for good reason. He had lived in the region his entire life and was respected by everyone on all sides, which, given the divisions and hatreds following the war, the revolution and now the civil war, defied all logic or common sense. Kozokoff was unique, a walking contradiction. Affable and authoritative, sensitive and stern, all depending on the circumstance. What made him so invaluable as a source of information for the Bolsheviks was that he had personal connections through family or marriage to all the camps.

An ethnic Russian, Kozokoff's grandparents had come from St. Petersburg aristocracy. His father had disavowed his family's lineage and become a radical Petrograd intellectual opposed to the Romanovs, eventually marrying the daughter of a fellow *re-*

fusenik. Kozokoff himself was married to a woman whose father was a German Catholic and whose mother was the daughter of a Russian Jew and a Muslim Romanian. As the local representative to the Bessarabian legislature, Kozokoff had supporters and admirers in all factions that were part of the struggle for Bessarabia's future. A Communist and admirer of Lenin, Kozokoff was also a Bessarabian nationalist who, in the wake of the fall of the Romanovs and the Soviets' seizure of power in Petrograd, wanted Bessarabia to be a independent soviet republic and not part of Moldavia or Romania.

"Kozokoff is the one who's been telling me what he knows of Fischer-Franzen. He's been watching closely," Popov answered. "I talked to him about this yesterday and he—"

"Watching closely? Watching closely isn't good enough. Does he corroborate what we heard from Sylowich?" Yulinov interjected.

"He does. That's why I have confidence in what our guy is telling us. He says that there are 12 of them planning the attack near the bridge to Strassburg. He was the one who told us about the Whites' ambush more than two years ago. If he hadn't tipped us off, we would have been fucked. Leonev here would likely be dead today, and it would have been our bodies burned, not theirs. So, yes, I have confidence in what he tells us."

Yulinov leaned back in his chair and put his hands behind his bald head.

"So, the German fuckers think they're planning the big hit, do they. Well, we'll see who gets fucked. If everything you say is true, this is going to be a lot of fun. I can't wait to see the look on their faces when the time comes."

Popov nodded and said nothing.

He and the others were uneasy about Yulinov's frequent reference to the reliability of the information Popov was supplying. It was a kind of caveat, the subtext being that it had better be reliable intelligence. They all knew it was a serious mistake to display any doubt or lack of resolve when dealing with Yulinov. To do that was to betray a weakness that Yulinov would not tolerate. And you never wanted Yulinov to question you in any way, let alone your commitment and dedication to the revolution. After all, there could be no doubting his soviet commitment, or pedigree. Yulinov was, without question, the leading Bolshevik in the region and his influence and reputation extended through the Kutschurgan, reaching across the Dniester into Bessarabia.

Yulinov's story was well known, so much so that it caused a certain reverential treatment from fellow comrades in the Bolshevik revolution.

IN THE FALL OF 1917, when he heard that Lenin had returned from exile in Finland, Yulinov left Selz and, in late October, made the long trek to Petrograd to join the unrest building in the capital. It was a grueling 1,400-kilometre journey on horseback. Normally it would take two weeks of 12-14-hour days. But Yulinov, passionate in his commitment to the Bolshevik cause, completed the journey in only 11. The story, which already had grown to the status of legend, was that Yulinov had quickly been brought to a small group of tacticians known as the Military Revolutionary Committee, who worked directly with Trotsky. The fact he'd come from Ukraine and travelled such a great distance had quickly given Yulinov stature with leading Bolsheviks in Petrograd. They were eager to broaden the scope of the revolution beyond the capital, which was the epicenter of the political and social unrest, into the far flung regions of Russia. So a passionate adherent to the cause like Yulinov, from the far-off Kutschurgan, was considered an important asset.

But Yulinov also knew he had to prove himself as a revolutionary before he could become a trusted Bolshevik. When he arrived in Petrograd, he quickly learned that the revolutionary forces were amassed near the Winter Palace, the opulent former home of the deposed tsars, which had become seat of the provisional government. Eager to prove his commitment to the revolution, Yulinov circulated through clusters of 20-30 men huddled about open fires to keep warm. He certainly looked the part of a revolutionary fighter. One bitter night during his trek to Petrograd, Yulinov had suffered frostbite to his face and fingers. When he arrived in Petrograd, his nose was still badly swollen. The skin of his nose and right cheek had turned a ghoulish purple and black before disappearing into the matted thicket of beard. Two fingers on his right hand, from the last knuckle through to the fingernails, were also discoloured from frostbite, the skin hardened like leather. He hadn't bathed in weeks and was pungent with his own sweat and urine.

At first, the Bolsheviks he met seemed disinterested, if not outright suspicious, of the man who claimed to be from Ukraine, anxious though he seemed to become a Bolshevik revolutionary foot soldier. Until he met a man named Yuri Lebedev.

It was on the cobblestone promenade running along the Neva River that Yulinov made his move. Hundreds of revolutionaries had gathered in anticipation of an assault on the palace that would signal the end of Kerensky and the provisional government. When Yulinov told one man he wanted to join them, the man looked at him impassively and simply pointed to Lebedev, who was standing nearby talking with two others. Yulinov waited until the other two had left before approaching Lebedev, who had turned and started to walk in the opposite direction.

"My name is Yulinov, Alexandre Yulinov. I've come from the Kutschurgan in Ukraine. I want to be a revolutionary," Yulinov said to Lebedev. At first Lebedev seemed oblivious to the stranger.

He didn't stop walking away or turn around to acknowledge the man speaking to him.

Yulinov quickened his pace so that he was only two steps behind Lebedev and repeated his plea.

"My name is Yulinov. I've come from Ukraine to join the revolution in support of the proletariat."

Lebedev stopped, took a package of cigarettes from his coat pocket and, without turning around to look the stranger, said, "How do I know you're not one of Kornikov's people?"

"Because I'm not. Because I've travelled for 11 days from Kutschurgan on horseback to join the revolution."

Lebedev lit a cigarette and kept his back to the stranger. "From the Kutschurgan, near the Dniester? I was there once. Mostly just Germans who have taken our land. Why should I believe you? How do I know you haven't been sent here to infiltrate our ranks?" Lebedev began walking away again, his back still turned to Yulinov.

"What do I need to do to prove myself?" Yulinov asked, hurrying to keep pace as he walked behind the other man. "I have already ridden far to join your ranks."

Lebedev didn't slow down and didn't respond.

"What do I need to do to prove myself as a revolutionary?" Yulinov asked again.

Still Lebedev kept walking, lengthening his stride, his back to Yulinov.

"I will do anything for the revolution. Anything!"

With that, Lebedev stopped, turned and finally set eyes on the stranger. He took a deep drag from his cigarette and exhaled a menacing cloud of smoke into Yulinov's face, his dark, coal-like eye expressionless.

"Why should I believe you? Why should I trust you? For all I know, Denizen sent you."

"Then test me," Yulinov said.

Lebedev was one of Lenin's most trusted lieutenants and a member of the revolutionary council. He was a tall, athletic-looking man with the wide shoulders, barrel chest, muscular arms and powerful legs of a labourer. Tufts of his long, curly blond hair sprouted from under the brim of a weathered brown leather cap. After ignoring him so thoroughly, Lebedev suddenly became consumed by Yulinov's presence. He narrowed his eyes at the stranger, scowling as he stared at Yulinov with piercing intensity.

"What the fuck's your name?"

"Yulinov," he said once more, "Alexandre Yulinov. I'm from the Kutschurgan, the Ukraine. I've travelled 11 days to get here. I want to join the revolution."

"Then join the fucking revolution," Lebedev snapped, pointing to a group of men huddled around a small fire across the road. "See those people over there? Tell them Lebedev sent you."

Lebedev flicked the cigarette over his shoulder in the direction of the Neva River, turned and walked away.

Yulinov approached the six men keeping warm around the fire. Each had a rifle slung over his shoulder. They looked at him suspiciously; one of them swung his rifle onto his hip, just in case.

"My name is Alexandre Yulinov. I've travelled 11 days on horseback from Ukraine to join the revolution," he repeated, for what he hoped would be the final time.

They stared at him but did not respond.

"Lebedev told me to join you," Yulinov said, making a fist and pointing over his shoulder with his outstretched thumb to where Lebedev was still visible, walking down the other side of the road.

Finally, one of them spoke.

"We need food. Find us food."

Taking this as his only chance, Yulinov simply said, "All right," and walked away.

What happened next became legend in the Kutschurgan.

THE SCENE WAS TRANQUIL, even breathtaking, in its serene beauty. The Winter Palace stood majestically bathed in the shimmering, light reflected off the Neva. The approaching night was cold and cloudless, the moon full. The Baroque columns of the palace glowed in the soft light, its recessed walls hidden in dark shadows, creating a momentary optical illusion. The palace seemed to be an empty shell, made up of columns and turrets—like a Russian acropolis—its walls invisible until the eye focused more clearly. The serenity was shattered by the hollow clomping sound of horses' hooves on cobblestone.

Soldiers, still loyal to Kerensky, stood arms' length apart in two lines that stretched from the front of the palace portico to the eight-foot wall at the edge of the Neva. The lines circled around the palace and down the middle of Druzinsky Prospect along the southeast side. Behind them, protecting the seat of government, were clusters of other soldiers on horseback. The Winter Palace was ringed by a secure perimeter, a cordon of soldiers on three sides, and the icy waters of the Neva on the other.

Yulinov raised his collar, pulled the flaps from under his hat to cover his ears and hunched his shoulders against the abnormally icy chill of the wind that swept across the square. Late October was always a somber and dreary time in Petrograd. Darkness didn't give way to sunlight until almost 9 A.M. and the deepening shadows returned by mid-afternoon, the swift oncoming of night erasing daylight shortly after 5 P.M.

He walked away slowly. Frustrated, physically exhausted after the gruelling days of travel and unsure what to do next, Yulinov knew one thing—he didn't travel 1,400 kilometres to be turned away by the Bolsheviks in their showdown with Kerensky. But in such moments of weakness, when he felt his personal resolve fading, he inevitably thought of the struggles of his father and his family. It always inspired him. Instantly he felt a current of energy and again shared the Bolshevik passion. He was determined to join the cause.

Grey twilight had already descended on the city. Instinctively, Yulinov turned his back to the cold dampness of the north wind that swept down from the Baltic, the Neva channeling it like a wind tunnel to sweep across Palace Square. Walking south, Yulinov turned a corner on to smaller side street. Needing a cigarette, he stepped into an alcove of what looked like a dreary government office building. It was littered with papers and pamphlets swirling in an eddy of wind. Hunching his shoulders against the chill breeze as he cupped his hands to light his smoke, Yulinov didn't notice the old woman crouched in the shadows, wrapped in a tattered woolen blanket.

"Can I have a cigarette?" she asked flatly.

Startled, Yulinov glanced at the huddled woman. Keeping his eyes fixed on her, he paused, then reached into the breast pocket of his coat. He pulled out a tarnished silver metal cigarette flask and, with a quick flip of his wrist, a cigarette emerged. He bent down and offered it to the woman. She took it, put it between her lips and, before she could ask, Yulinov held out the burning end of his cigarette to light hers. He noticed that her hands were those of a peasant, calloused and creased with wrinkles, the knuckles swollen from years of labour and arthritis. They reminded Yulinov of his mother's hands.

"Thanks," the old woman said, inhaling the smoke deeply.

Yulinov said nothing.

"I've been here for a week. Waiting."

Yulinov took a drag. "For what?" he asked, two bursts of smoke coming from his mouth as he spoke.

"Trotsky," she answered.

Yulinov assumed the woman was mad. He couldn't help but feel pity for her.

"He's coming, you know," she said.

Again, Yulinov said nothing but took time to look her over carefully. Despite the frayed blanket around her shoulders, a bright gold necklace hung from under a shabby woolen scarf, a bizarre adornment of elegance on an otherwise obviously poor, common woman.

"My son Yuri told me. He knows. He's with Lev Bronstein—Trotsky—at the Smolny right now. He told me they will be coming soon. So I wait."

Putting on his weather-worn and cracked leather gloves, Yulinov was about to step back onto the street and leave the crazy woman to her delusions.

"Will you tell them?"

"Tell who, what?" Yulinov wanted to know.

"My son and Trotsky. Will you go to the Smolny and tell them I'm here, waiting for them?"

"The Smolny?" Yulinov asked.

"The Smolny Institute. That's where they are. It's their headquarters. Near Taurade Palace. My son is a guard."

"What's his name?"

"Yuri Ragulin. Tell him his mother still waits for the salvation of the soviets."

"And what's *your* name?" Yulinov asked.

"Alexandra. He gave me this," she said, her calloused, dirty fingers gently stroking the necklace.

Yulinov said nothing. He stepped back out onto the cobblestone sidewalk, leaving the woman to the shadows as he moved towards a small cluster of people waiting for a streetcar.

"How much is fare?" Yulinov asked no one in particular.

"Three *kopeks*," an old man replied.

No sooner had the man answered than Yulinov heard the squealing of metal against metal and the clatter of a streetcar as it turned the corner and approached its next stop. The faintly lit sign in the window above the driver read SMOLNY STATION.

The streetcar was jammed with weary-looking passengers. Yulinov stood in the aisle, shoulder-to-shoulder with the others who climbed aboard before him. The people either gazed blankly out the dirty windows or stared at the floor, no one making eye contact. They travelled silently in a kind of metal cocoon of rattling, creaking and squealing iron wheels against iron rails. Five stops later, the driver shouted "Smolny" as the streetcar lurched to a noisy stop. All the passengers stepped off, Yulinov last.

Standing with hundreds of others at Smolny Square, he immediately sensed the energy of the throng. People walked to and fro in all directions, many more milled about in groups, some as few as three or four, others in clusters of 15, 20 or more. There was no way to know, but Yulinov guessed there were many hundreds of people in the square, probably a thousand. All those gathered in groups seemed engrossed in their conversations. The diversity of the people was striking, from what looked to be peasants to government bureaucrats; labourers to academics.

Across the square stood the Smolny Institute. It was an imposing sight, stretching for easily 100 metres and three storeys, its tall, arched windows rimmed in decorative gold trim. The former convent for the daughters of Russian nobility had the imperial insignia of the tsars etched into the grey concrete above its entrance. The massive wooden doors were propped open by what looked to be two logs wedged between the heavy gold latches, a block of concrete on each side. The dim electric light was enough to allow Yulinov to see people inside the lobby. Outside, two men, each armed with a rifle, stood guard at the front entrance.

Yulinov felt an unexpected tug on his arm.

"Here," a young boy, no more than 10, said, holding out a newspaper.

Yulinov took it. The headline of the *Workers' Road and Soldier* read: BOURGEOIS GOVERNMENT NEARS ITS END, PROLETARIAT RISES UP. Yulinov knew the headline was true. He could feel it. The contrast between the two extremes was palpable. The anticipation of the throngs forming a human garrison at Smolny Square. The fear and anxiety of the siege mentality among the troops who ringed the Winter Palace as a last line of defence against the revolution. The Kerensky resistance seemed futile.

The two guards standing at attention on either side of the entrance to the Smolny wore the green-grey garb of the Red Army, rifles slung across their chests. As Yulinov climbed the steps, they stepped together, closing ranks and blocking his path. Yulinov was not easily intimidated. He didn't stop until he was at the entrance landing, virtually nose-to-nose with the soldiers. They stared menacingly at each other in silence until Yulinov spoke.

With nothing more than his determination to join the Bolshevik cause, Yulinov had no idea how to go about doing so, or what to say. He wasn't even sure why he had come to the Smolny or what he hoped to achieve by being there. Now, face-to-face with the Red Army guards, their cold gaze making it clear they had no intention of letting him inside, Yulinov simply said the first thing that came to mind.

"I'm here to see Yuri Ragulin. I have a message for him from his mother."

The guards stared intently ahead, as if he wasn't there, and didn't move.

"Didn't you hear me? I said I'm here to see Yuri Ragulin—with a message from his mother."

"Who are you?" one of the guards asked.

"Alexandre Yulinov. I've travelled from the Kutschurgan in Ukraine to join the revolution."

"Wait here," he said, and disappeared around the corner inside.

A moment later he returned with a tall, thin man with a patchy black beard. He was dressed in what Yulinov recognized as the civilian clothes of the Bolshevik leadership cadre—a peaked leather hat, buttoned-up tunic, coarse woolen pants and black boots. His right sleeve was rolled up to display tattoos that covered his forearm.

"Who are you? What are you doing here?" the man asked sternly.

"Like I told your friends here, I'm Alexandre Yulinov, I've travelled 11 days from Kutschurgan to join the revolution. And I have a message for Yuri Ragulin from his mother, Alexandra."

The man's dour expression suddenly grew graver and more threatening.

"A message from his mother? A message from whose mother?"

"Yuri Ragulin's."

"Really? You better not be fucking with me or I'll rip your balls off with my bare hands and stuff them in your mouth. You understand? I'm Yuri Ragulin," Ragulin said, coming almost nose-to-nose with the stranger.

Yulinov could smell a blend of stale cigar smoke and rum on Ragulin's breath, his scowling face inches from Yulinov's own.

"I was walking from the Winter Palace and met a woman in a doorway. She was huddled in the cold and asked me for a cigarette. We spoke. She said her name was Alexandra and that her son Yuri Ragulin was at the Smolny. That you were with Trotsky and I should tell him that she's waiting for you, for the liberation of the proletariat."

Ragulin looked at Yulinov, unsure whether to believe the stranger or have the guards arrest him and take him away.

"How do I know you're not a fucking liar?" Ragulin snarled, "Why should I believe you? How do I know you're not a White from Ukraine, an infiltrator sent by the German *kulaks*?" Ragulin unsheathed a huge knife from his belt, pressing its serrated edge under Yulinov's chin.

"Your mother, she asked me for a cigarette. I gave her one. I saw her hands. They were the hands of a labourer, her knuckles swollen from arthritis."

Ragulin was not convinced.

"She said I was with Trotsky?"

"Yes. At first she said Bronstein. I didn't know who she meant. She called Trotsky by his family name—Bronstein, Lev Davidovitch Bronstein. She said Bronstein was Trotsky."

Ragulin began to believe the stranger was telling the truth. His mother often referred to Trotsky by his Jewish name.

"And your mother, she was wearing a gold necklace," Yulinov added. "It seemed odd, because she looked to be a peasant."

It was the necklace Ragulin had given his mother two weeks earlier for her 75th birthday, the day Kerensky had fled to Moscow as the Bolshevik grip tightened on the provisional government.

"So you want to join the revolution?" Ragulin said, abruptly putting his knife away but offering no apology. "You said you're from where, Ukraine? Near the Black Sea?"

"Yes."

"Come with me."

The two men walked through the entryway, down a long arched hallway of elegant marble, and up two flights of a wide staircase to the top floor of the Smolny. Ragulin led Yulinov to an unmarked office door and knocked.

"It's Ragulin," he said.

"Come in," someone answered, the voice barely audible from the other side.

Inside was a small dark office, a single lamp hanging from the ceiling glowing above the head of the thin man behind the desk.

Yulinov looked up to see the bushy hair, thick moustache, wire-rimmed glasses and thin, pointed nose of a face he instantly recognized from newspaper pictures and propaganda.

It was Trotsky.

He was dressed in a white shirt, sleeves rolled up, the smoke from a cigarette in his right hand curling up into the glow of the lamp above.

"Yes?" he said, glancing up only briefly.

"Sir, this is ... what did you say your name is?"

"Alexandre Yulinov."

"He says he is from Kutschurgan, sir, north from Odessa. He says that he wants to join us and the revolution."

Trotsky looked up and stared at Yulinov. "And you believe him?" he asked Ragulin, though his eyes were fixed on Yulinov.

"I do, sir. He says he has travelled 11 days to be here and then met my mother on the street. She told him that I was here with you. I believe him."

"So why did you bring him to me?"

"Because, Comrade Trotsky, the Kutschurgan is near your original home, and you've told me we need to strengthen our ranks there. I thought maybe you would want to meet him."

When he was born, Trotsky's family farmed in Mykolaiv Oblast, a province in Ukraine, northeast of Odessa on the Black Sea. His was not a typical Jewish family upbringing. They were not religious, did not experience the ghetto life like many other Jews of the time and farmed the land, unusual for Jews of any era. Moreover, his father was illiterate. Still, the family lived a comfortable life and, compared to many, were wealthy. As a young boy, Trotsky had been sent to a German boarding school in Odessa, an experience that ingrained in him two things: respect for the power of the Germanic ego and a deep resentment of the success of German immigrants in Ukraine.

One summer when he was a teenager, he worked for three months on the farm of a distant relative in the Kutschurgan. It was near Stepanowka, just 15 kilometres south of Fischer-Franzen. Bronstein's relatives were the only Jews to farm the land in what was an otherwise German region. He felt the isolation and alienation of being Jewish among Christian Germans, the powerful sense of being an outcast, resented for being a Jew farmer in a region settled and cultivated by generations of immigrant Germans.

This man Yulinov from the Kutschurgan, who wanted to join the cause of a Bolshevik Russia, interested Trotsky.

"Are you a Jew?" he asked.

"Yes," Yulinov lied.

"I understand. We need comrades in the Kutschurgan."

With that, Yulinov was anointed a Bolshevik, by no less than Trotsky himself.

CHAPTER 5

THINKING BACK ON IT NOW, I was actually lucky when they killed my father and brother. Don't get me wrong. I know that sounds unbelievably crass, even inhuman. But understand, I'm not saying there is anything good about watching, with your own eyes when you're four years old, your dad being murdered. Or that seeing your brother's body burned on the street in front of your house two days later is not something that haunts you for the rest of your life. It does, and it has me. What I'm trying to say is that, at a certain level, it was good because what actually happened didn't fully register with me at the time.

Let me try to explain.

Even now, many decades later, I can still recall the dread and fear I felt. I've never, ever forgotten the wrenching panic in the pit of my stomach when I saw them kill Dad, the feeling that made me throw up in my parents' bedroom. It haunts me still. There are times when, out of nowhere, that nauseous feeling overcomes me. Sometimes it's strong enough that I actually get sick. All of a sudden I feel a burning sensation in my throat as the vomit wells up out of my stomach and I have to find a toilet, fast. Other times it's just a kind of fleeting sickness that disappears as quickly as it comes. I've never been able to figure out what exactly triggers it because it happens when I least expect it.

So, in some ways, I have relived that moment countless times throughout my life. Years ago, I actually went to the doctor—a gastroenterologist—about it and he said I had what's called "acid reflux" and that it could damage my esophagus. He told me to watch my diet, avoid acidic foods like oranges, grapefruit and tomatoes, and that I should take a tablespoon of milk of magnesia twice a day for two weeks, then once a day three times a week for a year. I did and it didn't help. It just gave me the shits.

The other things that have never left me are the sound of footsteps, and the moaning and sobbing I heard when I was hiding in my parents' bedroom. Like I said before, it was unlike anything I've ever heard since. It was so intense, so painful, so haunting that it didn't quite sound human. Even now I can't really describe it. The only word that comes close is *forlorn*. Almost as if, somehow, the sound was detached from humanity. Just thinking about it makes me shiver, even now. And I remember the footsteps from below like an advancing dread, stalking me as I hunched over in my parents' bedroom. To this very day, when I hear sounds I don't immediately recognize, it makes me feel a kind of panic in my stomach.

Those are what I call physical memories. They trigger actual, real physiological effects, not so much *feelings*, in the sense of emotion. What I'm trying to tell you is that I'm left with more physical remnants of those days, and less emotional ones. At least, not that I struggle with today. Granted, I'm no shrink or expert on these kinds of things. But I think I know myself pretty well. Which brings me to my point.

It's like my brain is insulated from what happened to me when my life began. I know you'll likely think this is stupid, but it's like my head is covered with a tin foil helmet or Teflon or something, and all the bad thoughts from the outside just bounce off my head and can't get in. So what happens is instead of getting into my brain, the bad thoughts somehow get into other parts of my body, like my stomach or spine, and make me feel sick or shivery.

But the *really* strange thing is, other than what you might call those very real physical memories, I feel detached from it all, like it didn't really happen to me. At least, I don't get all emotional and feel sad, or sorry or depressed. Like I was saying, in other words I didn't get all messed up by what happened and have to see a shrink on and off for the rest of my life. Which, as far as I'm concerned, is a good thing. That's because I've long believed that psychiatrists are often pretty messed up themselves. It's only natural they would be. After all, they spend their working lives dealing with crazy people, and, if you ask me, some of that has to rub off.

Looking back now, I figure that being so young was the main reason I've been able to cope. So, that's why I say I was lucky when they murdered my father and my life began. The lucky part is that I was only four years old, and when you're that young things don't really sink in because you don't really understand what's happening or why or what it all means to you and your life. It's amazing how resilient little kids can be when they face adversity. It's because they don't really grasp things in a way they can fully appreciate. They live in a bit of a fantasy world that slowly but surely turns into the real world as they grow up and learn things, usually not very nice things, about other people and the world they live in.

So, I'd say being young was a good thing. That, and having Kaza as my best friend.

IT MIGHT HAVE BEEN THE DAY of my brother's funeral, but it was still perfect—sunny, hot, but not too hot or humid, with the slightest hint of a breeze. There were a few fluffy clouds way off just above the horizon in the distance. Standing with my mother, brother and sisters and a crowd of other people next to my brother's grave in the cemetery behind the church, I remember thinking it was just right for John's trip to heaven. With no clouds directly above us, the coast was clear all the way for him to meet up with God and Dad.

"Lord of all, we praise You for all who have entered into their rest and reached the promised land where You are seen face to face," Father Frederich said. "Give us grace to follow in their footsteps as they followed in the way of Your Son. Thank you for the memory of those You have called to Yourself: with each memory, turn our hearts from things seen to things unseen, and lead us until we come to the eternal rest You have prepared for Your people, through Jesus Christ, our Lord."

I thought it was going to be really neat seeing someone go to heaven, especially someone I actually knew, like my big brother. I couldn't wait for him to go and come back and tell us what it was like way up there above the clouds. I wasn't quite sure why John was in the box suspended on rope straps above the hole in the ground. I just figured the casket had wings that would automatically come out of the sides and it would start flying like a bird, with John steering from the inside. Either that or some angels would come down and lift it up to heaven.

Whatever the case, I couldn't wait to see it.

After Father Frederich finished saying prayers, he walked around John swinging a gold thing that looked like a lantern or something attached to a long chain. It was on fire. At least you could see smoke coming out of it and it smelled sweet. Next he shook a silver thing with a round bulb on the end. I could see drops of water came out and land on John's casket.

"From dust to dust ..."

Then, he turned and nodded to Mom. She was wearing a black

dress and scarf with a black veil over her face. But I could still see she was crying, tears dribbled down the sides of her chin. I remember wondering why she wasn't excited like me about John going to meet with God.

The priest handed Mom what looked like a miniature shovel made out of gold. It was about the size of the black metal one that I remembered seeing her use to dig in our garden. She took the little shovel from Father, bent over and scooped up some of the soil from the mound of earth next to the hole in the ground and John's casket. As mother sprinkled the dirt on John, she began sobbing loudly. I started crying too because whenever I saw someone else cry, it made me sad and nothing made me sadder than seeing Mom cry because I didn't want her to be sad. My uncle Victor, who lived down the road and across the bridge over the big river near Selz and had come to our house two days before to help our mother, put his arm around Mom's shoulders and she turned her face into his chest. A few minutes later, as we walked away from the cemetery, I remember that I could still see the wet stains from Mom's tears on Uncle Victor's white shirt.

After we walked back to our house, Mom went upstairs to her and Dad's bedroom to lie down. Our big sister, Eva, oldest of all the kids now that John was gone to heaven, called us together— me, Magdalena, Rachel, Theresa, Christina, Frank and even Mary, who was only two. Rachel sat down on the floor in the living room and asked us all to sit on the floor in a circle and join hands.

"I want to sit in the rocking chair," I said.

Rachel looked at me. She had tears in her eyes. "Please, Anton, no, just this once."

I felt like I might start crying too and sat down on the floor between Christina and Frank and held their hands.

"Where's Emma?" Frankie asked.

"She's not feeling well. She's resting in our room," Rachel said.

When Frankie asked about Emma it made me think she had hardly said a word in the four days since they killed Dad. She spent most of her time in her darkened bedroom with the window shutters closed and didn't even come down to eat with the rest of us. Instead, Rachel, Magdalena or Theresa would take food to her. A couple of times I saw them come into the kitchen with the plate of food they had taken to Emma's room and it looked like nothing had been eaten. I also noticed at the funeral that Emma wore a black veil over her face like Mom, which covered the bruise on her cheek and her swollen lip, which were slowly getting better. My other sisters didn't wear veils.

Frank was sitting too close to me and I could see extra space between him and Mary on the other side of him. So I shoved him on the shoulder and said, "Move over." He pushed me back and started crying. Then Mary started crying too and so did I.

"Stop it, Anton. See what you've done now? Be nice. Everyone stop crying, please," Eva said.

Mary stood up, crying loudly, tears streaming down her face. Rachel, sitting cross-legged on the floor, reached over to Mary's outstretched arms, took her hands and sat her down in her lap, wrapping her arms around Mary and pulling her close to her chest. Almost instantly Mary stopped crying and so did Frank, and then me.

Eva had the whitest skin, big brown eyes and beautiful dark red hair that spilled across her shoulders and caught the sunlight that poured through the living room window. "I know we all feel upset and sad. Dad and John have gone to be with God and we need to be strong for Mom, Emma and each other. We have to help each other."

"Eva, have Papa and John seen God already?" Frankie asked.

"Yes. They're with Him now."

"Will they be home for supper?"

"No, Frankie. They're going to stay in heaven with God and wait until we join them."

"When do we go?"

"God will decide."

"I wished we would have seen John fly up to heaven," I said. "There were no clouds in the way today, you know."

"I know," Eva said. "But listen, you kids have to promise me you'll be strong."

"We're older than Anton, Frankie and Mary, so you know that Christina, Theresa and I will do our parts," Magdalena promised.

"Why is Emma always in her room?" I asked.

"She isn't feeling good and needs time to feel better," Magdalena said.

"Kaza said Emma and Mama got raped by the scary men."

"Anton, I don't know where Kaza heard that, but you mustn't ever repeat it to anyone," Rachel said. "You have to promise me. Promise?"

"I promise."

It felt good to be sitting in a circle holding hands with my brother and sisters. I wasn't afraid anymore. Through the window I could see a few fluffy white clouds in the bright, noon-day blue summer sky.

Rachel, Magdalena, Theresa and Christina went into the kitchen to help make lunch. Uncle Victor and Aunt Felicia and Freda, a lady friend of my mother's who I saw at church every Sunday in the pew right in front of us, were already there helping prepare the food.

It was just after one in the afternoon and we were still sitting at the kitchen table, just finishing our soup and bread, when I heard Kaza's voice behind me.

"Kuh-can Anton come out and puh-play?" he asked.

I turned in my chair and saw Kaza standing on the back step through the screen door.

"All right. But, Anton, don't go far. And stay out of the Andre, you two. Mother has enough on her mind," Eva said.

"All right," I said.

Five minutes later our pantlegs were rolled up and we were standing knee deep in the Andre. Kaza had brought the small net that his mother had made for him to catch minnows. It was made out of thick hemp threads.

"Sometimes I wonder where the water kuh-comes from and where it guh-goes. Do you?" Kaza said, looking off in the distance upstream.

"Uh-huh."

"My dad says it kuh-comes out of the ground up in the huh-hills and goes all the wuh-way far down there to the Black Sea."

The Black Sea. I had heard others mention it and when I did it made me kind of afraid. I imagined an ocean with black water, monsters living in it and swallowing anyone who went into its waves. I instantly wanted to get my feet out of the Andre in case the monsters came out of the Black Sea and up the stream to grab me. I stepped back onto the shore and rolled my pantlegs down. Kaza did the same and we walked back into town to get a drink, this time going to Kaza's house, across the street and two houses down from our place.

Kaza's house always smelled funny. He had two older, fat twin sisters who had black hair and dark skin like Kaza.

Whenever I went to his house, his mother always seemed to be in the kitchen. She'd be ironing clothes, a cigarette hanging out of the corner of her mouth, with a big vat of something bubbling on the stove, the lid fluttering under the steam and vapours filling the house with a kind of smell that I always thought was some combination of sugar and vinegar. I didn't like the smell.

Kaza's mom had long, stringy, shiny, black hair that I was sure must have soaked in the smell of the kitchen. Her hair was pulled back tight into a braided bun. So tight, in fact, that when you looked at her hairline at the top of her forehead you'd think the roots were straining to hold onto her hair from being pulled right out of her scalp. She was quite tiny and thin, with scrawny arms and frail wrists that looked like they would break if someone shook her hand too hard. She had dark circles under her eyes. Sometimes when I was at Kaza's and his mom wasn't ironing—which wasn't often—she'd be sitting at the kitchen table, smoking, her hair hanging loose in strands. She'd take a puff of her cigarette, set it down and pick at the ends of her hair, like she was threading a needle or something. It was like she was in a trance.

"Mama, kuh-can Anton and muh-me get suh-something to drink? We're thirsty," Kaza asked after we walked into the kitchen. His mom was standing at the ironing table, staring out the window, smoking, a basket of wrinkled clothes sitting on the counter. She didn't answer.

"Muh-mom, kuh-kuh ..."

Kaza's mom turned and walked out of the kitchen. It was as if she didn't hear Kaza, or know we were even there. Without waiting, Kaza slid a chair over to the counter, climbed onto the chair, got up on his knees onto the counter and reached for two glasses from the shelf. He stepped back down onto the chair and took each glass and dipped it into the pail of drinking water in the sink. He turned, handed me a glass of water, got off the chair and reached for the other glass filled with water he had set by the counter's edge. Neither of us said a word as we drank the lukewarm water.

"Wanna play something?" Kaza asked as we stood on the walk in front of his house.

"Play what?"

"I duh-dunno. Wanna see my hi-hiding puh-place?"

"Sure. Where?" I asked.

A minute later we were standing inside a small, dark and musky wooden toolshed in the corner of Kaza's backyard. It was cluttered with mostly junk, pieces of metal and a few tools, like a wheelbarrow, sledgehammer and a scythe. A timber saw with rough, jagged teeth was propped up against a small crate that held two hammers and a metal tin filled with nails and wood screws. In one corner was what looked like a piece of dark green canvas tarp covering something.

"What's that?" I asked, pointing at the canvas.

"My secret hiding puh-place. I'll show yuh-you. But first I have to cluh-close the door."

When Kaza closed the door, we were enveloped in complete darkness. I instantly started to panic.

"Let me out! Let me out!"

"It's all right, Anton. Just wuh-wait. Pruh-promise?"

Within a few seconds, my eyes began adjusting to the almost total darkness. Light seeped between the cracks in the rough wooden planks of the walls, and after 30 seconds I could see Kaza next to me and gradually start making out the shapes of most things in the shed. In another minute I could see dust particles floating in the sunlight poking through the cracks.

Kaza took my hand and led me toward the canvas. He lifted a corner and crawled underneath. "Come," he said, holding the canvas back so I could get on my hands and knees and crawl in after him.

When we were both under the canvas, Kaza let the corner flop back and suddenly we were back in darkness. This time I could feel Kaza next to me as we sat close together on the dirt floor. But I didn't feel as afraid as before.

The thick, oily canvas had been hung over a wooden sawhorse, creating a crude sort of tent. It wasn't quite wide enough to completely hang down to the ground at the ends, so there was enough ventilation to let some light and air get in under the tarp. There was also a small knothole in the wall about two centimetres wide right at eye level from where we sat on the cool, dirt floor. Light streamed in through it. You could look out through the hole into Kaza's backyard and see past the corner of his house to the street to the front door of my house on the other side.

"This is my secret kay-cave," Kaza said.

"Neat."

"Now it is our suh-suh-secret. Right, Anton?"

"Uh-huh. Our secret, Kaza."

"Promise?"

"Promise."

We sat there talking for 15 minutes, about nothing in particular. Mostly just about how no one would ever find us in there and that it felt good to be in a secret place that only we knew existed. Kaza said sometimes when his dad was mad, he would sneak out and go to the secret place until it was all right to go back to his house. One time, he said that he was in there from suppertime until he had to go to bed.

Later that night, there were lots of people, mostly relatives like my uncles and aunts and cousins, at our house. The grownups had spent most of the afternoon in our summer kitchen, cooking and baking things like chicken, potatoes, corn on the cob and bread. I love corn on the cob with butter. When I came home from Kaza's, Mom was sitting with Aunt Heidel on a bench in the yard near the back door. I said, "Hi, Mama" and could tell she had been crying. She reached out to give me a hug and said, "You're such a big boy, Anton," which made me feel good. For supper, us kids got to eat outside sitting on two big blankets under the oak tree, while the grown-ups ate inside. Emma stayed in her room again, so Rachel took her a plate of food and glass of milk. I noticed later the plate was on the counter in the kitchen with the other supper dishes and most of the food was gone and the milk glass was empty. I remember it made me feel a little bit happy, but I'm not exactly sure why.

Even though they were girls and didn't like to catch frogs, mud turtles, tadpoles or garter snakes in the Andre with Kaza and me, I didn't mind my big sisters. At least, not too much. My biggest sister Eva knew how to do things, like milk the cows and help Mom cook. But she and Mom used to get mad at each other and argue sometimes, especially about Eva's boyfriend, Raphael, who Mom didn't like much. She said that he was part Gypsy. Rachel, who shared a bedroom with Eva, was 17. She had long dark brown hair and wasn't even as tall as Magdalena, who everyone called "Maggie," who was 16. Maggie had the same bedroom as Emma. Theresa, who was 12, and Christina, who was nine, had the most beautiful blue eyes and, I bet, a million dolls in the bedroom they shared. Everyone always used to say that Emma, who was 14, was the cutest, mostly I figure because her hair hung down in ringlets.

As for Frankie and Mary, there's not much to say about them, other than that we had the same bedroom, and Frankie, who had really thick, curly black hair, sometimes snored. He always wanted to follow me around, which was all right sometimes. I guess it was because I was his big brother and kid brothers always want to hang around their big brother. Mary had frizzy, reddish-brown hair that already covered her ears, even though she was barely two. Mom said that me and Frankie needed to watch out for our little sister, especially at night when she got scared of the dark. Sometimes, by the time I was five, I would get into trouble because when we would be lying in bed and not asleep yet and it was already getting dark outside, I would talk about Old Yellow

Tooth, *Yähl Tain*, the boogeyman. Frankie and Mary would get really upset and cry. Mom used to have to come into the room and sit on the edge of the bed they shared and tell them not to listen to me, that there was no such thing as *Yähl Tain*, tuck them under the covers and give them a goodnight kiss. Then she would tell me not to scare my little brother and sister, kiss me on the forehead and tell me to sleep tight.

That's the one thing I remember most about Mom. She never, ever really got angry or upset. Sure, maybe she might argue with Eva about her boyfriend Raphael sometimes, but it never ended badly. Mom would never raise her voice and in the end, Mom would always say: "*Herzchen*, remember I love you. I only want the best for you." There was a gentleness about her. In her touch, her words, her eyes. So, no matter what, Mom always seemed to be calm and strong, even when I knew she was suffering, like in those dark hours and days after Dad and John had been killed. Mom always found a way to be strong for her kids.

She came by it honestly. Her grandparents, my great-grandparents, were in the last of the migration by about 20,000 German immigrants to the Kutschurgan and Bessarabia in the early 1800s. They came believing a better life awaited them than the hard labour of my great-grandfather's job in the shipyards of Hamburg where he worked as a stevedore. The promise of his own 66-hectare plot of farmland on the Bessarabian steppes, when he was 34 and married with five children, was too powerful to resist. They were among what was known as the Danube migration, when mostly Protestant Swabian Germans settled in territory that had been reoccupied, then deserted by the Turks, following the Napoleonic Wars. My great-grandparents were part of only a handful of Roman Catholic German families in a migration that included mostly Lutherans from Germany. My mother was born in 1867, the oldest of five children, and used to tell the story of her grandparents' 2,000-kilometre trek across Germany, Austria, Romania and Ukraine to reach the Kutschurgan. They left in June and arrived six months later in the fierce grip of winter, with my great-grandfather forced to find jobs along the way to earn money for food and supplies while the family lived in a covered wagon pulled by two oxen. They and all their worldly possessions were in that one wagon. When they arrived, the Catholics were assigned to Krasna, a Catholic community founded in 1814 just southwest of the Dniester River in Bessarabia.

Other than for two years when she was six and seven, my mother never got the chance to go to school, at least not in any formal sense. School was simply out of the question in those days. The family needed to build a new life and, as the oldest child, Mom was expected to do her part helping Grandma care for the other children. So, my mom got a practical education, one derived from the expectations put on her young shoulders to help her family learn a new way of life, in strange surroundings in a place teeming with different cultures, languages, religions and ideas. Her classroom was the world she found herself in, where either you learned fast, adapted and understood your environment or simply didn't survive. It was an education that taught her the need for dedication, respect, kindness and, most of all, patience.

I remember a story she used to tell us. The first time was two weeks after Dad and John had been killed and we were sitting together around the kitchen table after dinner. I recall it so well because it was also the first time that Emma ate with the rest of us since what had happened to her. Mom said the story wasn't about her, but another young girl she knew when she was young and growing up in Krasna. But *I* think it was her own story that she changed a bit so we would believe it was someone else. She was just too modest to ever admit it was really about her helping someone.

She said the girl's name was Lena. For some reason, I've always loved that name, Lena. Anyway, Lena had one older brother who was mentally retarded—or mentally handicapped as you're supposed to say these days—and two younger brothers and sisters. She was nine years old when her mother got really sick from rheumatic fever. The fever was so bad that Lena's mother became almost completely paralyzed. She couldn't talk, feed herself or even go to the bathroom on her own.

For almost two years, Lena's mother was mostly bedridden and it was Lena's responsibility to care for her mother and brothers and sisters. Their father was a carpenter who had to find jobs in the district, which meant sometimes he would be away from home for days at a time. He built a chair with wheels so that they could take their mother outside and let her sit on the veranda in the summer or in the shade of a tree in the backyard.

Mom said that Lena was her best friend, but after her mother got sick she didn't have many chances to play because she had to look after her mother. So Mom would go to Lena's house. One day when she was visiting Lena, Mom said Lena's mom was in her wheelchair in the kitchen while Lena was peeling potatoes at the kitchen table. It had been almost two years since Lena's mom had been paralyzed and unable to say anything, other than to make sounds like whimpers, grunts or moans.

It was a hot summer day and with potatoes boiling on the stove, it was even hotter and stickier in the kitchen. Lena went to the cistern at the back door and pumped fresh cool water into a pitcher and poured a glass for her mother. She raised the glass to her mother's lips and she sipped slowly. But, with part of her face contorted by the paralysis, some of the water dribbled down her mother's chin.

Lena took a cloth, wiped her mother's chin, dipped the cloth in water at the sink, wrung it with her hands, mopped her mother's brow with the cool cloth and kissed her forehead.

She turned to go back to the sink.

"Thank you, *Herzchen*," her mother said, clearly and unmistakably.

Astonished and shaken by what she knew she'd heard, Lena turned to her mother to see her eyes filled with tears.

Lena's mother died the next week, and Mom always said that those two words from her mother meant more to Lena than anything else in the whole world.

Being so young, I remember at the time not thinking much of anything about the story. In fact, actually it seemed pretty meaningless to me. It wasn't until I was older, and more grown up, that slowly I started to understand the significance of how something that sounded so trivial could mean so much.

CHAPTER 6

THE TRUTH IS, I'm not exactly sure when I first realized what it was like for Kaza.

Just saying that, I know, will make you question my memory and the way I've been going on about how I remember everything since my life began, and all that. But, you have to understand something. When it comes to Kaza and knowing what he was up against—the kind of life he had—it's not like that. There was no specific moment that made me know, at that instant, the truth. It was more a gradual thing.

When I think about it now, the first and most important thing that helped me understand Kaza's life was his mother. I've already told you a littler bit about her, but you need to know more if you want to understand Kaza the way I do. Bit by bit, I slowly started to realize that Yazika was different from my mother. Not different in a way that is good or bad. Just different, as in odd.

For one thing, she smelled strange.

My memory of her is not so much an image, but an odour. It's as if what triggers my mental picture of her is first a sense of smell. When you stood close to Yazika you quickly picked up this scent. How to describe it? The best I can do is compare it to something else. A kind of blended smell, like a mixture of stale, damp clothes and the kind of sweetness from milk that's just started to go bad. You know, before there are lumps.

The smell makes me think of her hair. Like I said, it was black and when she didn't have it pulled tightly back into a braided bun, it hung in long, oily strands on either side of her face. Her eyes were dark brown, almost black. She had the kind of pupils with almost no distinction between her cornea and her irises. Dead eyes, surrounded by perpetual dark circles that made her look like she never slept. Her face was thin, with high cheekbones and her dark skin smooth. I remember to this day when she hugged me and kissed my cheek, how soft her skin felt against mine. Like the skin of my sister Mary when she was just a baby.

And Yazika had the softest, most delicate hands. Her long slender fingers, thin arms and wrists made her look fragile and defenceless, which she was. I would guess she was about five feet, four inches tall and, at most, 95 pounds.

The other thing you need to know about Kaza's mom was how sometimes she seemed almost disinterested in being alive. She would go through long periods when she hardly ever spoke, and when she did it was only when spoken to, and even then she would say the fewest words possible in a voice that was so weak you sometimes could barely understand her.

I knew Kaza really loved his mother, which likely sounds pretty stupid because all kids, especially when they're little, love their moms. But it was different with Kaza. He worried about her all the time. I remember one time, in 1920, 10 months after my dad and brother were killed, when we were huddled under the canvas tarp in our secret hiding place in the shed and, for no particular reason, he started talking about his mom.

It was mid-afternoon on a warm Saturday in late May. The air under the tarp was cool and musty from the damp, hard-packed earth floor. Sunlight lined the wooden planks of our secret place in the shed, a bright beam flooding through the open knothole that we used to spy on the outside world.

Kaza and I called our hiding place in the shed behind his house the Cave because we thought it felt like being in a cave, even though neither of us had ever been in one. We spent countless hours in the Cave, pretending we were spies. It was never clear who we were spies for, or what we were spying about, other than being on the lookout for bad guys. For me the bad guys were the men who had come to Fischer-Franzen and killed my dad, brother and the other men. But when you were five years old, it didn't much matter. Just being spies was good enough. For us, the Cave was a sanctuary, a refuge for Kaza when he wanted to insulate himself from his life. It was our special place only we knew about, where we could peer out through the knothole and through the slivers of light between the crude wooden planks of the wall to watch, talk about what we saw, or thought we saw, and what it meant.

We felt like we were invisible.

"I spied one of the bad guys yesterday," I said to Kaza as I squinted through the knothole. You could see directly out and partway down the main road that ran through Fischer-Franzen, see people walking or on horseback or riding in wagons pulled by horses, mules and even sometimes oxen.

"I was sitting on our front step and I saw this really mean and scary-looking man with a black beard and white hair come riding by on his horse. It was a pinto horse. I think pinto horses are my favourite. He went really slow and kind of stared at our house. I stared back at him, but he couldn't see me because I was hiding behind the hedge. He had a rifle, you know."

"Did he, he suh-say anything?" Kaza asked.

"No. And I wasn't afraid, you know."

"I wuh-wouldn't be ah-afraid either."

"I remember him. He was there the morning when they killed my dad."

"Really? For sh-sure?"

"Pretty sure."

"Do you think he will kuh-come back? If h-he duh-does, we could trap him."

"I've got my brother's slingshot and I've been practicing. See that tree in your yard, the one next to your house? I bet I could hit it with my slingshot from here."

"I've guh-got a slingshot too. It was my bruh-brother Omar's. He's dead now yuh-you know. If the bad man kuh-comes back we kuh-could shoot him with the, the slingshot. I bet we kuh-could kill him."

"I bet we could too. If we both shot him at the same time, like, he would fall off his horse maybe and the horse would step on him and squish him."

"Yeah," Kaza said, "squished like what happened to my bruh-bruh-brother."

"My dad made my slingshot for my big brother. But now that Papa and John are gone up to heaven, my mom says I get to keep the slingshot because *I'm* the big brother now. But I'll have to give it back when we go to heaven too, because it really belongs to John."

Kaza stopped looking out the knothole, turned around and sat with his back against the wall. We didn't say anything for a minute or so, while I kept looking out through one of the cracks.

"My mom is a good cook, you nuh-know," Kaza said.

"Mine too," I said. "She makes *gretcha* noodles. That's my very best favourite food. I could eat *gretcha* noodles every day."

"My mom talks to me at nuh-night when I'm in buh-bed," Kaza said. "She comes and sits on the edge of the buh-bed and touches me ruh-really softly right here on the top of my huh-head. She thinks I'm asleep, but I'm not, buh-but I-I pretend I am buh-because if I'm awake I think maybe she won't tuh-talk to me like that anymore."

The thing I haven't really told you about, at least not in any kind of explicit way, is the way Kaza stuttered. Usually he stuttered really bad, you know, where he would have lots of trouble saying almost every third or fourth word. I never, ever, said anything to him about his stutter or ask why he did it. My mom told me not to mention it and I never did. Besides, it didn't matter to me. I seemed to know what Kaza was going to say even before he said it.

But the thing about Kaza's stuttering was that he didn't do it as much when we were alone in the Cave, just the two of us. In fact, the longer we talked in the Cave, the less he stuttered. In fact, there were times in the Cave when we talked and talked and, after awhile, Kaza hardly stuttered at all. I never mentioned that to him either, because I thought if I did he might start stuttering again. Kaza was my best friend and I didn't want to say anything that would hurt him or make him stutter more.

"My mom reads stories to me, Frankie and Mary when we go to bed," I said. "My favourite is the story from the Bible about the loaves and the fishes. Do you know that one?"

"No," Kaza said. "What's the Bible?"

"It's the big book that God wrote. It's full of neat stories."

"You muh-mean the Koran? God wrote that buh-book, you know."

"I dunno. But in the Bible, God did magic and made more loaves and fishes in a basket when there weren't enough. People were hungry, so he did magic. God knows how to do magic. He can do anything, you know."

"I know," Kaza said. "Sometimes muh-my mom comes into my room at night when I'm in bed and tuh-tells me about Allah. I think Allah and God are the same. She says that if we do wuh-what Allah wants, if we are good and luh-love people, then we don't have to worry because we will go to heaven and be happy forever."

"In heaven we'll have wings and be able to fly, you know," I said.

"Uh-huh."

The thing about Kaza was he talked a lot about his mother but almost never about his dad. I remember wondering why, although me thinking that was a kind of gradual thing that changed as I got older and understood what was happening in his life at home. But now I realize it was another thing that helped me understand what it was like for Kaza. His father was really mean to Kaza and his sisters and his mom. This is how I know.

One hot afternoon in the summer of 1920, Kaza and me were down wading and swimming in the Andre in our undershorts. Like a told you before, Kaza had pretty dark skin, like his mother. She was from Turkey. But this time when we were swimming, I noticed that Kaza had two big dark blotches, one on each thigh, and another on his side, just above his waist. They were kind of purple. We got out and sat on a big rock to let ourselves dry in the sun.

"What's that on your legs?" I asked, pointing.

"Nuh-nothing," Kaza said.

"It's something. What made them?"

He didn't answer.

"Did someone hit you there?" I asked.

Again Kaza said nothing.

The reason I had mentioned it is because when I saw the marks it reminded me that just the day before, when Kaza and I were on the street in front of his house shooting slings at birds in a tree, his mom came out to tell us to stop because we might hit someone and hurt them. I noticed that Kaza's mom had a big mark on her cheek and her face was puffy on one side.

"Your mom had a mark on her face yesterday. How come?"

Right away, Kaza started crying.

"What's the matter?"

"I dunno. Nuh-nuh-nothing."

Kaza's shoulders jerked up and down with each ragged sob.

"Why are you crying? We're best friends, Kaza. You can tell me. My mom says it's not bad to cry. Sometimes it can make you even feel better."

Kaza's tears slowed a bit, wet tracks running down his cheeks and snot seeping from his nose. He sucked a deep breath through his nose in a vain attempt to pull the mucus back up and pushed the snot back into his nose with the palm of his hand. What he said next was interrupted by the gasping spasms that happen when you're trying to stop crying and compose yourself. It all made his stutter much worse.

"My duh-dad. He's me-mean to muh-my mom. He-he-he hit her on huh-her fuh-fuh-face and kuh-kicked her. I told him nuh-nuh-no, to stop hur-hur-hurting Mama and he kuh-kicked me tuh-tuh-too. See my leg? That's where huh-he kicked muh-me. He duh-did it on puh-purpose. My daddy kuh-kicked me. He said buh-bad words."

"Oh," I said, because I didn't know what else to say. Then I said, "Don't cry, Kaza. We're best friends. I'll tell your dad to stop being mean."

When I think about it all these years later, I wish I would have told Kaza that I loved him at that moment. Not in a homosexual way or anything like that. Just that I felt really connected to him emotionally. I wish I would have said that even though his dad was mean sometimes, it didn't mean that his dad didn't love him, too, and that I was sure that his dad was sorry for what he did.

Kaza's dad was an alcoholic and mentally unstable. But at the time I just thought he was mean. I was afraid of him. He wasn't really big and strong with muscles like my brother John. In fact he was kind of skinny. But he was tall, with a moustache and a goatee. He had a bald head and a tattoo of a horse on his forearm. Kaza's dad's name was Rudel Sylowich. He was Bessarabian.

Kaza couldn't stop the involuntary tremors of sobs. The tears kept running down his cheeks and dripping off his jaw. And snot kept running out of his nose no matter how hard he tried to suck it back up.

"Don't cry, Kaza." I wriggled around so that I was sitting beside him on the warm rock in the sunshine so I could put my arm around his shoulders. "I'm your best friend, you know. I won't let anyone be mean to you."

Kaza tried hard to stop but he couldn't. I didn't know what to do or say and I felt really sorry for him. So I started crying too.

Slowly, Kaza's sobs subsided and finally stopped, which had made me stop crying too.

You know something? Crying with your best friend because he's hurting and you feel sorry for him, makes you true best friends.

"Do you wuh-want to kuh-climb trees?" Kaza asked.

"Sure," I said.

We crawled out from the Cave and went to climb the big oak tree in our front yard. We called it Giant. There was what looked like a ʊ in the middle of Giant, about five metres off the ground, right where the big, thick trunk went in two directions. We had a ladder with three steps that we always left leaning against the trunk. It was high enough for us to climb up, reach the crux in the ʊ and pull ourselves up. The ʊ between the two big branches was a perfect place for us to prop ourselves up. We could lay back, cradled by the two big trunk branches, facing each other and look up at the tree's smaller branches as they spread out above our heads. We could even look through it in some spots, where the smaller branches spread apart, and see the clouds. But laying back in the tree wasn't ideal for looking at clouds because you would only get glimpses of the sky as the leaves fluttered in the breeze. But you could catch glimpses of the clouds floating by beyond the branches that reached so high into the sky. I always got a funny feeling when we sat in Giant's U and looked up. I'm not sure quite how to describe it, other than the movement of the leaves and the brief glimpses of the clouds in the sky.

There was a serenity to it, a kind of appreciation of nature, all by itself. You felt secure in the branches of such a massive tree and a sense of awe as you looked at what was above you. It reminds me of the poem that goes: "This tree is not only a tree, it is a friendly tree that's always watching over you."

Kaza and I sat in Giant for almost an hour. We didn't say much. We didn't have to because we felt safe in its arms.

I always remembered that time sitting on the big rock in the sun next to the Andre when Kaza told me about his mother and father. It made me feel like my friendship with Kaza was special and that he needed me to protect him and his mother because he had no one else he could turn to for help. It was special too because Kaza had talked to me about something that even then, as a five-year-old, I knew hurt him deeply. It made me feel like I loved Kaza like he was my brother, which I did, and still do today.

IT WAS 2:30 IN THE AFTERNOON on October 17, 1920 and I was helping Emma, Theresa, Christina and Mom wash clothes in the backyard. Well, it might be a bit of a stretch to say I was helping. I tried turning the crank on the ringer that squeezed the water out of the clothes after they had been rinsed so they could be hung on the clothesline to dry. But I wasn't strong enough to turn the crank for anything thicker than the linen tea-towels, and then I could only do one at a time and even that had to be flat and not bunched up or I couldn't turn the handle.

The weather was windy and chilly. Not a great day for looking at clouds. That's because they were kind of flat and wispy, fall kinds of clouds, not big, fat and fluffy cumulus nimbus ones like in the summer.

Ever since Dad died, Christina, Theresa and Emma had been almost inseparable. It made sense, because they were only about five years apart in age. So they shared clothes, the same bedroom and held hands when the three went for walks together. They were this way ever since I can remember, which was when Dad and John died almost a year-and-a-half ago and my life began.

Like I've been saying, I don't remember anything before my life began, so I don't really know what it used to be like, even though technically I was alive. But I knew a lot had changed in Fischer-Franzen because Mom said so. She didn't really say it to me, because, I guess, she thought I was too little and wouldn't understand. But I heard her tell it to the other moms after church, or when they talked on the front porch, and to my older sisters, like that day when we were in the backyard washing clothes.

"Mama, do you think we will ever get to have all the animals again, like the cows, goats, pigs and chickens we used to have?" Christina asked.

"I don't know, dear. We can only pray and maybe God will answer."

"But I don't understand. Why won't they let us have animals? We can only have one cow and a few pigs and chickens. We can't even have preserves in the root cellar like we used to. It's not fair."

"Things are not the same, Christina. They never will be now that Father is gone. The Bolsheviks now control all the food. We can't keep what we grow. They leave us with only a few bushels of wheat to make our own bread. If we have more than one cow for milk, they will take the milk from us. If we raise pigs and chickens, they will take them too."

"It's not fair," Theresa said. "Even our garden isn't really ours. I remember how we grew vegetables, like potatoes, tomatoes, radishes, lettuce and corn. Now they come and take most of it. We're lucky to get a basket for ourselves. It's not fair!"

"I know," my mom said weakly.

Unlike Theresa and Christina, who liked to talk a lot, Emma said very little. I asked Mom about that one time. She told me it was because of what happened to Emma on the day they killed Dad. I asked Mom what had happened, but she said I didn't need to know and that I should never ask Emma about it, which I never, ever did.

"Momma," Emma said, "do you think we could ever go and live in Canada with Grandpa? I know it's far, far away, but it would be better there, don't you think? We could grow our food there and we could keep it."

"I hope someday, my dear. Someday. I promise."

Mom used to talk about her father, who had left before my life began, to live in a country called Canada. So I'd never met him. Technically, I admit, you could say that I had, because he didn't go to Canada until after I was born. Still, in memory terms, that happened before my life really began, so as far as I'm concerned we'd never met.

I still remember vividly how sometimes, as my sisters, brother and I sat around the kitchen table, Mom would read letters Grandpa sent from the New World. We would all gather round and, as I listened to the words, I would imagine what Canada must be like. Don't ask me why, but I imagined a place where people wore white clothes and there were lots of horses, mostly pinto horses, cows, pigs, huge trees to climb, and big, white fluffy clouds in skies that were always blue. And I remember every word from my favourite letter from Grandpa Beler. It went like this:

My dear daughter Christina,

I hope and pray that you and the children are well. I think about you every day. I cannot imagine how hard your life must be since Nikolas and Johannes are gone. My heart aches for all of you. I only wish I was there to help you and the children.

Life in my new home in the country of Canada is at times not easy. I live on the great plains of Saskatchewan, where we grow wheat, vegetables and raise cows to milk. The winters are cold, the wind harsh, the summers hot. We have very little, live in sod huts and must work hard to till the soil and then pray that God sends rain from heaven.

But we live free from fear. We have food to feed ourselves. It is like being reborn. Someday soon, I pray, we will be together in the New World.

Love,
Dad/Grandpa

For some reason, I could never get the words "like being reborn" out of my mind. It made me think about what that meant.

Maybe I was only five going on six but I knew that being reborn would be like having a new life that started at a different time and place than when my life began. So, when I thought of Canada and a place called Saskatchewan, it made me believe that it was like heaven. And that God probably even lived there sometimes, when he wanted to go somewhere different from heaven. That must be why I imagined everyone wearing white clothes where Grandpa lived in Saskatchewan. And when God was visiting there, I imagined he had a beard and wore a long white robe and rode on a horse. Always a white-and-brown pinto horse, because they're my favourite horses.

We were still in the backyard washing clothes when Kaza came around the corner of our house. I didn't notice him for a moment as I strained to turn the crank of the wringer. Out of the corner of my eye he caught my attention as he waved for me to come.

"Do you wuh-want to play spuh-spy?" Kaza asked when I walked over to him. I looked back at my mom.

"Don't be long or go far. We will have supper soon," she said, without me even asking if I could play with Kaza.

For a chilly fall day, it was warm under the canvas tarp inside the Cave. There was always something soothing about being inside the Cave. Like I said before, it made Kaza and me feel safe. Maybe even invisible.

"I kuh-kuh-can see somebody," Kaza said as he peered out the knothole.

"Who do you see?" I asked.

"A man on the stuh-stuh-street. He's talking to someone."

"To who?"

"I dunno. The buh-bush is in the way."

Squinting through the cracks in the wall, I could vaguely make out the image of a man standing on the street near Kaza's house. He was waving his arms and talking loudly, but I couldn't really hear what he was saying.

Just then, the other man he was talking to came into view. It was Kaza's dad. They seemed to be arguing about something.

The man with the white hair grabbed Kaza's dad by the arm and began pulling him around the corner of the house. He roughly shoved Kaza's dad onto the wooden walk that went beside the house and pushed him forward from behind towards the backyard, and closer to us in the Cave.

For an instant, I felt really afraid. You know, the kind of panicky feeling you get in your stomach when you think something really bad is going to happen. Maybe they would come into the shed and find us spying on them. I could tell Kaza felt the same way as he squinted through the cracks.

"Luh-luh-look! I-I-I thuh-think they see uh-us."

"*Shusssh*. Be quiet!"

The two walked toward the shed and, just as it looked like they were going to come inside, they stopped, on the other side of the shed wall that Kaza and I were crouched behind inside under the canvas. They were literally inches away, so close that it suddenly got very dark in the Cave as they blocked the afternoon sunlight from streaming in through the cracks. They were so close that I could even smell them—the strong scent of tobacco and liquor, a smell that comes to me even now when I think about what happened.

We could hear them perfectly.

"Listen to me, Sylowich, you fucker. If you don't do this, you're dead. A fucking dead man. Fucking understand?"

"But, he's—"

"Shut up. Either do it or you're fucking dead, and so is your family. It's that simple. Understand? You know the deal."

"Why me? Why can't you? If it's gotta be done, then—"

"Look, asshole. Maybe you don't get it. Word has come down from Tiraspol. They spoke directly with Yulinov. He told them it would be done. This week. So fucking understand, I'm telling you. I'm not asking, I'm *telling* you. Get it done or you're a fucking dead man. Simple as that."

With that, I could hear the white-haired man turn and walk away. The sound of his heavy leather boots clumping along the

. wooden planks of the walk, leading from the shed past the house to the street, slowly grew fainter and finally silent.

The only sound was the whistle of the strengthening fall breeze through the cracks of the shed. Kaza and I stayed huddled under the tarp, trying desperately to be utterly still, fearing we would be discovered if we dared even to breathe. Kaza's dad did not move. He stood there for the next few minutes, leaning against the shed on the other side of us. He smoked a cigarette in silence. In the dimness of the Cave, I could see Kaza's eyes glistening with tears. I squeezed his hand as he struggled to suppress the sobs welling up inside.

CHAPTER 7

THE MULTI-COLOURED IMAGE OF CHRIST in the stained-glass window split the sunlight into glowing shafts of colour. Inset with chiseled pieces of what looked, to the naked eye, like tiny cuts of diamonds, the window became a prism, magnifying the light and intensifying the hues of the sun's rays into fluorescence. Particles of dust, caught in the sparkling beams, floated in the air as if the grace of God was shining down from heaven. Alone, the priest knelt at the altar rail, his head bowed, bathed in the warmth that shone like a spotlight against his back.

Alois Frederich always liked weekday mornings at 10:30. He cherished the serenity, knowing he would be alone. Seldom did anyone else enter the church at this hour. If they did, it would be to share the quiet tranquility, to pray and meditate. If someone came, almost certainly it would be one or two old women, their heads wrapped in scarves, arthritic hands clutched around rosary beads as they prayed in rapt silence to the statue of the Blessed Virgin Mary. It stood on a pedestal beside the altar, the figure's arms bent at the elbows, hands apart in a gesture of welcome.

On his knees, hands clasped as if in prayer, Frederich stared blankly ahead. He looked above the gold-painted, copper tabernacle at the life size figure of Jesus on the cross that stood above the altar. He gazed at the image and felt nothing. The very essence of his Roman Catholic faith, the crucifix—the icon of his church, the symbol of Christ's suffering and death so others might have eternal life—had been rendered meaningless. He wanted to care, but couldn't, and hadn't for more than a year.

Still, Frederich found comfort in the morning stillness of the church. If he was not moved spiritually, he was still able to reflect on his emotions. It had become like a drug, a chance to collect his thoughts and plan his next move. So, every morning, he would stop, kneel in front of the altar and silently consider revenge before retreating to the dark solitude of the confessional to wait.

"Bless me, Father, for I have sinned. It has been one week since my last confession," said the man in a hushed voice, barely more than a whisper.

"God bless you, my son, in the name of the Father, the Son and Holy Spirit. Amen. Tell me your sins."

"It looks like we're almost there."

"Almost? It's taken long enough. How soon?"

"Days. A week, maybe; 10 days at the most."

"Not before?"

"No."

"Why not? We've been hearing that this was going to happen for two months. What is taking so long? What else needs to be done?"

"It's Reichter. He says the word from Moscow is that he's still planning to come. So we need to make sure we have everyone in place. That it's clear what needs to happen and who does what. He says he needs a few more days to be certain. He says it's important to get it right when it does happen, that the longer we wait, the more time we have to be ready. He told me to tell you to be patient, to trust him. Just a few more days and we'll be ready."

Frederich felt a twinge of anger.

"Well, you tell him I'm a patient man. But my patience is running out. He keeps changing the timing. I'm starting to wonder if he's got good intelligence or is being fed a line of bullshit. I'm anxious and so are a lot of other people. Time is not on our side. Tiraspol sent a message last week. They want to know when this is going to happen, when we're going to make good on our promise."

"Tell them soon. Very soon."

"It better be. You tell Reichter that I don't want to be sitting here next week hearing another confession of further excuses why there is another postponement. About it being any day now. Understand?" ·

"Look, understand, will you? I'm only the fucking messenger. You know it's not my decision. It's not up to us decide. We don't control when it will happen, for crissakes."

"Get out. I'm tired of this."

The wooden kneeler creaked as the man grunted, got off his knees and left the confessional. He brushed past an old woman saying her rosary, waiting her turn to confess her sins, and walked out of the church into the bright sunlight.

The stooped old woman pushed back the heavy folds of the dark red curtain to step inside the confessional. As she slowly knelt, the kneeler creaking again under her weight, the priest slid open the small door behind the wire grate.

"Bless me, Father, for I have sinned. It has been five days since my last confession."

"God bless you, my child, in the name of the Father, Son and Holy Spirit. Amen. Tell me your sins," Frederich said.

"I have felt jealously," the old lady began.

The priest was not listening.

Frederich could think only of retribution. Of retaliation. Of punishment. Of vengeance. Of justice. He had become consumed by his own dark thoughts, preoccupied by an overpowering urge to strike back against the vile bastards who had inflicted so much harm, suffering and destitution on his people. At first, when he harboured such bitterness and anger, he felt shame for betraying his Christian beliefs of forgiveness and redemption. But that guilt had slowly evaporated, vanishing completely many months ago.

He had reconciled himself to these dark emotions and rationalized his actions. In fact, Frederich believed he was doing God's work by fighting violent oppression, thievery and murder. To do nothing, to make no attempt to protect his parishioners from the Bolshevik terror, would be a failure of his pastoral duties. He believed God's Word: "You have heard that it was said, 'Eye for eye, and tooth for tooth.'"

His mind elsewhere, Frederich was still able to feign his priestly duties and respond as if he was listening to the confession of the old woman as she asked for absolution. "In the name of God, I absolve you of your sins, my child. For your penance you must fast for two days by not taking supper and instead pray the rosary to replenish your soul in the grace of the Lord. God bless you."

The woman gone, Frederich was alone in the confessional of a silent and empty church. He sat in the utter darkness of the cubicle and closed his eyes, the only sound that of his own breathing. The splendid isolation, solitude and dark tranquility of the confessional was his place to think and brood—a cocoon that made him feel confident, determined. Unafraid.

It was always the same. Every time he sat alone in the confessional he was consumed by resentment. Years before he had thought that ordination into the priesthood had allowed him finally to erase those feelings. And, for a time, it had—or so it had seemed. He thought that letting Christ into his life had given him the perspective and spiritual grounding to help him not only forgive his tormentors, but accept them as part of the reason that eventually led him to find a life in Christ.

But not anymore.

He had felt himself steadily regress into a dark mental state of bitterness and hatred. The memory of that time as a young teenager was again so powerful, the emotion of that day so raw, his stomach churned when his mind reached back to that moment in Mannheim. Outwardly, he could still portray the public perception of a devout priest. His vestments, the long wooden rosary beads draped from the belt of his black cassock, the collar of a pastor, made him seem to others the priest he had once been. But Frederich was a changed person. No longer was he merely a man of the cloth. He had become an imposter. He knew it and didn't care.

The memory, long dormant, had returned.

THE TRAIL between the community pasture and Mannheim stretched for no more than a kilometre. It wound its way between a small wooded collection of trees and bushes clustered along a small stream that snaked along the bottom of a shallow valley. As part of his chores, twice a week, 14-year-old Alois would walk the path from town to the pasture when it was his turn to milk the two cows owned by his family. He slung two buckets at each end of a wooden pole he carried on his shoulders. He always dreaded the walk home. The weight of the buckets full of rich, warm milk pressed the pole into the back of his neck. At first, the burden didn't bother him, but unless he got the balance just right, the weight would quickly put painful pressure on his vertebrae and he would sometimes get a headache.

"Hey, Freak, what you doing?" came a voice from behind as he began the walk home with his haul of milk.

Alois recognized the voice and felt instant dread. He turned slowly, trying not to spill the milk, to see Alexi Kalanoff and

Velich Romocovich walking towards him with two other teenage boys he didn't recognize. He knew Kalanoff and Romocovich from school, but had not seen them since the two 16-year-olds had left a year earlier to find jobs.

"I asked you a question, Freak. What are you doing?"

"Nothing," Frederich said.

"Looks like to me you're doing *some*thing, homo. Ain't that milk you got in those pails?"

Frederich said nothing as the four surrounded him. Fear welled in his stomach. At school, Kalanoff and Romocovich had mercilessly bullied younger kids in school, German kids in particular. For more than a year, he had been their favourite victim. Though barely 13 at the time, Frederich had been open about his intention to become a priest, an admission that Kalanoff and Romocovich seized upon and ridiculed. They called him "Freak" instead of Frederich, or "Freak the Homo," claiming he wanted to be a priest because he was a homosexual.

"What you out collecting in them buckets, homo? Been visiting your homo friends?" Romocovich sneered.

"Hey, let's play spin the Freak," Kalanoff said, grabbing one end of the pole. Romocovich took the other and together the two violently spun it in a circle, with Alois desperately hanging on, trying to keep his balance. Milk slopped from the buckets before both handles slipped from the notches at the ends of the pole and the buckets fell to the ground with a thud, spilling it all.

"*Now* look what you've done, Freak. You've wasted all that milk. I think we should teach the homo a lesson."

What happened next was never a clear memory for Frederich. The mind has a way of blocking severe emotional and physical trauma, which can be a good thing.

As he thought of the assault now, Alois felt mostly revulsion. He recalled generalities more than specifics. He was more of an observer of the incident—an outsider looking at himself and the others—than a victim of the four teens. But some details were deeply embedded in his memory. He knew that he had been stripped naked, tied to a nearby tree and sexually assaulted by each of the four. He begged them to stop. They left him naked, bleeding, with his arms tied at the wrists around a tree. The skin on his chest and stomach was scraped raw from the rough bark, lacerated by the force of the assault. He didn't know how long he stayed lashed to the tree after they finally left. But it must have been at least an hour because it was getting dark by the time he had collected his senses and was able to wriggle his wrists free from the rope and gather his clothes that had been thrown in the bushes.

He remembered one other detail. The four had told him not to say a word to anyone about what had happened or they would be back. And next time, they would first cut off his testicles, then kill him. Alois believed them. He told his parents he had tripped and spilled the milk and never talked to anyone about what really happened, except God.

In fact, in the months and years that followed he talked to God a lot about it when he prayed. Frederich took great comfort from his conversations with God about the assault. It helped him to recover emotionally, and to forgive. Getting over it convinced him of God's healing power. Ironically, what he learned from that terrible experience helped solidify his ambition and propel him even more strongly towards the priesthood.

But now, as he sat alone in the confessional, Frederich knew something more powerful than faith had taken over his life.

Vengeance.

Recent events had stirred up the dark, dormant memory from his youth and together they made him a man who sought retribution at any cost. His faith had dissolved into a thirst for revenge.

The virulent nativism and xenophobia that had engulfed Russia for years didn't have a name. Eventually, with the hindsight of history and perspective, it was labeled *Slavophilism*. For German Russians, it was toxic. For Frederich, who knew the history well, it transformed him into the man he had now become.

As a group, the Volga and Black Sea Germans who migrated to Russia generations earlier and gathered in their own ethnic communities had succeeded in their adopted home. They had come to settle the virgin farmland, till the soil and improve Russia's agricultural production. But with their agrarian and economic success came growing resentment among the many ethnic Russians, who felt as if they had become second-class citizens in their own land.

The anti-German attitude simmered for decades but boiled to the surface with the outbreak of the First World War. When Russia found itself at war with Germany and the Axis powers, jealousy among Russians of the Germans in their midst turned to outright hostility. Germans in Russia were viewed as the enemy within, a fifth column. As Russian novelist Andrei Rennikov said: "We are waging war against the enemy within as well as without our borders."

In the final years of the tsars, legislation provided for the expropriation of German property. "My highest aim is the total destruction of everything German in Russia," decreed Alexis Khvostov, governor of Nizhni-Novgorod, who became interior minister for Tsar Nicholas. "We are waging a war not only against Germany, but against all Germandom," said Ivan Goremykin, the tsar's prime minister, at the outbreak of the war.

The German question, as it became known, which previously had been contained to a belief among some that the outsiders were intent on taking over Russia and her empire, mutated into outright hostility and hatred towards the Germans.

"The Great War is now beginning to expose the whole secret of the history of settlement in Russia," said Valeri Zimbirskii, a minister to the tsar. "One would like to believe that with the war the time has come to expose this plot at its roots, and finally to rid ourselves radically of the German tyranny."

This attitude was expressed too by Grant Duke Nicholas, the tsar's uncle, who said: "Russia's Germans must all be driven out, without respect of age, sex, any supposed usefulness, or their many years of residence in the empire."

What disgusted Frederich deeply was that the hatred found a new expression and legitimacy during the Bolshevik revolution. It took on the economic and social character of class justice. As landowners, the Germans became symbols of the exploitation of a capitalist system based on private property. The Slavophilism of the previous decades became rooted in the ideology of Marx, expressed in the Bolshevik revolution of Lenin and Trotsky. No longer was this simply the narrow, nativist expression of Russian xenophobia. It was elevated to the dogma of revolution, where the attainment of a classless, collectivist society made the elimination of the German landowning class a social and economic good in and of itself that had to be pursued. A simple, logical and chilling expression of the common good, a perverse morality that made genocide acceptable, even desirable.

Frederich understood perfectly. He had witnessed the vicious, cold-blooded execution of men in his parish. Under the threat of death, he had presided over funerals. He had watched the confiscation of land, the seizure of crops, the forced labour of children and the slow, miserable imposed famine of women and children as agricultural production fell and what little was produced was taken to be "redistributed," leaving families with barely enough to survive.

And, most importantly, he remembered that time as a 14-year-old in Mannheim. He had been radicalized by the Bolsheviks, transformed—from a priest who preached forgiveness and acceptance of God's will to a bitter counter-revolutionary who sought only to lash back at the perpetrators of such hatred and injustice against his people.

The cell of Fischer-Franzen insurgents never met together. Frederich knew better than to risk detection. The eight had initially formed their loose network in separate conversations in church on the margins of Sunday mass or when they shared thoughts in the cemetery, walking away after the internment prayers of another burial.

From that initial contact, Frederich's conversations with each happened only in isolation, or late at night and often in the security and privacy of the confessional. By circumstance, he had become the acknowledged leader of the cell. But always he had been cautious not to betray his intentions. He performed his duties as a priest, ever mindful that the Bolsheviks were watching for the slightest suggestion of subversion. Frederich never strayed from an outward devotional commitment to the gospel, his sermons always rooted in Christ's message of forgiveness, redemption and salvation. He tended to the emotional and religious needs of his flock by citing scripture, never publicly passing judgment on the morality of the revolution, its effects or the motives of the Bolshevik oppressors. In fact, he went so far as to preach that his parishioners needed to accept their fate as the will of God, to accept it and live their lives guided by the teachings of the gospel. Of course, he didn't believe a word of it.

And neither did Alexandre Yulinov.

A committed Marxist and revolutionary, Yulinov saw religion in simple terms. At best it was a useless emotional distraction for those who actually believed the rubbish of church dogma, a waste of time and energy. At worst, and more likely, it was a subversive counter-revolutionary force, the equivalent of a cult of vacuous ideology that needed to be monitored, contained and eradicated.

Ironically, Yulinov's atheism came in spite of parents who were devoutly Russian Orthodox. His father's itinerant and rootless life searching for labour actually made religion more important to his parents. It gave them a sense of belonging and a core set of beliefs that brought some emotional stability to their otherwise unstable and uncertain lives. But as a teenager, Yulinov could never reconcile the notion of a just God, and the Russian Orthodox belief in pious acceptance of fate as God's will, with what was manifestly an unjust world that ultimately led to the death of his father, who had literally collapsed and died under the burden of his labour. Those doubts blossomed into fully formed atheism when mingled with Marx's depiction of religion as a drug: "It is the opium of the people. The abolition of religion as the illusory happiness of the people is required for their real happiness." For Marx, economic realities prevented people from finding the true happiness they sought. Instead, they cleaved to religion, which told them they would find true happiness in the next life. Thus were they diverted from the real world, and revolution.

A deception and a perversion, Yulinov thought. *Religion is irrational. It dupes people, and people who are deceived can be dangerous.*

So, as the leader of the Andrejaschevski soviet, Yulinov saw religion as a direct threat to the revolution. It might be a delusional, fanciful ideology, but if allowed to fester and grow, it could become a focal point for anti-revolutionary thought and behaviour. It distorted perceptions, making people think the misery of this life would be relieved in some mythical after-life. Thus, religion was directly competitive with the struggle of the proletariat for the emotional loyalty of the oppressed.

Yulinov fully understood why many of the oppressed sought

refuge in religious belief. It was a means of simply surviving the misery of their lives. He pitied them.

But religion for the oppressors, in this case the landowning German Russian bourgeoisie, the *kulaks*, was something else entirely. Something far more sinister and dangerous. It was a competing ideology, in effect a private club that became a means for them to rationalize their lives and mount counter-revolutionary action.

And Yulinov was particularly suspicious of the German Catholics in Fischer-Franzen. There was something about the tiny village he had never felt right about from the moment of the purge two years earlier, when they swept through town and eliminated 12 men. This sense was not eased two days later when they killed eight more, two from Fischer-Franzen and six from other nearby villages, who had tried to ambush his Bolshevik brigade at the bridge to Selz. Luckily, he had been alerted to the murderous German counter-revolutionary plot. Ever since, Yulinov had paid special attention to the village. Not in an overt way. In fact, he was there only infrequently, maybe six times since he had been installed by Trotsky to head the Andrejaschevski soviet. But he made sure that he had intelligence of what was going on in Fischer-Franzen, who was talking to whom, who was meeting with whom, who was saying what about the revolution.

The period after the overthrow of Kerensky and the provisional government, specifically the first years of the new Bolshevik regime, were the most critical in ensuring the success of the revolution. It was a time when the counter-revolutionaries needed to be crushed with brutal force. There could be no sign of Bolshevik weakness in the midst of civil war. No doubts about the ruthless tactics of how the resistance would be dealt with, no glimmer of any wavering of the absolute and resolute commitment of the Andrejaschevski soviet to the goals of the Bolshevik revolution. Yulinov was absolutely determined to cleanse the region he was responsible for of anyone other than those absolutely loyal to the cause of the revolution.

His trusted friend and deputy, Leonev Kuzma, was key. Yulinov had assigned him surveillance responsibility for Fischer-Franzen. It was a task Kuzma accepted with his usual gusto, enthusiasm and profanity.

Kuzma was a logical choice. He knew many of the town residents from his days as a teenager when he worked the harvests as a hired hand for the German families. Although he had eventually moved to Odessa, where he spent 25 years working on the seaports loading docks, Kuzma loosely maintained contact with Fischer-Franzen through his friend, the Bessarabian Rudel Sylowich. The two had known each other since they were teenagers and had met working the fields during harvest.

They had lost touch for more than 20 years while Kuzma was in Odessa and Sylowich worked as an itinerant labourer in the Kutschurgan and Beresan regions. By pure happenstance, they reconnected in 1914 when they both joined the Russian army as the Great War began to unfold with conflict in the Caucuses. The two reported for duty the same morning at the Odessa barracks, where they were assigned to General Ilovaiskii's Eighth Regiment, Don Cossack Division. Even though Kuzma was in his mid-50s, he had the physical prowess and stamina of someone 20 years younger and had volunteered for the army.

They served together for almost two years, much of it along the bloody eastern front where the German-Austrian Axis powers poured more than two million soldiers, buttressed by heavy batteries of more than 1,500 artillery pieces. There is nothing like life-and-death combat to cement a friendship, and that's exactly what happened between Kuzma and Sylowich. They faced the Axis powers' onslaught in Galacia, where the dug-in Russian army was outnumbered, under-equipped and literally blown from their trenches. For two months in 1915, the epicenter of the war's eastern front was the battle for Gorlice in southern Poland. Eventually, the Russian army retreated, leaving oil- and resource-rich Galacia and Romania to the Germans.

During the battle for Gorlice, Kuzma and Sylowich spent four months in the same platoon, part of a Russian division that had been sent to help fend off the German offensive. For six brutal days, they literally shared the same trench. Twice when they were overrun by the advancing Austrian-German army, after being pounded by heavy artillery and then subjected to shelling of mustard gas canisters, they survived hand-to-hand combat by posing as corpses amid the multitude of muddy bodies.

Kuzma and Sylowich got some measure of revenge. Having lost dozens of their comrades, the pair killed at least six Austrian soldiers. They shot three in the back as the enemy made its way down the trench, mopping up their kill. Any surviving wounded Russians were shot in the head, gutted with bayonets, or both. Both Kuzma and Sylowich had been presumed dead by the Austrians. They feigned death by smearing their faces with the blood of their fallen comrades. Sylowich had actually taken the intestines of a dead Russian soldier whose body had been severed by a mortar, ripped apart his own tunic with a knife and made it appear as if his guts had burst through his uniform.

The other enemy soldiers heard the gunfire as Kuzma and Sylowich shot the Austrians in the back and assumed it was their comrades finishing off the wounded enemy. But when, after a few minutes, the three did not catch up with the others further down the trench, the remaining soldiers retraced their steps. When they turned a corner and came into view, Sylowich and Kuzma, hidden among the dead bodies, opened fire and killed them at point-blank range.

Alive, but with their platoon wiped out, their rations gone and almost all their ammunition spent, Kuzma and Sylowich spent the next 10 days wending their way back to Ukraine. After two days, they caught up with Ilovaiskii's defeated and retreating regiment. Once they crossed the border from Poland into Ukraine, the two deserted and returned to Odessa on foot, on the back of farmers' wagons or by jumping aboard passing trains. After three days in a drunken spree in Odessa, they parted. Sylowich returned to the Kutschurgan and his wife, Yakira. Kuzma moved in with an old girlfriend.

It was Yulinov who reunited them three years later. Following the October Revolution, the fall of Kerensky and the Bolshevik consolidation of power in Petrograd, Yulinov contacted Kuzma. It was only days after he had been named by Trotsky himself to head the Andrejaschevski soviet. Knowing that Kuzma would be totally committed to Bolshevism, Yulinov wanted him to help organize the soviet and stabilize the region. Kuzma eagerly embraced this offer and the two toasted his commitment with vodka in Kuzma's squalid one-room apartment in Odessa. The next day, the pair travelled 50 kilometres north to Selz, where Yulinov would direct operations. It wasn't long before Kuzma told Yulinov about his friend Sylowich, who lived up the road in Fischer-Franzen. Sylowich, Kuzma said, was battle-tested and bitter, someone who would be a useful contact and ally as Yulinov sought to control and transform the region.

And so, Kuzma recruited Sylowich as a "friendly." In return for his loyalty to the revolution, Sylowich was given access to a regular supply of vodka and whatever food rations he and his family needed. It proved to be a powerful and irresistible incentive. With food shortages endemic throughout Ukraine, having enough to eat satisfied a primal urge that assured Sylowich's fidelity to the Bolshevik cause.

CHAPTER 8

"**C**'MON," Joseph said. "Hurry up, move!" Kaza and I were having trouble keeping up, which wasn't surprising. Joseph Herle was nine-and-a-half, almost three whole years older than me and Kaza. And he was big for his age too, gangly, with long arms and legs. So he was good at scrambling up the hill. He scampered, using his legs and arms kind of like a monkey.

"If you guys wanna to be part of this, then you gotta move fast, c'mon! We don't want to get caught. We haven't got much time."

Both Joseph and Jacob Heidt were ahead of us, urging us on.

The four of us were climbing the side of a hill through thickets of trees and bushes, some of them prickly. Augustine Selinger had gotten a head start and was our lookout, waiting for us on top of the hill. We only had three minutes to make our escape before the gang of "Germans" would be coming after us. Joseph, Jacob and Augustine were regulars at this. They told me and Kaza how they had been chased by the Germans before and never been caught. They always said the chase was only for big kids like them and they didn't want us hanging around and getting in the way. They said that they'd never had anyone younger than eight involved before. But it sounded exciting and we asked if this one time they would make an exception and let us be part of it. They agreed.

This section of the Beresan hills was perfect for the chase. There was a coulee with rugged and sharp edges. The slopes of the coulee were steep enough that you had to, at times, hold on to branches to pull yourself up the incline. You couldn't just walk or run up the hill without reaching forward and using your hands to grab onto things to maintain your balance. At first, I felt intimidated by the steepness of the hill we were trying to scale and I know Kaza felt the same way. But we were anxious to be part of the chase with Joseph, Jacob and Augustine. It made us feel as if we were nine and 10 too, and belonged with the big boys like them.

The hide-and-hunt was pretty simple. Kaza and me had agreed to be part of the *Sheviks* with Joseph, Jacob and Augustine. In this game, as you might guess, *Sheviks* was short for Bolsheviks, so we were the bad guys being hunted by the Germans. The idea was they wanted to find us and "get even" for the bad things we had done, like kill Germans. If we could hide and the Germans not find us for a half-hour, then we'd win and the roles would be reversed—we'd be the German hunters and they would be the Bolshevik bad guys, the *Sheviks*, on the run.

At one point, I lost my footing and started sliding backwards. I skinned my knees and hands. The stinging sensation would have made me cry if wasn't for Kaza. He was coming up the hill behind me and grabbed my arm as I was sliding by to break my fall. I started to whimper and Kaza could tell I was going start crying.

"Don't kuh-kuh-cry, Anton. They wuh-won't let us puh-play if you do," Kaza whispered in my ear so the others wouldn't hear.

He was right and I knew it. I bit my lower lip and stifled my whimper so I wouldn't burst into tears.

When we made it to the top, a mixture of excitement and ex-hilaration went through me. Kaza and I hadn't climbed to the top of the coulee before. It always seemed too daunting. Now that we'd made it with the others, we felt more grown up. But there was no time to savour the moment.

"This way," Augustine said. "I've got the perfect hideout. The 'Germs' will never find us."

The five of us ran single file along a path on the top edge of the coulee for maybe 200 metres. Augustine, who led the way, stopped and we all gathered around him.

"This way," he said. "Follow me."

He pushed back the thick branches between two intertwined bushes and stepped through. He held the branches apart for Kaza and me to do the same, and then for Joseph and Jacob. We were standing in tall grass that came up past my waist and sloped down the hill.

Squatting down and going feet first, like he was going to slide on his bum, Auggie sank into the grass and began carefully down the side of the slope hidden by its tall blades. Like a crab, he used his feet and hands to keep himself propped up off the ground and control his descent. Very quickly he disappeared, as if he was swallowed by the thick grass into a hidden crevice on the side of the hill. "C'mon. There's nothing to it," he said from wherever he slid.

"All right, Anton, you and Kaza go next," Joseph said.

"It's too steep. I'm afraid," I said.

"Muh-muh-me too," chimed in Kaza.

"You guys want to play or not? Don't act like scaredy girls," Jacob said. "You saw Auggie do it. It's no big deal."

"C'mon!" urged Augustine from below, hidden somewhere beneath the grass in the crevice.

I grabbed Kaza's wrist. He looked at me and nodded.

We squatted down like Auggie and slowly inched our way side-by-side down the grassy slope. After a few feet, the side of the hill seemed to fall out from under us and we were instantly sliding on our backs into the shadow of thick tall grass. After no more than two, maybe three seconds, the slope leveled out, we stopped tumbling and found ourselves next to Auggie in a bowl-like hollow. The thick grass blocked much of the sunlight and was high enough that we were completely out of sight, sitting in what from the edge of the coulee above was an invisible depression on the side of the hill.

Moments later, Jacob, then Joseph, slid down to join us.

"You guys still scared?" Auggie asked.

"No way. I wasn't scared at all," I said.

"Me, nuh-neither," Kaza quickly added.

There was a strange serenity to the hiding place. We were no more than three or four metres below the top of the ridge, yet it felt like we were completely invisible.

"So, now you guys know. This is our secret hiding place. The Germans won't find us here. But we have to keep quiet and listen for them."

We crouched together in a circle, silently staring at one another, waiting and listening.

"I don't hear them, do you?" I said.

"Shut up and be quiet," Jacob snapped in a voice slightly louder than a whisper. "They only way they can find us if they hear us. If they find us they're going to kill us."

"No way, you're making that up," I said.

"I'm not. Believe me, this is no game"

I suddenly felt afraid. Jacob sounded like he was serious. These were big boys and so were the Germans hunting for us. I didn't like this chase. It reminded me of when my life began and made me scared. "I don't want to be killed. I wanna go home."

"Just shut up, Anton," Joseph said. "If you're quiet they won't find us and we won't get killed."

I looked at Kaza. He said nothing, but his lips were pressed together and turned down, a tinge of fear in his eyes. I started to shiver, even though it was hot out—close to 30 degrees—and I wasn't cold. Both of us were fighting back tears when we heard the first faint sound of voices.

"*Shhhhh,*" Joseph said.

At first the sound was a far-off unintelligible chatter. For a few moments it faded away entirely and then came back, louder. It sounded like four or five people, the voices of big boys the same age as Auggie, Joseph and Jacob—maybe even older.

"I'm sure they went this way," we could hear one of them say. "We saw them make for the side of the hill. They had to climb up here somewhere. We need to track them down. I think we should torture them before we kill them."

"We'll find them, all right. I really want to get my hands on those two little prick bastards, Anton and Kaza. I'm going to poke their eyes out before I shoot them with my bow and arrow," said another voice, louder as the Germans came closer. "Fan out. Look for footprints."

It sounded like they were almost directly above us on the same ridge we had run along.

Hearing them made my shivers turn to quakes of fear. The swear words scared me a lot. I don't like swear words. They sounded serious. I had thought this was supposed to be hide-and-seek, a game. But suddenly it felt very real, as if Kaza and I were actually being hunted. Joseph put his finger to his lips, signaling us to keep quiet.

The voices above us were silent. When we heard them again, it sounded like they had walked past the spot on the trail where we had gone through the bush and slid into our hiding place. But I was still shivering and Kaza had tears in his eyes. The voices faded until we couldn't hear them anymore.

"Kuh-can we guh-guh-guh-go home now?" Kaza said, barely above a whisper.

"Not yet. Sit tight," Auggie said. "We need to make sure the coast is clear before we go back up to the ridge. You heard them. If they catch us, they're going to torture us and kill us. They've got a bow and arrow."

So we sat, and listened for voices or sounds of the Germans.

After three minutes of silence, Joseph nodded his head towards the slope we had come down. "All right. I think it's safe. We can go now, but be really quiet in case they're close enough to hear."

Again, Auggie went first. "Follow me. Do what I do," he said.

Kaza went next and me after. It was impossible to climb back up the steep slope we had tumbled down. So Auggie showed us the way back. We went to the left, slowly crawling on our hands and knees in the tall grass. After maybe 10 metres, the slope back to the top became less steep and we gradually made our way back up, emerging through another bush onto the path we had followed. Jacob and Joseph were right behind us.

The Germans were nowhere in sight.

But instead of going back the way we had come along the path, Auggie said he knew a shortcut. "There's a path down the side of the coulee up ahead we can take. It's easier to go down than the way we came up."

"I think that's the way they went. Maybe we'll run into them," Jacob said.

"Naw, I don't think so. They're gone, I'm sure," Auggie replied.

So we followed Auggie slowly along the path, stopping after 30 seconds to listen for the voices of the Germans hunting us. The only sound was the wind whistling though the trees and the melodic calls of a meadowlark. Another 25 metres along, the path made a sharp turn to the right, away from the coulee. As we came around the corner, five older boys stood waiting for us—

the Germans—one of them holding a thick piece of wood in one hand and slapping it with rhythmic menace into the palm of his other. Another boy held a bow and arrow.

"Oh shit," Auggie shouted and we spun on our heels to run back down the path. But three other Germans burst out from behind the bushes to block us. We were trapped.

It was weird. Even though I recognized most of the Germans as teenagers from Fischer-Franzen and Strassburg, the sharp, raw pang of fear curdled my stomach. I knew they were Germans like me and my family. But Jacob had said this was "no game." Thinking about it now, I realize something else made me afraid. It had to do with Kaza being from "the other side."

"So look who we've found," said the one with the stick in his hand. Right away I could tell he was leader of the Germans because he was the oldest, I'd say maybe even 15 or 16. He stood tall, his feet astride the path in front of us, four other Germans behind him.

"Good work, you guys," he said, looking at Auggie, Joseph and Jacob. "Let's go."

"I wanna go home," I said, on the verge of crying.

"Fine kid, You can go," the German leader said.

"C'mon Kaza, let's go."

"Hold it, hold it. I said *you* can go, not him," he said, pointing the wooden stick at Kaza. "He's coming with us."

Kaza, frozen in fear, stood next to me.

"Pluh-pluh-pluh-please, I wuh—"

"Shut up, kid. You're coming with us."

"But why can't he leave with me? He's my best friend. We just wanna go home. We don't want to play anymore."

"What's your name, kid? You're a Schergevitch, aren't you?" the German leader asked.

"He's Anton, Anton Schergevitch," Joseph Herle said.

"I suggest you just leave now and go home. Don't worry about your little friend here. We'll take good care of him, believe me. You're Sylowich, right?" he said to Kaza.

Kaza didn't respond.

"I think I asked you something, kid. You're Sylowich, right?"

Kaza, staring at his feet, looked up and nodded.

"Your father, he's that Bolshevik drunk, isn't he?"

Again Kaza said nothing, only stared at his feet.

"You deaf, kid? I asked you something. Your old man, he's a Bolshevik drunk, right?"

Kaza kept his head down and stayed quiet.

"Well, well," the German gang leader snarled. "Seems like Sylowich here can't talk. But I bet you he's got a tongue. Seeing how he doesn't know how to use it, I think maybe we should just cut it out. Whaddaya say, guys?"

The others burst out laughing. "Sounds good to us," said one of the other German kids.

I'm not sure where the courage came from, because I was shaking with fear, but I suddenly blurted out, "Leave him alone! He hasn't done anything."

"Shut the fuck up, you little shit, and get out of here. *Now.* Or else we'll treat you like a Bolshevik sympathizer. And believe me, you don't want that."

"Hey, Schergevitch, wasn't your dad killed by the Bolsheviks?" the German with the bow and arrow asked. "Well, wasn't he?"

"Uh-huh, I guess so."

"You guess so? What do you mean you *guess* so? Either he was or he wasn't. Which is it?"

I didn't respond but glanced at Kaza, who looked horrified and had tears running down his cheeks.

"Schergevitch, I asked you a question. I'm not asking you to guess. So tell me, was your old man killed by the Bolsheviks or not?"

"Yes," I said.

"So you're not going soft on us now, are you? You're not trying to defend the bastards who killed your dad, are you? Is that what you're doing here, trying to save your Bolshevik friend's ass now, are you? Because if you are, you're no better than the Bolshevik bastards. Are you a fucking traitor? Are you?"

"No," I said.

"Well then, you must agree with us that Sylowich's old man is a drunk Bolshevik bastard. You agree?"

I didn't say anything.

"I asked you a question. Is your friend's old man a drunk Bolshevik·bastard or not?"

"Yes," I said.

"Well say it, then. If you're not a traitor, say 'Sylowich's old man is a drunk Bolshevik bastard.' Say it!"

Without hesitating, I repeated, "He's a drunk Bolshevik bastard." Then I said, "But I don't even know what a bastard is."

"Don't worry, you'll know soon enough," the German leader said. "Do you think your friend Sylowich here is a Bolshevik lover? Do you?"

"I dunno."

"You don't *know*? But you just said his old man is a drunk Bolshevik bastard. Doesn't that mean his kid here is likely a Bolshevik lover? Huh?"

"I dunno. I guess, maybe."

The moment I said the words, I knew I had betrayed Kaza. Ever since, I have been haunted by immense guilt of that moment. Even after these many years, it stays with me, lurking in a corner of my conscience and never, ever leaving. I know I said it because I was afraid, was trying to get away and just wanted to tell the older German boys what they wanted to hear. But knowing I did it for such selfish reasons only makes the guilt of abandoning Kaza worse.

"Well then, Schergevitch, I suggest you go home now and let us big guys deal with this Bolshevik lover we've got on our hands. So get going, right now."

As I turned to walk away back down the path, I only glanced at Kaza. His face was etched with fear. "Nuh-no, it's nuh-not truh-truh-true," he said.

"Shut the fuck up. We'll see what's true and what ain't, you stuttering little bastard. Get lost, Schergevitch."

There are moments in your life that haunt you, that you always regret and always remember. For me, this was one of them, the first one and maybe one that I regret more than anything else in my whole life. I am still overcome with feelings of remorse, regret and shame when I remember how I betrayed Kaza, how I didn't stand up for my best friend, how I only cared about myself and being able to get away, even if it meant abandoning Kaza to the hands of bullies.

Often I've wondered if other people would have done the same thing when they were little—betrayed a friend to save themselves from a threat. The older I got and the more I thought about it, the more guilty I felt. I always remember the Bible story of Judas and his betrayal of Jesus. At least he got 30 pieces of silver. Me, I got nothing but the shame and guilty conscience that haunts me to this very day.

Leaving the others, I began running down the path along the edge of the coulee to get away. But after running for a minute I stopped. I don't know if it was my conscience that made me turn back, but I felt I needed to find out what they were going to do with him. Maybe I could sneak up and distract them and Kaza and I could get away together. Maybe I could save him.

I started back, walking quickly but trying not to make any

sound so they wouldn't hear me. By the time I got back to the place where I had left them, they were gone. So I stayed on the path, going very slowly, listening.

Maybe another 50 metres along, I started to hear voices. They were coming from behind the same clump of bushes we had slid down through into the depression with the deep grass when we were hiding from the Germans. I couldn't make out what they were saying very well, other than when they shouted out "Bolshevik bastard" or swear words like "fucker" and "cock-sucker."

But what I did hear were Kaza's cries. When I think about it now, I would say he was whimpering, a mixture of fear and desperation in his voice. He wasn't saying real words, but I knew what he was trying to say. He was begging for mercy.

"Nuh-nuh-nuh. Pluh-pluh-pluh."

Instead of going down and helping my friend, I did a terrible, horrible thing. I turned and ran away, not stopping until I got to my house, which was about two kilometres away. I abandoned Kaza instead of helping him and to this day have not forgiven myself. I never will.

That night I hardly slept, only in short fits and starts. I kept hearing Kaza cry for help. My mind raced with images of what the big boys might have done to him. Did they torture him? Maybe they poked his eyes out. Maybe they even killed him and hid his body somewhere in the trees. The more I thought about it, the more I was sure that Kaza, my best friend, was dead.

And it was my fault.

"ANTON, ANTON, WAKE UP!" It was my mother's voice. I could feel someone's hand on my shoulder and opened my eyes to see my mom, sitting on the edge of my bed shaking me awake in the middle of the night.

"Anton, when did you last see Kaza? He hasn't come home and

it's midnight. His mother just came to the door. She's frantic. Do you know where he is? Do you know what might have happened to him?"

I looked up at my mother and, feeling absolute dread in the pit of my stomach, I lied.

"I dunno."

"When and where did you last see him?"

"I dunno. At his house," I lied.

"When?"

"I dunno, right before lunch."

"You didn't play with him in the afternoon? His mother said she saw you two together on the street in front of our house after lunch. That you guys said you were going down to the Andre."

"I dunno. I decided not to go with him. He went by himself."

"By himself? Did you see anyone with him when you left him?"

"Uh, no. He was all by himself."

"Why didn't you go with him? You guys always go to the Andre together."

"I wasn't feeling so good."

"You didn't tell me you were sick. I didn't see you for a couple of hours. I was sure you were with Kaza. Where were you after you left him?"

"Uh, I dunno. Climbing trees and looking at clouds."

"Was anyone with you?"

"No. Just me. Alone."

"Well, all right. I hope you're telling me the truth. Go back to sleep. I just hope Kaza is all right. If you know anything, Anton, about where Kaza might be you have to tell me. Promise? This is important. You don't have to be afraid."

"I told you, Mama. I dunno."

As she got up from the bed and turned to leave the bedroom, I pulled the covers up over my head and started to shiver with fear.

A minute later, I heard the door to our bedroom creak open. I was still under the covers, shaking and crying.

"Anton, Anton, why did you leave me?" It was Kaza's voice.

I pulled down the covers to see Kaza standing in front of me.

"Look what they did to me," he said, holding his hands out from his body.

He had on only his underwear. His body was covered with red marks; there was blood dripping from his nose and mouth. His eyes were dark shadows, his eyelids closed over what I instinctively knew were empty eye sockets. They had poked his eyes out.

"Why, why did you leave me, Anton? I thought you were my best friend. Look what they did. I'm blind now."

I tried to say something but couldn't. I felt like I was choking. Kaza turned and walked out of the bedroom.

MY SISTER EMMA called me in the morning to get up for breakfast. I told her I didn't want breakfast. That I wanted to stay in bed. But she said that Mom had breakfast ready and I needed to wash up and get downstairs right away because we were going to the 8 A.M. mass and we only had half an hour. She said Frankie and Mary were already having breakfast and I had to "get with it."

But I didn't want to face my mom. I didn't want her to ask me again about Kaza and what I knew. I was sure she knew what had happened to Kaza, that she saw that his eyes had been poked out and that I was lying, that I had been with Kaza and left him instead of staying to protect him from the big, bad boys.

So I stayed in bed. But a minute later I heard my mom calling me from the bottom of the stairs.

"Anton, get down here for breakfast. We have to go to mass. Hurry up."

She didn't sound mad at me or upset that Kaza was missing. It was at that instant I realized she hadn't been in my room in the middle of the night, and that Kaza hadn't really been in my room either with blood coming out of his nose and mouth, and his eyes poked out. That part had only been a dream.

I felt an instant rush of relief.

"All right. Coming," I said.

On the way to church, we walked, as always, down the sidewalk on our side of the street. Kaza's house was down a bit and on the other side. I looked across at his house and could see his mother on the front step, pouring a bucket of soapy water onto the ground. I figured it was likely dishwater from doing their breakfast dishes. My mom and her waved to each other, which made me feel a bit better.

But all through church, I wondered about what had happened to Kaza. I knew that being in the Beresan hills the day before was no dream. I kept hearing his cries for help and thinking about how I ran away instead of helping him. I asked God to forgive me.

"Dear God," I said in my mind while I knelt in the pew after getting communion. "Please don't be mad at me. Please forgive me for doing a bad thing and not helping Kaza. Please make Kaza okay. I'm sorry and promise to be good from now on."

It was weird in church, because both Auggie Selinger and Jacob Heidt were there with their parents, and I even saw one of the teenagers who was one of the "Germans" who caught us. They saw me too, but didn't say a word, although Auggie, two pews in front of us, did turn around right after the Lord's Prayer and glanced at me for a second with a kind of blank look on his face.

After church, I looked at Kaza's house again when we walked home. This time I didn't see Kaza's mom or anyone else. But the front door was open behind the closed screen door.

I didn't know what to do. I was anxious and nervous, afraid about what happened to Kaza. Had he come home? Did they tie him up and leave him in the forest? Did they maybe even kill him and throw his body down the side of the coulee? Then the fact my mother didn't seem to know anything seemed to me to be a good thing, I thought. And his mother was out on the front step and waved to my mom when we were going to church. She wouldn't do that if Kaza was missing or dead, would she?

So, I decided I would sit on our front step, watch and wait. I could see Kaza's house clearly from our front step. Sooner or later someone would know what happened to Kaza and they would tell me.

I sat there for 20 minutes, and other than kids playing in the street and two wagonloads of potatoes and corn going by, not much was going on.

Then I saw Kaza. He came out of his front yard with his father, who held him angrily, clutching Kaza's upper arm, forcing him to walk kind of tilted because his dad was sort of lifting him up by the arm on one side.

I could tell his father was saying something to him, but they were too far away for me to hear exactly what. I think I saw Kaza glance quickly at our house, but I don't know if he saw me before his father tugged him roughly down the street.

To this day, I don't know what Kaza's dad was doing to him that morning. It sure looked like he was mad at Kaza about something, but I don't know why and Kaza never told me, and I never asked.

The main thing for me was that Kaza was alive and not missing. I could tell his eyes weren't poked out and he could see because after a few steps his dad pushed Kaza in front of him and let go of his arm. So obviously Kaza could see where he was going. That made me feel a *lot* better because I had been sure that if he wasn't dead he would at least be blind.

It was an hour or so later when I decided to walk down the

street to Kaza's house, hoping that I might see him. I knelt down, picked up a small branch lying on the ground and used it to draw faces in the dirt. Every few seconds I would glance up at Kaza's house, hoping he might come out the front door.

After five minutes, I saw Kaza standing behind the screen door. He pushed it open, stepped out and waved to me. I waved back.

Quickly, I jumped to me feet and ran across the street and got to his front gate by the time he had come down his front walk.

"Hi," I said. "You all right?"

"Luh-let's go to the kuh-Cave," Kaza said. He had a scratch on his face and one eye was swollen almost shut.

Like I told you before, the Cave was our refuge. A sanctuary where we felt insulated and safe from the outside world. Sure, maybe we were only sitting on a dirt floor under a canvas tarpaulin thrown over two sawhorses, but it still gave me and Kaza this sense of security, even invulnerability.

What added to that was the grey darkness. We would open the latch to the shed in Kaza's backyard and often leave bright sunlight for the relative gloom of the shed, which had one small, grimy window that allowed in some measure of light. But in our Cave, under the tarp, it was much darker—an inky kind of blackness that gradually gave way to a kind of gray gloom as your eyes adjusted to it. The knothole, where sunlight streamed through into our Cave, provided enough light so that by the time our pupils dilated, we could see each other and our surroundings well enough to have a sense of perspective.

"I'm sorry," I said to Kaza once we had sat down in the Cave.

"How kuh-come? What do you muh-mean?" Kaza asked.

"Because I left you yesterday."

"Naw," he said.

"What happened? You've got marks on your face. What happened to your eye?"

"Nuh-nothing."

"You can tell me."

Kaza just sat quietly for a moment.

"I'm sorry, you know," I said again.

"It's nuh-not your fault," Kaza said.

"I was afraid. But I should have stayed. We could have run away together."

Kaza never did tell me what happened. All he said was that they were mean, that they pulled his pants down and did bad things. But he said he didn't want to talk about it, that it was no big deal. I know now the fact he wouldn't tell was because he *couldn't* tell me. It was too difficult for him to talk about it, even to me, his best friend, and it was because of me he suffered alone.

Then we talked about going down to the Andre and maybe catching turtles or frogs or something.

"Have you noticed the kuh-clouds today?" Kaza asked. "They're real buh-big and fluffy. I buh-bet it would be fun to look at clouds for awhile."

"Me too," I said.

Kaza and me always felt better when we looked at clouds. Somehow it always seemed to make bad thoughts go away.

CHAPTER 9

D O YOU KNOW what it's like to go hungry? Not *be* hungry. Everybody feels hungry some time or other. That's no big deal. I'm talking about "going hungry." In other words, being hungry all the time, as in never having enough food to not feel hungry. Basically, when being hungry is normal.

It's a kind of dull gnawing in your stomach. You feel this constant emptiness, like your body needs something you can never give it. It's not a feeling you ever really get used to, but you do learn how to live with it. At least you do when there is no other choice.

Well, that's what it was like for my family and most everyone in Fischer-Franzen. We never had enough to eat, so in our case Mom would improvise. For example, we ate a lot of *borscht* soup. I hate borscht soup. That's because it's made from beets and just the smell of beets makes me want to barf. When my mom made borscht, it would stink up the entire house with the smell of beets. I hate *borscht* and beets to this very day.

Funny about that, but when I think of being hungry—even like now when I've just had a big meal and I'm not the least bit hungry—I smell *borscht* soup. That's right. I actually get the smell of boiling beets in my nose.

So right now, when I talk about "going hungry" I smell *borscht*, and I feel like I'm going to puke.

All that makes my memory of going hungry when I was a little kid all the worse. It's not like I remember, in a kind of abstract way, the feeling of being hungry. Thinking about not having enough to eat all those years ago actually makes me ill, right in the here and now. Needless to say, those aren't good memories. But, like it or not, I have them.

Not having enough to eat is what it was like growing up in Fischer-Franzen after the revolution. It was just the way it was, and for me that's all I knew when I was kid. In that sense, I guess, I was lucky because from the time my life began until we went to the New World, going hungry was something I accepted because I didn't know any better. It was no big thing, I guess, because for me it was normal, just the way things were.

So, don't get me wrong. I'm not looking for sympathy or anything about going hungry when I was a kid.

But it was a big deal, a very big deal, for those whose lives began before mine. That's because they remembered when there was lots to eat and people weren't going hungry, so they had something to compare going hungry to, and that was having food and not going hungry. From what I've been told by my mother and older sisters, before the revolution there was plenty to eat at our place. We had a big farm with horses, cows, pigs, goats and chickens and a huge vegetable garden.

"We used to have vegetables coming out of our ass," was the way I remember Rachel describing it one time when I was almost five.

That struck me as a kind of really sick. I mean, could you imagine eating a potato or a carrot or a rutabaga that came out of someone's ass? I know I can't. In fact, just the thought of vegetables coming out of someone's rear end made me not want to eat them, just like I didn't want to eat beets. Just think about that for a second. Beets taste bad enough, so having them coming out of someone's ass makes them taste even worse, at least they did when I was like four and five years old and I thought vegetables really did come out of our asses. How gross is that?

Sure, I know now that Rachel was saying that as a way to emphasize how big a vegetable garden we had. But at the time, I actually thought our family—my mom and sisters and brother—had vegetables coming out of our asses. And for a while I thought that's where all vegetables came from— from other people's asses —and that was why I remembered how my mom and sisters used to scrub the vegetables and then boil them. You had to kill all the ass germs before eating them. At least, that's what I thought.

I know, it sounds really stupid now. But you have to remember, I was really little when Rachel said it—I was only four going on five—and I had no reason to believe it wasn't true.

The reason I'm telling you this is because now I realize why we went hungry when I was young. I started to figure it out kind of gradually, and by the time I would say I was six-and-a-half, I pretty much understood what was going on. It all kind of crystallized for me one night when I was with Theresa, Christina and Emma in the kitchen. Believe it or not, I was helping them scrub potatoes before we put them into a big vat of water on the stove. I asked Rachel how come the scary men killed Dad and she explained why. Which was this:

The reason the Bolsheviks killed our dad, and the other men, was because we were landowners and had lots of food. They didn't like that because they believed in communism, where there would be no private property and people would share everything, especially food.

I remember thinking, "How stupid is that?" They didn't have to kill our dad. Why didn't they just ask and we likely would have shared our food with other people.

As you can see I was still pretty naive and didn't really understand what was going on in Fischer-Franzen and throughout the Kutschurgan. It took a while longer.

What really helped me figure things out was what happened next.

It was 9:20 Saturday morning, August 14, 1922 and I was six, going on seven. I kind of had this ritual every Saturday morning. I would get up—usually around eight—have breakfast and then play soccer on the road in front of our place with the other kids.

I'd go down to the kitchen and have a bowl of wheat cereal and a piece of bread with jam. During the week we didn't get bread for breakfast because we didn't have enough to go around, so Mom would save it for the weekend. If we were really lucky, on Sunday after church we'd get a slice of bread and maybe even a hardboiled egg. But on Saturday and Sunday we also didn't get lunch. So breakfast had to hold you over until supper, which, wouldn't you know it, inevitably included *borscht* soup.

After breakfast on Saturdays, I would go outside and play, usually with Kaza or some of the other kids. Almost always, there would be kids playing soccer in the road and just before I turned seven I started to join in.

But on this Saturday, Kaza was away at his uncle's in Tiraspol —you know, the one who called us *Nushniks* I told you about a while back. And, because it had rained the day before, the road was muddy, so no kids were out playing soccer. But it was a beautiful warm, summer morning. So, I decided to climb Giant, the big oak tree in our front yard. I used the small, three-step ladder at the base of Giant to shimmy up its trunk. It was such an old tree that the bark on the trunk had deep crevices that you could get your fingers and the toes of your shoes into. That way you could shimmy up to the crotch where the main trunk separated into two major boughs to form a perfect u shape, an ideal place to sit back and straddle one of the branches with your back propped against the other. This time, though, I climbed a little higher, to a secondary branch.

It was high enough that no one would notice me on the street, unless they actually looked up into the tree, and hardly anyone ever did that, except maybe me and Kaza and the other kids. Making it even better, I was also camouflaged a bit by the leaves. Sitting in the crotch of the tree made me feel pretty neat, like a spy—almost invisible and with a great vantage point to watch what was going on below.

Actually, not much was going on. So I just tilted my head back and looked at the clouds floating by through the leaves as they rippled in the slightest of a breeze.

Other than the chirping of birds, it was very quiet. Kind of one of those tranquil mornings you always appreciate, even when you're a kid.

The first sound that distracted me was the distant neighing of horses. Nothing unusual about that, as there were always horses around, either pulling wagons or people riding them.

But then, I heard a strange sound. Kind of a rumbling or a grinding. At first I didn't know what it was, but as it became louder I realized it was something I had heard a couple of times before. One of those wagons with a motor instead of a horse. What people called a truck.

I bent down to try and look below the branches down the street towards the church where I could tell the sound was coming from. At first I couldn't see it, just hear it. But in a few seconds it came into view and I could see the truck slowly coming up the road. In front of it was a man on a horse. There were two other men on horseback on each side of the truck and two more on horseback following it.

As the truck got closer I could tell it had a big wagon-like box on the back. I could hear pigs squealing and chickens squawking. It stopped halfway up the road in the middle of town. Our house was on the east side, so the truck and the men on horseback were maybe 50 metres or so from where I was in the tree.

Each of the men on horseback, except for the guy in front, dismounted. There were six of them. They went in pairs, each pair walking to a different house on our side of the road. Each of them carried a rifle. I could hear the sound of heavy thuds, like wood pounding on wood, and voices shouting, "Collectivization! Open!" The two closest to me were three houses down from ours. As I leaned and peered down, I could see them slamming the butt ends of their rifles against the door of the Selinger house.

Without waiting for an answer they opened the door and disappeared into the house. I could hear voices coming from inside, but couldn't make out what they were saying A few minutes later they came out carrying burlap sacks full of something that they tossed onto a pile of other sacks on the back of the truck next to the crates with the squealing pigs and squawking chickens before moving to the next house, two doors down from our home.

At that moment I realized this was not happening just to other people. That the men were making their way down the street and were coming to our house as well.

I knew I had to warn Mom.

Sliding down the tree trunk, scraping the insides of my arms and legs in the process, I rushed into the house and ran down the hallway to the kitchen at the back. Mom, Rachel and Christina were there, still doing the breakfast dishes.

"They're coming, Mama! I saw them, the Bolsheviks, and they're coming here. I know they're coming here too. I'm afraid. We should hide!"

Mom calmly lifted her hands from the wash basin, picked up a towel, slowly dried her hands and looked down at me.

"I know, Anton. Don't worry. They won't harm us if we give them what they want. They just want food."

"It's all right, Anton. It's all right," Rachel said.

But it didn't make sense to me. I knew enough to realize we didn't have extra food. Except, that is, *borscht* soup. I wouldn't mind if we gave them all the *borscht* soup Mom had stored in sealer jars in the root cellar. I hate *borscht* soup.

Then came a loud pounding at the front door. "Open up! Open up! Collectivization!"

Before Mom was able to leave the kitchen and get down the hall to the front of the house, three men opened the unlocked door and stepped inside. Two of them had beards, they all wore similar grey shirts and each had a rifle over his shoulder.

"Do you have your production quota ready?" one of the men asked. He didn't say it in a mean or threatening way. More kind of matter-of-fact.

"Yes, we do," Mom said. "Follow me."

She turned and walked through the kitchen past me and my sisters to the back door. They followed her as she stepped outside. Next to the back steps, Mom lifted the trap door to the root cellar. She held it open while one of the Bolsheviks attached the latch to a hook on the side of the house that kept the door wide open. My sisters stayed in the kitchen, calmly doing dishes and acting like nothing was going on. I watched from behind the screen door as Mom and the three men disappeared down the stairs into the dark and damp root cellar under the house.

I could hear muffled voices from below. In less than two minutes they re-emerged, the men first, each carrying a full sack of what I assumed were vegetables. Mom followed, carrying a cardboard box. I couldn't tell what was in it because there was a lid on it. But it looked heavy. Then another of the men went back down and brought up an even bigger and heavier cardboard box of something. A second man went down below and carried back up a heavy silver can that I knew was full of milk.

Instead of coming back through the house, they carried the sacks, boxes and milk can around the side of the house to the front. But as they walked past the screen door, they were close enough that I picked up the smell of fresh meat from the cardboard boxes. I couldn't tell what kind of meat, but if I was guessing, I'd say it was pork, which I realize now made sense. That's because the only animals we had, other than our old plough horse Blackie and Little Red, our milk cow, were five pigs—a great big fat mom pig everyone called "Sow," a dad pig we called "Ben" and their three little pigs that had grown to become pretty big, but not as big and fat as Sow and Ben. There used to be nine little pigs when they were born in the winter, but now there were only three. Mom said they went to live with other pigs. Rachel says pigs are really smart. I don't know how smart, but what I do know is they stink because they fart a lot.

Of course, I know now what happened to the pigs. They were killed for food, which isn't nice, but is just the way it is. We ate some of them, but most of them we gave up to collectivization. None of them went to live with other pigs, at least not for long, before they were killed and people ate them.

I ran through the house to the front screen door so I could see what was going to happen next, after my mom and the three men came around the side of the house from the back. The truck had moved up the street and was now on the road in front of our house.

The men threw the sacks of vegetables onto the back of the truck and lifted the boxes and milk can onto the truck bed. Then they grabbed a silver milk can from the back of the truck that I could tell was empty and handed it to Mom before they loaded the full milk can onto the truck with the rest of the food.

I sort of realized then how it worked. When they came back we would have filled the milk can, they would take it and give us another empty can for us to fill up again with milk from Little Red.

"Mama, why did you give those men our food?" I asked her when she came back into the house.

"It's what we have to do, Anton. Come back to the kitchen and I'll explain."

When I sat down with Mom at the kitchen table, Rachel and Christina joined us.

"Rachel, dear, will you go get the others," Mom asked. Rachel went to the foot of the stairs and called for the others to come.

A moment later, Eva, Magdalena, Theresa and Emma, with Frankie and Mary tagging along behind, came down from upstairs. Mom took Mary and put her on her knee. All of us, the whole family, were now sitting around the table.

We waited for Mom to speak.

"Kids, I want to talk to you about things."

"What sort of things, Mama?" Frankie asked.

"Just about what it's like for us and what we might do that will be best for our family. Anton just asked me why I gave our food to the men who come to our house. We don't have enough to eat for ourselves, yet I give them our food. Anton doesn't understand."

"It's all right, Mama. I'm not mad or anything that you gave it to them," I said.

"I know for you little ones, this is going to be hard to understand, but I—"

"I'm not little anymore. I'm six-and-a-half."

"I know, Anton. You're a big boy now, which is why I want to explain. Frankie and Mary are probably too young to understand, but I think it's important we talk as a family."

"I'm five-and-a-half," Frankie said.

"All right, Frankie," Rachel interjected. "Let Mama talk."

Mom smiled. She tugged on her *babushka*, tucking some strands of hair back under the fabric and put her hands on the table. They were the sturdy hands of labour, her fingers and wrists strengthened by a life of child-rearing and hard work.

"I know it's difficult for you kids. We often don't have enough to eat and have to make do with very little. And I know it is even more difficult when you see me give away our food to the men who come every few weeks.

"But much has changed since your father and John went to heaven. We can no longer keep all the food we grow for ourselves, or sell it to others. We now have to share almost all of it with the men who come to collect it."

"Share it?" Rachel said. "That's a nice way of putting it. They steal it from us. We're forced to give it to them. If we don't give it to them when they come, then terrible things would happen."

"Would they kill us?" Frankie asked. Mary quickly turned and put her arms around Mom's neck.

"No, no, no," Mom said, hugging Mary on her lap. "They wouldn't do that. I don't want you kids to worry about that. We just need to share our food. The food we give them goes to help feed people who don't have their own food."

"It's called communism," Rachel said.

"Listen, *kinder*. I know it's not easy and it doesn't seem fair. But it is just the way it is, and we have to live with it and make the best of it. At least for now."

"What do you mean, for now?" Emma asked.

"Well that's what I want to talk to you about. That's why we're all here, sitting around the table. I want to talk about what we should do, whether we should go to the New World and start a new life, one where we have enough to eat."

"Do you mean across the ocean? Going to the United States of America?" Christina asked.

"Well, yes. But not the United States, to Canada, a place with a funny name called Saskatchewan, where Grandpa and Grandma have gone, with two of my uncles and some of their families, to start a new life."

"Suskachin?" I said.

"I have a letter here from Grandpa Beler. They left Mannheim more than two years ago and now have a farm in the New World of Saskatchewan, Canada. Let me read it to you kids."

She read:

My dear daughter Christina,

> *I am writing to you from our new home in Canada. We live in a great farming province named Saskatchewan, in a tiny village called Billimun. Mother and I love our new life in the New World. God has taken good care of us.*

> *The land stretches for as far as the eye can see. It is rich and fertile. It reminds me very much of the great Steppes. There is not as much rain as we enjoyed in the Kutschurgan, so it is dry and not humid. But the land produces much wheat.*

> *Our homestead is 160 acres. We were given the land for a registration fee of five Canadian dollars, which is the same as nine rubles. We are growing wheat and oats, have two milk cows, a sow who produces many pigs a year, a draft horse for the fields, a coop full of*

chickens and a vegetable garden of two acres. The food here is plentiful.

Our church—St. Martin's—was built only three years ago, so it is new, a beautiful structure with a steeple that reaches 25 metres into the sky. Our priest is Father Joseph. He is German, and came here just six months ago from the state of North Dakota in the United States. He comes from Baden.

We love our new life here. But I must also tell you that there have been hard times. The weather can be harsh—very hot and dry in the summer, bitterly cold in the winter. Agnes and I spent the first winter in a sod hut. It had two rooms that we heated with a wood stove that we borrowed from Hans, our neighbour. There was a terrible blizzard and I thought we might not survive. For three days the snow was so deep we could not get out our door.

But now we have built our new farmhouse. It has three bedrooms, an attic, root cellar and barn. We have a stove that burns wood or coal we can get in the town of Mankota, which is not far away from Billimun. We are very comfortable and happy.

How is life in Fischer-Franzen? I encourage you to consider coming with the children here to the New World. We could help by being your sponsor. There are many others from the Kutschurgan who have come from across the ocean and settled in this district.

Our life here is much different. We are free. There is no fear. We feel safe and have a life that is complete. One can ask for nothing more.

Your father and grandpa, Joseph

Mom folded the letter and set it on the table. For a moment, no one said anything. It was as if we were all imagining what life was like in the New World. I know I was. The image I had was of golden wheatfields as far as the eye could see and the biggest, bluest sky, nice fluffy cumulus nimbus clouds floating lazy over head like great big balls of cotton. And for some reason, I have no idea why, I also imagined that everyone in Suskachin was riding a horse, even me. I was sure that my horse in the New World would be a pinto. Pinto horses are my favourite.

"I want to go to the New World," Christina said.

"Me too," I said. "Would we go on a big boat? I bet Frankie and Mary want to go too."

"Yes. Can we, Mama?" Frankie asked.

Our mother looked around the table, taking turns glancing at each of us.

"I know how you kids feel. And I feel the same way too. I wish right now all of us were together in the New World with Grandma and Grandpa, where we would have a new life together, with enough to eat."

"So why don't we go?" Emma said.

"It is not that easy. We would need money for passage. We need health certificates. We need someone to sponsor us in the New World. And the government would have to allow us to leave. We would need to convince the right people that they should let us leave for the New World. That would not be easy."

"Grandpa said he would sponsor us," Rachel said. "He said in his letter that he wants us to come where he lives in the New World."

"Please, Mama," Emma said. "I want us to live in the New World."

"We'll see," Mom said. "All right, everyone. Time for those of you with chores to get going. You little ones can go outside and play."

From that day forward, I often thought about the New World, about what it would be like to travel across the ocean and live in a place that sounded so perfect. My mom often told us that many people said Canada and the United States were "the Promised Land," a place where everyone was happy and there was never any shortage of food to eat.

I would lie in bed at night and think about the Promised Land. The image I had was of us living in a town like Fischer-Franzen, only our house would be bigger. In the Promised Land, I would have my own bedroom, with a door to a balcony where I could look out at fields growing with wheat and big stalks of corn. There was a giant tree standing right next to my balcony. I could easily step from the balcony railing onto a big tree branch and either climb down to my pinto horse, who was tied up at the bottom of the tree or I could climb to the top of the tree and see for miles in all directions.

And one other thing, in the Promised Land all my friends would be living there too, especially my best friend Kaza. He and I would each have a hammock tied to the trees in our backyard where we would gently sway back and forth in the warm breeze and look at clouds together.

The next afternoon, when Kaza was back from his uncle's, we talked for the first time about the Promised Land. We went to the Cave. We always had our best conversations when we were in the Cave. But I noticed that Kaza seemed afraid and stuttered more than he usually does when we're alone in the Cave.

Kaza had heard about the New World too. But he had never heard of Suskachin before.

"It's like here, only a lot nicer. There is food for everyone, no one is mean to each other and everyone there has their own pony," I explained.

"I wuh-would like to have a pony," Kaza said. "If we had puhponies we could go riding tuh-together. My uncle has horses, you know. I saw them wuh-when I was there yesterday."

"Really. How many?"

"I dunno. There were a whole buh-bunch. They duh-didn't all buh-belong to my uncle though."

"How do you know that?" I asked.

"Because I saw the other men kuh-come riding to my uncle's huh-house on horses. There was a whole buh-bunch. When they got there, they went inside thuh-the buh-barn with my uncle and my dad."

"Uh-huh."

"You nuh-know what, Anton?"

"What?"

"I heard what they tuh-talked about."

"Really? How come?"

"Buh-because I went out to look at the horses. They were tuh-tied up next to the barn.

"Uh-huh."

"I could huh-hear them tuh-talking in the barn. They were tuh-talking about kuh-kuh-killing people. Anton, they wuh-wuh-were talking about kuh-kuh-killing people. Ger-German people. I heard them."

"Really? What German people?"

"People in muh-Mannheim and Selz. Thuh-they think the Germans are bad because they're against the ruh-ruh-revolution. So thuh-they are going to kuh-kill them."

I didn't say anything. I knew Kaza was telling the truth because we had always promised each other that we would tell each other the truth. So I trusted Kaza and knew he wouldn't exaggerate what he heard or make things up that weren't true.

"And suh-suh-something else, Anton."

"What?" I asked.

"I heard them tuh-talk about suh-someone else."

"Who?"

"Fuh-Father Frederich, from the chuh-church you go to with your muh-mom and sisters and bruh-brother. I huh-heard them say thuh-they were guh-going to guh-get him too. Thuh-they said that he was a kuh-cunt. Do you know what a kuh-cunt it?"

"No. I think it's a swear."

"I *nuh-know* it's a swear," Kaza said. "My duh-dad says it wuh-when he's mad at muh-Mama."

"Did they say when they were going to kill Father Frederich?"

Kaza said he didn't know. That he got afraid and ran back into his uncle's house because he didn't want to hear any more.

"Are yuh-you afuh-afraid, Anton?"

"No, because we're going to go and live in the Promised Land on the other side of the ocean. You can come too, Kaza."

"I'd luh-like that. I wuh-want to guh-go to the pruh-Promised luh-Land," Kaza said.

Later that night, as I was lying in bed, I felt both guilty and afraid. Guilty because I didn't tell Kaza the truth when he asked if I was afraid. I *was* scared by what he told me he'd heard the men say in his uncle's barn. But I said I wasn't afraid because I thought it might make Kaza not feel so scared.

As I shivered under the covers from fear, I was hoping that maybe this was just a dream and that I would wake up in the morning and be in the Promised Land. And sure enough, I did wake up in my own room with a balcony, next to the big tree at our giant house in the Promised Land. At least, that's what I thought, until I heard Mom calling from downstairs and I realized I was only dreaming. We hadn't moved to Suskachin in the Promised Land, and what Kaza had told me was true, because we're best friends and always tell each other the truth.

CHAPTER 10

Y ULINOV tugged back on the reins slightly, slowing his horse to a stop. He stepped down from the saddle and led his horse from the road onto a barely visible path that led off through a clump of trees into a small clearing. Guiding his horse, he walked quickly, disappearing from sight, stopping when he reached a small pond where the tired animal could have a drink.

As his horse lowered its head to the water, the sinews in its neck growing taught as its lips began lapping at the cool surface, Yulinov let go of the reins. He reached into the breast pocket of his shirt to pull out the tarnished silver cigarette case.

Before lighting a smoke, Yulinov ran his thumb over the initials VSY etched into the silver. The case had been given to him by his mother after he had enlisted to fight the advancing German army in the Great War. "Keep it close to your heart," she had told him, squeezing his hand and kissing his cheek as he left with his regiment.

She died alone and destitute, a pathetic beggar on the streets of Odessa, while he was trying to survive the brutality of trench warfare against the advancing German army on the Romanian front. It was almost a year before Yulinov learned that his mother had died. After he deserted and made his way back to Odessa,

Yulinov learned his mother's fate from a shopkeeper who had felt pity for the old woman and given her scraps of meat and cast-off vegetables. Her rigid body, hunched and curled under a soiled, fifthly blanket, was discovered in an alleyway. She had been dead for days, parts of her corpse gnawed at by rats and dogs. She was buried in an unmarked grave Yulinov could never locate in a cemetery with hundreds of other faceless and nameless dead.

He traced his thumb over the barely perceptible etching of the letters vsy, the initials of his father—Vaclav Sergei Yulinov. A silver cigarette case was the only remnant he had of his parents, the lone reminder of them, the sum of their lives lived, their single earthly possession. For Yulinov, it was evidence of the injustice and futility of their lives. Whenever he felt his spirit weakening, when his conscience began to question his own brutality, Yulinov would pull out the cigarette case and rub his fingers across the initials. Every time, he could feel passion rise and his determination return.

It was the same now.

For six days, Yulinov had been travelling on horseback alone throughout the Kutschurgan. His purpose was twofold. Meet with those loyal to the revolution and kill those who were not. As soviet head, nothing was more important to Yulinov than loyalty to the cause. During his four years as Trotsky's choice to oversee and sustain the Bolshevik revolution in the Kutschurgan, Yulinov had developed a powerful, fearful and quizzical reputation. He was known to have utter loyalty to Bolshevik ideals and would not tolerate indifference, let alone opposition to the Bolshevik struggle. Known enemies would be killed, as would those whose loyalty was not beyond doubt. Conversely, Yulinov's own loyalty to those faithful to the revolution was already legendary. He was a man whose ruthlessness with anyone less than utterly devoted to the soviet was matched only by his devotion to those who embraced the cause.

This was the last part of his journey. He had turned off the road between Selz and Strassburg to travel the eight kilometres to Fischer-Franzen, where he would meet Smenev and Popov. They were to rendezvous in the small clearing next to the pond where he now silently smoked his cigarette. They were to meet at noon. Yulinov took out his pocket watch. It was 11:40.

There was something about Fischer-Franzen that bothered Yulinov. He couldn't quite explain why he felt the way he did about the small, nondescript village. It was just a feeling he had. Certainly there were other, larger towns of Germans that were more challenging, that were pockets of counter-revolutionary sentiment. Places like Kratz or Hilzendeger or Selz or Mannheim, which Yulinov and others knew had been prime recruiting areas for Deniken's White Army. But slowly, using brute force, the Red Army had gained the upper hand in South Russia, and now in the fall of 1922 seemed on the verge of military control over the Kutschurgan.

Still, Yulinov remembered more than three years earlier when Germans from Fischer-Franzen tried to ambush a Red Army platoon he was leading as part of the suppression of counter-revolutionary Germans. It had been a particularly brutal clash that came a day after Yulinov's platoon had gone into Fischer-Franzen and exterminated 12 Germans known to be White sympathizers and counter-revolutionary activists.

Yulinov and his men were not surprised by the ambush. They had come to expect fierce backlash to their suppression and extermination efforts and that time was no different. But then, Yulinov had been forewarned of what was being planned by the German enemy. Sylowich had been able to alert him minutes before the ambush.

Yulinov's memory was vivid.

HE AND 12 OF HIS MEN had been camped next to the Kutschurgan River, eight kilometres upstream from Selz. It was the day after the Fischer-Franzen operation, which had gone well. Twelve men executed, all shot in the back of the head, the village traumatized. To ensure word didn't leak out about what happened in the village, the single road in and out of town was sealed off by six Red Army regulars.

Yulinov's platoon, one of three operating as execution squads in the region, had camped for the night before carrying out their last planned assault for the next day. They were to ride into Selz and eliminate 18 men identified as enemies of the revolution. It was early in morning, just after daybreak, and they were preparing to mount up for the ride into Selz when an excited and breathless Rudel Sylowich rode up, his horse lathered and panting from what had obviously been a long gallop.

"They're coming. They killed the others. They're all dead. I saw them," Sylowich said as he scrambled down off his horse. "They're coming."

Yulinov leapt to his feet. "Who? What?"

"The Fischer-Franzens and others. They killed our comrades on the road from the village. Now they're coming for us. They want revenge."

"How many," Yulinov asked.

"Twelve. I dunno. Maybe 15."

"How far behind you?"

"I think maybe 30 minutes. Fuck, I don't fucking know. They were still hacking the bodies."

"Did they see you?"

"I don't think so. I heard screams and gunshots as I was approaching. I hid in the trees. They didn't see me."

Yulinov knew they would be coming up the road to Selz. They

would either try to find and kill him and his men, or at least get to Selz and warn the townspeople of the coming execution squad.

With no time to waste, Yulinov ordered his men to mount their horses. Less than a kilometre towards Selz the road cut through a small, heavily wooded area, the perfect blind spot for an ambush.

A surge of adrenalin coursed through his body and Yulinov began to feel excited, almost aroused at the thought of the coming conflict. He loved the anticipation of killing. Especially killing those who opposed the revolution. Especially the despicable German *kulaks* who took Russian land and saw themselves as superior to native Russian peasants. These same vermin who now sought to resist the Bolsheviks. And what added to his excitement was knowing that his platoon would surely be better armed and trained than the ragtag band of Germans. So not only would they have the advantage of surprise with this ambush, they would also have greater firepower to eradicate the enemy.

His heart pounded. He could hardly wait for the kill.

They rode ahead to the place where they would launch their surprise attack. Yulinov quickly dispersed his men into the dense cover of trees and bush. He stationed his comrades so that they encircled about a 70-metre stretch of the road, enough room to ensure that all the Germans would be surrounded before they opened fire. The men took their horses out of sight, deeper into the forest, and tied them to trees. The platoon waited in silence, hidden from their prey.

As if on cue, less than an hour later the Germans rode slowly, cautiously, into sight. There were 11 of them, all silently and carefully surveying their surroundings left and right for any sign of the enemy. Each carried a rifle. The lead horseman, a young man of maybe 20 in a red and black checkered shirt, also had a huge hunting knife sheathed on his hip. Another of the Germans had a long-bladed sickle, its razor-sharp edge honed for harvesting, slung over his shoulder.

Just seconds before the Germans were about to be perfectly encircled and the trap sprung with Yulinov's order to open fire, one of the Russian's horses neighed loudly. Instantly, the advancing Germans stopped. Sensing the trap, the lead rider signaled the men to dismount and Yulinov realized he had lost the chance to fire while they were still mounted, which made them much easier targets and at the mercy of what would have been panicky horses. He was about to lose the advantage of surprise too, so he ordered his men to open fire.

What happened next was 90 seconds of utter chaos and bloodshed. The opening volley of shots from all directions mortally wounded three of the Germans; four others were only grazed and still capable of returning fire, along with the other four who had not been hit. Unable to see their attackers, the Germans fired blindly and wildly into the trees where they believed the shots had come from. Before they were able to dive into the cover of tall grass in the ditch next to the road, two more were dead. But another two managed to flee out of sight into the trees, including the lead German with the red-checkered shirt. Bursting into the trees, he came face to face-to-face with Andropov trying desperately to reload his rife. The German sprang at him with the ferocity of a wounded predator, plunging his hunting knife deep into the Russian's chest. The blade made a sickening sound as it cracked through ribs and cartilage, slashing Andropov's aorta. Yanking it free, the young German sliced open the Russian's throat, almost severing his head.

Hidden not three metres away, and with no time to react, Yulinov could only witness the carnage. Before the German could turn around, Yulinov acted on instinct. His chest felt like it was going to explode from the pounding of his heart. He took aim and fired into the back of the German's head. Skull fragments and pieces of brain matter burst out of the man's forehead as he dropped dead to the ground, his body twitching involuntarily on top of the Russian he had just killed. Yulinov pulled the dead German off Andropov. He pried loose the knife from the dead man's hand, turned him over and, for good measure, plunged the blade through the red shirt, deep into the German's heart. Yulinov loved the sensation of the knife piercing through the ribs into the softness of the dead man's heart. It was as if a jolt of electricity ran from his hand up his arm to trigger the spasm of pleasure in his brain. A moment later, when the ecstasy subsided, he felt warm and tranquil inside, even though his heart still pounded.

By the time Yulinov finished savouring the moment, it was over. His comrades had sought out the other Germans, wounded or not, and rounded them up. Captured, they all were shot in the head then stabbed in the heart.

Other than the one the red-shirted *kulak* had killed, none of his men had been seriously wounded in the frenzy. For a moment, Yulinov considered his next move. He could leave the scattered bodies of the Germans to rot in the grass or he could deliver a message. Earlier they had passed a burned and abandoned farmhouse, no doubt that of a former German landowner, where he remembered seeing a small flatbed wagon. He told his men to retrieve the wagon. When they did, he had them pile the bodies onto it and sent three of his men to deliver the dead to Fischer-Franzen.

"Dump them on the street for all to see. Then set them on fire," Yulinov had said. "I want no more trouble from this village. I want them to understand who the fuck they're dealing with."

FOR THE PAST TWO YEARS, Fischer-Franzen had been quiet. There had been no overt signs of counter-revolutionary activity, no doubt the result of the trauma of July 1919 which left so few adult men alive. The community had become acceptably compliant, meeting its food and livestock redistribution rations. But food production had also plummeted. With no incentive beyond fear to grow the traditional crops of wheat, oats, corn and vegetables, and a lack of manpower due to the executions, the village was a pathetic shell of the once vibrant and productive farm community it had been. In that sense, Fischer-Franzen was a microcosm of what was happening throughout Bessarabia, Ukraine and across Russia. Famine and malnutrition were epidemic, death by starvation, particularly for the vulnerable—newborn infants and the aged—was common.

In spite of the obvious failings of the revolution, Yulinov remained as committed as ever. Twice he had received personal handwritten letters from Trotsky himself, thanking Yulinov for his work in the Kutschurgan and encouraging him to continue the transformation of Russia into a Bolshevik communist society.

"I know we are in a difficult time. The failures of our economic policies and the suffering of the masses are undeniable," Trotsky said in a letter whose opening salutation read: "Dear Comrade Alexandre."

"But we are at a critical juncture and must not lose sight of our goal. The magnitude of our task is apparent, and has been since the outset. Still, we have made progress and will succeed in building a revolution that transforms the lives of all Russians for the better."

Yulinov found it mildly interesting that Trotsky had written about "the failures of our economic policies." It was the truth, and Yulinov knew it.

Indeed splinter factions had developed within the Communist party hierarchy, with the likes of Alexandra Kollontai and Alexander Shliapnikov, two prominent Bolshevik revolutionaries, forming the Workers Opposition. The discontent with the unfolding economic calamity across Russia had spurred peasant uprisings, like the Tambov rebellion of peasants in the Tambov and Voronezh regions southeast of Moscow. And it was Trotsky himself, as head of the Red Army, who oversaw the brutal repression of the food uprisings, which were led by Alexander Antonov. A one-time radical Communist and vocal supporter of the revolution, Antonov became disenchanted with the Bolsheviks' ill-fated grain requisition policy. Word of the brutality of the repression, including the use of chemical weapons against the peasants under the direct orders of Trotsky, had spread quickly throughout the country.

Still, Yulinov thought it curious that Trotsky would admit to failed policies. He couldn't help but speculate that if Trotsky was willing to concede the mistakes in something as fundamental as economic policy, how many others must share the same view and how deep the discontent must run within the Bolshevik leadership itself.

But Yulinov was never one to dwell on such fleeting doubts. To do so would be a sign of weakness. Of course there would be setbacks and adjustments. A revolutionary project of such scale— nothing less than the fundamental and radical transformation of Russian society, culture, economy—would face challenges and encounter the doubts of the weak-minded. But being weak of mind was not one of *his* frailties.

Which is why he couldn't help but consider his nagging doubts about Fischer-Franzen. Yulinov always trusted his own mind, never questioned his instincts, and there was *some*thing about the village that troubled him. Not in an aggressive or continuous way. It was more a case of remembering the band of Germans who had come to seek their revenge and the ferocity of their response. In particular, he remembered the absolute viciousness of the young German in the red-checkered shirt who had gutted then slit the throat of his comrade. The same German he shot in the back of the head and stabbed through the heart. It made Yulinov think that Fischer-Franzen should not be taken for granted, even now.

At that moment, he heard the voices. He recognized them immediately as belonging to Petr Smenev and Sergei Popov, who were to meet with him. The two, on foot and leading their horses, emerged through the trees as Yulinov himself had done.

"Comrades, how was your journey?" Yulinov asked the pair, who he knew had travelled from Mannheim.

"Uneventful," said Smenev.

"There have been no signs of activity. The people seemed resigned," Popov added.

"Good," Yulinov replied.

The three spent the next half hour eating food they confiscated from people and carried with them. They talked about Fischer-Franzen, the last village they would visit as part of their sweep of the Kutschurgan. There was no specific action to be taken, other than perhaps a visit with the local priest. The purpose of their appearance in the town at this point was more for mental intimidation than physical confrontation.

Yulinov was of two minds about how to deal with the priest. He didn't know much about him other than what he and others had heard from Sylowich, which wasn't a great deal. But what he had heard made him suspicious.

First, he didn't like or trust this priest, for two pretty obvious reasons. One was the simple fact he was German, so he could not be trusted for all the reasons Yulinov was charged with quelling and controlling the Kutschurgan. Yulinov believed Germans were loyal only to themselves and to Germany, which made them enemies of the revolution and the Russian motherland. They were landowning *kulaks* who had resisted the revolution and, he believed, many had been complicit with the invading German army during the war. But more importantly, there could be no greater enemy to the revolution than religion. It amounted to a competing ideology that could not be tolerated. Nothing less than utter and total commitment to the cause of Bolshevism was acceptable.

So a German priest was someone to be closely watched, neutralized and eliminated, if necessary. But Yulinov was no fool. He also knew that to kill the priest would be a major provocation in a community traumatized into compliance. It could be the tipping point, the spark that ignited the kind of passion that would radicalize people unnecessarily, an act that would ultimately be counterproductive to the cause.

That's not to say German priests had not been executed as part of the pacification of the region. Many had "disappeared," a few strategically found dead, shot in the back of the head—the signature of Red Army hits—as a warning to others that no one was safe if they opposed the Bolshevik cause. But Yulinov was wise enough to know there were limits to terror. To simply eliminate all the German priests, to eradicate fully their religion, would again only risk the kind of backlash that made pacification and compliance even more difficult. Better to let the fools have their religion and a few of their holy priests as a gesture that, if they obeyed, they would be allowed to cling to their pious beliefs and their God. But these beliefs had better not get in the way of the revolution. It was a kind of measured terror.

"Tell me about Fischer-Franzen. I haven't been there for more than a year," Yulinov said to Popov and Smenev as the three sat cross-legged, taking turns reaching into a sack of vegetables to eat carrots and radishes.

"I would say it's not a problem, at least not right now," Popov answered.

"What do you mean, 'not right now'? That sounds a bit ominous," Yulinov said.

"Petr, you explain. You're a young guy," Popov said, nodding to Smenev.

An interesting comment, Yulinov thought. *Why would Smenev's age have anything to do with it?* In fact, Yulinov was less than always comfortable with Smenev's impulsiveness. At times, the erratic behaviour of someone in his late twenties could be used as an asset for the intimidation of others. But if not managed wisely, it could become a source of problems. Bad judgment was not something Yulinov tolerated, and he was far from convinced that Smenev always acted rationally.

"So, Petr, tell me what I need to know," Yulinov said.

"To put it bluntly," Smenev answered. "Fischer-Franzen is basically neutered. We cut the town's balls off more than two years ago when we swept through and did our thing. When we killed that bunch of them—what was it, I forget, 10 or more?—we basically ensured the town was not going to be an issue."

Yulinov didn't especially like the answer. Too glib.

"Oh really? Then if we cut their balls off that day, how come the next we barely escaped an ambush by the young men of the town? I still fucking remember what happened. This so-called castrated town would have cut *our* balls off if Sylowich didn't warn us they were coming."

"That was just their last gasp ..."

"Fuck you, Smenev. Listen to me. Neutered? I watched those bastards come after us. They were ferocious. One of them killed Andropov, fucking slit his throat and stabbed him in the heart. We lost a comrade to the bastards from Fischer-Franzen and you're telling me we neutered them the day before? What the fuck is that?"

"Well, uh, sir, I meant that after we killed those guys the next day and dumped their carcasses in the street, then the town had its balls cut off," Smenev said, his voice less confident than it had been a moment earlier.

Yulinov didn't reply. He stared coldly at Smenev for several seconds until the younger man looked down in capitulation.

Minutes of icy silence passed. The quiet was broken only by the almost-comic crunching sounds of the three Bolsheviks eating raw carrots and radishes they kept pulling from the burlap sack.

Eventually, Yulinov decided to restart the conversation.

"So what's been happening in the town?"

Smenev looked at Popov, who nodded.

"It has been quiet. There are few adult men left in Fischer-Franzen and not many in the outlying region. If we didn't kill them, they fled and haven't returned," Smenev said.

"Who's left?" Yulinov asked.

"Mostly women and kids. There are some teenage boys, I'd say 30 or so. Maybe seven or eight are now in their twenties. But the only real men are the Jew, Podnovestov, Sylowich and the priest."

"Tell me about the priest."

"His name is Frederich. What can I say? Typical fucking German priest. He hasn't caused any trouble."

"How do you know?"

"Because we've been watching him. Got good intelligence. When he preaches, it's all about accepting God's will, that kind of bullshit. We've never heard him say anything threatening about the revolution. In fact, he never talks about it with his German sheep. Keeps talking about being rewarded in heaven. Regular religious crap."

"Don't you find that kind of strange?" Yulinov said to Smenev.

"Strange? No, why?"

Yulinov didn't answer immediately. He waited, staring at Smenev for a few seconds before replying.

"Well, let me see. You say we have this town that's been castrated. There are very few adult men left because we have eliminated them all. People are compliant and accept their fate and the fact that the men are all dead. Right?"

Smenev nodded.

"What I see is a town with a bunch of teenage boys, most of whom watched as we shot their old men in the head. They also saw a second set of bodies dumped in the middle of town the next day, bodies of young men they knew, who wanted revenge. Teenage boys who are now more than three years older and three years angrier.

"And we have this priest, a priest who *you* say is preaching religious bullshit and not stirring up shit, not feeding the resentment and anger of teenage boys who want revenge. Nope. Just this nice German priest telling his people to forgive and forget, let bygones be bygones. Just telling those teenage boys not to get all twisted about us killing their old men and brothers. Telling them to be good boys, to behave and listen to their mamas and they'll get their reward in heaven."

Again, for the sake of emphasis, Yulinov made sure there was another awkward silence before he continued.

"So, I hear what you're saying about the town's balls being cut off. But you know what? A town can grow new balls, and if there are 30 or more teenage boys in Fischer-Franzen, and some now in their twenties, my guess is they've got big balls and they've grown a lot bigger over the last couple of years.

"And this priest. I don't trust him. He's not going to say anything in public. I mean he's not going to stand at the pulpit and say, 'We have to get the Bolshevik bastards, we have to fight back, let's kill them.' He's not that stupid. But does he think it? Does he say that privately? Does he talk that way to those teenage boys with the big balls? That's what we don't know. But if you asked me. I'd say you bet your sweet ass he does. So you might think Fischer-Franzen is deballed and everyone is all still traumatized. Me, I'm not so convinced."

Impulsive as ever, Smenev wanted to sneer at Yulinov's sarcasm and call him an asshole. But he wasn't crazy and had enough self-control to say nothing and simply nod his head meekly.

An hour later they rode into Fischer-Franzen, three abreast, Yulinov in the middle, just slightly ahead of the other two, as if to signal his stature as the Bolshevik in charge. They came from the south. As the road veered to the right in front of the church and then turned back straight into the centre of town, Yulinov cast a quick glance over his shoulder at the church. As with everything Yulinov did, it was a purposeful gesture. Just in case Frederich was peering out from a window in the small rectory in the yard between the church and the cemetery, Yulinov wanted to make sure the priest saw him gazing over his shoulder at the church.

The town was quiet. Other than a handful of young kids playing soccer on the street, one woman sweeping her front step and another old lady in a rocking chair under the shade of a tree on the front walk of a house, the town seemed deserted.

The three stopped and dismounted at the small water well that marked the centre of the town. As the young boys who had been playing soccer stood rigidly and looked on from a distance, Yulinov turned the iron crank on the well that lowered the bucket noisily into the cool water below. Retrieving it, each took turns sipping from a full ladle, glancing up and down the street as they did.

Out of the corner of his eye, Yulinov caught sight of a man coming out of the town's only small general store. He wore a black apron and walked casually over to the three of them.

"That's Podnovestov," Smenev said quietly.

Yulinov felt certain there were many hidden eyes watching the scene unfold, which was exactly what he wanted.

"Hello. Can I help you gentlemen with anything? Need supplies?" Podnovestov asked.

"Nope," Yulinov said. "Just visiting. Want to make sure that things are under control here and everyone is all right."

"Everything is just fine. The vegetable crop was good this year so people are feeling pretty good about things. They've got enough to eat."

At that moment, Yulinov saw Sylowich coming out of his house. Each raised a hand in greeting as Sylowich approached.

Quickly, Yulinov sent Podnovestov on his way back to his store with a curt, "We don't need you. Get lost."

Podnovestov quickly turned and walked away.

"So, Comrade Rudel, how are you? Kuzma tells me you're doing a good job keeping tabs on this place."

"I do my best," Sylowich said.

The four of them—Yulinov, Popov, Smenev and Sylowich—stood around the well for the next quarter hour in quiet conversation. The young boys slowly returned to their soccer game, although they regularly cast nervous glances towards the men at the water well.

They talked about nothing of particular importance. But that wasn't the point. What Yulinov wanted was to create a scene that would quietly get the attention of the townsfolk, who, he had no doubt, were cowering in their homes watching them conduct their very visible, but private conversation.

This was about style, not substance.

Sylowich reported that the latest collection of food for redistribution had gone smoothly and that it seemed the townsfolk had finally accepted the reality of collectivization. He said there were no signs of counter-revolutionary behaviour.

"If every town was like Fischer-Franzen, we'd have nothing to worry about, "Sylowich said.

"The priest. Tell me about the priest," Yulinov asked.

"Oh, Frederich. Not much to say. Publicly he seems to mind his own business. Keeps a very low profile. Only time I really see him is on the steps of the church Sunday mornings when he's greeting the people who go to mass."

"His sermons?"

"I listen sometimes. Of course, not every sermon. But sometimes I sit at the back of the church. Sometimes, I'll stand outside when it's warm and the windows are open and I can hear him preach. Nothing other than 'God loves you,' that kind of crap."

Yulinov did not prolong the conversation. His skepticism of Frederich's true motivation was not weakened by Sylowich's report. But he felt there was no purpose in challenging his informant. Sylowich might be naive but he seemed otherwise dependable and was certainly someone whose commitment to the cause he did not question. At least not yet.

He thanked Sylowich and told his two comrades it was time to leave, that he was satisfied with what he had heard and seen in this visit to Fischer-Franzen.

Together, the three mounted their horses and slowly began to leave the town the way they had come. Again, Yulinov was in the middle, slightly at the head of the trio. This time, Yulinov purposefully set a much slower, much more exaggerated pace. The horses ambled almost painfully slowly.

The scene unfolded in what seemed like slow motion. It was a hot and humid, dead calm afternoon. As the three made their way back down the road out of town, they again rode past the young boys playing soccer. The game paused as the strangers passed, the boys standing silently, one of them holding the ball under his arm, gazes never leaving the three men on horseback.

As they reached the curve in the road that headed out of town, Yulinov nodded in the direction of the church. The three slowly rode their horses up onto the wooden sidewalk that ran in front of it. A small white fence followed the sidewalk, marking the church property line. With the other two holding their horses a couple of steps back from the fence, Yulinov, using his knees, gently nudged his horse to step forward so that its front hooves were on the sidewalk and its head extended out over the low-slung fence.

For at least three minutes, Yulinov sat on his horse and stared at the church, his piercing gaze never leaving the heavy wooden front doors. He lowered the reins so his horse could drop its head over the fence and begin eating the delicate flowers still in full bloom in the priest's flowerbed.

Inside, from high above, Frederich peered through the slats of the church bell tower and watched.

CHAPTER 11

D ON'T LAUGH, but for the longest time when I was a kid, I
thought altar boys were priests in training.

Let me try to explain. I used to think that if you were an altar
boy, you had to move into the rectory, eat hosts, drink wine and
live with the priest. Now I know that these days, with what happened in the Roman Catholic Church involving priests sexually
abusing altar boys, just me saying that might sound all ironic
and everything. But that's got nothing to do with it. I'm just
telling you what I thought when I was a little kid and it's got
nothing to do with some priests being perverts.

Don't ask me why, but I figured that in your spare time you
squashed grapes by stomping on them with your bare feet in big
wine-making vats the priest had in the basement of the rectory.
And as for the hosts, I thought they were actually made from the
wax drippings of candles in the church. Oh, and one other thing.
I also believed that if you were an altar boy, you were pretty
much guaranteed a place in heaven because you worked for God.
I figured God would always take care of the people who worked
for Him. It was part of the deal.

I know now that sounds pretty crazy. But actually when you

think about it, it's perfectly logical. I mean, logical if you look at it from the perspective of how a little kid's mind works and how kids that age see the world.

All I knew was what I thought I knew. And what I knew was what I saw. And what I saw were altar boys dressed up like junior priests, praying with the priest in Latin, handing him water and wine and holding patens under the chins of people who were getting communion hosts that tasted like wax. That looked pretty impressive and holy to me. So it only made sense that the reason kids were altar boys was because they were becoming priests and were learning the ropes, so to speak.

I even believed most of that stuff when I turned seven and was old enough to become an altar boy. My mom was big on me being an altar boy. In fact, truth was she was big on me becoming a priest. I could tell she really wanted one of her sons to be a priest because it would make her feel proud that one of her kids was holy enough to become a priest and for sure get to heaven. No doubt it would make her feel holy too, because obviously if she was holy enough to raise a son who became a priest, it raised the odds she'd get into heaven.

The other thing was that my brother John never became a priest before he was killed. So I became Mom's oldest son—even though I was just seven—and the next best hope to become a priest. It was kind of taken for granted that as soon as I turned seven, I would become an altar boy and, as far as I was concerned, begin my training to become a priest.

So that's what happened, and I was fine with it.

On my seventh birthday Mom took me over to the rectory to meet with Father Frederich so I could begin learning how to be an altar boy. He told my mom that a new training class for altar boys was beginning in two days and he looked forward to me joining his "army of God's little soldiers."

I thought that sounded pretty neat, being in God's army. I remember wondering if Father Frederich had a gun hidden under his cassock.

On the way home, I asked Mom if I was going to have to live at the rectory now that I was becoming an altar boy. "No Anton. You'll still live at home, for now. But when you get older I hope that you will go to a seminary, where the young men go before they become priests. I'm very proud of you, Anton," my mom said to me.

That made me feel pretty good, my mom being proud of me and everything. I really loved my mom and was getting old enough to understand she had a hard life, especially since Dad and John went to heaven. Whenever she talked about me going "into" the seminary, I wasn't exactly sure what she meant. I knew it was some kind of grown-up school for priests. And maybe because seminary sounds a bit like cemetery, I thought the seminary was a building in a big cemetery in Odessa or someplace.

I've got to tell you, the altar boy training was pretty intense. I had to go four times a week after school—I was in Grade 2—for four weeks to get my "habit" and officially become an altar boy.

The toughest part was I had to memorize all my Latin lines from the mass, things like: *e cum spirtu tuo* and *en numero patra, filio, sancto, amen*. The other one that I always liked, and don't ask me why, was: *Glória Patri et Fílio et Spirítui Sancto. Sicut erat in princípio, et nunc et semper et in sae´cula saeulórum. Amen. Ad Déum qui laetíficat juventútem méam.* That one took me almost three weeks to memorize.

I had no idea what the words meant, but, boy, I felt really holy when I said them.

The other cool thing was ringing the bell chimes at the point in the mass when the priest held up the big host, which was actually some kind of really bad-tasting bread and not candle wax like I thought, and then the chalice of wine. It was all part of turning the host and wine into the body and blood of Christ, which people then ate and drank as part of communion. When I think about it now, how weird is that? When we went to communion we were actually eating the body and drinking the blood of Jesus Christ. Gross.

I know the host was supposed to be bread, but if you asked me it had to be the worst-tasting bread imaginable. The year before, when I was six, I got to have First Communion and make my first confession. You had to do your first confession before you had your First Communion because you wanted to get rid of all your sins before you went to communion. So you went into the confessional, told your sins to the priest and he gave you your penance and then absolution, which meant your sins were erased from your soul. The way it worked was you could have "venial" sins—which are little minor sins that wouldn't keep you from going to heaven if you were to all of a sudden die—on your soul when you went for communion. But you couldn't have "mortal" sins, which are the really bad ones, like missing mass on Sunday, or eating meat on Friday. Those ones ranked up there with, for example, murder, and definitely meant you were going to hell if you had them unconfessed on your soul when you died and there was no way you could have communion without first going to confession. I figured if you missed mass on Sunday and didn't go to confession and do your penance, and then went to communion, you would for sure choke to death on the host.

There was no way I was going to let that happen to me.

I remember my first confession like it was yesterday. I told the priest I had two sins to confess. My first one was being jealous of Jacob Heidt because he had a bicycle and I didn't. The second one was being mean to my brother Frankie and not sharing my apple with him when he asked if he could have a bite. My penance was three Hail Marys, which I figured was pretty easy and only took me maybe one minute to do after I got out of the confessional.

Anyway, after getting rid of my sins I was clear to have my First Communion. That's when I discovered the host, which was supposed to be bread, tasted like it was wax or something. It didn't really taste like anything I had eaten before, and certainly not like bread, and the thing was the priest said we weren't supposed to let the host touch our teeth. Apparently your teeth touching the host would ruin everything. We had to just let it dissolve on our tongues, which I hated because it just made the bad taste linger. I actually remembered gagging a bit as I knelt in the pew after getting communion, trying desperately not to let the host touch my teeth and hoping it would dissolve faster on my tongue. But instead it got stuck to the roof of my mouth, which is what made me gag.

I'm telling you all this for a reason.

Early on, I realized that in Fischer-Franzen, St. Joseph's Church was a really, really important place. It was where everyone would come together on Sunday morning. Well, almost everyone. Kaza's family, the Sylowichs, didn't come to St. Joseph's and that's because his mother was Muslim and his father was an atheist, which means he didn't believe in God, even though he used to be a Muslim. And neither did the Podnovestovs, because they were Jews. But I learned they believed in God too, but just did it in a different way than the way we did it when there was mass at St. Joseph's. It wasn't until I became an altar boy that I realized why they didn't come to St. Joseph's like everyone else.

None of this mattered to me, at least not as far as Kaza was concerned. He was my best friend, and just because he wasn't Catholic didn't mean anything as far as I was concerned. Kaza was a really, really good guy and I loved him like a brother. Sure, maybe sometimes I might have wished Kaza was Catholic like me, because then he could have been an altar boy too and we could have served mass together. But other than that, I didn't care he was Muslim. Those things don't really mean anything between best friends when you're a kid.

The thing about the church was that it felt like a safe place. Every time I walked into St. Joseph's it was like stepping into a different world. It was as if it was disconnected from the world outside. Pull open the heavy wooden front door with the gold latch and it would be like entering this kind of sanctuary, insulated from everything else that might be going on outside. It would be quiet, serene and even smelled different, mostly the lingering after-effects of incense burned during high mass. I used to think that going into church was like stepping into the waiting room for heaven.

So, when I turned seven and became an altar boy I became much more aware of the church as a kind of refuge from the world. Just by being in church and realizing how it felt different there, and how it seemed insulated from the outside, also made me more aware of the world out there. St. Joseph's started to put things into perspective for me. I began to understand better.

Only a month after I had officially become an altar boy I started to notice things that made me realize how the people of Fischer-Franzen were suffering. Up to that point, my understanding was limited to basically two things. First was that never having enough to eat was just the way it was for everyone in town. Second, it was the fault of the Bolsheviks. But what I didn't understand was how it was affecting people in other ways. It wasn't until I started to hear conversations between Father Frederich and other people in the church that I began to figure things out.

I remember two conversations in particular.

It was just after the 7 A.M. mass on a Wednesday morning.

When I first started serving mass, I often got to do the early morning weekday masses. That's because there were not that many people in the church and it was a pretty basic mass. No sermon, hymns, no incense-burning. Nothing like that. Just lots of droning in Latin. So there wasn't as much of a chance to screw up as a beginner altar boy. And if you did flub your Latin lines it didn't much matter because probably no one, other than Father Frederich, would notice. And Father Frederich was always really nice about it. He never got mad and would thank the altar boys after every mass, give us a blessing, pat us each gently on the top of the head and send us on our way.

So early morning weekday masses were not like serving the high mass at 11 A.M. on Sunday. Now *that* was a big deal. For one thing, the church would be packed. There would be a procession up the aisle to begin. Lots of incense-burning, stuff like that, not to mention a long mass because instead of saying our Latin lines, much of it was sung, which really slowed down the process. And the sermon at the high mass was always longer for some reason. My first year as an altar boy I never got to serve at high mass, other than a few times as an acolyte carrying a candle in the procession at the beginning and end. The older boys, the ones who were 10, 11 and 12, and more experienced as altar boys, were the ones who got to serve high mass.

The sacristy was the area in the back of the church behind the sanctuary, where the priest and altar boys got ready for mass. There were basically two rooms connected by a small hallway. The priest's area was on one side and the altar boys' room, where we stored our black cassocks and white surplices with square-yoked necklines that we wore when we served, was on the other. We kept our vestments hanging in a closet with the larger to smaller sizes going from left to right.

After mass, our job was to sort of clean up. By that I mean

snuff out the candles, bring in the water and wine crucibles from the small table beside the altar and pick up the big mass book from the altar and put it on the priest's table. I had been serving with Andrew Getzlaf, who was eight and in his second year of serving. So, because I was junior to him, I had to clean up after the mass and Andrew was able to leave before me.

It was while I was hanging up my cassock and surplice I heard the voices coming from the other side of the sacristy where Father Frederich was taking off his mass vestments. At first I didn't think anything of it, because sometimes people would come to the back of the church after mass to talk with Father Frederich.

But then I heard a word that really caught my attention, and scared me. The word was "fuck."

I knew it was a really, really bad swear. What scared me was that I heard it in church. I was sure that whoever said it had committed a mortal sin because he said it in church. I carefully hung up my vestments and was going to quietly leave when the voices became louder. I realized then that Father Frederich thought I had already left.

"Tell me this, do we have the numbers to pull it off?" I heard Father Frederich ask.

"There are seven of us, eight if we count you. Are you in?" the other man said.

"You know, for Christ's sake, I'm in, but I can't be part of the ambush. I'll be here," Father Frederich replied. When I heard him say a swear, instantly I felt sick. It was like someone punched me in the stomach and I couldn't breathe. I almost threw up right there, but choked back the bile that had risen and was burning in my throat.

Then fear and panic took over. I didn't want to hear any more. I wanted to run from the church, but I was afraid Father would hear me. So I stood frozen by fear—fear of hearing more, fear of being found out.

"I'll tell the others we will meet at midnight," the other voice said.

"Good," Frederich said. "The fucking bastards are finally ..."

I couldn't stand it. I stepped into the closet to try and disappear into the altar boy vestments, covered my ears with my palms, crouched down and put my head between my knees to block out the voices. I'm not sure how long I stayed like that, likely three or four minutes. I tried not to make a sound, not even to breathe, so that I wouldn't be discovered. When I finally took my hands away from my ears I listened, but the voices were gone. It was totally silent. I waited another five minutes until I was sure Father Frederich had gone, peeked out into the church and saw only one old lady doing the stations of the cross. I quickly walked out of the church and into the bright morning sunlight.

Hearing Father Frederich say swear words, and in church, had a profound effect on me. I realize now it shattered my childish sense of the world. You might say, and I don't want to sound overly dramatic here, a big piece of my childhood ended at that moment.

As I left the church, I felt confused and suddenly very uncertain about the world I found myself in. The church never felt like a safe place again. My notion of trust, which is so much of being a child, had been rocked to the core. Although I didn't appreciate or understand it at the time, I had been introduced to cynicism.

"WANNA GUH-GO TO THE CAVE and be spuh-spies?" Kaza asked as we sat on his front step. It was a week after I had heard Father Frederich swear and I hadn't told anyone about what happened.

"Sure, I guess. Why not," I said.

Walking around to the shed in Kaza's backyard, I wondered if

I should tell him about what I had heard in church. It was still bothering me a lot and I really wanted to tell Kaza to see what he would think. But then I thought, *Kaza doesn't go to church and he won't likely understand.*

But once we got under the tarp and in the Cave, I started to feel different. I guess it was the sense of safety and isolation, our secret hiding place, that gave me the confidence I needed to tell Kaza. And besides, he was my best friend and we never kept secrets from each other.

"You know how I'm an altar boy and everything," I said.

"Uh-huh. But I don't really nuh-know what you do. Are you going to be a priest when you're gruh-gruh-grown up?"

"Maybe, dunno. Used to think so, but now I dunno."

"How come?" Kaza asked.

"Can you keep a secret?" I asked.

"Sure. Have you guh-got a secret? I wuh-won't tell anyone. Promise."

So I told Kaza about how I heard Father Frederich say swears.

"But lots of people say buh-bad words," was Kaza's reaction.

"This is different. Father Frederich is holy. He's like God's assistant. He works for God and doesn't make sins like other people. He's going to heaven."

"Well, muh-maybe not if he says swears. God doesn't like that, you know."

"I know. That's why it's so bad. I feel kinda sick when I think about it."

Kaza didn't have any advice for me, beyond not to worry. He said maybe the priest didn't mean to say bad words but couldn't help it because he was so upset about something.

At first, I didn't think anything about what Kaza said, except the part about Father Frederich saying bad words because he was really upset. That made sense, and I could tell from the little bit I heard that Father *was* really upset, mad enough to say what he did. Actually that helped me feel a little better. Everyone gets upset, I guess even holy people like priests. He was so bothered by something he couldn't help himself and the swears just slipped out. But it made me wonder, too, how Father Frederich went to confession. Did he do it like ordinary people, in a confessional? And if he did, who does he tell his sins to? I figured it must be God, Himself.

I didn't think anymore about the reason Father Frederich was so upset until I heard the second conversation 10 days later. This time it happened when I was delivering a loaf of bread my mother baked for Father Frederich to the rectory next door to the church.

As I climbed the stairs to the front door one of the windows was slightly open and I could hear voices from inside. Just as I was going to knock, I heard a man's voice that I didn't at first recognize. I decided not to knock and was just going to put the bread on the front step.

"What our people have been through—the killing, the suffering, now the starvation—it's unbelievable. It cannot go unanswered." It was Father Frederich's voice. "Sometimes I ask myself, as a priest, maybe I should only be concerned with their spiritual lives and not be part of the struggle with the murdering, thieving Bolsheviks. But I look at what's been done to the German people. How our lives, our families have been torn apart, our futures destroyed and I realize there can be no faith in God, that for those who have lost their faith, they can't regain it if we do not first have justice. The will of God demands justice."

"You don't have to convince me, Father," said another voice.

"Or me," said another.

"Unless we fight back, there can be no justice and there can be no justice without revenge."

I didn't fully understand the specific meaning of some of the words they were saying. But I understood enough to sense the anger. I felt a terrible sense of dread, set the bread on the step and carefully tiptoed down the steps of the rectory so the men inside wouldn't hear me. When I got to the street I ran as fast as I could, all the way home.

"Hi, Anton. Did Father say anything when you gave him the bread?" Mom asked me as I came through the front door.

"No," I said.

"No? You did take the bread to him, didn't you?"

"Uh-huh."

"And he didn't thank you? Why are you so out of breath?"

"I ran all the way home. I heard Father talking to people in the house, so I just left the bread on the step."

"You should have at least knocked. I hope he notices the bread or someone else might take it. You can play outside until suppertime."

I went back out the front door where Frank and Mary were playing in the dirt. Mary was drawing lines and circles with a stick. Frank was using one of Mom's wooden spoons to dig a trench around the big tree in our front yard. "I'm building a moat," he said. "I'm going to pour water in it so the tree can have a drink."

"Good idea," I said before shimmying up the trunk of the tree to reach the lowest branch and then pull myself up to the crotch between the two big boughs that were perfect to sit back and watch the world go by in.

"I wanna come up too," Frankie said, looking up at me.

"You're not old enough yet. It's pretty high up here. You have to be seven. I couldn't climb it until I was seven. Just build your trench and give Giant a drink."

"I'm almost six-and-a-half," Frank said.

"I'm five-and-a-half," Mary said.

As I sat in the tree, reclining between the two big branches, it made me think about things. I remember that moment so well. Like it was right now. You know how, when you're a little kid, your life is pretty much about playing and using your imagination to transport yourself into another world. You kind of live two separate lives. One is your real life, with your family, at school, when you eat supper together or when you have to clean your room or make your bed. That's real stuff. The other is your imaginary life, the one that you make up in your mind, where you kind of enter this other place that is all about your fantasy world and what you make yourself imagine to be true.

Basically, that was what it was like hanging out with Kaza. For the most part, we lived our imaginary lives together. We'd be lying on our backs looking at clouds, swimming in the Andre, climbing trees, being spies in the Cave. When I think about it now, it was a good imaginary life, one where we were able to retreat from reality and create a different, uncomplicated-by-adults world for ourselves.

But that all changed for me on that day in October 1922, when I was seven years old and sitting in the tree. That's when I started to understand what part of my life was real and what was fantasy. The difference between what I believed, or maybe should say what I *wanted* to believe, and what was true.

It was one of those rare moments in your life that comes upon you like a revelation, when your perspective changes forever. That's what happened to me.

As I looked down from the tree at Frankie and Mary playing, I suddenly felt disconnected from them and everything else below. The best way to describe it is like when you're watching a movie. You're observing but not participating physically, even though you are emotionally involved in what you see. Of course I didn't think of it in those terms at the time, because in Fischer-Franzen in 1922 there were no such things as movies. But come to think of it now, in some ways, the imaginary world of children is really movie-making of the mind, a way to transport yourself from the real world into a fantasy of your own making.

I could see Mary drawing a face in the dirt—at least that's what I think she was trying to do. Being so young, her motor skills weren't great. But as she sat on the ground and struck up a conversation with the misshapen circle she had etched, I realized she had created a make-believe person in the dirt. I couldn't hear well enough to know exactly what she was saying but I could tell it was a two-sided conversation. She talked to the face in the ground in her voice and then changed her voice to speak back to herself as the face in the dirt. It was quite an animated conversation she was having with her imaginary friend. As near as I could make out, they were talking about each other's dolls being sick and how they had to get the doctor.

Meanwhile, a few feet away, Frankie was totally lost in his own world, digging a moat around the base of the tree with the wooden spoon. He was completely silent, entirely focused on the chore at hand, carefully carving the trench, stopping regularly to make sure the moat was the same depth by measuring it with the handle of the wooden spoon.

Down the street I could see the older kids playing soccer. There were five a side. Each of the goals was marked by two rocks. Standing on the sidelines were four girls, sisters of the boys playing the game. They weren't paying attention to the game, being instead more interested in their own conversation as they huddled together to talk as if they were sharing secrets, often breaking out into giggles.

Just beyond the street soccer, at the community well in the small town square, were two women—my mom and Mrs. Heidt—collecting water. My mom turned the noisy crank to raise and lower the bucket and Mrs. Heidt would empty it into a big silver metal tub with handles on both sides. As I watched them, I counted six buckets to fill the tub.

Together, one on each side, they lifted the tub by its handles. You could tell it was a heavy load as each used both her hands to lift it before awkwardly walking sideways to carry it up the street and eventually to the Heidt's house, which was two doors down from ours. They had to walk slowly, synchronizing their steps, so the water wouldn't splash over the sides of the tub. You could see the strain on their faces from the heavy load as they silently lugged the tubful of water.

After disappearing for a minute into the house, they emerged with the empty tub. This time they carried it easily, one on each side, walking straight ahead and not sideways, talking to each other as they made their way back to the well. The scene repeated itself, this time with Mrs. Heidt turning the well crank and my mom pouring each of the six buckets into the tub. When the tub was full, they struggled with it again, straining to deliver the water this time to our house, which I knew Mom would heat on the coal stove and use to do the wash.

Thinking about a tub of water to wash clothes simmering on the stove made me feel nauseous. It reminded me of the smell when Mom boiled beets to make *borscht* and how much I hated the smell of boiling beets. It also reminded me of what it was like to go hungry.

As I describe these things that I watched unfold, and how I reacted, I realize it all sounds quite unremarkable and insignificant. But what made it meaningful for me, even memorable, was that I experienced all this in the wake of the two conversations I had overheard between Father Frederich and the others.

For some reason, sitting in the tree that day changed the way I perceived the world. Maybe not in a good way for me, as a seven-year-old kid. But in a more realistic way.

I was, at that moment, able to differentiate between my life as a child and the adult world. These things are never easy to explain, or even logical. They just happen.

The only way I can explain it is like this.

First, being in the tree gave me a different physical perspective on the world. I was able to watch things from above without feeling like I was part of what was happening. So I was kind of detached from what I saw.

Second, seeing Frankie and Mary playing in their imaginary world allowed me to witness the fantasy world of young childhood. Even though I was still very much a child myself who, like all young kids, used my imagination to create my own make-believe life, I suddenly saw it for what it was. It was the same with the kids playing soccer and the girls giggling and talking together about whatever it is young girls their age talk about. I don't say any of this in a negative or bad way. It wasn't as if I was being judgmental of the imaginary world of children. It was just that I recognized it for the first time.

Third was watching Mom and Mrs. Heidt struggle to carry the tubs of water so they could wash clothes. I suddenly realized this was the real world of Fischer-Franzen. This was a town gripped by famine, where hunger was simply a way of life, where women did the work of men because most of the men had died and gone to heaven. A town so burdened by violence, inhumanity and hate that even the priest was filled with anger and a thirst for revenge.

A town, I realized sitting in that tree as a seven-year-old, still trying to cope with what happened on the day when my life began.

CHAPTER 12

I T HAD BEEN A LONG TIME since he was last in Odessa. A very long time. You might say, and it would be true, that it had been a lifetime ago.

In those days, his name was Lev Davidovich Bronstein. But more than his name had changed in the 24 years since he had left school in Odessa. Much more.

Gone was his naiveté. Gone were his teenage populist instincts. Gone was his petty bourgeois lifestyle. Gone, too, was his outward Jewish heritage. They all disappeared into the designed persona of Leon Trotsky, his new Russian name that embodied a burning revolutionary zeal and the rejection of who he once had been.

But much about Trotsky remained the same as those days of his youth. It's not easy to escape the imprint of your past. Trotsky knew as much. So his journey was less about rejecting who he had been and more about defining who he would become. And there could be no doubt about who Leon Trotsky was now.

His parents had farmed near the Jewish village of Yanovka on the steppes of southwest Russia, in Ukraine. It was a region defined by its ethnic enclaves—Jews, Russians and Germans. The Bronstein family was well-to-do, considered landowning peasant farmers or *kulaks*. Even though Trotsky had grown up largely free from want, his family did not enjoy the luxuries of life. His father was obsessively frugal, not the sort to spend money, even though they had more than most others of the district. David Leontievich Bronstein, his wife Anna, who had grown up in Odessa, and their eight children, lived in a simple mud home, with a thatched roof and earthen floor.

One of the most enduring memories Trotsky had of his early youth was the rhythmic cadence of raindrops on metal. It reminded him of the many evenings his mother spent reading to her housebound children. In fact, if there was one overriding image of his past that remained with him through the years, it was of how his mother had instilled in him a love of knowledge, ideas and words.

So committed were his parents to the education of their children, that at age nine Trotsky was sent to live with his mother's nephew so he could attend school in Odessa. Moisey Filippovich Shpenster was a young journalist who had come to spend a summer vacation with his aunt Anna Bronstein in the country. He was impressed with young Lev's sharp mind and saw great possibilities for the boy should he receive a proper, formal education. A year later, Shpenster married the principal of the school for Jewish girls and wrote to the Bronsteins to encourage them to send their son to live with him and his wife and attend St. Paul's grammar school in Odessa. David Bronstein, hoping his son would become an engineer, agreed. So, before this 10th birthday, Lev Bronstein had left home to begin the journey that would turn him into Leon Trotsky.

At school in Odessa, Trotsky was recognized for two things: his good looks and his sharp mind. Endowed with thick black hair, brilliant blue eyes and a gift for dressing well, Trotsky had many admirers at school. But his obvious intellect also made him egocentric, a trait manifest in a condescending personality. So, while he might have been admired for his appearance and his intelligence, he was not well-liked because of his egotistical, superior attitude.

For his last year of high school, Trotsky had to transfer to a school in nearby Nikolayev to study classes not offered at St. Paul's. It marked a turning point in his intellectual development, and his life.

At Nikolayev, he lived with a family whose sons were committed socialists. At first, demonstrating his typical intellectual disdain, he heaped scorn on their "socialist utopia" and dismissed their radical ideas as fanciful and naive. But as he debated against socialism, Trotsky demonstrated a characteristic that would display itself throughout his life. The more rigorous his opposition to an idea, the more he internalized the ideas and arguments he fought against. Suddenly, Trotsky would reach a point where he felt he had fully confronted and probed the concept he was debating and convert utterly to it. He would then become a complete adherent, which was how he was brought to Marx, his adherence to communism and the notion of inevitable worldwide communist revolution.

He and his friends met regularly with a group of radical students on the outskirts of Nikolayev. They gathered in a small hut located in an orchard owned by a poor gardener named Franz Shvigovsky. Young Trotsky was quickly enthralled by the idea of revolution. He was particularly captivated by a young woman named Alexandra Sokolovskaya, who introduced him to the ideas and dogma of Marxism

The air of superiority Trotsky displayed in his youth did not only remain, it become an even more dominant aspect of his personality. He did not suffer fools gladly and considered virtually everyone his intellectual inferior. The same was even true, he felt, of Lenin. But Trotsky was wise enough to never betray that belief to anyone else. He knew that disagreeing with Lenin about ideas, tactics and policy was tolerable, providing it was done with respect and deference. But open defiance of Lenin's intellect was the equivalent of disloyalty to the cause. It irked Trotsky that he was made to feel subservient, or even equal, to anyone else's intellect. But he was wise, cunning and pragmatic enough to realize it was necessary.

But there were limits to his deference. If there was one from whom Trotsky did not disguise his disdain, it was Josef Stalin. What a crude and shallow man. As far as Trotsky was concerned, Stalin was little more than an uneducated brute. A cunning and manipulative thug whom he despised, but also recognized he must respect, if only for his ruthlessness as an adversary.

Now, alone in his room at the Tsentralnaya Hotel in Odessa, Trotsky was ridden with frustration, anxiety and anger. He felt no particular nostalgia or warm memories at returning to the city of his youth. As he sat at a small desk and peered out the window onto the street, the city seemed strangely foreign, like a place he had never visited, let alone lived in, before. The reason for the disconnect with his past was simple—he was too preoccupied with the here and now of his life.

It had been almost five years since the Bolsheviks had seized power and, by all accounts, Trotsky should have been basking in the revolutionary glow of communism. Not only had the revolution succeeded and taken root across Russia and many of its neighbouring republics—not only here in Ukraine and its regional appendages like Bessarabia—but the bloody civil war had been won. The Whites had been crushed and ethnic uprisings quelled. Sure, there were still pockets of insurgency, and a few sporadic incidents with the bourgeois and *kulak* Germans in this very region of Ukraine. But clearly there was no turning back. Power had been consolidated, revolution embedded in the Russian psyche and society.

Yet instead of contentment and a sense of achievement, Trotsky found himself in a dark mood, brooding in an Odessa hotel. He had ostensibly been dispatched to Ukraine by Lenin to assess the situation on the ground. As the head of the Red Army and the commissar of war, Trotsky was the logical choice to determine whether or not the anti-revolution insurgency in Ukraine required any additional suppression by the military. If anyone knew about the effectiveness of brute force in crushing anti-revolutionary uprisings, it was Trotsky. But he was also there for other reasons—as bait to lure the remaining anti-revolutionaries and insurgent *kulaks* into a trap, and, more importantly, to consolidate his political position in the coming struggle with Stalin.

A year earlier, in 1921, he had unleashed the full power of the Red Army to brutally crush the Kronstadt rebellion, led by mutinous sailors, soldiers and civilians in the Baltic seaport. The rebellion had been triggered by many factors—the complete exhaustion and ruination caused by the First World War, the revolution and subsequent civil war, and the utter economic failure of the Communist revolution. The destitution and famine that resulted spawned an uprising that Trotsky dismissed as part of the bourgeois counter-revolution. The bloody toll of suppressing the rebellion was huge. Its leaders were summarily executed and hundreds more sent to forced labour camps.

But success in ending the rebellion left Trotsky feeling more resentment than satisfaction. In the wake of the conflict, Lenin succumbed to the belief the social unrest demonstrated that unless the revolution changed its economic policies in fundamental ways, it was doomed to fail. The result was Lenin's New Economic Policy, which Trotsky saw as nothing more than a sop to the bourgeois capitalists. Ironically, it had been Trotsky who had proposed reforms to agriculture production, which would allow farmers to sell their surplus production on the open market as a means to stimulate productivity. At first Lenin rejected the notion, but was later forced to accept it, along with other liberalization measures under the guise of the New Economic Policy. While the state retained control of large and medium-sized production facilities, the NEP allowed private enterprise back into agriculture and small industry with some control by the state. The result was the intermingling of state socialism with state capitalism and private enterprise.

What Trotsky hated was the scope of the economic reforms. He believed Lenin had gone too far—it was economic capitulation. But he hated Stalin even more.

The rivalry between the two had become intense, especially after Lenin suffered a stroke and was left partially incapacitated and in a feeble state. As General Secretary of the Communist Party, Stalin saw Trotsky as his rival to replace Lenin, whose fragile health made it clear that his days as leader of Russia, the Communist party and the revolution were numbered. For Trotsky, the challenge was to overcome the perception of some that he was a latecomer to the Bolshevik cause, first a socialist revolutionary, then a *Menshevik* before finally embracing the Bolsheviks in 1916. While his intellect was never doubted, his adherence to the view that the Bolshevik revolution should seek to inspire world communist revolution was not shared by many, least of all Stalin.

The tension between Trotsky and Stalin simmered for years, but as long as Lenin was healthy and fully in charge of his faculties and the party, the rivalry had been held in check. Lenin's illness fundamentally and irrevocably changed that dynamic.

As the feud broke into the open, Trotsky accused Stalin of promoting policies such as the NEP that would deliver Russia back into the hands of the capitalists. With Lenin now in the background, Stalin formed a powerful inner circle that included Gregory Zinoviev and Leo Kamenev, who had been Lenin loyalists stretching back to the days before his return to Petrograd from Finland and the advent of the revolution. A year earlier, Zinoviev had proposed that Stalin assume the newly created position of General Secretary to the Central Committee of the All-Russian Communist Party. A resentful Trotsky, realizing he could not block the move, reluctantly agreed. When Lenin offered Trotsky the position of Deputy Chairman of the Council of People's Commissars, Trotsky refused, even though technically the position would have nominally installed him as second in command to Lenin. The reality was two others already held the title and Trotsky saw the offer as a slight.

Excluded from the inner circle now controlled by Stalin, Trotsky felt isolated. He lacked the power base to mount a serious effort to counter what was clearly Stalin's growing influence as Lenin faded from prominence in the party and the government.

This visit to Odessa gave Trotsky the opportunity to reflect on his options. As he stared out onto Preobrazhenskaya Street he could see throngs of people gathered around wagons where local farmers were selling their produce in an open market. It was visible evidence of the NEP, a return of street capitalism, unencumbered by government control over prices or distribution. Those with the money were able to buy. Those with production were able to sell at prices set by a crude, free market. And those who did not have the means simply had to do without. Trotsky could see some milling on the edges of the crowd, people clothed in little more than rags, who could not afford to buy food and were reduced to begging for scraps and leftovers from the street merchants.

There was a knock at his hotel door.

"Who is it?" Trotsky said.

"Yuri, sir," came the reply.

"Come in."

Yuri Stelmanov was a tall, heavy-set man with powerful arms and meaty hands. He had the intimidating physique of a bodyguard, which is exactly the service he provided Trotsky. But Stelmanov was also much more. Trotsky trusted him implicitly as an aide-de-camp, advisor and confidante. Given his growing isolation from power, Stelmanov became more and more a critical ally and friend. Trotsky always travelled with him, and sometimes two other plainclothed bodyguards, as he had on the train to Odessa from Moscow.

"Sir," Stelmanov said. "He's here, waiting in the lobby. I just spoke with him. He says we can leave any time you're ready."

"Go get him. Tell him I'd like him to come to the room so we can talk before we leave."

Stelmanov nodded, turned and disappeared out the door. A few minutes later there was another knock.

"Enter," Trotsky said.

The door opened and Stelmanov walked in, this time followed by a tall, imposing figure.

Trotsky was stretched out on the bed, his back against the headrest, his hands clasped behind his head.

"Comrade Yulinov. It is good to see you again," Trotsky said, getting up off the bed and extending his hand.

Yulinov quickly took off his leather cap in a show of respect and shook Trotsky's outstretched hand. The two embraced, kissing each cheek.

"Welcome home, to Ukraine and to Odessa, sir," Yulinov said.

They had met only one other time since that night at the Smolny on the cusp of the overthrow of Kerensky and the provisional government. Yulinov had travelled to the 1920 party congress in Moscow. By that point, Trotsky and other party *apparatchiks* were well aware of Yulinov's effectiveness in managing the Andrejaschevski soviet. His discipline, control and commitment to the revolution were well-known and admired by many, including Trotsky. In fact, Yulinov had risen in stature to the point that he was considered not only a key party functionary, but a revolutionary strongman in the region. These days, Trotsky needed all the friends he could get, and Yulinov was someone whose utter loyalty and dedication Trotsky could trust.

So for Trotsky, the visit to Odessa was about expanding and consolidating his power base in Ukraine. It was, after all, his home turf, and just as Stalin dominated the party in his home state of Georgia, so too did Trotsky have to ensure that he was seen as the party strongman in Ukraine for the post-Lenin era looming on the horizon. And Yulinov would be key to the venture.

"Tell me how things are. My reports are that you have made very good progress. The countryside is mostly calm, people have accepted the regime," Trotsky said, lighting a cigarette and flicking the still-burning match out the open hotel room window.

"I believe that is true, Comrade Trotsky. We faced some vicious opposition from the Whites and the Germans. But we acted quickly and decisively to quell any insurgency. The message that resistance was futile and that those who did not support the revolution would be eliminated was clear. But much of the credit goes to the Red Army. They were superb."

Yulinov knew that by complimenting the Red Army he was complimenting Trotsky, the army's commander in chief. Trotsky took it as such.

"That's nice to hear," Trotsky said. "But I also understand there are still some pockets of resistance in the ethnic German enclaves. True?"

"Some, but very few. Nothing we can't manage."

"Who are the some?"

"Mostly German *kulaks* who still try to avoid their duty. And I watch the priests closely. You can't trust the German Catholic fuckers. But there are those in the pews who tell us what is happening, what they are saying, what people talk about when they gather after mass on Sunday mornings."

"You're wise to be suspicious. We must be ever vigilant," Trotsky said.

The conversation then turned to the extent of the famine in the region and the impact of the New Economic Policy. Yulinov conceded that hunger and food shortages remained a problem, but the scale of famine had receded.

"The worst is over, I believe," Yulinov said. "People are not starving to death any longer."

Trotsky nodded.

It was true. The famine of the three previous years had eased. Although the stark failure of a Communist command-and-control system had been an undeniable factor in bringing the economy to its knees, there were other causes as well. Russia had been a country wracked by upheaval for almost a decade. The physical destruction and economic ruin caused by the First World War, the turmoil of the Bolshevik Revolution, the ensuing civil war, the policies of war communism and other Communist policies that sapped the economy of incentive to produce, had all conspired to wreak havoc on the nation. Now that conflict, both external and internal, had subsided and Lenin's initial harsh economic constraints had been eased with the New Economic Policy, the signs of a very modest, grassroots economic revival were evident. Indeed, they were apparent outside the hotel where they planned Trotsky's stay in the region, visible on the street where food and produce were being sold in an open market.

The plan was for Trotsky and Stelmanov to go with Yulinov for a brief visit to a tiny place called Blumenthal, where they would meet with the others from the Andrejaschevski soviet, namely Popov, Kurbesky, Smenev and Kuzma, as well as Georgy Pyatakov, a powerful figure in the Ukraine Communist movement. The purpose of the visit was twofold: to allow Trotsky to assess the situation on the ground in the Kutschurgan, and to elevate his stature with party loyalists in the region, bolstering his campaign in the power struggle with Stalin.

A wagon led by a team of two white Arabian horses was waiting in the laneway behind the hotel. Yulinov had been told that Trotsky wanted to travel anonymously— in fact, Trotsky had been registered at the hotel by Stelmanov under the name of Anatoly Borshikov—and so he tied the horses to a post near the rear entrance to the hotel. Normally, as a powerful figure of the Soviet regime, Trotsky would travel with all the trappings of that power: a private salon car on the train or in a Russian-made Moskvitch car or truck, which were rarely seen other than as official vehicles for senior Communist party *apparatchiks* in Moscow or Petrograd.

The trio emerged for their journey through the back door of the hotel, Trotsky wearing a wide-brimmed black straw hat as a disguise, and climbed aboard the wagon.

The trip to Blumenthal would take three hours, passing through Mannheim, Strassburg and Fischer-Franzen along the way. As he snapped the reins and the two horses started forward, Yulinov took a watch from the pocket of his leather vest and flipped open the cover. It was 10 A.M.

Trotsky sat next to Yulinov. At their feet was a rifle, lying on its side. Stelmanov, who had a pistol holstered on his belt and a rifle across his lap, was on the raised bench behind them, serving as lookout. Behind them were two rifles under an old woolen blanket on the wagon's flatbed. With the horses' hooves clopping on the cobblestone, the three men headed through the winding streets of Odessa, finally going northwest into the countryside along a well-travelled dirt road that ran adjacent to the Dneister River.

On the outskirts of the city they were met by two Red Army regulars in plain clothes on horseback who Yulinov had recruited as outriders for extra security.

AT THAT MOMENT, Father Frederich slid open the wooden panel in the confessional. In the dimness he could barely see the shadowy outline of a man's face on the other side of the grate.

"Bless me, Father, for I have sinned. It has been ..."

Unfortunately, the darkness did not diminish the priest's sense of smell. Frederich couldn't help but recoil from the reek of the man's breath, a pungent mixture of vodka, chewing tobacco and garlic.

"Cut the crap," Frederich said.

"Thought I might kill two birds with one stone. You know, confess my sins and then tell you what you want to hear," the man said, his voice betraying the smirk on his face.

"Very funny. Not to mention sacrilegious. Just tell me, is it today or not?"

"Imagine that," the man responded. "You accusing someone else of sacrilege. I don't even care about your stupid religion and all its superstitions—but even I get the irony of you, of all people, saying that."

Frederich could barely stand the man. He found him crude and repulsive. But there was little choice but to tolerate him because he was too valuable, too good an informant to alienate. So Frederich had to tolerate his smart-ass comments, not to mention his foul breath, the many times they spoke in the confessional.

"Just tell me. Is it today?" Frederich repeated calmly.

"It's today. He arrived in Odessa yesterday. They just left and are on their way."

"How many of them?"

"Three pieces of shit in total. Trotsky, Yulinov and some other jerk-off, some guy who's Trotsky's bodyguard. Apparently Trotsky goes nowhere without him. I figure they're homos."

"How do you know? Are you sure? Can we trust whoever told you this?"

"What, that they're homos?"

"Don't be an ass. You know what I mean."

"I just spoke with the hotel clerk. Amazing how this telephone invention works. He saw them leave. They're in a wagon. A team of two white Arabians."

"How long?"

"Two hours, two-and-a-half at the most. Depends if they stop in Selz. They're not supposed to. Plan is for them to be in Mannheim this afternoon. Everyone is already in place, just as you wanted. Six of 'em. This is going to be a thing of beauty."

"At the place we discussed."

"Yup. Three at each end. It's going to be like shooting trapped skunks. Nowhere to run. Nowhere for the fucks to hide."

"Godspeed," Frederich said.

How fucking twisted is that, thought Sylowich as he got off his knees, pushed back the heavy drape, stepped out of the confessional and left the church. A priest wishing him godspeed to go and kill three people. It just added to his contempt of religion.

As he mounted the horse he had tied to a tree near the church, Sylowich saw Kaza playing soccer with other kids in the street. Sylowich rode over and called out to his son.

"Kaza, tell your mother I won't be home tonight."

With the shouts and clamouring of the youngsters caught up in their soccer game, Kaza didn't hear.

Angry that Kaza had not responded, Sylowich rode into the midst of the soccer match, the kids scattering, and Kaza knocked to the ground in the scramble.

"I said, tell your mother I won't be home tonight," Sylowich repeated, as Kaza struggled to his feet. "Understand?"

"Yes, Papa," Kaza nodded.

Sylowich turned his horse and rode south out of town towards Strassburg.

"Where's your dad going?" Anton asked Kaza.

"I-I dun—I dunno," Kaza said.

Once he was beyond the turn in the road at the edge of town, heading south and out of sight, Sylowich urged his horse into almost a gallop. He set a pace that he knew the horse could sustain for some time before exhaustion.

The duplicity of it all made Sylowich smile to himself as he rode. For the last year-and-a-half he'd felt like a new man. Finally, he had power and influence. Finally, there was meaning to his life. Finally, he felt important.

It had all begun with a chance encounter on the road to Mannheim. Stopping so his horse could drink from a small pond next to the road, Sylowich sat down on a large rock to have a cigarette. A few minutes later, Alexandre Yulinov came riding from the other direction, heading towards Fischer-Franzen. The two knew each other but not well. Yulinov recognized Sylowich as someone from Fischer-Franzen who, because he was one of the few non-Germans in the village, was seen as being unopposed to the revolution. Yulinov knew Sylowich was someone he wanted to recruit. Moreover, Yulinov remembered what Kuzma had told him about his experience with Sylowich in the trenches against the Germans. Like most people, Sylowich knew Yulinov mostly by reputation. That is, as the local Communist revolutionary strongman who issued orders others carried out. And he had heard the stories, too, of how Yulinov had been in Petrograd during the overthrow of Kerensky and had become a friend of Trotsky himself.

"Rudel Sylowich, Fischer-Franzen, correct?" Yulinov had said as he swung out of his saddle.

"That's right, sir, er, Mr. Yulinov," Sylowich replied.

"How are you, Comrade? Kuzma has told me much about you. I hope all is well, that your family has enough to eat and your life is better than it was."

"It is better, sir. But it is still a struggle to feed my family. Thank you for asking," said Sylowich, feeling both intimidated and pleased that Yulinov would express an interest in him.

And so the partnership began. Yulinov always believed he was a good judge of character. He could assess another person quickly and seldom were his instincts wrong. This was his opportunity to judge Sylowich.

As the two talked—the conversation lasted more than a half-hour—Yulinov saw in Sylowich exactly the kind of person he needed. Someone in Fischer-Franzen he could trust, someone who could be his eyes and ears. In return, Yulinov promised Sylowich that his family would never go hungry and, if he faithfully did his duty, that Sylowich would be rewarded with money, food, alcohol and tobacco.

But Yulinov wanted more from Sylowich than merely someone who kept his eyes open and reported back. He wanted an infiltrator, an agent who would become a confidante of the Germans by winning their trust; a conduit who would feed them the information they sought about Yulinov and the activities of the Andrejaschevski soviet. In other words, a kind of double agent.

Yulinov knew Sylowich was mentally unstable, subject to unexpected mood swings and often drank too much. But curiously he saw those as positive attributes for the assignment. The Germans would perceive his weaknesses and think Sylowich someone they could control and manipulate for their own purposes.

Which was exactly what happened.

The first step was to establish Sylowich's credibility in German eyes. It required the visible public disgrace of Sylowich at the hands of Yulinov and his people in such a way that would allow Sylowich to ally himself with the German resisters.

The scheme wasn't very elaborate. In was, in fact, rather crude and simple.

One day in November 1920, Yulinov and three of his henchmen road into Fischer-Franzen at midday as planned. They went to the well at the middle of town to draw water for themselves and their horses. Sylowich, and his wife and son, were already there, filling a large wooden tub. Completely unaware of the choreographed encounter, Yakira and Kaza were unwitting pawns in what transpired next.

Yulinov and his men quickly became interested in Sylowich's wife, making lewd comments as she bent over to pour water from the well's bucket into the large washtub.

"Leave her alone. Just take your water and leave," Sylowich said.

The response was swift and brutal; Yulinov slapped Sylowich across the face, knocking him to the ground.

Young Kaza, stricken with fear, burst into tears and ran to his mother's side. One of Yulinov's men grabbed the boy by the upper arm—yanking him hard away from his mother, who clutched at his shoulders—and flung Kaza to the ground. Another man reached over and ripped open Yakira's blouse, exposing her breasts. He slapped her face and she fell to her knees.

The four men laughed loudly as Kaza sobbed on the ground next to his mother and Sylowich staggered slowly to his feet.

"Let that be a lesson to you," Yulinov had snarled.

Each of the four then had a drink of water. Laughing loudly, they pushed over the half-filled tub of water before mounting their horses and riding away.

It was a perfectly planned and executed spectacle. Perfect because the scene had been witnessed by dozens of the town's residents, who looked on in silence from their doorsteps. They couldn't help but feel compassion for Sylowich and his family, even though he was not one of them.

If they only knew.

He met them, as planned, a little more than a kilometre south of Strassburg. Sylowich had ridden hard for almost 20 minutes, his black horse panting and lathered in sweat. He came around a slow turn in the road and pulled back on the reins as he saw the two Red Army soldiers on horseback, and approached the wagon carrying the three men rumbling slowly towards him.

Yulinov brought the team of horses to a stop. Sylowich rode up next to the wagon. The two exchanged nods, while the men on horseback looked suspiciously at Sylowich.

"Comrade, it's good to see you. Right on time," Yulinov said.

"Yes, sir. I take it your journey has been uneventful?"

"Indeed," Yulinov said.

Trotsky, seated next to Yulinov, stared intently at the stranger but said nothing. He reached for a cigarette in his breast pocket, lit it, took a deep drag and exhaled the smoke menacingly towards Sylowich.

"I assume everything is in order?" Yulinov asked.

"Yes, sir. Our men are in place. All 16 of them, as planned. They spent the night together and have been at their positions since sunrise."

"Good," Yulinov said. "And the Germans?"

"There are seven of them and they expect you and Comrade Trotsky to arrive in less than an hour. My role is reconnaissance, to ride towards Selz, make visual contact with you and then circle back to report to them on your progress, describe the wagon, what Comrade Trotsky is wearing, so they can be certain of their target.

"Their plan is for one of them with a supposedly lame horse to stop you. He will be on the side of the road and will ask for a ride to Fischer-Franzen. The others will be hiding in the bushes and will emerge with their rifles drawn. They want a capture, not a kill."

"How can you be sure?"

"Because I have been part of the planning from the beginning. They want Comrade Trotsky as a hostage, to be dealt with later."

"Later?"

"Yes. They want to create a spectacle, for others in the village to see. A public execution on the street, in revenge for July 1919 in Fisher-Franzen."

It was a surreal scene. There, on a desolate road, far from Moscow, Leon Trotsky sat stone-faced, his gaze never leaving Sylowich as the stranger talked in an expressionless voice about the capture and execution of the man second in command during the revolution. The putative successor of Lenin himself.

But none of this came as a shock to Trotsky, who had been told before he left Moscow that his visit to the region was likely known by the Whites. Yulinov had also forewarned him of the German plot before leaving Odessa, and had given his word that all was in hand and he was in no danger. With Stelmanov on hand, Trotsky never doubted his personal safety. Stelmanov had been at his side since the October Revolution and had been intimately involved in the planning of the Odessa visit. He had complete faith in his protector, who had assured him that everything was in place not only to thwart the ambush, but to capture and kill the German plotters. Trotsky would never be in harm's way, even though knowledge of his presence in the Kutschurgan was what made it all possible.

Yulinov had told Trotsky that capturing and killing the German *kulaks* would be a bitter blow to the few active anti-revolutionaries who still operated in the Kutschurgan. This would surely sound the death knell of the remaining resistance, particularly because they would be able to use this event as a means to rid the region of the key figure who orchestrated the anti-revolutionary efforts. Moreover, the fact Trotsky would be on the ground and involved in a final, critical blow to the few remaining resisters would greatly add to his revolutionary stature in Ukraine and across Russia.

The plan was simple.

A few kilometres up the road, the group was met by four others, handpicked by Yulinov from the Andrejaschevski soviet. They were on horseback. One was Petr Yakushev, a thin man with glasses and thick curly hair. He was to pose as Trotsky. One of the others was a stand-in for Stelmanov. Trotsky took off his black straw hat and handed it to Yakushev. The two imposters took Trotsky's and Stelmanov's places on the wagon while Trotsky and his bodyguard mounted their horses and rode off with the other two, who took them to a nearby farmhouse to await word from Yulinov that the mission had been accomplished.

Yulinov and the two decoys then continued toward Fischer-Franzen, nine kilometres distant. The trap for Trotsky had been set less than a kilometre and a half from Fischer-Franzen.

The seven *kulaks*, along with Sylowich, had gathered early that morning in the St. Joseph rectory with Father Frederich to discuss, one final time, their plan to capture Trotsky. Guns drawn, they would take the trio by surprise and overpower them. They would bind their captives' hands behind their backs, lash their legs together, blindfold them and force them to lie face-down in the wagon to be carted into Fischer-Franzen and killed in front of the townsfolk. Trotsky would be executed last.

Yulinov held the team of horses in place while Sylowich rode off quickly to rejoin the Germans. He waited five minutes to give Sylowich a head start before allowing the wagon to begin lumbering ahead. It was a leisurely pace, slow enough to ensure Sylowich plenty of time to meet with the Germans lying in wait. But by the time the wagon carrying the decoys arrived, a much different ambush would already be over.

Sylowich rode hard and fast to get as large a head start as he could, leaving the wagon to follow slowly behind. In less than 10 minutes he came to the spot where the seven Germans waited for their Communist prey. It was a place shielded by heavy trees, where the road narrowed after a sharp turn. It was chosen specifically because it would provide both cover and the element of surprise as the wagon came around the turn to find a man with a lame horse at the side of the road.

"They're on their way. No more than 20 minutes behind me!" Sylowich said breathlessly, his horse rearing as it came to halt after the long, punishing gallop.

Two men, each with a rifle, stood at the side of the road, one next to a horse. The others, each with a rifle and knives sheathed on their hips, stood a few steps beyond them.

"How many are there? Three as expected?" asked Georg Becker, a bald and bearded man from the town of Kandel, and the leader of the German insurgent group.

"Three," Sylowich confirmed, "Yulinov is driving the team. Trotsky is next to him and a third—I don't know his name, but he's an associate of Trotsky's who doubles as his bodyguard—is sitting behind them."

"Are they armed?"

"I saw only two rifles. The man in the rear is carrying one on his lap and has a pistol in a shoulder harness. Another rifle was lying on the front panel at Yulinov's feet. Trotsky, I believe, is unarmed."

"Good. All right, quick, get over here, listen up." Becker gesturing the others to come together.

As the Germans gathered around, Sylowich dismounted as if he was going to join them. But instead, he took a few steps back.

"You, too, get over here," Becker said motioning Sylowich over.

Sylowich ignored him.

"For Christ's sake, did you hear me, Sylowich? Get the fuck over here!"

At that instant gunfire erupted in a staccato-like blaze from all directions. It was impossible to react. The Germans didn't stand a chance. There was a kind of sickening echo, a whizzing sound, as bullets, some fired from four hand-cranked machine guns and others from 12 rapid-fire long guns, ripped into their unsuspecting targets. The shooters, hidden only metres away in the dense bush, included six Red Army marksmen from Odessa. They shot to kill, aiming at the heads of their targets, while 10 other accomplished riflemen fired at the chests and upper backs of their prey.

Brain matter spewed as skulls exploded and blood burst from the mouths, ears, eyes and upper bodies of the victims. Four lucky ones died instantly. Two others fell to the ground in spasms. They writhed on the ground, one struggling to his feet in a hopeless attempt at escape. Seconds later, the swarm of gunmen emerged from the trees. Two quickly rushed to the gravely wounded man tottering on his feet. One calmly and deliberately shot the German in the knee. As he screamed in agony and bent forward to clutch his leg, the other Russian shot him in the head and the man collapsed face first into the dirt, dead before he hit the ground. The other wounded man was on his back, gurgling and grasping at his throat where a shot had penetrated his windpipe. He stared at the Red Army soldier standing above him, who lowered his pistol and shot his victim between the eyes.

Rudel Sylowich stood back, at a safe distance, and marveled at the efficiency of the kill.

CHAPTER 13

I N THE STILLNESS of the night there was a mesmerizing quality to the sound of the old clock on the mantel above the fireplace. A duel between silence and sound, nothing and something; *silence ... tick ... silence ... tock ... silence*. Christina Schergevitch always found it soothing, and slightly hypnotic.

She cherished these moments alone in the sitting room late at night. The children were asleep in bed, stillness had descended on her home and she felt a calmness in the tranquility of the moment. It was her time. The sound of silence interrupted by the cadence of the clock was a powerful drug.

"Christina. Christina. Christina."

The voice haunted her still. Only if she focused on the competing solitudes, silence then sound, silence, sound, would the voice no longer echo in her mind. It would dissolve with the vision of the young face and hand, disappearing into murky darkness.

They had gone together, as they always did. They shared the same birthday, the same age, which emotionally made them feel like sisters, even twins. But they were joined by more than just their age. They shared the same secret, which gave them an emotional bond far stronger than a mere accident of birth.

"Do you feel guilty?" Valerie would always ask.

"I try not to think about it," Christina always responded.

"But when you do. How do you feel?"

"Valerie, please."

"I just need to know. I can't help it."

"You always ask me. What's the point? There's nothing to be gained."

"But it matters. It matters to me."

"All right, yes. I feel guilty. Of course I do. You know I do. Are you happy now?"

"No," Valerie replied, her voice weakening. *"I don't think I can ever be really happy again."*

The conversation, almost word for word, had been repeated countless times since that serene day in the spring of 1877 when they ventured to the liman. Christina and Valerie were both 10 years old, and Joseph, Valerie's younger brother, was seven. They had been warned many times by their parents to stay off the ice once spring had arrived. But each year they could not resist the temptation of treading out onto the thinning crust that still covered most of the small lake. Other than a small open area of water in the middle, the ice remained intact. The crackling sound beneath their feet, the air bubbles that silently appeared from the pressure of their cautious footsteps, added to the allure of walking on the ice.

"Where are you going?" Joseph asked.

"None of your business," Valerie said.

"I know. You're going to walk on the ice. I'm going to tell. Mama says you're not supposed to. You might fall through."

"Don't be silly, Joseph. We're only going to see if the ice has melted, see if we can break it with rocks. You wanna come too?" Valerie had asked her brother.

"Well, all right. I guess so."

"But you've got to promise not to tell."

"I promise."

At first, the three stood at the edge of the liman, gazing out to the small body of open water more than 20 metres from the shore. Christina was the first to step onto the ice. It seemed solid. Valerie and Joseph quickly followed. After a few cautious steps, the girls gained confidence and moved more than halfway towards the open water in the middle of the partially frozen lagoon.

Christina took another step. The ice cracked beneath her feet and water gurgled silently into air bubbles trapped between two layers of ice. She stopped.

"I don't think we should go any further."

"Just step slowly. Look over here, the ice is thick," Valerie said, pointing to the right.

Joseph, scared by the sound of the groaning ice, started walking backwards, slowly retreating towards the shoreline.

"C'mon, Joseph, don't be afraid," Christina said.

"I don't want to fall through the ice. The water is cold and it's over my head," he said.

"Go over there," Valerie said, gesturing her brother towards what she thought looked to be thicker ice.

Slowly, Joseph moved further out to where his sister had pointed, taking cautious steps until he was a few metres from where the girls were standing. As he walked, the ice crackled.

He stopped, motionless.

"Don't worry. It won't break," Valerie said.

Joseph took one more step. The ice cracked loudly. He stopped again, then slowly began to turn so he could retrace his steps.

Suddenly, the ice collapsed under him, splintering into pieces and plunging him into the water.

"Help, Valerie, Help me! Christina!" Joseph screamed as he fell. He reached out, flailing to find something to cling to. For a moment he caught a piece of ice, which slowed his descent and kept his head and shoulders above water.

"Oh my God!" Valerie screamed. She started towards her brother, but the ice beneath her started to crumble. Instinctively she turned and fell to her hands and knees, scrambling towards the shoreline and safety.

Christina stood frozen, watching helplessly as Joseph flailed in the frigid water, his heavy water-soaked jacket slowly pulling him down, his chin now at the water line.

"Valerie, Christina, help me!" he begged before disappearing into the water and ice surrounding him.

The girls panicked. They ran to the shoreline and safety. There was no sign of Joseph. Just the broken ice where he had fallen only moments earlier.

"Oh God, Joseph! Oh God, Christina! We have to *do* something!"

Immobilized by terror, Christina was unable to act, able only to stare in horror at the place where Joseph had vanished under the ice. The girls stood on the shoreline, gripped by fear, and screamed Joseph's name.

Christina was always haunted by the memory, never quite knowing how long they stood there, crying and hugging each other and calling out to Joseph, but making no effort to go back out to try and reach into the water and pull him to safety. They stood there—shivering, paralyzed—and did nothing as Joseph's lungs slowly filled with water and he died.

But what made the guilt so much greater was the knowledge that she and Valerie had never told the full story. They had kept secret the fact that they had invited Joseph to go walking with them on the ice. That they had lured him further out from shore to the place where he died. In the horror of that day, they agreed not to tell how they had encouraged Joseph to join them in doing something they knew was wrong. They lied, saying Joseph had run onto the ice in spite of their warnings.

Other than Nikolas, her husband, the only person Christina had ever told the truth to was Father Frederich, in confession many years later. She had needed to relieve her guilty conscience with someone other than God, to whom she had prayed every night, asking for His forgiveness.

It had been a burden she carried alone for many years; Valerie had killed herself on their 17th birthday. She had suffered immeasurable anguish, a relentless guilt, and this was the reason she constantly asked how Christina felt. It was a way to ease her pain, knowing she did not suffer alone. But Christina had never thought Valerie would take her own life. Her suicide on their shared birthday meant Christina was destined to be haunted by her friend's death and Joseph's drowning—the two tragedies were inextricably linked—for the rest of her life.

Many believed Valerie's death to be an accident.

Christina knew better.

Valerie had drowned, just like Joseph. She had been missing for two days before her body was found, floating in the reeds and bulrushes along the shore of the Dniester River. Her parents said Valerie must have slipped on a rock while sunning herself, hitting her head and falling into a swift-flowing part of the river.

Christina never believed it. Valerie couldn't swim and had a pathological fear of water since Joseph's death. It was clear to Christina that Valerie had taken her own life. She died as Joseph had. It was, Christina believed, Valerie's way of escaping the torment of living and repaying the debt to her brother.

Sitting alone in the darkness, Christina often thought of her life. The candle flickering on the table next to her in the sitting room, the silence interspersed with the ticking clock, created a kind of irresistible reflective ambience. Memories of her childhood, her marriage to and life with Nikolas, the birth of their children, the family's early struggles, their successes, the murder of her husband, the death of their son John, the hard times that followed, would flood her mind.

She came to realize there were two deeply tragic and defining moments in her life.

One was the day many years earlier when she had watched Joseph drown. The guilt was deeply ingrained in both character and conscience. It shaped her in fundamental ways. She had lost her innocence in an instant. From that day forward, she saw life and the world around her in a completely different context. Gone was her childhood naiveté, to be replaced by a constant dread of the tragedy life might bring.

The other was that day four years ago. July 1919. It was not surprising that the execution of her husband in front of her and her children would leave a second life-altering imprint. But his murder did not make her bitter. It merely confirmed the grim expectations of life she had learned as a child. It actually gave her strength. What that awful day had done was to convince her that she and her children had to take control of their future, that they had to escape. She clung to the belief that there was a better place, truly a kind of promised land. Not in the biblical sense, although as a deeply religious woman she believed absolutely in the salvation of Jesus Christ and the reward of heaven. No, she was convinced there was a better temporal world out there in the here and now, somewhere that offered the two essential ingredients of a decent life—faith and hope—and a place where people believed in each other and their future together.

Her parents, George and Magdalena Beler, were modest farmers, much like their parents had been after emigrating from Germany to settle in Russia. Christina was the third of seven children—four boys and three girls. The family had lived in a small, overcrowded log and sod house in Selz. They farmed 50 acres of land on the edge of town where they grew mostly wheat and corn, raised chickens and pigs, and had two milk cows. It was a mostly uneventful life, dominated by the constant need to grow the food and raise the animals they needed to survive. With nothing remarkable about Christina's childhood, Joseph's death was the dominant and most important memory of her youth.

She had known her future husband, Nikolas Schergevitch, by name for years but didn't really meet him until she was 17. Her father needed help harvesting a bumper crop of corn and hired Nikolas, who was two years older than Christina and did odd jobs around town. Beler paid him 20 cobs of fresh corn for the day's labour.

All Christina knew about Nikolas was that he had been adopted by the Schergevitch family when he was a young child. His mother had died from consumption when he was two and his father had put their only child up for adoption and apparently moved to Kiev, never to be seen again. The Schergevitch family was considered well-to-do by the standards of their community. They owned a small hardware store in Mannheim and operated a thriving 150-acre mixed farm that produced wheat, oats, corn and a herd of milk cows and beef cattle.

Christina wasn't immediately attracted to Nikolas. He was outgoing and gregarious; she was quiet and reserved. At first, she didn't care for his extroverted personality. And he was also rather too short for her liking, maybe 5'7", barely an inch above her own height. But she did admire his obvious dedication to hard work, something her father complimented him about when the day's chores were done. When Christina brought drinking water to them in the fields, Nikolas smiled at her and said "thank you very much." Their eyes met for a moment and Christina couldn't help but be captivated by his clear, blue eyes. The moment had obviously ignited a spark in them both.

A week later, Nikolas came by their house and asked Christina if she would like to join him for a walk. They strolled aimlessly for three hours, making small talk at first but gradually opening up to each other. By the time evening came, Christina knew that Nikolas was a kind and decent young man who carried with him the regret of never really knowing his mother and father. She told him about her life, sharing with him even the secret burden of guilt she felt over Joseph's drowning and the suicide of her friend Valerie. This gave their relationship a great depth and meaning from the start. They quickly became soulmates and were married four months later.

With the help of Nikolas' parents, who gave the young couple 50 acres of farmland at Fischer-Franzen as a wedding gift and loaned them the money to buy another 50 acres, Nikolas and Christina were very fortunate newlyweds. A year later they had their first child—a son, John—and, 18 months after that, they had their second child—a daughter, Eva. Again, with the help of Nikolas' parents, they were able to buy another 50 acres. They had built themselves a new two-storey home, with four bedrooms and a separate summer kitchen in the backyard.

The future looked bright, indeed.

How my life has changed, Christina thought as she stared at the faint outline of the mantel clock in the flickering candlelight. Strangely, she felt no particular anger, or even resentment, over what had happened. She had long ago put her trust in the Lord, and believed whatever pain she encountered was all part of His plan. It was this deep faith that gave her amazing inner strength, reflected in the calm, personal fortitude that allowed her to remain steadfast in the belief that, with God's help, she could make a better life for herself and her children.

In fact, she harboured no bitterness towards the Bolsheviks at all. She would never forget what they had done to Nikolas and John; how they shattered her life, the lives of her children and countless others; how their cruelty had brought untold suffering and starvation to millions. But she had long since forgiven them because she knew from the New Testament that forgiveness was God's commandment. As Matthew said: "Love your enemies, bless them that curse you, do good to them that hate you, and pray for them which despitefully use you, and persecute you."

Tonight, as she had every night in the dark and quiet solitude of her home, she prayed for the souls of Nikolas and John, her grandparents, young Joseph and Valerie. She sought forgiveness for her sins and asked God, if it was His will, to guide her and her children to a better life. And she prayed that He would forgive the Bolsheviks and lead even them to enlightenment, redemption and salvation.

IT WAS A SINGLE SHEET OF PAPER. She kept it in the drawer of the night table next to her bed. The edges were curled and the words faded. Every night since it had come in the mail three months earlier, Christina took the paper from the drawer and gazed at it before she turned down the lamp to go to sleep.

In the middle of the page was a picture of a wheatfield, the tall and bountiful crop cut by a thresher pulled by a team of two horses. Stooks of threshed wheat stood throughout the field where the crop had been harvested. The horizon stretched into the distance. Above the picture were the words: CANADA WEST, THE LAST BEST WEST, HOMES FOR MILLIONS. In the lower left corner:

RANCHING, DAIRYING, GRAIN RAISING, FRUIT RAISING, MIXED FARMING. At the bottom: FARMS IN WESTERN CANADA, FREE.

The paper had been sent by her parents, who had left with eight others from the Kutschurgan seven years earlier in the hopes of finding a better life in the New World. The instability and growing unrest in Russia and the advent of the Great War convinced them to emigrate and settle on the great farming plains of Canada, in a province called Saskatchewan. Two of Christina's sisters had gone with their parents, but Christina, like her brothers and other remaining sister, had a young and growing family and was unwilling to uproot it. But with their parents settled in the New World, the option to leave Russia had at least become feasible.

As Christina looked at the sheet of paper once more, she imagined a land where people lived in harmony and amid plenty. A place of security and prosperity. A place of faith and hope. A place where she longed to take her children to give them the opportunities taken from them in the Kutschurgan.

The need to find a way out was now firmly embedded in her mind. Christina had the resolve to do whatever was necessary to take her children and move to the other side of the world. Her last emotional anchor to life in Fischer-Franzen had vanished more than six weeks earlier. No longer did she feel connected to the community. Her last lifeline had been severed.

It had disappeared along with Father Frederich. She was made aware that something was wrong when Frederich did not appear for the 7 A.M. weekday morning mass. Christina had been there in church with several others, mostly other women, waiting for the mass to begin. But the priest never appeared. After a while, the only man in the congregation went next door to the rectory to see if Father Frederich was ill or had somehow overslept, which was very unlikely.

There was no response to knocks on the front door. The man had tried the door and found it unlocked. There was no sign of Father Frederich inside the rectory, nor any evidence of forced entry. The only things out of place were an overturned chair in the kitchen and pieces of glass from a shattered drinking glass strewn on the floor. The priest's white collar, which he always wore when he left the rectory, was on the kitchen counter.

What had happened to Father Frederich remained a mystery. But his fate was not in any doubt. Christina and the other Catholics in Fischer-Franzen knew their parish priest was dead, murdered by the Bolsheviks. They knew it because there could be no other explanation. Frederich would not simply vanish.

And they knew it because the day before the priest went missing, so had six other men, two of them from Fischer-Franzen.

The confirmation that something dreadful had occurred came a week later when the bodies of the six men were found, bloated and rotting, in a heavy thicket of bushes and trees. The gruesome discovery was made by a man from Mannheim who had stopped to relieve himself at the side of the road. A foul odour made him suspicious and, when he pushed back branches to investigate, he saw the pile of corpses.

One body, separated from the pile, lay a few steps away. Like the others who had died from multiple gunshot wounds, this body had been shot several times. It had also been beheaded; the head nowhere to be found.

Neither was Father Frederich.

CHAPTER 14

Y OU COULD TELL right away he was an oddball. For one thing, his clothes were different, which made him look out of place. A quick glance was enough and you knew he was kind of strange. Not in a particularly weird or menacing way. Just strange, a misfit. Like he belonged somewhere else other than Fischer-Franzen, or the Kutschurgan, or even Russia, for that matter.

The first time I saw him was when Frankie and me were sitting on the stone fence in our front yard, waiting for Kaza. It was a really hot day, like 35 degrees Centigrade or something, which is in the 90s Fahrenheit for those of you who still live in the mid-20th century. The plan was we were going down to the Andre to catch some frogs and have a swim to cool off. We were waiting for Kaza, who had gone home to tell his mom where we were going. Kaza's mom always wanted Kaza to let her know if he wasn't going to be playing in the street or with me over at our place. She always seemed to be afraid that something bad would happen to him or something if she didn't know where he was.

At first, I used to think Kaza's mom was kind of strange the way she kept Kaza on such a short leash. But as I got older and turned seven, I started to think differently when it came to Kaza's mom. I started to feel sorry for her. I began to realize she was actually a very nice, kind lady who was just messed up in her mind because of her life and everything. It wasn't as if I knew explicitly that her mental problems made her so insecure and fragile. It was more than just a child's intuition. The only way to explain it is that instead of thinking she was weird, I began to feel sorry for her. I realize now she was seriously paranoid, although at the time all I knew was that she was always afraid. I didn't even know what paranoid meant until I was really old, like 18 or maybe even 20.

Just as Kaza came running across from his house, I noticed the man out of the corner of my eye. He walked up the road, stopping at the town well to lower the bucket for a drink of water.

"Let's go," said Kaza, as he ran to join us. "Muh-Mama suh-says it's all right."

"Yeah, let's race," Frankie said, jumping down from the fence.

"Who's that guy?" I asked, pointing to the stranger at the well.

Both Kaza and Frankie turned to stare at the man.

He was dressed like he came from the city, wearing a white dress shirt with a black tie. Even from a distance you could see his gold cufflinks glistening in the sunshine, the kind of fancy cufflinks that once in a while I'd see some men wear to mass on Sunday mornings. Slung over his shoulder was a black leather bag. He had on black pants and suspenders, with pant legs that didn't go down quite far enough to cover his white socks. He wore shiny black leather shoes you'd only see on special occasions. His hair was cut short, almost like he was a soldier or something.

The three of us stared at him, me still sitting on the fence, Kaza and Frankie standing on either side of me, none of us saying a word. As the man raised the water bucket with both hands to his lips and began sipping the water, he looked up and our eyes met for an instant. When he finished his drink, he set the bucket down on the edge of the well, slung his leather bag over his shoulder and looked back directly at us. Then he smiled and waved.

The three of us felt the same instant impulse—run. I leapt from the stone fence and we raced through our front gate, down the side of the house and out the backyard. We didn't stop until we reached the Andre, panting and out of breath.

"Think he's a bad guy?" asked Frankie as the three of us doubled over trying to catch our breath.

"I dunno. He's weird though. Whaddaya think, Kaza?"

"I dun-dunno either. He luh-luh-looked fuh-funny."

"Maybe he's a vampire."

"Frankie, don't be stupid. Vampires don't come out in the sun. They're asleep in caves until it gets dark. I think we should be spies and spy on him," I said.

"But it's hot. I wanna go swimming," Frankie said.

"Me too," Kaza agreed.

"All right, but after we can spy on him. I bet he'll still be around. Did you notice he was walking? He didn't have a horse."

"That's true," Kaza said. "Luh-luh-last wuh-one in is a ruh-rotten egg."

With that, the three of us stripped to our underwear and jumped into the Andre. It was only just over waist deep in the middle, just enough for me to dunk Frankie while Kaza dove underneath, grabbed my legs and pulled me under. Frankie broke free and tried to hold me under water by sitting on my submerged head while Kaza kept his arms locked around my knees. That's the other thing about Kaza I don't think I've mentioned. He could hold his breath underwater like he was part fish or something. Sometimes we'd see who could stay under the water longest while the other person counted. Kaza's record was 54. We'd count like this: "A thousand and one, thousand and two, thousand and three," and so on. I never made it past 38, but Kaza went all the way to 54.

We did it again this time. Frankie couldn't count high enough, so he was kind of like the referee. His job was to make sure no one was cheating by counting too slow when the other person was under the water and holding their breath.

"So we count like this: 'a thousand and one, a thousand and two, thousand and three, thousand and four.' You got that, Frankie?" I asked before we started the holding-our-breath-underwater contest.

Frankie nodded.

This time, Kaza made it to 52 and I got to 37.

After 30 minutes in the water, we climbed up on three big rocks we always used to let the sun dry us as we laid on our backs staring into the sky. It was another great day for looking at clouds.

"I think clouds are made out of mashed potatoes, like what Mama makes sometimes in the kitchen." Frankie said.

"No way. Don't be dumb. They're made out of fluff from the cotton trees. You know, the stuff you see floating in the air some-times. It gets sucked up into the sky to make clouds."

"How does it get way up into the sky like that?" Frankie asked.

"The wind takes it up there and it gets so close to the sun that it starts to melt and gets sticky, which is why the cotton fluff sticks together and makes big clouds."

"Oh," said Frankie.

"I like cluh-clouds that are really tuh-tall. You know, thuh-thick," Kaza said. "They look like thuh-things. That wuh-one there luh-looks like a muh-muh-mountain."

"Yeah, I like big fluffy ones too."

"How come some clouds get black sometimes, like when there's a storm?" Frankie asked.

"That's because of the rain in them," I said.

"But water's not black. You can see right through it."

"I thuh-think the sunshine reflects them and muh-muh-makes them buh-black-looking. That's what my muh-mom says."

"Where does the water come from before it gets into the clouds?" Frankie wanted to know.

"God puts it there so it rains and the plants grow," I explained.

"Oh," Frankie said.

"See those ones?" Kaza said, pointing directly overhead. "It luh-looks like they're guh-going to smash tuh-together."

"Do you think they'll bounce off each other?" Frankie asked.

"No way. They never do, because clouds float and when they get close together they float either up or down so they don't smash together."

"Oh," said Frankie.

We stared into the sky, feeling the warmth of the sun-soaked rocks radiating against our backs, and watched the clouds drift overhead in a kind of slow-motion procession. The warmth of the rocks was always a comforting feeling, one that made looking at clouds even more special. Above you was this kind of magical panorama of heaven and beneath you the soothing warmth of Mother Earth.

"Did you ever nuh-nuh-notice how clouds almost always seem to muh-move in one direction?" Kaza asked.

I had never thought of that, but the moment Kaza said it I realized it was true.

"It's the wind," I said.

"Where does the wind come from?" Frankie asked.

That was a good question, I thought. In fact, I had never thought about that either and it made me wonder.

"I thuh-think it's God's bruh-breath. It's Him breathing," Kaza said.

That seemed to make sense to me. With God up there in heaven,

I always imagined Him as being really, really big—bigger than anything on the earth. But I never thought about God breathing. Obviously He had to breathe and it only made sense that's where the wind came from.

"How come sometimes its windy and sometimes it isn't? Sometimes it blows hard and other times there is hardly any wind at all," Frankie said.

The answer seemed pretty obvious to me. "That's because sometimes God is running and He's breathing fast, so it's windy. Other times He's resting and He's breathing real easy, so the wind hardly blows at all."

"Muh-makes sense to me," Kaza said.

"Me too," said Frankie.

By now we were dry from the sun, so we put on our pants and decided it was time to go and spy on the strange man we had seen in town.

We walked back in our bare feet. That's one of the amazing things about being a little kid. In the summer you spend so much time in your bare feet that before long you can pretty much walk on anything and it doesn't bother you at all. The soles of your feet get to be almost like leather. That's the way it was for us. We'd be in our bare feet almost the whole summer, except when we went to church on Sunday morning and Mom made sure that we wore shoes, freshly polished, and that we had our bath on Saturday night. "You don't want to go to church with smelly, stinky bare feet with yucky toe jam. What would the good Lord think of that!" Mom used to say as she scrubbed us with soapy water in the tub.

Frankie and I always bathed together on Saturday nights in a big, silver metal tub that had handles on the side. The tub would be on the floor in the middle of the kitchen. Mom would heat water in two big kettles on the stove. When the water started to steam, she would pour it into the tub to mix with the water that our sisters had hauled from the cistern on the town well.

Even to this day, I've wondered why the dirt between your toes is called toe jam and not toe dirt or toe yuck or toe gunk or something. It actually used to bother me when I was a kid because I liked eating jam sandwiches, especially with the jam Mom would always make in jars and keep in the root cellar. So, the whole idea of calling it toe jam kind of made feel like I was going to be sick.

Just to bug me, because she knew I didn't like the words "toe jam," sometimes my sister Christina used to ask me to "pass the toe jam" when we were having breakfast. She thought it was a big joke, but I didn't, and Mom would always tell Christina "don't talk so silly" when she said that.

There was no sign of the stranger when we got back to town. He wasn't at the well and we didn't see him walking anywhere on the street. It was the middle of the afternoon and the only people we saw were the Herle brothers, Jacob and Joseph. They were older than us, 12 and 11, and always acted like we were beneath them because we were younger.

"What are you little turds up to?" Jacob said. He always called us "little turds" and when I was five I didn't even know what "turd" meant. So I asked Mom. She said it was a bad word and that I shouldn't say it. When I told her that Jacob Herle always called me and Kaza "little turds," she said we should just ignore him and not repeat the word. It wasn't until I turned six that I learned "turd" was another word for "poop" or the even worser word "shit." Robert Klein, who was 16, told me when I asked him. I knew Robert was an expert when it came to bad words because he said so many of them, so I figured he would be the perfect guy to ask. He thought it was pretty funny that I didn't know what "turd" meant. My mistake was asking him in front of Kaza, Frankie and three other kids.

"Are you kidding me? What are you, some kind of idiot?" he said. "Hey, Johnny," he said, waving over his friend John Schmidt, who was on the other side of the street. "Get this. Idiot Anton here asked me what 'turd' means? Fuck me. Can you fucking believe it? A turd is what comes out of your ass. A turd is a *shit*, you turd."

That only made things worse.

"What does fuck mean?" Frankie asked no one in particular, just kind of to all of us. "Is that a bad word?"

Robert burst out laughing and even bent over clutching his stomach, he was guffawing so loud.

"Ha, ha, ha. 'Fuck,' a bad word? Naw," said Robert. "It's actually a nice word. Say it to your mom. She'll think you're a good little boy for saying it."

My mistake, then and there, was not telling Frankie that it was a bad word and he shouldn't say it ever, especially to Mom. I didn't know exactly what it meant, but I knew that it was a swear and that only bad kids said it, or grown-ups when they were really mad about something.

Instead we just walked away to play, with Robert laughing at us. He said, "Get lost you loser turd-shits" as we were leaving.

Sure enough, that night all 10 of us were sitting around the dinner table. Mom, as she always did, was serving us our dinners one at a time. It was the one big meal of the week we had on Saturday nights, something I always looked forward to because I knew I wouldn't have to go to bed hungry like on other nights. I remember we were even having meat at that meal, a bit of beef Mom had managed to save from the Bolsheviks. Mom always started with the youngest first. So Mary got her plate and then she handed Frankie his.

"Fuck, thanks Mama," Frankie said.

I thought my older sisters, Magdalena, Eva, Rachel, Emma,

Theresa and Christina, were going to die right there on the spot. The six of them gasped together out loud and turned as white as the tablecloth. But Mom, she was cool as a cucumber.

She didn't miss a beat.

"You shouldn't say that word, Frankie. It's a bad word and nice boys don't say that," she said as she served me my food.

"But Robert Klein said it's a nice word and I should say it to you so you'll think I'm a good boy," Frankie said.

"Well, Frankie. Who are you going to believe? Robert Klein or your mom?" she said.

"I believe *you*, Mama. I won't say that word anymore."

'Thank you, Frankie. Because if you do, I'll have to wash your mouth out with soap and I don't think you'd like the taste of that," Mom said, and she kept on serving dinner.

"Yuck," said Frankie.

"What is fuck?" asked Mary, who was a year younger than Frankie.

Mom looked over at her. "Never mind, *Herzchen*. Like I told your brother, it's just not a nice word and you shouldn't ever say it. All right?"

"All right," Mary answered.

It was the next day when the stranger showed up again. Just like before, he came walking down the street and stopped at the well for a drink of water. He was dressed the same—soiled white shirt, black tie, suspenders, gold cufflinks, white socks and shiny black shoes.

Kaza, Frankie, me and our cousin Jerome Frulach, who lived in Selz and was visiting for the day with his parents, were playing soccer in front of Kaza's place. It was Kaza, playing goal and facing the town well, who noticed him first.

"Look," he said, pointing past us.

The four of us turned to look and, just as we did, the man looked at us, waved and started walking towards us. Instinctively, part from fear and part from excitement, we ran to our house and stopped on the front step. We looked back and the stranger was still walking towards us. The four of us stood motionless and watched him approach.

"Hi kids," he said when he got to our front gate and stopped. "Don't be afraid. I'm not going to hurt you."

"Mama, Mama! Come quick!" I shouted, never taking my eyes off the man.

A few seconds later Mom appeared behind the screen door, wiping her hands on her apron.

She looked at the stranger. "Can I help you?" she asked.

The man tipped his hat.

"Thank you, ma'am. I didn't mean to frighten the *kinder*, or anything. But I'd sure be appreciative if you were able to offer a hungry man something to eat. I haven't had a square meal in three days."

The man spoke German in a strange kind of lingo, quite unlike anything I had heard.

"Where are you from? What's your business? What brought you here?" Mom asked.

"I'm here doing God's work, the work of the Lord. I'm travelling in these parts and spreading the good news of the Lord Jesus Christ."

Mom stopped wiping her hands, pushed open the screen door and came out to join us on the front step. As a devoutly religious woman, the moment she heard talk of Jesus and the Lord, her interest was piqued.

"You didn't tell me where you're from."

"I apologize, ma'am. I'm from Ohio, in the United States of America and I've come to Russia and this region to do my missionary duty for the Lord and my church."

I was mesmerized by the stranger. I had heard of the United

States of America, but had no concept of what it was, beyond being an almost mythical far-off land that many people, my mother included, often called the "New World." In my imagination, the New World was a place of great happiness. I wasn't even sure if it was on Earth or was a kind of otherworldly place like heaven. So to see this stranger and hear him say he was from the New World made him an endlessly fascinating character to my young mind.

"Well," Mom said. "If you're doing the Lord's work you're certainly welcome at our dinner table."

We sat in the dining room that evening because we needed a larger table to accommodate all of us. Aside from the 10 of us— Mom, me and my seven sisters and brother—we also had the Frulachs. With the stranger, that made 14.

He said his name was John Carter and he was from Dayton, Ohio in the United States. At the time, he seemed to me to be pretty old, but I realize now he was maybe 25, 30 at the most.

"Are you a priest?" Mom asked him.

"No, ma'am, I'm not. I'm a missionary for my church. You might say, I guess, that I'm a lay preacher. I have committed myself to spending two years spreading the new gospel of the Lord."

I could tell Mom and the Frulachs were very interested in the stranger and his talk of the gospel.

"What church are you? Are you Roman Catholic, like us? Or Lutheran or Mennonite?" Mom wanted to know.

"No, ma'am. My church is the Church of Jesus Christ of Latter-day Saints. Some people call us Mormon, for short."

Mom sat at the table, the expression on her face a cross between puzzled and shocked. I could read her mind: *"Latter day saints? What is this man talking about?"*

There was this long, silent pause, and I could see the Frulachs and my mom exchange quizzical glances.

"We've never heard of your religion," Mr. Frulach said.

"I'm not surprised. I realize this is largely a Roman Catholic village and I know it's the same for many of the German-speaking towns in the Kutschurgan. But I also understand you have lost your parish priest, a Father Frederich, I believe. I'm told he vanished a few weeks ago. It must be difficult for you," the man called John Carter said.

Again, an awkward silence.

"The priest from Selz comes to say mass for us three times a week," Mom replied. "Is that why you're here, because of what happened to Father Frederich?"

"I must be truthful. In part, yes," the man said. "But I was already in Odessa doing my missionary work when I learned of what happened in Fischer-Franzen. So I decided to come because I believed there might be a need, that people might want to hear the new gospel, to learn about Joseph Smith and the Latter-day Saints."

Again, there was an awkward silence.

"There is no need to preach conversion to us," Mom said, the Frulachs nodding in agreement. "We are devout Catholics and we will die devout Catholics. It is, as Jesus said, the one true church. All others are imposters."

Carter had heard similar comments many times from others. He had become, if not almost oblivious to the resistance, certainly unaffected by it.

"I respect your beliefs. The Roman Catholic Church is a great church. I greatly admire your pope. And I agree it was founded by Jesus Christ Himself. I would never seek to weaken your faith. My faith is not about rejecting your faith, it's about expanding it, to help you understand the revealed word of God, of Jesus Christ, as told to Joseph Smith."

"Joseph Smith?" Mr. Frulach said. "Who is this Joseph Smith?"

Thus began a long evening of rambling conversation dominated by the stranger from the New World. I was too young to fully understand but I was old enough to be enthralled as I listened to him tell his story. As my mother and the Frulachs listened, what I remember most was how the mood of my mother and the Frulachs changed as they listened to the stranger, at first with disbelief, then great skepticism and gradually with curiosity, if not belief itself.

A very condensed version of the story he told went like this: Joseph Smith was a young boy of 14 who lived in the state of New York. His was a religious family, and by 12 years of age he had already studied the scriptures, become aware of the darkness of the world, his own sinful ways and was concerned about the welfare of his soul. His revelations came first with a vision of God and Jesus Christ, together. The first vision occurred in 1820, when young Smith went into the woods to pray. Carter read from a thick, tattered book with a frayed dark brown leather cover, quoting Smith's description of his vision:

> *I saw a pillar of light exactly over my head, above the brightness of the sun, which descended gradually until it fell upon me. When the light rested upon me I saw two personages, whose brightness and glory defy all description, standing above me in the air. One of them spake unto me, calling me by name and said, pointing to the other —'This is my beloved Son. Hear Him'.*

My mother said nothing, as the stranger told his story of Joseph Smith. She sat motionless at the table, her hands folded together on her lap, her gaze fixed on the man and occasionally glancing to her left at the Frulachs, who also sat silent and listened. There was this eerie kind of quiet around the table, with only the sound of the stranger's monotone voice as he told his story.

"It was three years later, on the night of September 21, 1823 when young Joseph was visited by an angel. After his vision with God and Son, Joseph had grown concerned about his human sins and transgressions, the weakness of his spirit, the vanity of his mind.

"On the night of September 21 he was praying for forgiveness and seeking guidance when the angel Moroni appeared before him. The angel was the last prophet of a race of people that had vanished. Moroni told Joseph his sins were forgiven and said there were gold plates of religious history from a forgotten race engraved by Moroni and his father Mormon.

"This was the first of many visits from Moroni, who eventually led Smith, by his 21st year, to the place where the plates were buried. Through divine inspiration, Joseph translated the scripts engraved on the plates. It took many years.

"The plates tell the story of an ancient people, a band of Hebrews who, in the year 600 BC, were inspired to leave Jerusalem. Divinely guided, they travelled to the Indian Ocean where they built a boat and sailed to the promised land on the west coast of what we now call the New World. Eventually, conflict divided the people into Nephites and Lamanites. Following his crucifixion, Christ appeared to His people in the Americas to organize his church. His message was that people had lost their way, that we needed to return to the lessons of the gospel and remain true to the word of the Lord Jesus Christ."

Even though I was only seven years old, I could tell Mom found the story of Joseph Smith, and the visions of God and this angel guy Moroni, fascinating. At first skeptical, soon she was listening intently, the way she did Father Frederich's sermons at mass on Sunday mornings.

"I have in my hand the word of the Lord that was on the plates," Carter said, holding up another book, this one black-leather bound and not as big as the other he had quoted Smith from. "This is the *Book of Mormon*, the revealed word of the Lord. Its message is clear. We must restore our faith to the teachings of the Lord Jesus Christ as told to us by the revelation of Joseph Smith.

"And Moroni tells us, the Lord said: 'Behold I say unto you, Nay, for it is by faith that miracles are wrought; and it is by faith that angels appear and minister unto men; wherefore, if these things have ceased, woe be unto the children of men, for it is because of unbelief, and all is in vain.

"'For no man can be saved, according to the words of Christ, save they shall have faith in his name; wherefore, if these things have ceased, then has faith ceased also; and awful the state of man, for they are as though there had been no redemption made.'"

The stranger stopped, lowered his eyes for a moment and looked at my mother and the Frulachs.

A long pause was broken by my mother's voice.

"Who are you? Why are you here? Why have you come from the New World to tell us this? We have our own religion. We are Catholic. It is the one true Church, founded by Jesus Himself," she said.

"I am a simple man doing God's work," John Carter answered. "It is my missionary duty, all of us in our Church are obligated to spread the word of the restored gospel in the Book of Mormon."

"But why have you come here, so far from your home, to the Kutschurgan?" asked Mr. Frulach.

"It was my choice. I know of the suffering you have faced, the pain you have endured, your struggle to survive. I am here to give you hope in the face of fear, to tell you the Lord loves you and if you follow His word you will escape the darkness of your lives."

"How did you get here?"

The stranger, as if in reflection, paused, closed the *Book of Mormon* and laid it on top of the brown book he also carried.

"I left my home eight months ago. I travelled by train to the city of New York and gained passage on a steamship to Amsterdam, doing whatever chore was asked of me as a deckhand. In Amsterdam, I met with two members of our Church, who took me in, and gave me food and shelter for a week. They gave me fare for the train to Petrograd and then to Moscow.

"I was two months in Moscow, preaching the word of Mormon on the street corners until the Bolsheviks threatened to shoot me if I didn't leave. The Bolsheviks hated me.

"I had nowhere to live and spent nights sleeping in alcoves and doorways. Luckily it was spring and a person could survive the outdoors. I found a place adjacent to the square on a walkway in Ismailovsky Park, where people came to gather and relax, often with their children. There was a small pedestal I used as my pulpit. At first, people thought I was mad and kept their distance, as I preached the Lord's word. But in time, some people felt sorry for me and they would give me scraps of food that they brought with them to the park.

"One elderly woman, who would bring me food and listen briefly to me, took me in. Her name was Svetlana and she had an apartment near Gorky. She told me that she had been born in Odessa and came to Moscow as a young married woman. Her husband, she said, was of German heritage and had died 20 years ago. Since his death she had earned a meagre living by sewing clothes.

"I stayed with her for a month and she listened to me in the evenings as I told her about the word of the Lord. It was she who told me about her home in Odessa, that she had sisters and brothers who still lived there and who would help me if I came. She gave me fare for my passage to Odessa, where I heard of Father Frederich's disappearance. She told me too about what had happened in the German villages in this region, stories she had heard from her cousins on her father's side of the family."

"What did she say happened?" my mother asked.

"She said that life is harsh and famine widespread. That many innocent men had been killed in cold blood by the Bolsheviks, murdered simply because they were German farmers, and that many more have died from starvation in the years since the Communist Bolsheviks have taken power over the land."

"Well, it's true," Frulach said. "It's true."

There was another brief moment of silence before the stranger spoke once more. "But some of you survived. Some German men were not killed by the Bolsheviks. How was that?" he asked, looking directly at Frulach.

Again silence.

"I was in the field, baling hay, the day they came. God spared me. I know not why."

As I sat at the table, hearing this exchange, the realization suddenly struck me that most, but not all, of the men in the nearby villages had died like my father that time four years ago when my life began. I had never wondered about that before; in fact, the thought never occurred to me until I heard Mr. Frulach's explanation.

I understood, for the first time, that life is unfair.

CHAPTER 15

THE END CAME with measured, focused deliberation. It was purposefully slow and excruciating. To the brink, then back. Over and over. A kind of sado-masochistic dance to death. But when it did come, the final act was chillingly brutal.

He died of asphyxiation from his own regurgitated blood. Technically speaking, he drowned. He was hemorrhaging internally from his liver, stomach and kidneys, which had been slashed and torn open by the repeated plunging of a nine-inch knife blade into his midsection. With each thrust, the knife was twisted to do the most damage possible.

But what ultimately killed Father Frederich was when Petr Smenev sliced open his esophagus and carotid artery with one deep, rapid slash across the throat. With blood already welling in his abdomen and rapidly draining from his brain, each pump of his feverishly beating heart spurted more, some of it spraying the front of his shirt in grotesque artistry, the rest gushing into his windpipe and down into his lungs. The last sound he made was a kind of gurgling rasp.

"Pig," Smenev snorted as the priest slouched to the side in death.

Frederich's limp body was propped up in a wooden chair, his

hands tied behind his back, his ankles lashed to the back legs of the chair, contorting his lower limbs. The edges of an oily rag, jammed into his mouth to stifle his cries, protruded from between his teeth. His pants and underwear were around his calves, his bloodied and mutilated genitals evidence of the torture inflicted before death found him.

Yulinov had stood back throughout the entire procedure that had lasted for nearly half an hour. It had begun when he and the five others took turns butting their cigarettes on the doomed man's cheeks and forehead.

Now that it was over, Yulinov rolled and lit another cigarette. He took special delight in each deep drag, looking at the priest's blood-soaked body. It was hard to believe, he thought, the human body could contain so much blood. It was everywhere; the floor, the walls. Smenev was covered in it; his shirt, arms, hands, even his face was speckled with blood splatter.

Yulinov enjoyed the slaughter. Not in a particularly twisted, macabre way. Nor did he revel in the brutality or sadism of the gruesome spectacle. Rather, it gave him a sense of satisfaction knowing a key enemy of the revolution and the proletariat had been eliminated. He felt no pity for the priest. In fact, strangely enough, he was serenely content in the knowledge that another small, but important, objective of the revolution had been achieved. The cult of religion needed to be neutralized, if not completely eliminated, from Russian society. It amounted to an opposing ideology, one that sought the loyalty of its believers. The very notion of a God and some glorious afterlife as a reward for suffering in the world was a direct threat to building a classless society.

Sure, maybe this *was* personal for Yulinov, who had long felt that Frederich was mocking him, using his status as a priest for protection while he tried to sabotage the revolution. Yulinov had long detested Frederich and wanted him dead. But now that it was over, he realized it was just business.

He took one last drag on his cigarette, then stubbed it out on the dead priest's ashen thigh, the sweet, acrid smell of burnt skin immediately filling the air.

"Get rid of the carcass. Somewhere not obvious. I want his body discovered, but not for a while," Yulinov said.

The other four untied the body and Smenev dragged it out the door, feet first, smearing blood as he pulled it across the wooden floor planks. Together they flung the priest onto the back of a flatbed wagon and rode off.

Yulinov left the small, one-room wooden storage shed and walked back to the farmhouse. Inside, sitting at the kitchen table drinking vodka and smoking, was Trotsky.

"Well?" Trotsky asked as Yulinov walked through the door.

"It's done."

"Good," he replied.

It hadn't been a pleasant day for Trotsky. To put it bluntly, this was not exactly the kind of experience that arguably the second most powerful person in Russia would enjoy, or should necessarily endure. Granted, there never was a moment when he had been in any direct personal danger. Yulinov had made certain of that. Trotsky had been kept at a safe distance from the ambush of the German *kulaks*, a kind decoy that laid the trap for the hapless victims. But still, being this close to the bloody reality on the ground in revolutionary Russia was a new and slightly unnerving experience for him. It was far removed from his role as head of the Red Army, which was about military strategy and action. It was always more of an intellectual abstraction: the planning and execution of worldwide Marxist revolution.

He and his bodyguard Stelmanov had waited in the safe house near Selz—a small farm Yulinov had owned then donated to the local soviet and was now part of the collective. It sat mostly vacant, other than when Russian peasants were assigned to work the land; production had become part of the Andrejaschevski soviet's contribution to the Kutschurgan food quota. Or when Yulinov held his twice weekly meetings of the local soviet council in the very shed where Frederich had been butchered.

Trotsky and Stelmanov had waited there for almost five hours, while Yulinov and his men orchestrated the ambush and the abduction of the priest from Fischer-Franzen.

The entire operation had gone well, even flawlessly. They had quickly and efficiently eliminated the Germans along the road and had then taken Frederich swiftly out of town without anyone noticing. The church and rectory were on the southern edge of town so they were able to ride up behind the rectory and leave their horses hidden in a cove of trees. Sylowich had been sent to the back door to summon the priest while the others waited out of sight around the corner, only a few feet away. When Frederich saw Sylowich he greeted him with a huge smile, expecting the man to report on the Germans' successful ambush of Trotsky. Sylowich played along for a moment.

"We got the bastard. He's alive. We have him handcuffed and blindfolded," Sylowich said.

"Wonderful. Where is he?" an excited Frederich asked, swinging the door open and inviting Sylowich into the rectory.

At that moment, Sylowich lunged forward, his shoulder hitting the priest in the middle of the chest, knocking him backwards off his feet and onto his back with Sylowich on top. The other three rushed around the corner and pounced on the priest, roughly turning him over to pin him face down on the floor. One quickly gagged him, jamming a piece of cloth into his mouth and tying a rope around his face to keep him from screaming. Another straddled his back, wrenching Frederich's arms behind his back, dislocating his shoulder, tying his wrists together and then wrapping rope around the trunk of his body, lashing his arms to his sides so he was completely immobilized.

Tossing a burlap sack over his head, they roughly led the staggering priest out of the rectory and into the trees where they had left their horses. They had brought an extra horse, without a saddle, which they flung Frederich over, face down. They strapped him to the horse's girth to keep their victim in place while they headed back to the safe house six kilometres away to begin the ritual of torture and execution.

Yulinov couldn't help but feel proud of himself. Things had gone extremely well, even better than he had hoped. In fact, it was hard to imagine a better outcome—eight dead Germans, including the priest who had been ringleader of the Fischer-Franzen resistance. There could be little doubt the killings would deal a fatal blow to counter-revolutionary activity in the Kutschurgan. And all of it planned and carried out by Yulinov and his core group, witnessed firsthand by Leon Trotsky himself.

But Yulinov also knew the successful elimination of counter-revolutionaries was not the sole, or even key, purpose for which Trotsky had come to the Kutschurgan. His visit might have had the intended effect of serving as bait to draw out the enemy. And neutralizing the Fischer-Franzen cell of German insurgents was certainly an important step forward in Yulinov's pacification of the region. But the real reason for Trotsky's presence was far more political than a single effort in counter-insurgency. It was about the future leadership of Russia and the revolution, about who was going to lead the Bolsheviks and rule the Kremlin in the years ahead once the already debilitated Lenin had either died or been deposed as ruler.

The visit to Odessa and tour of the Kutschurgan was part of a three-day plan that would connect Trotsky to key members of the regional revolutionary cadre, most of whom would be delegates to the Thirteenth Congress of the Soviet Union a year later in 1924. It was already evident the next Congress would be pivotal in that it would determine Lenin's successor, he having been further incapacitated by a second stroke. He was no longer able to walk, his left side completely paralyzed, and his speech seriously impaired. So, while he remained the titular ruler of both the Communist Party and Russia, in reality the duties of governing had been dispersed to Lenin's chief lieutenants: Leon Trotsky, Josef Stalin, Gregory Zinoiev, Lev Kamenev, Nikolai Bukharin and Georgy Pyatakov. Within that group, there were two tiers. Trotsky and Stalin held the most clout in government and influence in the party and had the power base to be considered Lenin's likely heirs. The other four lacked similar stature, and unless there was some alliance among them to throw their support behind one in particular, the chances of one of them overtaking Trotsky or Stalin to replace Lenin were slim at best.

For Trotsky, the challenge was to outmanoeuvre and out-organize Stalin with key party regulars. He needed to expand his support within the party by reaching out to key regional figures, who would provide him with the influence and depth of power across the country to defeat Stalin.

It was no small task.

The problem was that many saw him as a latecomer to the Bolshevik cause, which was true. A socialist and a revolutionary, yes. But he had not officially joined Lenin and the Bolsheviks until 1917. Up to that time, Trotsky had been aligned with Julius Martov and the Mensheviks. Martov split with Lenin in 1903, and Trotsky was among the Martov supporters. Ironically, the schism had been driven by relatively minor differences. The Mensheviks took a more liberal view of who should be considered members of the Russian Social Democratic Labour Party and the two sides were split over editorial control of *Iskra*, the Communist party newspaper. But the great rift had come in 1917 when the Mensheviks supported Kerensky and the Provisional Government, which the Bolsheviks perceived to be bourgeois-inspired and ideologically corrupt, and therefore sought to overthrow.

So, although Trotsky joined the Bolsheviks in the summer of 1917 and played a key role in the October Revolution and subsequently as commissar of foreign relations and head of the Red Army, he was never able to fully overcome the doubts many Bolsheviks had of him. He was constantly trying to escape the shadow of his Menshevik past.

The Kutschurgan visit was another step in Trotsky's effort to prove his loyalty to the cause and solidify his quest to replace Lenin. What made the trip to Ukraine of particular importance was the chance to win the support of Pyatakov. A native of Ukraine, Pyatakov was a powerful figure in the region who headed the Kiev committee of the party and helped form the Red Army Cossacks of Ukraine. But, most significantly, Pyatakov had been a strong opponent of Lenin's support of national self-determination. He saw ethnic nationalism within the Soviet Union as dangerously destabilizing and inherently counter-revolutionary. It was a view ardently shared by Trotsky.

The two were closely aligned in the belief any sign of nationalism needed to be forcefully suppressed. And both fervently believed that any evidence of German nationalism in Ukraine and Bessarabia needed to be ruthlessly crushed. Trotsky and Pyatakov shared the crude conviction that Germans in Russia were aliens to be either eliminated or controlled into irrelevance. Germans could not be trusted. It mattered not that they had lived peacefully and productively for generations in the Kutschurgan. German-Russians were interlopers who should be quarantined, exiled or executed.

Thus, the small but successful Fischer-Franzen operation, with

its killing of Frederich and the others, carried far greater significance than its relative size might suggest. This was Trotsky himself making a clear and unequivocal statement at the heart of
the German counter-revolutionary resistance in Ukraine. There
could be no mistaking the message it sent of both strident anti-
nationalism and commitment to the Bolshevik cause. Surely it
would help increase his chances of defeating Stalin in the struggle
to replace Lenin.

THE MEETING TOOK PLACE at Yulinov's safe house. After Smenev
and the others had disposed of the priest's body, they returned to
the farmhouse. When they arrived, Pyatakov was already there
with two of his key Ukraine operatives—Yurgi Kozakov and
George Kopelchuk. They were sitting at the kitchen table along
with Trotsky and Yulinov, smoking and drinking vodka.

The conversation was at times intense, light-hearted, passionate and profane. But always political.

Trotsky's objective was obvious: solidify and expand his support
within party ranks in southern Russia, and especially Ukraine.
It was crucial to show he had political momentum in the region
where he was born and raised if he was to offset Stalin's overpowering strength in his home state of Georgia on the south-
eastern shores of the Black Sea. But the fact Trotsky had left
when he was young and largely lost contact with Ukraine did
not give him the political roots in the region that Stalin enjoyed
in Georgia and its neighbouring states.

In fact, Trotsky was seen as someone whose ego and ambition
exceeded southern Russia. So, instead of a native son whom people in the region took great pride in for his political success, Trotsky was more often viewed as someone who had deserted Ukraine
because he felt himself superior to the people he left behind. The
key was to re-cast his image, to make him a product of the region

who had neither lost touch with his home nor considered himself anything other than a son of Ukraine.

And that's where Pyatakov came in.

If Trotsky was to be first rehabilitated in the eyes of Ukrainians, then embraced by them, he needed someone like Pyatakov at his side as a supporter, advocate and organizer.

"I doubt Ilyich will finish out the year," Pyatakov said of Lenin. "He should be gone now. The man is nothing much more than a vegetable since his last stroke."

"I agree," Trotsky said. "But I don't believe anything will happen until the next Congress. In fact, I live in fear that he will have another episode or even die sooner and the party will be forced to act. We need time, so I hope he hangs on."

"Maybe so, but I think it would be a mistake to assume we are going to have much time. If he doesn't die then I wouldn't doubt that Stalin will try to force the issue. Not in an official way, but just by continuing to concentrate power in his own hands. His strategy is apparent. The fucker intends to make his selection as the new party head a foregone conclusion because, by the time of the Congress, he will have effectively been doing the job for a year."

Trotsky knew as much himself.

"It's why we need to show our strength quickly, if we're going to stop the bastard."

Yulinov sat expressionless at the table, keeping silent. He knew enough not to speak unless someone asked his opinion. It had been a long and emotionally draining two days. As much as he took great pride and satisfaction in the elimination of the enemy German priest and the Fischer-Franzen scum, it had taken its toll. This was, after all, *his* operation, undertaken with Trotsky's full support and cooperation. It had gone superbly and Trotsky was clearly impressed. But had anything failed, it would have been Yulinov who was called to account. The responsibility was entirely his own, and with it came enormous stress. Without question, Yulinov had proven how valuable he was to both Trotsky and the revolutionary cause.

Now on his third glass of vodka, Yulinov was feeling more relaxed. But he was also somewhat stunned and even unsettled by the conversation. It wasn't so much the plotting against Stalin that surprised him, but the outward disdain, even contempt, they had for their political adversary and their dismissive attitude towards Lenin. For all his hardened life experiences, Yulinov was still something of a neophyte in the reality of politics. Just as he was a Communist ideologue, so too was he a party stalwart, someone who had great admiration for the party leaders, whether it be Lenin, Trotsky or Stalin. He might be—ever since that night at the Smolny almost six years earlier—a Trotsky acolyte, but he also had nothing but respect for the others in the higher ranks of the party. So to hear Trotsky and Pyatakov, members of the very echelons of the party he so admired, speak with such disdain and personal disgust of Stalin, and to refer to Lenin himself as a "fool," came as something of a slap-in-the-face revelation. A revelation that he could feel deflate some of his Marx-inspired idealism.

"I need you," Trotsky said, looking directly at Pyatakov. "I need you if I am going to hold Ukraine and strengthen my support. I need you if I am going to defeat Stalin."

Pyatakov ran his hand through his long, thick hair, adjusted the wire-rimmed glasses perched on the end of his nose and stared back at Trotsky. "I know that, you know that."

"So what will it take?" Trotsky asked.

There was a brief silence. Pyatakov took a long sip of vodka and a drag from his cigarette. As he blew out the smoke, the two candles on the table flickered to the verge of going out and the room momentarily dimmed.

"You know, Lev, I was wondering when you would ask."

"What do you mean?"

"It's pretty obvious, isn't it? You asked what will it take. I assume you mean what will it take for me to be on-side and deliver Ukraine?"

Trotsky didn't take his eyes off Pyatakov and said nothing.

There was an awkward and uncomfortable silence as the two men stared at each other. A nervous Yulinov slurped noisily as he took another sip of vodka.

"You have nothing to say to me, comrade?" Pyatakov finally asked sarcastically.

"I asked you what will it take," Trotsky said coldly. "I'm waiting for *your* answer, comrade."

A man of rigid beliefs and fierce determination, Pyatakov was not going to let the moment pass. He knew Trotsky needed him, more than he needed Trotsky, so he wanted Trotsky to squirm. Pyatakov relished being in a position to savour the situation, to let Trotsky feel uncomfortable, knowing that he wasn't in control of the conversation or the terms of their burgeoning political relationship.

This was Pyatakov at his manipulative best. A leader of the radical left communists in Ukraine, Pyatakov was nothing if not skilled at using others for his political ends. He was a member of the intelligentsia that Stalin and many other Bolsheviks so despised. A Communist well-schooled in the works of Marx, Pyatakov was among the elite in the party who knew nothing of the reality of labour because they had never worked a day of physical labour in their lives. Like Trotsky, he considered himself a strategist, a tactician and a man of great intelligence who was above the proletarian masses he sought to control. His job was to mould and manage the revolutionary mob, to direct the course of history by the sheer force of his intellect.

Pompous yes, but Pyatakov was also smart enough to know he

could not overtake Trotsky as the party's alternative to Stalin. He resented Trotsky's stature but also respected his intellect, which wasn't easy for an intellectual egotist like himself.

It was little wonder that Stalin considered the likes of Trotsky, Pyatakov and their fellow travelers in the "intellectual" wing of the party to be beneath contempt. They were elitists who knew nothing of the reality of the masses of the workers; posers, if not imposters; leeches on the body politic of Marxist revolution. In Stalin's mind, they were pretentious, self-important and self-centered, a kind of despicable elite lumpen proletariat.

"It's not what I want, my friend. It's what I expect and deserve."

"And, I repeat, for one last time—what is it?" Trotsky asked, arms folded across his chest, not averting his gaze from Pyatakov's.

"I expect without question to have my choice of roles, to have control of economic policy and foreign policy, to be your direct liaison to the party. In short, to be—without doubt—the second in command."

Trotsky smiled.

"Really? Why piss around? Why not just be supreme leader while you're at it?"

Pyatakov wasn't amused, enraged, in fact, by Trotsky's sarcasm. He stood straight up, kicking his chair back, slamming it noisily into the wall. Yulinov's eyes widened in a mixture of amazement at what he was witnessing and fear of where the confrontation might lead.

"Well then, comrade, fuck you and your grand ambition. I don't need you and I can think of others who do," he said.

"Jesus Christ, for fuck's sake, Georgy, relax. I'm not serious," Trotsky said. "Sit down. Let's talk this through."

Pyatakov didn't move, only glared down at Trotsky.

"I said relax. I was just trying to get under your skin and it seems like I did. They say the best way to get a glimpse of the real person is to get them angry. But I like emotion in a person. Passion matters, especially in matters of politics and revolution." A smile slowly emerged on Trotsky's face as he looked up at Pyatakov. "Now I can't figure out if you're an ally or an adversary. Which is it?"

As Pyatakov reached for his overturned chair without taking his eyes off Trotsky, Smenev quickly grabbed it and slid it upright behind Pyatakov, who sat back down.

"Ally or adversary?" Trotsky asked again.

"That depends on you," Pyatakov said. "You heard my expectations. You might have been kidding. I wasn't. So you will determine which I will be."

"Of course. But this is not a one-sided negotiation, my friend. You know, I give, you take. You told me what you want and I am willing to consider it, maybe even meet your expectations. After all, I am a reasonable person. But, comrade, I have certain expectations as well. Things that I will demand of you. How do the Greeks say it, a *quid pro quo*, I believe."

Pyatakov nodded, almost imperceptibly. It was the slightest of gestures but it was enough to break the tension, and Yulinov felt a small surge of relief.

"Yes," Pyatakov said.

"Very well, then," said Trotsky. "If I were to meet your demands —and notice I said *if*—then I would expect some specific things in return. As we both know and have already discussed, I need your help in Ukraine. But I need to clearly define what I mean when I say that I need your help. Specifically, the help I would not only expect, but demand, and receive, if there is to be this *quid pro quo*, as they say."

"Yes."

Trotsky raised his left hand and began counting, his right index finger touching the fingers of his other hand.

"One, I would expect, demand and receive your utter loyalty.

"Two, I would expect, demand and receive the massive support of members from Ukraine at next year's Congress in Moscow.

"Three, I would expect, demand and receive your high-profile, active and visible support throughout the region, support that will cast me as a loyal son of Ukraine and deserving of admiration.

"And, four, you will lead and carry out the campaign to undermine Stalin by showing him to be the buffoon and thug he is, not only unworthy of high office, but unfaithful to the cause itself.

"If, my dear comrade Pyatakov, you agree and my expectations are met, then I too will meet your expectations and our *quid pro quo* will have been carried out to our mutual benefit."

Witnessing this discussion was nothing short of a revelation to Yulinov. The thought that personal ambition, ego, accumulation of power and self-advancement was what fuelled the passion and determination of the revolutionary leadership had never occurred to him. He had actually believed, foolishly it seemed, that the likes of Trotsky, Pyatakov, and even Stalin, were driven by idealism and the ideological commitment to Marx and a classless, communist society. To a society that would bring equality and social harmony. Only now did he begin to grasp his naiveté.

Pyatakov leaned back in his chair and looked down his nose across the table at Trotsky.

"Hmm. I find this all very interesting. I've heard you say what you expect from me. But not a word on what I have asked of you, or what—"

"Did you not listen?" Trotsky interrupted. "I said that if you met my expectations, that if you delivered what I set out, I would meet your expectations."

"You said that, indeed. But I did not hear you repeat what I expect and say that you will deliver your end of the *quid pro quo*, as you like to call it. I want to hear it from your mouth, here, in front of our comrades. They can be our witnesses."

There was another awkward silence. Again Yulinov slurped from his glass of vodka.

"Our *quid pro quo* is this," Trotsky said. "You give me your complete support, deliver Ukraine, be my vocal and loyal deputy in this region and be my agent against Stalin and I will make you my designate for foreign and economic policy, the liaison from the Kremlin to the party, my unquestioned second in command. Agreed?"

There was a brief moment before Pyatakov responded.

"Agreed," he said.

Trotsky stood up, leaned forward and stretched out his hand. Pyatakov did the same and the two shook hands. Relieved, Yulinov smiled, ever so slightly.

And so it was done. In one brief meeting, Trotsky had taken great strides to solidify his political hold on Ukraine, enhance his chances of defeating Stalin and become ruler of Communist Russia and the burgeoning Soviet Union. In Pyatakov, he had, without question, the best-known and respected member of the Ukraine Communist revolutionary elite in his camp.

"This visit has been very productive. I thank you, Alexandre, for helping to make it happen," Trotsky said after Pyatakov and the others had left and he and Yulinov sat alone at the table. "You are an important part of my team, comrade, and will be in the future."

Yulinov felt a powerful mixture of satisfaction and pride. He could hardly believe this was happening. Here he was, sitting across the table from Leon Trotsky, who had just paid him a great personal compliment and acknowledged him as one of his inner circle. It was a long, long way from that cold night in Petrograd when they had met at the Smolny, an unlikely alliance formed because of a chance meeting between him and an old woman huddled under blankets in a bleak and cold doorway.

Alone, they talked and drank vodka together for more than an hour as Stelmanov, acting as sentry, dutifully waited outside the front door.

"Tell me about the Muslim." Trotsky said.

"You mean Sylowich?" Yulinov asked. "Our mole? The one who lured the Germans into the trap?"

"Yes."

"He's been a valuable asset. A drunkard and a bully, but dependable. And, I would mention, not a Muslim. His wife, yes. But he's a non-believer."

"How did you come to be associated?" Trotsky asked.

"He lives in Fischer-Franzen, has very little, does odd jobs for people. He's far from being a *kulak*. But he's the sort of person who always knows what's going on, who's talking about what, who's talking to whom. A natural as an informant."

"Are you paying him for his loyalty?" Trotsky asked.

Yulinov thought it an odd question.

"In what way do you mean, sir?"

"Are you paying him? Has his loyalty been purchased?"

Yulinov knew the conversation was heading to an awkward conclusion.

"Not in the sense of money, per se," Yulinov said. "I supply him and his family—he has a wife and three children: a young son and two daughters—with steady rations so they never go hungry. Sometimes I give him bottles of vodka. But I have not given him a single ruble."

"So his loyalty *has* been bought," Trotsky said.

Yulinov did not respond. He thought it best to remain silent to see if the subject of the conversation might change.

"We have no more use of him. I want him dead," Trotsky said, as he reached to refill his glass with vodka.

CHAPTER 16

LIKE I WAS SAYING, the Mormon fellow was totally a fish out of water in Fischer-Franzen. I mean, here was this guy from Ohio, U.S.A. who travelled halfway around the world to convert us into believers of some character named Joseph Smith. Not only did this Smith fellow have visions of God and then some angels, but, in the process, discovered gold plates in the backwoods of upstate New York with the new word of God inscribed on them, which became the *Book of Mormon*, a new kind of Bible.

You have to admit, that's pretty weird stuff for someone to be doing in a devoutly Roman Catholic, conservative, German-speaking farming village on the fringes of Bessarabia in southern Russia in the wake of the Bolshevik revolution.

Don't get me wrong, I'm not saying anything against Joseph Smith, the Church of Latter-day Saints, the Mormons or their beliefs. As religions go, I'm sure it's fine and they're decent, good folks. I'm just saying that it was strange having this guy in our midst.

But you know what? I kind of liked him.

There was nothing pretentious or phony about John Carter. Sure, he didn't dress like other people and he might have been a bit odd. But he had a likeable quality to him, if you know what I mean. He was the kind of person who seemed to completely lack guile. Of course, back then as an eight-year-old, I had no idea either what guile was, or meant. All I knew was that Carter struck me as being totally straightforward and honest. There was no sense that this guy had a deceptive or cynical bone in his body.

Let me explain.

It was a crisp Saturday—the second Saturday of the month—in October 1924 at, I'd say, 10 A.M. to be precise and, as usual, we were playing soccer in the street. We had this ritual that, for as long as I can remember, the kids would play soccer every Saturday morning, starting at 10 A.M. There was nothing official about this. In other words, no specific organization or plan to the game beyond a few basic rules. As near as I understand it, the routine had developed organically and been handed down from one generation to the next.

So, as you grew up, you came to understand that Saturday morning was when the kids played soccer in the street. Just as the game itself was a tradition, so too were the rules around the game and how it was organized. I never quite grasped the logic of any of it, but that didn't seem to matter. What did was that the rules were strict and always explicitly followed.

First of all, you had to be at least seven-and-a-half years old to play and then only as a spare. To be a regular you needed to be eight. I have no idea why seven-and-a-half was the cut-off age. It just was. Kids younger than that could only watch and were expected to retrieve the ball when it went out of bounds, which tended to happen a lot. Sides were picked by the two team captains who, get this, had to be 10 or 11 years old and girls. But the girl captains also could only be goalkeepers and no other girls could play.

When you got to know the rules just by growing up with the Saturday morning soccer game custom, you tended not to think about them or question why they were the way they were. They just were. That's not to say I didn't wonder on occasion why only girls aged 10 or 11 could be team captains. I did. But it just wasn't important and the few times I thought about it I figured it was because 10 and 11-year-old girls were so out of it when it came to knowing how to pick good soccer players that it tended to make sure that no team had a skills advantage. And, you know what? It appeared to work, because our teams always seemed to be fairly evenly matched. Granted, we never really did keep score, so I'm only going by the feel of the games and a vague sense of the goals each side scored.

Anyway, on this Saturday morning, I remember the two opposing team captains—Heidi and Valerie—were busy picking sides from the dozen or so of us old enough who had come out to play. This was mine and Kaza's first year playing Saturday morning soccer because we had both just turned eight.

"Hey, kids, do you need a referee?" John Carter asked, just as we had finished picking sides.

He kind of startled us because none of us had seen him coming up the street. For a moment we all just kind of looked at him and no one said anything.

"Well, kids, whaddaya say? Want a referee? I've even got what every referee needs," Carter said, holding a wooden whistle in his outstretched hand.

"Ah, we've never, kind of, had a referee in the past," said Jacob Height.

"I bet that's because no one ever offered before. Am I right?"

We all looked at each other and no one said anything.

"Well, what do you say we get started then," Carter suggested, as he picked up the ball and walked to the middle of the road that we used as our soccer pitch. "Line up and I'll throw the ball in. Let the match begin."

It turned out we had a great game that day. For one thing, Kaza and I were on the same side, which was only the second time in the five games we had played as regulars since turning eight that we got picked on the same team. But aside from that, Kaza scored a goal and I assisted on it. It was a pretty cool assist, even if I do say so myself. That's because I, on purpose, kicked it through the legs of Hans Seidl, who was 10, right to Kaza, who redirected the ball past Valerie into the goal. Of course, we didn't have goal nets or anything like that. We just used two rocks for goalposts at each end.

But aside from Kaza's goal and my assist, what made the game memorable was Carter. He was a great referee. Not in the sense that he was blowing his whistle all the time because we were offside or tripping each other, or something like that. The truth is we didn't know anything about offsides. It was more that John Carter was like a one-man cheering section for all of us. When he wasn't gladly chasing down the ball when it went out-of-bounds, he was congratulating kids on making good plays or passes, or just trying to make plays or passes even if they didn't quite work out. It didn't matter to him. What mattered was that we were playing soccer and having fun doing it.

You could tell he was having fun being the referee and that added a lot to the game for us kids. Just having this man out there helping us with the game and cheering us on made it all the more fun. His enthusiasm was infectious.

We had so much fun that we played for a good 90 minutes, which was at least 20-25 minutes longer than normal for our Saturday morning matches. And when we were done, we all went over to the town well, where John cranked up a bucket of water for each of us to have a drink.

It was as we were taking turns using the ladle to scoop water from the bucket to drink when Jacob Height brought up the subject of the New World.

"Are you really from the United States of America?" Jacob asked.

"I am. It's true. I come from one of the states in the United States called Ohio. You know what they say about Ohio?" John Carter asked.

At first none of us said a word as we stood staring at the stranger.

"What?" Kaza asked.

"Well let me tell you," John Carter said. "What's round on the ends and high in the middle?" He paused for a moment and we silently stared back at him.

"Ohio. Get it? O, hi, O."

It was a joke but none of us really got it at first, though I still laugh when I think about it now.

"What's it like there? It's the New World, right? Is everything new, like the houses and buildings and schools?" Jacob asked.

John Carter smiled. "Well, kids, why don't we all sit down and I'll tell you about the New World."

So, John hopped up to sit on the edge of the well and we all sat on the ground in a semi-circle to hear him tell us about the New World.

Me and Kaza sat right at the front, just a few feet away, looking up at him. Frankie and Mary were next to me, and Christina, who had watched the last bit of the soccer match, came over and sat with the bigger kids at the back.

"All right, can any of you tell me what you know about the New World, or do you have any questions?" John Carter asked us.

I was surprised to see that Kaza was the first to put up his hand. Usually, Kaza is pretty shy, especially when it comes to talking out loud in front of a bunch of other kids. I think it was because of his stutter, which got even worse when he was nervous, and I knew Kaza was nervous around other kids, especially older boys. But in this case, I could just sense that Kaza didn't feel so nervous and it was because he knew that John Carter was a nice, kind man who we didn't need to be afraid being around.

"Yes," John Carter said, pointing to Kaza. "What's your name son?"

"Kuh-Kaza," Kaza said.

"He's got a stutter, you know," Frankie said.

"That's all right," John Carter said. "In fact, you know what, Kaza? I had a stutter too when I was a young boy like you. There's nothing wrong with that."

Out of the corner of my eye I saw Kaza's smile.

"God makes us all different. He makes each of us special and unique. Not better, or not as good as another person. Just different in our own special way. So you're all special and you should be proud of who you are, just the way you are. And you should re-spect other people, just the way they are too.

"You know what, Kaza? I still stutter a bit sometimes. When I was young like you, I used to stutter when I was nervous. But eventually, when I got older, I didn't do it as much and I realized it wasn't something to worry about. It was just who I was—the way God made me."

I leaned over to whisper in Kaza's ear. "He's nice man," I said very quietly and Kaza nodded without taking his eyes off John Carter.

"Why, thank you for the compliment, Anton," John Carter said to me. I was surprised he heard me because I had tried to whisper. But, at the same time, I felt kind of proud that he knew my name.

"You had dinner at my house, didn't you?" I said.

"That's right. All right then. Kaza you had your hand up. Did you want to ask me something about the New World?"

"Yes sir. I wuh-was wondering. Are there clouds in the New World?"

"Clouds? You mean like, in the sky?"

"Uh-huh," Kaza said.

"Why, yes, there are, Kaza. The clouds there are the very same as the clouds here. There are big, fluffy white ones that look like pillows in the sky, ones that are more streaky and then dark ones when it's going to storm. So when you look at clouds here, it's the same as looking at clouds where I come from in the New World."

"Me and Kaza, we like looking at clouds," I said.

"I like looking at clouds too," Frankie said.

"Me too. Especially ones that are all fluffy," said Mary.

John Carter smiled a big smile.

"You know something, kids? Looking at clouds is a special thing to do. You know why?"

We all looked at each other and shrugged our shoulders. Then Kaza raised his hand again. "I know why, I thuh-think," Kaza said.

"Go ahead, Kaza. Tell us why you think looking at clouds is special," John Carter said.

"When I look at clouds it makes me feel and thuh-think different," Kaza said.

"Different? What do you mean by that, Kaza?"

"I, I dunno. It's just when I'm lying on muh-my back looking at kuh-clouds everything seems to chuh-change," Kaza said. "I feel different. You know, kuh-kind of calm inside."

As I listened to Kaza talk about how he felt when he looked at clouds, I realized he was describing how I felt too. And I think all the other kids were thinking the same thing as me.

Even though Kaza and me laid on our backs and looked at clouds all the time, we didn't really talk about how it made us feel. We just did it because we liked it. When I think about it now, I liked looking at clouds because it made me imagine things and feel good inside, like Kaza said.

"Do you other kids agree with Kaza?" John Carter asked.

When no one said anything for a few seconds I put up my hand.

"Mr. Carter," I said. "Me and Kaza are best friends and we look at clouds a lot. When we lay on our backs and see the clouds, it makes me imagine things."

"What kind of things?"

"I dunno. Maybe that the shape of a cloud looks like a horse or a goat, or something; you know, like that."

"I saw a cloud yesterday that looked like a dog with three legs," Mary said.

"Really," John Carter said. "When I was young like you kids, I used to lie on my back and look at clouds too. It made me feel the same way as it does for you. And you know what, I still do it whenever I can now, even though I'm all grown up, because it still makes me feel the same way as it did when I was young like you. I've got an idea, why don't we all lay on our backs and look at clouds together right now?"

"Yeah!" some of us shouted in unison.

"Not me," said Jacob. "That's for little kids. I've got better things to do."

So Jacob got up and left, with four of the older boys going with him.

The rest of us spread out and laid down on our backs in a circle with our heads pointing inwards. It must have been quite a sight. John Carter and eight kids lying in a circle in the middle of the road and staring at the sky.

"Let's not say anything for awhile, all right?" Carter suggested. "Let's just look up at the clouds and the sky and let your mind free. We can talk later."

We stayed that way, quietly looking at the sky for, I bet, five minutes. It wasn't the best day for looking at clouds, mainly because there weren't many of them and the ones that were there were those swishy, streaky kinds of clouds you see in the fall when it's windy and the weather is getting cooler. But the sky was also a brilliant, translucent blue.

"You know, kids," John Carter said, "from now on when you look at clouds I'd like you to think about not just the clouds, but the sky. When you look up like this at the blue sky and the white clouds, you know what you're looking at? You're looking at heaven. That's why, like Kaza said, it makes us feel different and calm inside. Because when we look at the white clouds in the blue sky, we're looking at heaven."

"You mean heaven where God lives?" Alois Dietz asked.

"That's right," John Carter said. "Right now, we're all looking at heaven."

I felt very relaxed, like I was almost floating, as I looked up at heaven.

We never saw John Carter again.

Mom said that he had left and gone back to his family in the New World. I wanted to believe her, because I liked John Carter. But deep inside me I thought that maybe it wasn't true. Don't get me wrong, I'm not saying that Mom was telling a lie about what happened to him; my mom would never tell a lie. I just thought that maybe someone hadn't told her the truth about what really happened to him, but she thought it was the truth. Therefore, when she told other people, she thought she was telling the truth because someone had told her. So even if it wasn't true what she said, it wasn't a lie because she thought it was true, even if it wasn't. Do you follow me?

Anyway, I had this feeling that what Mom said about John

Carter going back to Ohio was maybe not true, except she didn't know it.

I know what you're thinking. How could an eight-year-old kid like me think I knew the truth about what happened to John Carter and my mom, who was all grown up and a lot smarter than me, not know it too?

My answer is I don't have an answer, except maybe for one word: intuition.

Oh sure, you're saying to yourself right now—a little kid who doesn't know the meaning of the word is capable of using intuition to know something that smarter grown-ups don't.

But intuition isn't the same thing as knowledge or knowing something for sure to be true. For example, if I'm holding a stick in my hand, I know it's true because I can see it, touch it and feel it. And so can anyone else.

When it comes to intuition, I figure it's about perceiving something to be true, without knowing if for certain. So in the case of John Carter, I perceived that instead of him going back to his home in the United States, like Mom had said, something bad happened to him, something *really* bad.

I intuitively believed that he was dead.

I didn't know this for a fact. I didn't even want to believe it to be true. But my intuition told me that it was likely the case.

There were two reasons why I believed that John Carter was dead. First, he left behind his leather bag that he had carried into town a week earlier. I know he left it because I saw it under the bed in Mom's bedroom one afternoon when I crawled under there while playing hide and seek with Frankie and Mary and Mary was "it."

I admit that the fact John Carter's leather bag was under my mother's bed suggests my mom knew about what really happened to him, which was more than she might have been willing to admit. Except, I asked my mom about the bag and she said: "He forgot it when he left. I'm sure someday he plans to come and visit again so I'll keep it for him until then and we can give it back to him."

I believed Mom believed that. But my intuition made me suspicious. Of course, I realize now that Mom knew more and wasn't telling me because she knew I liked John Carter and didn't want me to be upset by telling me the truth.

The second reason was that I was old enough to realize that everything that had happened and was happening in Fischer-Franzen were interconnected and fit together. There was a pattern to life, one experience after another that helped me to understand the reality of my world. When people disappeared, it usually was because they were dead.

The memories of my father's death and my brother John's body on the back of a wagon in a pile of other dead men were etched into my memory. So was the famine of the past years, the lack of food for us to eat, the fact that what we grew on our farm and the animals we raised didn't belong to us and we had to turn everything over to the "soviet." The fact that Father Frederich had disappeared and I had heard Mom and others talk about how they feared "the worst." The talk of life in the New World we heard when Mom read the letters we received from Grandma and Grandpa in someplace called Saskatchewan. How the idea of a "New World" far away across the ocean, with its unstated but powerfully understood promise of a better life, and how the idea of going to the New World and leaving our troubles behind, was more and more becoming part of the daily fabric of my family.

I might have only been a kid but I wasn't stupid.

You get to a point in life when more and more you wonder about things. Come to think of it, if you ask me, wondering is the key to knowledge and understanding. You know how people say that little kids are like "sponges"—they soak up everything they see and hear? Well that's true. But it isn't until they get a little bit older that they start to wonder more and more about the world around them and their experiences. They wonder why and seek explanations to understand why things are the way they are.

That's what happened to me. I wondered more and more, which made me think rather than just perceive.

So, I wondered about John Carter and how he suddenly vanished. I wondered why he would do that, why he would go back to the New World and not tell me or the other kids. It didn't seem right, especially after that day when he was our referee and we all looked at clouds together. He had stayed a couple of nights at our house in the small spare bedroom we had in the summer kitchen and had dinner with us in the evening, so for him to go without saying goodbye made me wonder. And when I wondered, him suddenly being gone didn't make sense.

I guess you call that intuition.

In the back of my mind you might say I "feared the worst," the way I heard my mom and others talk about Father Frederich suddenly being gone. The worst for me was for John Carter to become another victim of our world, as I knew it, in Fischer-Franzen.

And it wasn't just me who thought that. Kaza did too. We talked about it one afternoon when we were in the Cave, which was where we always went when we wanted to be alone and talk about things.

"I wonder what happened to John Carter," I said, as we crouched under the tarp and peered through the small cracks into the sunlight of the outside world.

"Me too," said Kaza.

"My mom says he went back to Ohio in the New World, but that he will come back someday to visit. He left his leather bag. It's under my mother's bed, you know."

"I don't thuh-think he's coming back," Kaza said.

"How come? Why not?"

"Because I think he didn't ruh-really go back to the New World. Buh-because I thuh-think he's dead."

I didn't flinch or say anything in response, and just kept squinting to look through the peephole in the wall towards the street past Kaza's house.

"What do you thuh-think?"

"My mom wouldn't lie to me. So she really thinks he went back to the New World. But I dunno. How come he never told us?"

"You nuh-know what else," Kaza said.

"What?"

"Muh-my dad says a muh-man with a name like Trotty or suh-something was near here. Thuh-that he's from Moscow and is really important. You know, with the Bolsheviks and everything. I heard him tuh-tell my mom that about him. Thuh-that some German people from Selz and Strassburg were killed. Even the pruh-priest."

"You mean Father Frederich?"

"Uh-huh."

After that, we stopped talking for awhile and just sat quietly in the Cave, looking out through the cracks in the planks on the wall. I was thinking about what Kaza said and I could tell he was thinking about it too.

"Do you think that maybe they killed John Carter too?" I asked.

"Uh-huh, I think maybe," Kaza said.

It was two days later when I was talking with Alois Deitz, who sat in the row across from me in our school. Alois was in the third grade and I was in the second. There were two classrooms in our school and each one had kids all the way from grades one to six. We didn't have kindergarten like they do today. If kids wanted to go to school after the sixth grade, which not many did, they had to go to a school in Mannheim and stay in the dormitory where they slept in bunk beds. I always used to think that sleeping in the top bed of a bunk bed would be really neat, which made me want to go to the seventh grade or even further so I could get to sleep in a bunk bed.

I was sitting on our front step when Alois came walking up and motioned me to come over to the sidewalk.

"Have you heard?" he asked.

"About what?"

"About what Robert and Joseph found in the river?"

"No, when?"

"Today, this afternoon, about two hours ago. They were down at the Kutschurgan, you know, under the bridge."

"Uh-huh."

"And they found a dead man's body floating in the water. I guess it was all kind of purple and blue and bloated like a balloon or something. You know, really gross and everything from being dead and in the water for so long. They said at first they couldn't even tell it was a dead body. They thought maybe it was a piece of wood or something," Alois said.

"Did they touch it?"

"Are you kidding? They were totally grossed out when they got close to it and could tell that it was a dead person. You know how sometimes there'll be dead carp floating along the side of the river and when you get close to them they really stink from being dead and everything. Well, when they got close to this body, thinking at first it was something else, it really stunk and when they realized it was a dead body they shit themselves and Joseph puked and everything. I bet he's still puking."

I could feel myself starting to shiver and it wasn't even cold outside.

"But you know what else, Anton?" Alois said. "I heard my mom and dad talking to Jacob's dad, who went down to the river to see for himself. He said that the dead body is Father Frederich. I heard it with my own ears."

My mother never, ever mentioned anything about Father Frederich being dead and found in the river and I never asked her about it. It was like it never happened. Not once did it ever come up at the dinner table, nor did any of my sisters or brother ask Mom about Father Frederich being dead. There were a few times when I wanted to ask her but never did. I decided that it was better not to mention what Alois had told me or to say anything about what happened to Father. I figured if she didn't want to mention it, there must be a good reason, which was good enough for me.

But that's not to say it didn't bother me, because it did—a lot.

At night, when I would lie in bed, I'd have trouble getting the image of Father Frederich's dead and bloated body floating in the Kutschurgan out of my mind. One time a few weeks later, Jacob told me and a few of the others kids about what it was like finding a dead body. We were all gathered around him in the schoolyard.

"It was really, really gross," Jacob said. "It's not like a normal dead person like you'll see at the back of the church in a coffin at a funeral, like when an old person dies or something. You know, how they're lying there in nice clothes like they're asleep or something, their hands folded across their chest with a rosary and everything.

"No way. This was way different. It was all kind of this purply black and kind of grey, sort of. I almost can't describe it. What made me realize it was a dead person was when I saw his hand. At first I didn't even realize it was a hand. But I poked at it with a long stick, still thinking it was this piece of wood with some kind of clothes tangled up with it. But when I poked it with a stick, this hand popped up. It was all purply and the fingernails were black. Then it rolled over and we saw the face with eyes bulging out of the eye sockets. That's when we both started screaming and Joseph puked."

I know it sounds weird, but for the longest time Jacob played his role of finding Father Frederich's dead body to the hilt. It was as if it somehow made him special, that he was more grown up than the rest of us because he had seen a real dead body, which was way different from just seeing someone who's dead at their funeral.

At night, when I went to bed, I would have to try and figure out ways to trick my mind so it wouldn't imagine what Father Frederich's dead body looked like or else I couldn't sleep. I would do really weird and pretty elaborate things, like when there was still light in the room, count the little squares painted on the ceiling in my bedroom; or close my eyes and imagine I was with Kaza looking at a blue sky with the best clouds ever; or that I was in a soccer match and the score was tied and when Kaza headered it to me, I bounced it off my knee, took it down the field and scored the winning goal. The only problem was when I looked at the ceiling to count the squares, Father Frederich's face, all bloated and purple with eyes like a monster, would suddenly appear in one of them. Or a cloud I was imagining suddenly looked like his dead face or the goalie I scored on was Father Frederich who was alive but still looked like he was dead and a kind of living monster.

I never told anyone about those things. It was something I kept to myself, other than when I would pray to God asking Him to make the bad thoughts go away. But they never really did, ever, for the rest of my life, right up to now.

CHAPTER 17

YURI PODNOVESTOV was a businessman. The only one in Fischer-Franzen who wasn't also a farmer. It made him unique and gave him a certain status in the community, a kind of unstated measure of respect. Even though Podnovestov was a native Russian Jew, and not a descendant of the Germans who had settled in the Kutschurgan, he was appreciated for who he was, instead of being less appreciated for who he was not.

But it didn't happen by mere circumstance. Podnovestov had earned the respect of his neighbours and was known as a man of great humility, kindness and sincerity. He was recognized as a man of character, someone who understood the personal merit inherent in hard work, the importance of being dedicated to your enterprise, the value of thrift and the meaning of commitment to others. In short, Podnovestov was the kind of friend and neighbour everyone wished they had. So the people of Fischer-Franzen felt lucky to have him in their village.

Podnovestov owned the local general store. It sold everything, from hardware to household goods, food to fertilizer. And if you needed something that Yuri didn't have, he would always find a way to get it for you, either by ordering it from a supplier in

Odessa or Tiraspol or by making it himself. Indeed, Podnovestov was the ultimate innovator. He had an uncanny ability to fashion hand tools in the shop at the back of his store, where using a coal-fired furnace, he worked as a blacksmith, forging iron into usable steel implements for the farmers who frequented his store. You might call him a problem-solver. If you were looking for something or needed help, Yuri would find a way to be of assistance.

So "Yuri's," as everyone called it, was a favourite place for customers from the area and townsfolk to gather in the back to talk about whatever was on their minds. Everything, that is, except the Bolshevik revolution.

Politics was the one subject off limits around Yuri's hot stove. People could talk about farming, the weather, even the famine, but no one was to broach the topic of what had happened since October 1917.

It wasn't that Podnovestov wasn't interested or unconcerned about the revolution and its unfolding aftermath. He cared deeply. But he also realized that if his store became a place where politics was discussed and debated, if it was anything more than just a place where people could purchase what they needed to farm, his business would be confiscated and his life threatened. For that matter, Podnovestov was puzzled by the fact his business still existed, that he had not been stripped of its ownership and it had not been turned into a state enterprise. He could only assume that his business was too small to matter, and that as long as it served the low-level function of supporting local agricultural production, the Bolsheviks would tolerate his existence.

But he knew that if he was ever suspected, even in the slightest, of being an anti-revolutionary, if his store was perceived as a place for the expression of discontent with the revolution and

Bolshevik barbarism, his business, and maybe even his life, would be over.

People in Fischer-Franzen understood it as well as Yuri did and did not want to do anything that might harm their good friend and neighbour. They respected Yuri too much to risk putting him in jeopardy. So Yuri's became a tiny island of normalcy, a kind of snapshot from the past, where people acted as if nothing had changed in their lives from those days before it had all begun. Walking under the wooden sign above the door with the red-painted letters Y. P. GENERAL STORE and across the threshold into Yuri's was like stepping into the past, into a happier, more tranquil and far more comforting time. It was a reassuring place.

The other thing about Yuri's was that, quite literally, it had always been there. Almost from the day the village was founded in 1814, there had been a general store run by someone named Podnovestov. It was Yuri's great-grandfather who had started the store in 1815. Recognizing the business potential of the rapidly growing population of German farming immigrants, Jacob Podnovestov had moved from Odessa and started a small general store in Fischer-Franzen, a business that was passed on to his son, grandson and eventually his great-grandson, Yuri. It was the kind of enterprise that gave the town a sense of its own roots and recognition of the Podnovestov family as people with a deep commitment to the community and the Kutschurgan.

Christina Schergevitch had long felt a strong personal friendship with Podnovestov and his wife, Andrea. It stretched back more than 20 years, to the days when, as a newly married couple, Nikolas and Christina had begun to raise a young and rapidly growing family. They felt the kinship of the Podnovestovs, who also had a young family and understood the pressures of trying to raise children, put food on the table and make ends meet.

The moment Christina realized the depth of the bond that had been created with Yuri and his wife was when she and Nikolas went to the general store one spring day in 1902 to ask if it would be possible to borrow a shovel. Unable to afford one, Christina needed a shovel to dig her garden in the spring after the family's only shovel had gone missing, apparently stolen. Nikolas and Christina had gone together to the general store and browsed awkwardly while Yuri and Andrea stood behind the counter waiting on a customer.

An intensely proud man, Nikolas Schergevitch finally summoned the courage after the other customer had left.

"Yuri, I'm ashamed to ask this," Nikolas said.

"You shouldn't ever be ashamed to ask anything, my friend," Yuri responded before Nikolas could finish his request. "How can we help you?"

"Christina and I were to begin planting our garden today, but our shovel has gone missing. I'm sorry, but I don't have the money to buy one from you and I was wondering if you might lend us one for a day. Or, if possible, extend us credit. I promise we will repay you the moment I have earned some money. And as security, I can give you my winter sled."

Podnovestov smiled at the young Schergevitch couple.

"Nikolas, don't be silly. Of course we will extend you credit. And don't worry, we don't need security. You're our friends. We're glad to help. If I can't trust you, who can I trust? Pick the shovel you want over there," he said, pointing to a row of new shovels leaning against the wall.

It might seem like a small favour that, in the grand scheme of things, was not particularly unusual or generous. But often those are the moments that matter most. It's not so much the magnitude of the generosity, but the manner and the moment in which it is extended that makes it far more significant than it might seem as a simple act of kindness.

At least, that's the way it was for Christina Schergevitch. She never forgot it and the Podnovestovs became her dearest friends. It didn't matter that they were from "the other side" or weren't German Catholics. Or that they were Jews. They were good people she could count on in time of need and they knew they could count on her.

And it was again a time of need.

In the April darkness at nine o'clock at night, Christina Schergevitch left her house through the front door. Carrying a candle burning in a small lantern to light her way, she walked across and down the street. She could see a light in the store window and knocked on the door. A moment later, Yuri Podnovestov lifted the latch and opened the door, surprised to see her.

"Christina, is there something wrong?" he asked. "It's late."

"No, no. Nothing. But I need to talk to you. I apologize for coming when it's dark. I didn't mean to startle you."

Inside, Yuri invited Christina to the back of the store and into his family's modest living quarters. Andrea was sitting at their kitchen table, mending clothes.

"Christina, my dear. What brings you over? Is everything all right?" Andrea asked.

"Yes, yes, Andrea. But I did want to talk with you and Yuri."

"Of course, of course. Let's talk, please," Yuri said as he offered Christina a chair and the three sat around the table. "The children are asleep."

"I'm wondering if you can help me? I don't know where to turn."

"You know that Yuri and I will do anything we can to help," Andrea said. "What can we do?"

Christina Schergevitch paused and took a deep breath, as if to summon her courage.

"I want to take my children and leave, to start over in the New World, to get away from our lives here. I want to give my children a chance at a better life than what they can expect if we stay. Ever since Nikolas was killed, I've known in my heart that we must go, that it will never be the same under the Bolsheviks. As their mother, I feel that I must do something to give them a life they can live in peace and security, a place where they feel free and unafraid of what might happen to them. It can never be that way in the Kutschurgan. Not anymore."

Andrea Podnovestov reached across the table to squeeze Christina's hand.

"I understand. Believe me, I understand," she said.

"Can you help me, please? I'm told, Yuri, that you might know people who might be able to help, people who have helped others go to the New World," Christina said.

It was true. Podnovestov had helped two other families in the region who wanted to emigrate by putting them in touch with someone in Tiraspol who knew someone else who worked for the railway. Podnovestov had been led to believe that the railway worker was able to book passage on the railway out of Bessarabia and through Romania. Apparently the same person had contacts who could get the exit papers people needed to get all the way via rail to Antwerp, Belgium, where they could book passage across the Atlantic to the New World.

But what Podnovestov didn't know was whether their escape from Russia to the New World had been a success. Both families left, but he had never heard if they made it to their destination, so he was not certain his contacts had been reliable. For all he knew, it was a scam for money; the families were expected to pay dearly for the papers and passage they needed for freedom and a new life. He didn't know how much. All he knew was that his contact in Tiraspol, a man who worked for the local police, had told him that the price would have to be directly negotiated between those fleeing Russia and his contact with the railway.

He had met the police officer by pure chance on a trip to Tiraspol two years earlier. Once a year, Podnovestov took the train from Strassburg to Tiraspol, where he met with suppliers of farm implements for his store. One evening, he had gone for a drink and ended up sitting next to a stranger who had turned out to be a police officer. They struck up a quick friendship, helped along by a series of drinks, that eventually led to a conversation about the upheaval of post-revolution civil war in the Kutschurgan, as well as across Bessarabia and Ukraine.

The stranger brought up the subject of people, especially persecuted German farmers, seeking escape.

"There are ways for people to leave. I know someone—he works for the railway—who can help. He has very good contacts and has helped many dozens of people flee to the New World. Of course, freedom comes with a price. But if people are willing to pay it, there are others who know how to make it happen."

Podnovestov was intrigued by the notion of an underground railway to freedom. He had witnessed firsthand the horrors of recent years, the indiscriminate killings, the ruthless plundering of homes and farms, the scourge of famine and starvation from the confiscation of food production, the unconscionable suffering of children. He took down the man's name—Mircea Lucinschi—and his address.

But Podnovestov knew nothing more about the man who claimed to be a Tiraspol policeman. He had the impression that the stranger was legitimate. But, truly, he had no idea if the man was merely running a scam, was some kind of lunatic, or was actually capable of helping people reach the New World. He told this to a young man from Strassburg who occasionally came to his store and once mentioned his dream of reaching the New World with his young wife and two children. Yuri gave him the Tiraspol policeman's name and address, and never saw him again. The same was true for the widow Schmidt, who was left with six children after her husband was killed south of Selz during the civil war clashes between the White and Red armies two years earlier.

"Christina," Podnovestov said now. "I don't know if I can help. It's true that I once met a man in Tiraspol who said he could help, for a price, and I referred a couple of people to him. But I have no idea what happened. For all I know, he's an agent for the Bolsheviks and does this to lure people to their deaths."

"It doesn't matter," Christina said. "I'll take the chance. I have no choice."

"But this man, he said the services come at a price. I don't know how much. It might be too much."

"No price is too great," she said. "I don't have much but I've been saving money for years, especially since Nikolas died, in the hope that someday I can buy freedom for my family. We cannot stay. There is no future for my children here."

Podnovestov wasn't sure what to do. As much as he wanted to help Christina and her children, he was uneasy about putting her in touch with someone he knew from only one chance meeting in a bar. The man might be a complete fraud. For that matter, he might no longer be at his Tiraspol address, or might even be dead. But by chance, Podnovestov was planning his annual trip to Tiraspol in a week's time. It would be an opportunity to see if he could reconnect with Lucinschi, determine if the man really was who he said he was and legitimately had the contacts to help people escape Russia for the New World. He didn't want to recommend the man to Christina and put her and her children's fates in the hands of someone he didn't know could be trusted. In fact, Podnovestov's conscience had been troubled already, knowing he had put others in contact with the Tiraspol policeman with unknown results. He was not going to take the same risk with the Schergevitch family.

"Christina, I want to help you and I will in any way I can. But I need to make sure that anyone you speak to about this can be trusted," Yuri said.

"I trust you, Yuri," she said.

"I know that, Christina. But I don't want to do anything to betray that trust. So I need to make sure that if I put you in touch with someone, that someone can be trusted, by me, and by you and your family. Next week I will take the train to Tiraspol. It's my yearly visit to speak with my suppliers. I can find out more when I'm there. Hopefully, when I come back, I will be confident that there is someone who will help you and your children reach the New World. I know your parents are waiting there for you."

Christina nodded. "Thank you, Yuri, thank you, Andrea," she said.

THE VIEW from the Timoty Hotel was impressive, which was more than you could say about the decaying hotel. One of two hotels in the centre of Tiraspol, the Timoty sat across the street from the banks of the Dniester River. Outside the hotel's front door was a striking panorama of the river, stretching in both directions, with people walking and riding bicycles up and down the promenade next to the Dniester.

The inside of the hotel was a whole different matter. The heavy wooden front door sat ajar, its top hinge separated from the doorframe so that the door tilted awkwardly, its bottom edge jammed hard against the concrete front step.

The small, dimly lit lobby of the hotel, such as it was, consisted of two wooden chairs right next to each other against the wall, and a desk where an old man sat under a single gaslight hanging straight down from the ceiling, the smoke from his cigarette curling up as if drawn to its hazy radiance.

Podnovestov had arrived an hour earlier and walked the two

blocks from the rail station to the Timoty, where he checked into a second floor room. There was a narrow bed with one old, grey, worn woolen blanket, and a table with a washbasin, but no towel. The toilet for all the guests was behind the reception desk in the lobby.

"Excuse me, sir," Podnovestov said to the old man at the front desk who moments earlier had checked him into his room. "Could you please direct me to the police station?"

The man, slouched over on his elbows, head down reading what looked like a newspaper, did not look up.

"Out the front door. One block to the right, turn right. Go a block, on the left," he said.

"Thank you," Podnovestov said.

There was nothing to identify the police station, which was in a small one-floor brick building attached to a two-storey building that looked like what could be the city office. The only marking was a small wooden sign above the door with POLJJCIJA carved in it. Podnovestov walked in.

Other than a long, impressive counter and three rows of wooden chairs across the room, separated by an aisle down the middle, the room was empty. There was a rather pungent odour, a kind of damp, sweet smell, which Yuri found quite unpleasant. He noticed a closed door behind the counter and was waiting for someone to appear when he saw what looked like a cow bell sitting on the counter. He walked over and shook it, making a loud clang, then set the bell back down on the countertop.

A moment later a short, squat man with a full beard wearing a dark grey tunic and cap came through the door. He looked at Podnovestov and kind of grunted, as if to say "what do you want?"

"I'm looking for Mircea Lucinschi, who I believe is with the police here," Podnovestov said. "I'm wondering if you might tell me where I might reach him."

"Who are you?" the man asked.

"My name is Yuri Podnovestov. I've travelled here from the village of Fischer-Franzen where I have a store. I'm here to meet with suppliers and I—"

The man laughed loudly, slapping the palm of his hand on the counter.

"Suppliers? And you want to talk with, who was it, Mircea somebody? Pray tell, for what, dare I ask? "

"Nothing other than to say hello. We met in a bar when I was here last year and I thought I would be good to renew acquaintances," Podnovestov said.

The man erupted into another belly laugh and slapped the counter yet again.

"Right. I get it. You're looking for a whore, right?"

Podnovestov didn't know what to make of this strange man.

"Look, if you don't know Mircea Lucinschi, then fine. I'll be on my way."

As Podnovestov turned to walk out of the station, the man spoke again.

"As you can see, we've set up for court here. Trial begins in about an hour. You're welcome to come back. Maybe we'll pick you for jury or something," he said. "Who knows, maybe the guy you're looking for might even show up."

"Thanks, but no thanks," Yuri said over his shoulder as he headed for the door.

"Well, in that case, I'll mention to the judge that you stopped by. What's your name again?"

"Forget it," Yuri said.

"Whatever you like, but Judge Lucinschi will be disappointed he didn't get to renew acquaintances with his friend from, where was it, Fischer something?"

Podnovestov stopped and turned.

"Are you serious? He's the judge?"

"Would I lie?" the man said, laughing and slapping the counter a third time.

Watching Bessarabian justice in action was quite a spectacle, Podnovestov thought, as he sat through six "trials" in the span of three-quarters of an hour. Three were for murder; two, robbery; and one, assault. The process was brutally simple and efficient, if utterly lacking due process.

The accused were led in through the door behind the counter in leg irons and handcuffs by the short man who had greeted Podnovestov.

They stood in front of Judge Lucinschi while the man read the charges.

"Dinu Silviu is charged with the heinous offence of murder. He was arrested as he was taking the wallet of a dead man in an alleyway. Next to the deceased was an iron rod that had been used to crush the victim's skull. Silviu had been seen drinking with the man earlier that night."

Lucinschi looked straight ahead at the accused.

"Do you have anything to say in your defense?" he asked.

The man began a long, rambling and vain attempt to claim his innocence. He talked about growing up without a mother or father from the time he was eight and living mostly on the street or off the charity of others. He had fought alongside the Romanians with the Bessarabian infantry during the war and served in the Bessarabian Red Army and been loyal to the revolution. It was true, he said, that he had been drinking earlier with the man and that he was stooped over the body when the police saw him in the alley and arrested him. But he denied taking the victim's wallet and said that he'd only knelt down over the body to see if the man was still alive.

"We were drinking inside. He said he had to relieve himself

and went into the alley. When he didn't come back after 10 or 15 minutes, I went out to see what happened and that's when I came across him."

Lucinschi seemed unimpressed. Even though no corroborating evidence was presented and the case against Silviu was simply the statement read by the squat man, it was apparent what the verdict would be.

"I find you guilty and sentence you to death by hanging. Next case," Lucinschi said matter-of-factly, rapping a wooden gavel on the counter in front of him.

And so it went through each of the six cases, all were found guilty, two were sentenced to death and the four others to long prison terms of hard labour.

An hour later, Podnovestov and Lucinschi were sitting together in the same bar where they had met two years earlier. When the trials ended, Podnovestov had approached Lucinschi and re-introduced himself. Initially, the judge was skeptical about this stranger. But when Podnovestov mentioned the people he had referred to Lucinschi who wanted to escape from Russia, he remembered their earlier meeting. When Podnovestov said he would like to talk, Lucinschi had offered to meet him in the bar in half an hour.

"I have to ask you," Podnovestov said as the two sat at the same table in the corner of the bar where they had met a year earlier, each with a glass of vodka. "How did you become a judge?"

Lucinschi grinned and took a sip of his drink.

"You seem surprised, my friend. Do you think I'm not qualified?"

"No, it's not that. It's just that I, I dunno, I guess I just assumed you were in the police and never expected you would become a judge."

"What better judge than someone who knows the criminal mind?" Lucinschi replied.

Podnovestov was not about to argue and, besides, he had other things to ask of his police-turned-judge friend.

"When we first met, you told me you knew those who, for a price, can help get people to the New World. Do you remember?"

"Of course I do. In fact, I remember well the families you sent to me. You did send them to me, is that not true?"

Podnovestov felt a small surge of optimism.

"That is true. Do you know what happened to them?" Podnovestov asked.

"Of course. Both the young man and his wife, as well as the widow and her children, are in the United States of America. They made their voyages safely and are very happy indeed with their new lives."

Podnovestov could hardly believe what he was hearing. He immediately became skeptical.

"How can I believe you?" he asked.

Lucinschi was offended. "What? You think I'm lying? Me, a judge, *lie*? What the fuck is that?"

Podnovestov backed down immediately. "No, no, it's just that no one in our region has heard anything from them. We thought maybe they didn't make it, that they might even have died."

Lucinschi reached inside his jacket and from the breast pocket pulled out a letter. He unfolded it, picked up his glasses from the table and began to read aloud.

My dear Mircea,

I write with my heart overflowing with gratitude. You have saved my life and the lives of our children. We will never, ever, be able to repay you.

After a journey of two months that took us to Bratislava, Berlin and London and by sea to New York and the New World of the United States, and finally by train across this great land, we are now in our new home in the state of North Dakota. We live in a small town named Mandan, where I have work as a housemaid and cleaner. It is hard work, but it is enough for us to have a small home and food on the table. My children are all healthy and now in school. I know a great and wondrous future awaits them and it is all because of you.

I hope to meet you again one day, in heaven.

With deepest thanks,
Frieda Schmidt

Lucinschi slid the letter across the table to Podnovestov for him to look at. He picked it up and saw the handwriting. It was dated three months earlier, March 14, 1924. He also noted the stamps of the United States of America, which he had never seen before, and the imprint of the United States post office.

"By coincidence, the letter arrived today," Lucinschi said. "Kind of makes the ol' judge feel pretty good about himself. Proud even."

Podnovestov nodded.

"This is very good. You *should* feel proud. And I feel relieved because for many months I had feared that the widow Schmidt and her children might have perished. No one had heard from them, even their cousins who live in Mannheim had not heard a word from her. I remembered our conversation, and a year ago gave her your name when she asked for help. To be honest, I wondered if I had made a terrible mistake."

"You had no reason to worry. I'm a man of my word."

"I can see that now," Podnovestov said, handing the letter back to Lucinschi. "Are you still able to help those who want to leave?"

"I do my best. There are people who can help facilitate the process. But, as I told you the last time we met, this is not something I or others do for simply humanitarian reasons. It's a business. And we offer no guarantees. There are many factors at work, and success is not certain. People don't get refunds if they do not reach the New World. We keep our part of the bargain by doing our best. But what happens once people begin the journey happens. It is not our responsibility."

Unlike their previous conversation, Podnovestov sought more details—how much it cost, what services exactly did people receive for their money, how were they transported and to where?

Lucinschi told him the price was 100 rubles per person. Each would be given a Romanian passport, with temporary visas to enter Hungary, and train passage from Tiraspol to Budapest. In the Budapest train station they were to find the kiosk in the main terminal where a bald man sold newspapers. He would tell them where to find a nearby trucking company that would put them in the back of a truck and transport them to the Austrian border, where the driver would bribe the border guard to allow his shipment to pass without inspection. They would then be taken to the Austrian town of Oberwart, where they were left to fend for themselves.

"What happens from that point on is not our concern," Lucinschi said. "We commit to get them out of Romania, across Hungary and into Austria. But from that point on, they are on their own. There are immigration agents in Oberwart who work for the governments of the United States and Canada in the New World. They are anxious to recruit people to settle the new land and will offer incentives. So, as you can see, there are no guarantees they will make it to the New World. But what we can offer is the chance. The rest is up to them. And, as the letter from the widow demonstrates, it is not an impossible journey."

Podnovestov thought it sounded like a credible scenario. But he also knew it would be immensely challenging to get from Austria across Europe to a seaport, and secure the necessary papers and passage on a ship to get to either the United States or Canada. Immensely challenging, but not impossible because he also knew the New World was not simply welcoming, but seeking immigrants. He had even heard there were offices of immigration agents for the United States and Canada in cities such as Amsterdam, Paris and London who were actively recruiting people to immigrate to North America. In some cases, he was told they were even offering free passage on ships headed to places like New York and Halifax.

"I have spoken with my contact in Tiraspol," Podnovestov told Christina Schergevitch four days later when he was back in Fischer-Franzen. She had come into the store to buy a small sack of flour and Yuri asked her to step into the back next to the coal furnace where they could talk privately.

"He tells me that he can help people to get to Austria, via Romania and Hungary. But once in Austria, people are on their own and will have to find their way to the New World."

Christina Schergevitch stood silent for a moment, then simply nodded her head.

"He also said the price is 100 rubles for each person, whether child or adult. He said it needs to be paid in full before he can get the proper papers and train passage."

"Thank you," Christina whispered, then turned and left carrying her sack of flour.

CHAPTER 18

ONE THING I haven't told you much about was school. That's because there wasn't much school to talk about. It was a kind of hit-and-miss sort of thing. Not like today, when kids, by law, have to go to school and get educated and if they don't show up, the school has people who check where they are and why they aren't in class. Truant officers, I think they call them. Although, you don't hear much about truant officers anymore these days. In my day, it wasn't like that at all.

Fact of the matter was, in Fischer-Franzen I only went to school on-and-off for maybe four years. If you added it all up, by today's terms it probably amounts to a couple of years at most. I guess you could say I'm pretty uneducated, at least in a book-learning sense. Most of my learning came from watching what was going on and trying to understand why things are the way they are.

It reminds me of that saying by Yogi Berra, the one that goes: "You can observe a lot just by watching." That's true you know. If you just kind of pay attention to your life and think about things, it can be an education in itself. Speaking of Yogi Berra, don't you just love all his Yogisms? I think my favourite one is "we made too many wrong mistakes." The thing about Yogi's sayings is they are all rooted in an ironic truth that you can't deny. That's what I like the most about them.

The school in Fischer-Franzen was in what doubled for what today you might call a community centre. It was a white wood-framed building next to the church and had two rooms—a big one and a smaller one. I was in the bigger one. The other things it was used for were wedding and funeral receptions.

We didn't have desks per se, at least not what you think of as desks where everyone has their own chair and a flat surface to write on and a place to put your stuff, like pencils and paper and books. We didn't even have books. We sat on benches on each of the four sides of a wooden table. There were five tables in the room and kids used to sit at tables based on their age and how much they already knew or, more likely, didn't know. Our teacher was Mrs. Hopfauf, who Mom said had gone all the way to Grade 8 in school, so she was the most educated person in Fischer-Franzen. We used to call her Mrs. Fauffyhoppy, but not to her face, of course.

Basically the curriculum was reading, writing and doing additions and takeaways. Pretty basic stuff. Like they say, the three RS—readin', 'ritin' and 'rithmetic. Once kids were able to do those three things, they're schooling was pretty much finished.

I never much got the hang of arithmetic; it just wasn't my thing. But I got so that I knew all the letters of the alphabet and could print them, and write them in a kind of crude way. Not only that, but I could read sentences in my head and out loud when Mrs. Hopfauf put words together on the blackboard. For example, I could read things like: "the weather today is hot," or "it will not be a long time until it is winter." That's not to say that's all I could read, but that gives you some kind of idea of the level of my reading after going to school in Fischer-Franzen.

Kaza was a lot smarter than me. He was really good at doing

additions and takeaways and he could print and read really good too. In fact, Kaza and I always sat together at the same table in the classroom and he'd help me with arithmetic or writing a really big, hard word like, say, *grandfather* or the hardest word of all: *hippopotamus.*

When Frankie started school, he used to sit at the same table with me and Kaza. Like all little kids, at first Frankie didn't know anything. But before too long he was really good at arithmetic, but not so good with reading and writing, so kind of just the opposite of me.

The reason I'm telling you this is because of what happened one day at school. Mrs. Hopfauf had to go to the toilet, which meant she had to go to the outhouse in back of the school. So the students were left alone. And you know what happens when the teacher leaves the classroom and the kids are by themselves—trouble.

I was sitting at a table with Kaza, Frankie and five other kids, all of them older than us—Joseph, Robert, Karl, Anna and Johann. You might recall from what I told you before, but Joseph and Robert were real jerks and shit-disturbers, especially Robert. They liked to pick on me and Kaza, but mostly Kaza. The moment Mrs. Hopfauf said she had to "step out of the classroom for a few minutes," I knew we were likely in for it from the two of them.

"So, Sylowich, I hear your dad's a drunk and a commie," Robert said, out of the blue.

Kaza was looking down, printing on a piece of paper and didn't look up or respond.

"I'm talking to you, Sylowich," Robert snapped, grabbing the paper away from under Kaza's pencil as he tried to practise his letters. "Your old man, he's a Bolshevik, ain't he?"

"I dun-dun-dunno," Kaza said, still not looking up.

It was one of those rare moments in your life when you feel incredible anger, so much so that you have no fear, which was how I felt. Robert was 13, five years older than me, likely a foot taller, but at that moment it mattered nothing.

"Leave him alone, Robert," I hissed through gritted teeth.

"Fuck off, Schergevitch," he snapped back.

With that I went slightly berserk. I literally leapt out of my chair and across the table, scrambling on my hands and knees to get at Joseph. He obviously wasn't expecting it, which is not surprising because I wasn't expecting it myself. With a final lunge, using my knees to spring forward off the table, I flew towards him, both my hands grabbing him around the throat, landing against his chest with the full weight of my 73 pounds. It was enough to knock him backwards, off the bench and flat onto his back on the floor with me on top.

Pandemonium ensued.

Anna and the other girls were screaming and so, apparently, was I, although I don't remember that part of it. But after people told me that I was making a kind of shrieking, banshee kind of howl as I alternated between punching Joseph's face and scratching at his eyes with both my hands as I knelt on his chest.

Unfortunately, as you might expect, I only had the upper hand briefly. Once the element of surprise was gone, I was in trouble. Big trouble.

Joseph was able, after a moment, to grab both my wrists and kind of fling me off him to the side. As I scrambled to get on my feet, he lunged forward and punched me square in the right eye. I saw an instant explosion of sparks, got dizzy and stumbled backwards. The next thing I knew, Joseph was on top of me with his right hand clutching my face in a craw grip, his fingernails digging into my cheek and forehead.

I could hear the other kids screaming and yelling and caught a glimpse of Kaza, who had jumped on Robert's back and had his arms wrapped around his head. It was enough to get Robert to let go of my face as he tried to get Kaza off his back.

Luckily, at that moment, Mrs. Hopfauf, having heard the shouts and screams, had rushed back into the classroom.

"Stop it! Stop it this moment!" she shouted loudly, grabbing Kaza with one hand and Robert with another, pulling the two of them off me.

Quickly, I jumped to my feet and in the same motion lunged at Robert again, trying to scratch his face. Mrs. Hopfauf, still hanging on to Robert and Kaza, got between us and blocked me before I could get another shot at Robert.

"I said stop it, Anton! Stop it right now!"

With that, just as I had momentarily lost my senses, I regained them. The adrenalin rush stopped and I backed away. Robert and Kaza seemed to have the same reaction and just as quickly as the scrap had started, it was over. Robert had scratch marks on his face and a bit of a bloody nose, all, I assumed, compliments of me, which made me feel good. Kaza seemed unscathed. In a moment I discovered my nose and lip were also bleeding and my right eye was soon going to have a major shiner. I could taste my own blood, which was running from my nose into my mouth.

The funny thing about all this was it had exactly the opposite effect than what I expected. Later that night, as Mom was putting cold, damp cloths on my eye, which was swollen shut and turning purple, I figured I was in deep trouble. Sooner or later Robert would get his hands on me and beat the living crap out of me.

But you know what? It was just the opposite. From that day on, I never had a lick of trouble with Robert, and neither did Kaza. Beats me why, but it was like he respected me for sticking up for Kaza and Kaza for sticking up for me, even if it was two against one. He never said a word to us about it and treated us both just fine from then on. It goes to show you that standing up for your friend against a bully is always the right thing to do.

To this day, I'm really happy I did what I did: fighting Robert because of the way he was treating Kaza. Not because I think I'm a big hero or something, but because I know it made the bond between me and Kaza even stronger. The other thing was I always remembered that time when I didn't stick up for Kaza when we were playing with the big boys in the Beresan hills and they were mean to him and I ran home like a little chicken-shit. This was a bit of redemption for me. And the other thing was it couldn't have come at a better time given what happened two days later.

That's when they killed Kaza's dad.

It happened in the middle of the night, right in Kaza's house and Kaza heard everything. He didn't exactly see it happen with his own eyes, like the way I saw my dad get killed. But he heard it, and if you ask me, hearing it but not seeing it is just as bad and probably worse. It messes with your mind more. I know it did for Kaza.

The way I found out about Kaza's dad being killed was from my sister Magdalena. I was in the kitchen getting a drink of water out of the pail on the counter when she came in and asked me what I was doing, which seemed kind of odd because it was obvious, she could see I was getting myself a cup of water.

I figured something was up.

"Getting a drink," I said. "Why?"

"I don't think you and Kaza will be playing together for a few days," she said.

"Why not?" I asked.

"Mama said to tell you that Kaza's dad died last night. She said you shouldn't go over to Kaza's for awhile. You should wait until he comes to see you."

"He died? How?"

"I dunno. All I know is what Mama said and she wanted me to tell you and said that she'll talk to you about it later."

"Why can't she talk to me now?"

"Because she's gone over to see how Kaza's mom is doing."

It was weird. When I heard that Kaza's dad was dead, the first thing I thought was not how sorry I felt for my best friend. It was how I thought that maybe it wasn't really such a bad thing that his dad was dead because I knew he was mean to Kaza and his mom. I always remembered the bruises I saw on Kaza the day we were swimming in the Andre, and the mark on Kaza's mom's face. I knew the marks were because Kaza's dad had beaten them. So, in a way, a part of me was almost happy that Kaza's dad was dead.

I know that sounds really cold and crude, but it's the truth.

I didn't get to see Kaza for two days until they buried his dad. There was no funeral or anything like that, and they didn't even bury Kaza's dad in the cemetery by the church. It was because Kaza's family was Muslim and only Catholics like us could have funerals at the church and get buried in the cemetery next to it.

At first my mom didn't want me to go to the burial, but I pleaded with her to let me. I said that Kaza was my best friend and I wanted to be there because Kaza needed to have his best friend for something like that. Finally, she agreed.

It was a beautiful day, sunny with fluffy clouds in another brilliant blue sky. The burial was in a small plot of land on the edge of town where I counted six other graves. There was no statue at the entrance to the grave plots with a prayer etched in stone like at the cemetery next to St. Joseph's church, not even a fence around the graves. There were only small wooden markers with names and the years they were born and died. None of the "Rest in Peace" or "Gone to the Father in Heaven" they had on headstones in the church cemetery. Some of the markers were barely even visible because of the overgrown grass.

Mom and me walked to the burial site and when we got there, counting us, there were nine people: Kaza, his mom, two sisters, my mom and me, and three other men—two of whom I recognized as seeing before, although I didn't know where they lived. The one I didn't recognize at all stood at the end of the open grave holding a black book. At the bottom of the grave I could see something wrapped in a white sheet, which I realized was Kaza's dad. It made me shiver, seeing Kaza's dad in the cold ground without a casket.

Kaza was standing next to his mom, holding her hand. His two sisters were on the other side of his mom, one holding her mom's hand and her sister holding *her* hand. Right away I felt a kind of crushing sadness. The suffering was palpable. Kaza's sisters were sobbing quite softly and Kaza's mom, Yakira, looked to be in some kind of catatonic state. She looked pathetic—frail, weak, hollow, empty—an utterly spent human being. Kaza never lifted his head as he clutched his mother's hand, but I could hear him faintly whimpering.

"Glory be to thee, O Allah, and I praise Thee. Blessed is Thy name and Thou art exalted. Thy praise is glorified, and there is no God other than Thee," said the man at the head of the grave, reading from the book he held open with his outstretched arms.

"O Allah! Have mercy on Muhammad and on those related to Muhammad, just as Thou hast mercy and Thou sendeth peace and blessings and hath compassion on Abraham and on those related to Abraham. Surely Thou art praiseworthy, the Great!

"O Allah! Forgive those of us who are still living and those who are dead; those of us who are present and those who are absent, and our minors and our elders. O Allah! Let the one whom Thou keepest alive from among us, live his life according to Islam, and let the one Thou causeth to die from among us, die as a believer.

"Peace be upon you and have Allah's Mercy."

With that, Yakira, Kaza and his two sisters each bent over and picked up a handful of soil from the mound next to the grave. Together they tossed the soil into the open grave and Kaza's mom said in a weak voice I could barely hear: "Out if it we created you. And into it we deposit you. And from it we shall take you out once again."

We stood there for maybe a minute, in total silence. It was one of those situations where you dared not move until others did. You even tried not to breathe for fear someone might hear you. The only sound was the distant, melodic call of a meadowlark and faint rustling of leaves in a soft breeze.

The signal we could move came from the man at the head of the grave who had read the prayer. He closed his book, walked around to the side of the grave and embraced Kaza's mom. Kaza never once raised his head through the entire ceremony and he kept his head bowed even as his mom led him and his sisters away from the grave and began their walk home.

"Can I catch up with Kaza and walk with him?" I asked my mom as we waited for the others to leave.

"Not right now, Anton. You need to let Kaza be with his mom and sisters. This isn't the time."

"But I can tell that Kaza needs me. I can help him not feel so sad."

"You'll have your chance. But now isn't the time," my mom said.

We waited for Kaza and his family to get a long head start before we began the slow walk home. When we got to our place, I told my mom that I wanted to sit on the front steps and wait to see if Kaza would come out.

"All right, Anton. You wait for Kaza. I'm not sure if he'll want to come out today or not," Mom said. "But when he does, you need to be there for him. I'm sure this is a very hard time for him. You're his best friend and this is when being someone's best friend really matters. The difference between a friend and a best friend is that best friends are there for their friend in good times and bad. This is one of those bad times for Kaza."

I've always remembered that.

For more than an hour I sat on our front step, watching for Kaza and thinking about things. But mostly just thinking.

You know how there are times in your life when you remember being able to kind of understand things better than before? I'm not saying some revelatory moment or anything dramatic like that. More just a particular point when you have a chance to think things through and, for whatever reason, you find yourself making more sense out of your life than before. Well, sitting on the front step the day that Kaza's dad was buried was one of those moments for me. Just being there, waiting to see if my best friend was going to come out, gave me a chance to think in a way I had never thought before.

It's hard, maybe even impossible, for me to explain in a way that makes sense, but I'm going to try.

I'd say the key was what my mom said to me about how best friends are there for each other in good times and bad. As I sat there and thought about what that meant, it made me think about what had happened since my life began and how Kaza was always there for me. What it did was make me not simply recall all the things over the last few years, but to think about them as part of an interconnected chain of events, how what happened in Fischer-Franzen was part of something much bigger.

Now, I'm not saying as an eight-going-on-nine-year-old that I truly understood the magnitude of what was going on in the Kutschurgan, or Bessarabia, or Ukraine, or Russia or anything that grandiose. But sitting on the front step that day, and thinking about my friendship with Kaza and everything that had happened, I felt like I was starting to finally understand what was going on in my life, if not make sense of it entirely.

This is likely going to sound bizarre, but what connected things for me that day was the meaning of clouds in my life. I don't mean to sound all profound and everything, as if there is some kind of deep, esoteric meaning to clouds. There probably isn't for most people, who no doubt see them as nothing more than what they are—droplets or water vapour frozen as water crystals floating in the sky. Nice to look at sometimes, but no big deal.

For me and Kaza, though, clouds were much more. They had become an integral part of our lives as young kids, something we associated with our friendship because whenever we felt insecure, or afraid or uncertain, we would lie on our backs and look up at the clouds and talk about how we felt. It was kind of like therapy.

I didn't mention that as I stood with my mom in the small cemetery plot where they buried Kaza's dad, I almost started to cry when I saw Kaza with his head bowed and heard his soft whimpers as he held his mom's hand. One way for me to stop myself from crying is to look up at the clouds, so that's what I did then, and it worked. I didn't cry. Don't ask me why looking at clouds keeps me from crying, but it does. The only way I can explain it is it seems to have some kind of special effect that makes me feel at ease. It's as if I get lifted up into the air and, at least mentally, leave what's happening on earth behind.

As I sat there, thinking, I remembered almost five years earlier in the church cemetery when we buried my brother John. Kaza was there too and I had this vivid memory of looking up at the clouds as I stood next to my brother's grave thinking that I was going to watch John fly up to heaven and how, a little bit later, Kaza and I laid on our backs in our yard and looked up at clouds together and talked about what we saw floating in the sky.

At that moment I realized how clouds had been such an important part of my life living in Fischer-Franzen. How clouds offered Kaza and me fleeting but soothing relief and escape from our lives as kids when we faced the reality of the world around us.

Sitting on our front step, hoping Kaza would come out so we could talk and hang out together, I looked up. The sky was heavy with clouds, big, thick ones stacked on top of one another. It was one of those days where much of the sunlight was filtered by the clouds, casting a broad blanket of shade over the town. Looking south down the street, far out towards the Karstal Hills, I could see sunlight illuminating the high ground where there was a break in the cloud cover and the sunlight shone through. You could actually see the sun's rays beaming down from between the clouds. The sight of the sunlight at that moment made me remember how Mom had told me that when Dad was alive he said you could talk to God when you climbed up to the Karstal Hills. It looked like it was one of those days, with the grace from God flowing down between the clouds from heaven. I wondered who might be in the hills that day talking with God and receiving His grace.

It's hard to be sure how long I sat there looking at clouds. You know how it is when you get kind of mesmerized in thought and you lose track of time and your surroundings. It could have been maybe only 20 or 30 seconds, although my guess is it was more like minutes because the next thing I knew, Kaza was standing at our front gate. I hadn't even noticed him walking over to our place because I was still looking towards the Karstal Hills and the sunlight streaming down from between the clouds.

"Hi, Anton," Kaza said.

"Hi, Kaza. How you doing?" I said, a little surprised and feeling awkward, not knowing what to say to my best friend on the day his dad was buried.

"Uh, all right, I-I guess," he said.

"Sorry about your dad and everything. How's your mom doing? And your sisters?"

"All right, I guess. Muh-muh-Mama's being ruh-really quiet. She's pruh-pretty sad, I guess. My suh-sisters are duh-doing all right, I guh-guess."

I could tell how nervous and upset Kaza was because his stutter was worse than ever. It made me feel sorry for him.

Kaza walked to the step and sat down beside me. I put my arm around his shoulders and sort of hugged him for a moment. We didn't say anything for a minute or so, just kind of looked out at the street together.

"Lots of clouds today," I said looking up at the sky and not knowing what to say.

"Uh-huh, big, fat wuh-ones," Kaza said. "I like big, fuh-fat ones."

"Yeah, me too."

So we sat there, saying nothing for at least a minute, and stared at the sky. You could tell that it was windy up in the clouds, even though there was only the slightest breeze on the ground. The sky was alive with movement, a kind of ever-changing dynamic vista, as clouds constantly changed their position and gradually altered their shapes. The shadows on the earth kept changing too. Sunlight would break through, spilling onto the ground and advancing quickly in one place and retreating in another spot as shadows from the clouds spread elsewhere.

"See over there," I said, pointing towards the Karstal Hills in the distance.

"Uh-huh," Kaza said.

"Before my dad got killed, he used to tell my mom that you could talk to God if you went to the Karstal Hills. I bet there is someone there now and they're talking with God. You can see that it's open, I bet all the way to heaven, between the clouds, because the sun is shining through."

"Duh-do you muh-miss yuh-your dad?" Kaza asked.

I realized it was a good question because it made me think and, to be honest, I had never really thought about my dad and whether I missed him before. At least not in the way that makes you focus on it like when someone asks you the question directly. This might sound callous, but as I wondered about Kaza's question I realized that in some ways I didn't miss my dad.

But I don't think I felt that way because I'm selfish or insensitive or anything like that. I'd say it had to do with the fact that I didn't really know my dad. I had this vague recollection of him— a kind of faint image in my mind—but I had no strong and vivid memories of being with him. I didn't have a personal relationship to give shape and meaningful context to my feelings about him being gone.

The only real memory I had was one that left me with an overpowering blend of fear and sickness that came with that moment when my life began. It has stayed with me through the years, always lurking somewhere in the back of my mind. The memory of seeing a man being murdered, shot in the back of the head, a man that I didn't really know but who I understood to be my father, left me with a deep sense of dread but no particular sense of loss. How can you feel loss over someone you really never knew, at least not through your personal memories, but only through what other people told you? Does that make sense? I hope so, because I don't want you to think that I don't have feelings like other people. I do, but like I've said all along, for me, all my feelings start from the moment my life began.

"I dunno, Kaza," I said. "I want to say that I miss my dad and I do, like that I wish he hadn't been killed and he was still living with us and everything. But I don't really miss him because I didn't know him because I can hardly remember him.

"Like, I don't miss him the way I would miss you if you moved away somewhere else. That's because we do stuff together, lots of stuff, and we're best friends and everything. So it's different. Do you know what I mean?"

"I do," Kaza said.

We sat there for a couple of minutes and kept looking at clouds. The sky was getting darker and looked like it could rain.

"Anton, I fuh-feel afraid. Wuh-wanna go to the Cave?"

"Sure," I said.

As I've told you many times before, the Cave was our special, secret place that gave us this incredible sense of isolation and security from the rest of the world. Sure, it was mostly just our imagination, but imagination really matters when you're a kid. Imagination becomes your reality when haven't got the world figured out yet.

The still air was heavy from humidity inside the Cave and, with the growing darkness from the gathering storm clouds, it was darker inside than it was on sunny days. It felt kind of somber.

I could tell Kaza wanted to tell me something. We sat quietly for a few minutes, peering through the cracks and the knothole.

"When you, you told me about your duh-dad and how you nuh-nuh-never really knew him, I felt suh-sorry for you," Kaza said.

"Thanks," I said. "And I feel sorry for you too, about your dad dying. Did he have, like a heart attack?"

"No, no. He got kuh-killed in our house buh-by bad guys. I huh-heard them," Kaza said.

I knew Kaza wanted to tell me what had happened and how he felt, so I told him that I remembered seeing my dad killed almost five years earlier.

the leg of one of the two sawhorses that held up the canvas tarp and formed the Cave.

"Anton, I'm afuh-afuh-afraid. They kuh- came to our huh-house in the nuh-night. I huh-heard my muh-mom skuh-scream. They shuh-shot my dad."

We sat there for the next 30 minutes, just me and Kaza, and talked. But mostly Kaza talked, more than he had ever talked before.

He described to me how he had been asleep in bed when he was woken up by a loud crash at their front door, then the sound of heavy footsteps, followed by strange voices and yelling in his parents' bedroom, which was next to his. He said that he heard his mother screaming, that he pulled the covers over his head, closed his eyes tight, and prayed to Allah, hoping he was only dreaming.

Then he heard three loud gunshots.

He stayed in bed, shivering from fear under the covers. The noise and voices stopped after the gunshots and he heard his mother wailing quietly before there was the sound of footsteps leaving his house. Then there was only the faint sound of his mother weeping and nothing else. For the entire night, Kaza stayed under his covers, paralyzed by terror, until his mother came into his room in the first light of dawn in the morning. She was in a trance-like state, taking Kaza by the hand and leading him to his parents' bedroom where he saw his father's body on the floor, wrapped in a white sheet stained with blood. His mother opened the sheet and Kaza saw his father's face, his eyes wide and mouth slightly open, like he'd died trying to say something.

Yakira knelt down next to her husband's body, leaned over and kissed him. She motioned to Kaza, who did the same, feeling his lips against the cold, lifeless skin of his father's forehead.

Kaza told me that he loved his father, but he feared him even

Yakira knelt down next to her husband's body, leaned over and kissed him. She motioned to Kaza, who did the same, feeling his lips against the cold, lifeless skin of his father's forehead.

Kaza told me that he loved his father, but he feared him even more. He described how his father would be kind one minute and cruel the next. He told me about how his dad treated his mother the same way; how he didn't know why his father could be so different; how it was impossible to know what kind of a mood he would be in; and, how he would become quiet and mean when he drank vodka, which he did every night.

When Kaza told me the story he didn't cry. Even though he stammered worse than I ever heard him before, he spoke steadily and without stopping for 10 minutes and I just listened. It was only when he was finished and it became totally silent in the Cave that he began to cry, very, very softly. There was enough light coming through the cracks in the wall that I could see tears glistening on his cheeks in the darkness.

I reached over and squeezed his hand.

CHAPTER 19

I T WAS IN THE BEDROOM WALL, next to the door frame. Nikolas had purposefully put it there when he built the house 24 years earlier. From start to finish, it had taken almost three months to build the house in 1901. It was an impressive structure by any measure—from its arched, oak-trimmed front doorway to its sweeping, curved staircase off the small entryway; its brilliant hardwood floors to the parlor-sitting room with a bay window. But what made Nikolas most proud was the secret hiding place. When he showed it to his young wife the day they finally moved into their new home, he could barely contain his excitement.

"This is where we can keep our valuables," he said to Christina, as he carefully, using fingertips, pulled out one of the many small wooden panels in the wall. The uncovered 12-by-six-inch space revealed an 18-inch deep wooden cubicle recessed into the wall. When Nikolas gently set the wooden panel back in place, there was no visible sign of the hidden space in the wall of their bedroom. Even better, the wall area itself was often out of sight behind the open door to the bedroom.

Nikolas and Christina had tucked into this alcove valuables like the nacre mother of pearl necklace Christina received as a wedding gift from her mother, and the diamond earrings handed down from her grandmother. But mostly the couple used the wall cubicle as a place to save money over the years. It had been a slow and painstaking process, especially during the early years of their marriage as they struggled to make ends meet and raise a family. But they agreed that every week they would find a way to add something to the small stash of money, even if it was a mere kopek. They kept this promise to themselves faithfully.

On only rare occasions would they take money from the safe place in the wall. They agreed from the beginning that the money would be used only for necessities, and then only when there was no choice. And always, the money must be used for the good of the family. For the most part, the few times the couple had dipped into their secret savings was for medical reasons. One was an emergency appendectomy at the hospital in Selz for Theresa when she was eight and almost died from the fever. Another time was when Emma, at age six, needed eyeglasses to correct her vision, impaired at birth by strabismus—a condition that misaligned her eyesight. But just as spending the money was a rarity, saving it was a weekly ritual.

Christina never counted the money they had saved. There was no need to. She knew her husband regularly kept track of the amount and, besides, for some reason she felt more comfortable being uncertain of their total savings. It was, as if not knowing, added to the suspense that the amount might actually be more than she might expect. Nor did she ever open the secret hiding place herself and add to the amount. If she had a kopek or two for savings, she would always give it to Nikolas, who would put it into the safe place.

The first time Christina opened the wall alcove herself was in August 1919, three weeks after Nikolas and John had been murdered. She remembered feeling guilty, as if it was a horribly crass thing to do while she and her children were still deep in shock and mourning the loss of their husband and father, son and brother.

But she and Nikolas had saved for the good of their family. If ever they were at risk, Christina thought, it was now, in the wake of her husband's death; the family's future had never been so bleak and uncertain, so peering into the hiding place and counting the money was what she must do to fully understand the resources her family had. She blessed herself with the sign of the cross and carefully pulled away the smooth wooden panel that opened the hidden recess.

The money was in a tarnished silver tobacco tin. A small, red velvet sack held her jewelry safe, its drawstring pulled tight. Her heart sank as she pulled out the container; it was very light, hardly big enough to hold all the money they had saved over the years. Sitting on the bed with the tin in her lap, Christina pried off the metal lid. Inside was a roll of bills, wound tightly inside an elastic band. On the bottom, she could see a few kopeks.

As she pulled off the elastic band and unfolded the money, Christina saw the bills were rubles. The first few were singles, but as she peeled back more bills, the rubles unfolded in denominations of 10s, 20s and even hundreds. She could scarcely believe her eyes. Hands shaking, she counted carefully and deliberately. A woman of little education, Christina went slowly, pausing after each grouping of 10, and to avoid losing track she wrote down a running tally of the total. She counted 893 rubles, 6 kopeks. It was more money than she had thought possible, even in her wildest hopes. Nikolas must have gone repeatedly to Yuri Podnovestov's to trade kopeks for rubles and single rubles for larger denominations as the family's small savings accumulated.

Christina gripped the money tightly, suddenly felt fearful. The Bolsheviks would surely take it if they discovered it, so just holding it in her lap seemed dangerous and made her feel vulnerable.

She had quickly wrapped the elastic band around the rubles again, put the money into the tin and set it back in the alcove, gently slotting the panel back into place so that it was perfectly aligned with the rest of the wall.

With her husband gone, and the Bolsheviks in control of her family's farm, the secret hiding place became a small source of comfort for Christina. It sheltered a remnant of her previous life, untouched by the upheaval of revolution, and offered the faint hope of escape to a new and better life for herself and her children. But it also brought anxiety; fear that it would be discovered and her hope for the future destroyed.

Faithful to the pact she and Nikolas had made, Christina never wavered from the commitment to save a few small coins whenever she had the chance. There were many weeks, even months, when she had nothing to save, unable to find a single kopek to add to the silver tin. Just feeding her family was often beyond her meagre resources. Seldom did she have any currency, depending on barter as a means of exchange for food or clothing.

But there were occasions when the food quota allotted to her family allowed her to sell some of the vegetables from her garden. A small black market in the region provided access to hard currency now and then. Acting as middleman, Yuri Podnovestov was able to take Christina's vegetables and, for a small commission, sell them in Mannheim, Selz or even Odessa where there were people who had the cash to pay for food.

But at the most, Christina could only sell her fresh vegetables or some of the preserved food in her root cellar three or four times a year. It wasn't much, and rarely resulted in more than a few rubles. But it was something, enough that she was able to occasionally add to the savings she and her husband had started. If nothing else, it helped her feel she was honouring the legacy and memory of her husband.

By the spring of 1925, it had been many months, perhaps even a year, since Christina had last gone to the secret hiding place, opened the tin and looked at her family's savings. She always feared taking even a few moments to retrieve the savings, afraid that she might be discovered, that one of the local Bolshevik enforcers might suddenly appear at her door and discover her secret. For almost six years she had been able to keep her secret from the Bolsheviks and, with it, keep hope alive for her family's future.

Yuri had told her what it would take to get out of Russia and to the New World—100 rubles for each person: man, woman or child. For that price they would receive the papers they needed and passage to Austria through Bessarabia, Romania and Hungary.

It was late at night, all her children were asleep and the house was silent. Nervous, worried that someone outside might be watching, Christina blew out the candle in her bedroom. Darkness engulfed her. Slowly, the gloom subsided as her eyes adjusted to the faint light of the full moon on a cloudless night.

She closed her bedroom door and slid her hand along the wall, feeling for the panel she knew would lead to the safe place. Carefully, she pulled it off, reached in and brought out the silver tin. It glistened slightly in the moonlight. Christina sat on the bed, and with the tin on her lap, prised off the lid, and reached in for the roll of bills. Turning slightly to take advantage of the limited light, she began to count, slowly and carefully. It took her awhile, but by the time she was finished she had counted 964 rubles, two kopeks.

"HELLO YURI. How are you? How are Andrea and the *kinder*?" Christina Schergevitch asked as she walked into the general store. No one was there other than Podnovestov, who was sitting behind the counter, carving a piece of wood.

"We're all fine, Christina. It's good to see you. How are you and your family?" he asked in return.

"We're doing all right, too, Yuri, all things considered."

Summoning her nerve, Christina browsed the few sealers of preserved vegetables on the store shelves for a moment. Glancing up from his effort to whittle a wooden plate, Podnovestov sensed that Christina was there to talk, not browse.

"It's good to hear the children are well," Podnovestov said. "It's not easy for so many."

Christina put the glass jar she had been looking at back on the shelf and nodded.

"I know. It's a constant struggle just to find enough food to feed ourselves. And I see nothing to make me believe the future will be any better. As a mother, that's what troubles me the most," Christina said. "It would be easier to accept our life now if it was possible to believe things might get better. But I feel no hope."

It was so true, Yuri thought. *Life is less about the here and now and more about hope for the future. Without hope, life becomes mere existence.*

"I understand completely," he said, knowing that Christina had more she needed to talk about.

"You know when we talked about how some people have been able to leave for the New World, and how you know people in Tiraspol who can help?"

"Yes, of course," Yuri nodded.

"Well, I have thought a great deal about our conversation and I've decided that I must do something. That my children deserve more and it is my duty as their mother to do whatever I can to give them the opportunity for a better life—the chance at hope for their future," Christina said.

"Yes, of course," Yuri repeated. "And as I said, if there is some way that I can help you Christina, I will."

And so the plan for the Schergevitch family's escape to the New World began. It was a decision Christina had felt was inevitable ever since that day in July 1919 when her husband had been killed in cold blood in front of her children. Executed, not because he had actively resisted the Bolsheviks and their revolution, because he had done nothing of the sort. Executed because he was a German *kulak*. Executed because he was a landowning farmer. It mattered nothing that he was a good, God-fearing man, a hardworking father, a dedicated husband who believed in the Christian principles of sharing with others less fortunate. There was no place for him in the Russia of the Bolsheviks. At that moment, Christina knew there was no place for her family in this country anymore either, a country gripped by political psychosis and the inevitable extremism that results.

It was hard for her to express the fear, anxiety and excitement she felt when she thought about what might lie ahead for her family. Once she had made the firm decision to begin the effort for their escape from the Kutschurgan, Bessarabia, Ukraine and Russia, virtually her every waking moment was affected by thoughts of what the future might bring. The risk and uncertainty of their escape was impossible to determine, in either practical or emotional terms.

What if the effort failed and she forfeited her family's life savings? What if they became separated? What if they were captured by the Bolsheviks before they reached Hungary and were executed? What if her children became ill during their long voyage to the New World? What if she died before reaching their destination and her children were orphaned? What if they reached the New World and life was not what they had expected?

The uncertainty was immeasurable, the doubts palpable. But for Christina, this was more than offset by two other factors, one very real and measurable, the other unknowable.

There was the objective reality of their life in the Kutschurgan. This was something they knew and experienced every day. This was a life that was not imagined, but lived in the here and now. It was, moreover, a life that offered not a single reason to believe it would ever be any different, any better.

The unknowable was the hope of a better life in the New World. Admittedly, this hope was based on the uncertainty of an imagined life. But when people face the day-to-day reality of lives hardly worth living, lives utterly consumed by the prosaic, hope becomes an incredibly powerful force of motivation. Hope and the pursuit of a better future, even an imagined one, is what makes life worth living.

For almost six years, Christina had clung silently to hope. It had given her the strength to continue against the odds stacked against her and her children.

Even with all the uncertainty, from the moment she opened the secret hiding place after her husband had been murdered, and discovered the amount they had saved, her decision to leave was never in doubt; the family's flight from Russia predetermined. It was as if her husband spoke to her from his grave. She and Nikolas had agreed the money was to be used for the good of the family. What greater good could there be than freedom from oppression and the pursuit of hope and happiness?

No one other than Yuri and Andrea Podnovestov knew of their plans. The last thing Christina had done before visiting Podnovestov to ask him for help was to sit down with all her children to talk about their future together.

They had finished their supper of soup and bread at the kitchen table. She had made certain that all nine of her children were there—Eva, Magdalena, Rachel, Emma, Theresa, Christina, Anton, Frank and Mary. It was becoming difficult to gather them all together, especially the two oldest girls, Eva and Magdalena, who were 21 and 20 respectively—both with boyfriends and marriage on their minds.

Before Eva and Magdalena got up to begin clearing away the dishes, Christina asked them to wait.

"We can do that later. Now that we're together, I want to talk to all of you about something," she said.

"Aw, Mama, you're not going to lecture us again about ..."

"No, Rachel. This is not a lecture. I want to talk about something very important—our future as a family. About what we need to do to have a chance at better lives."

"Aren't we going to be a family anymore, Mama," Mary asked, sounding on the verge of tears.

"No, no, *Herzchen*. We'll always be a family. I want to talk about how we can start a new life together, as a family."

"Do you mean in the New World? Is this about us going to the New World to live with Grandpa and Grandma?" Emma asked.

"In Saskchin?" Frankie added.

Christina smiled at her children.

"Well, yes, perhaps. That's what I wanted to talk with you about. You kids need to know that I only want the best for you."

"Mother, we know that," Eva said. "You don't have to tell us."

"Thank you for saying that Eva. Every night when I go to bed I pray to the Lord to protect us and give us strength as a family to do what is right. It's not always easy to know what is the best thing for us to do.

"But ever since your father died I have been thinking about the New World. Grandpa and Uncle Joseph tell us about a better life there, a life with hope, where all you kids will have the chance for an education, a life where we don't have to worry who will come knocking on our door anytime during the day or night. If there is anything I want for us, but especially for you kids, it is to give you the chance at a better future than what we have here in Fischer-Franzen."

"Would we take a big boat to get to the New World?" Frankie asked.

"Yes," answered his mother. "But first I want to know what you think of the idea of going to live there. Is it something you want?"

For a moment, there was quiet as the children looked at each other. They turned to Eva, the oldest, to say something.

"Mama, we know how hard it has been for you since Papa died," Eva said. "I know there is no reason to believe the days we remember, when we had our farm and Papa was with us, will ever come back. Our family changed, our life changed when all that happened. So I think if there was some way to go to the New World, to be with Grandma and Grandpa, to start over, it would be a good thing.

"But Mama, I need to tell you that Raphael and I plan to get married. He has a job in Odessa, working in the shipyards. I love him and he loves me. We want to be together, to start our own new life together, to raise a family."

Christina looked at Eva and smiled. "I know, *Herzchen*," she said.

Then Magdalena spoke.

"Mama, I feel the same. Christian and I love each other. He wants us to marry. I can't leave him. We need to build a new life together here."

Christina was not surprised. She had fully expected her two oldest daughters would not want to leave their serious relationships with boyfriends; they had already begun their own, independent lives. She understood and did not intend to interfere.

"I understand, Magdalena. I felt the same when I was your age and would never ask you to leave behind someone you love. You and Eva are both adults—you will make your own choices.

"But it's not the same for your sisters and brothers. They are younger; their futures less certain. As their mother, I need to do whatever I can to give them a chance for a better life than what we have here. Only the New World gives us that hope."

Again there was brief silence before Theresa spoke.

"Mama, I think we should go."

"So do I," said Christina.

With that, it was quickly agreed that the family should emigrate to Canada, to the province of Saskatchewan in the New World where their relatives lived with others who had left the Kutschurgan to start their lives over.

"Mama," Anton asked. "Can Kaza come too?"

"No, Anton," she said. "I'm sorry. He can't leave his mother and his sisters. But maybe someday, if we go to the New World, he and his family will come too."

Anton's eyes grew sad.

"But Kaza is my best friend," he said.

THERE WAS A GRIM MOOD of resignation in Fischer-Franzen, a kind of dreary monotony in the village. Such had been the fabric of life for years. But it became especially pronounced with the discovery of Father Frederich's body in the Kutschurgan River. It was as if the last link to the past, the final fibre of resistance, had been severed with the death of the parish priest. All that remained was the struggle to survive from one day to the next.

If it were to be judged by the transformation of economy and society, the Bolshevik revolution was a success. What had been a farming economy in the Kutschurgan, based on a land-owing petty bourgeoisie class, had been virtually eradicated. Commercialism had all but disappeared, taking with it most private property, private production and a market-based economy. In its place was a crude, forced collectivization, a command-and-control society where incentive had been replaced by an abstract notion of collective welfare. But there was a fatal problem in this communist model where each received according to their need, from each according to their ability. It failed to take into account human nature, namely the truth that personal reward for one's effort has been at the core of human progress through the centuries of mankind's existence.

Marxist abstractions about materialism, labour as a commodity, the alienation that results, the fact that all human preoccupations could be reduced to economic determinants and that history is driven by clashing economic forces proved to be powerful intellectual stimulants for adherents. But this kind of economic reductionism, like all worldviews that seek to declare a single organizing principle for human behaviour, is, at its core, simplistic and dangerous. People are far more complex creatures.

The people who embraced the Marxist worldview, architects of the Bolshevik revolution like Lenin, Trotsky, Stalin and Plekhanov, believed they not only understood the world, but more importantly, human nature. Convinced of their ideological beliefs, certain of how to change world history, of how to build a classless, egalitarian society, they became populist demagogues, the most dangerous of all politicians. It became easy for them to identify enemies to the revolution, those they saw as impediments to the greater good they espoused. For such idealists, the end always justifies the means.

In such a reality, anything and everything can be, and is, rationalized. Elimination of basic human rights, murder, genocide, forced collectivization and resettlement, all of it was for the revolution and the higher purpose they sought. Or, as Marx said, the key to reaching the ultimate phase of world history, human development and the organization of society, is the elimination of class struggle. If that is the objective, the means merely become a necessary tool to achieve this greater good, this higher moral purpose.

Of course, Christina Schergevitch understood nothing of such Marxist ideology. She was a simple, barely-educated woman whose expectations matched her modest upbringing. She sought a peaceful life for her family, free from persecution and excessive want, a life rooted in the Christian principles of charity, humility and forgiveness. Her life was guided by a simple tenet: live simply so others might simply live.

She had long ago forgiven the men who murdered her husband, raped her and her daughter and seized control of their farm. She harboured no anger, felt no hostility and sought no vengeance. She had come to terms with her past and sought only to give her children hope for their future. But although she knew nothing of Marx, what she understood fully was the practical reality of life under the Bolsheviks, who appropriated his philosophy and sought to apply his abstractions to the real world. In this she was an expert.

The last decade had been a steady deterioration into hopelessness. A modest life on the land turned into a constant struggle for existence. War, revolution, civil war, repression, economic upheaval, famine, ethnic hatred and drought had created little but despair. Even the proletariat, those whom the Bolshevik revolution was supposed to help, had seen their already miserable existence sink further into despair.

But of course, this, too, could be rationalized by the proponents of the revolution. It was the cost that must be paid, the inevitable stages of the unfolding revolution—all part of the process towards the highest state of human development: communism. A price worth the cost, because the end justified the means. People were merely pawns, disposable in the larger chess match being played out across the land. And some pawns were more disposable than others.

Christina didn't know any of this explicitly, but understood it all implicitly. She had learned it through experience. And practical knowledge gained from real life is always more powerful than the abstractions of political theorists.

So, in the end, the decision to seek refuge in the New World, was not a difficult one. It was the only realistic option for her family, because at least it offered uncertainty and the potential of hope. There was no uncertainty in remaining in the Kutschurgan, only the certain knowledge that their suffering and struggle to survive would continue.

Leaving Russia was not going to be easy. It would require careful and subtle planning. Their intent had to be closely guarded—only a very few of the most trusted could be aware of the Schergevitch family's plan. Should the Bolsheviks learn of it, the family would be in great jeopardy. They could travel with only a very few of their personal belongings, so aside from leaving the house Nikolas and Christina had built, they would also have to abandon most of their belongings.

The journey to Canada and Saskatchewan would be long, dangerous and filled with imponderables. How long it might take would depend on many, many variables. But it could easily be six months. How would the family cope, would they be struck by illness, could they depend on safe passage out of Russia through Bessarabia and into Romania? After passing through three border checkpoints and reaching Austria by train, the plan was that they would somehow make their way to Germany and Belgium. But just how that would happen was uncertain; details of the trek across Europe were not known and wouldn't be until they met with Austrian authorities, who were supposed to be in touch with Canadian immigration agents. They were to board a ship in

Antwerp that would sail for Northampton and then spend seven days on the North Atlantic before reaching Halifax, on the eastern shores of Canada. At the pier in Halifax, they would board a train and travel west across Canada for five days, finally reaching their destination, a small town on the great plains of Saskatchewan called Hodgeville, where they would be greeted by Christina's father and mother. Finally, the last grueling leg of their journey would begin, a 57-kilometre trek by horse-drawn wagon to the village of Billimun, where their new life in the New World would finally begin.

When she thought of it in those terms, Christina was overwhelmed by the magnitude of what lay before her and her children. She could not begin to contemplate the risk or assess the danger without being stricken by fear. She couldn't help but question whether she had the personal fortitude and strength to lead her family to a new life.

But always, hope would emerge and her fears subsided.

CHAPTER 20

EVERYONE HAS THEIR MEMORIES, good and bad, happy and sad. Come to think of it, when all is said and done, that's what life is all about. It's a collection of memories.

But the ones you really remember are also those that never really leave you. They become a part of who you are, your identity, so to speak. The reason some stand out and stay with you forever is because they're rooted in powerful emotions. The joy they gave you at the time comes back with a kind of warm sense of contentment or fulfillment when you recall the moment. The same is true of the painful memories, those moments in your life you regret or wish you had never experienced because of the hurt you felt at the time. Sure, the actual physical hurt might disappear and the emotional pain subside, even vanish, when you're distracted by other things. But the emotional damage never actually leaves you. It stays locked away in your mind, just below the surface, and unfailingly re-emerges every time the memory returns, even years later. It might be less raw, diminished by time, but it is never gone forever.

If you ask me, I figure it's memories that make us human. What gives us our emotional depth is because we remember our lives, think about our pasts and dwell in our memories. The way you can tell our memories are so important to who we are is by the way we think about the future. Basically, having a future is what makes life worth living because what is the future other than anticipated memories? That's why you always wish for a good future, so that you will have positive and happy thoughts of the past when the future is over and you know you're dying, when all you have left is your memories.

So, when it comes right down to it, life *is* memories.

You might think I'm crazy and trying to sound all brainy like Freud or something, but I'm not. And besides, I don't care if that's what you think. I'm too old for that now. It's just the way I feel about things.

If you want to know, the very worst part of my life, the experience that left me with the most painful of my memories, came the day after I turned 10. Even now, a lifetime later, it's hard for me to tell you about it. But I'm going to try because it's not good to keep the hurt locked up inside all the time. Sometimes it's healthy to let it out.

"Do YOU want to go down to the Andre?" I said to Kaza. It was July 9, 1925 and it was a really hot summer day, perfect for swimming.

Kaza and I hadn't been swimming much that summer, partly because the weather had been pretty lousy—lots of cloudy, gloomy, rainy days. But the other thing was that Kaza always seemed to have to spend more time at home with his mother ever since his dad got killed. It didn't make me mad or even upset or anything like that. I realized that his mother wasn't doing so good. In fact, my mother told me to be patient with the situation and not expect Kaza to spend as much time with me as before, at least not until his mother started feeling better.

At first I thought that Kaza's mom was like, *sick* sick, you know, with the influenza or the gout or consumption or fever or something. But it didn't take me long to realize she was a different kind of sick, the kind when you're feeling blue all the time and can't snap out of it because your mind is weak. To make matters worse, she *looked* like she was sick, I mean physically. Like I said before, she was a very frail and fragile woman, who I'm sure didn't weigh more than 90 pounds soaking wet. I had slowly realized over a few years that Kaza's mom was not well, but I wasn't exactly sure what the problem was.

For as long as I had known Kaza, I knew how much he cared for his mother. I could tell he felt very protective of her, so I didn't want to do anything to interfere with him doing what he could to help her after his father was killed in his own bed in the room right next to Kaza. I kind of instinctively got it, so to speak, when it came to Kaza and his mom. By that, I mean I was able to understand there was a special emotional attachment between the two of them that I needed to respect, never question or interfere with, because Kaza was my best friend and I owed it to him.

"Sure, I-I guess," Kaza said.

As we walked to our usual spot on the Andre, I didn't say anything. For some reason I felt I needed to let Kaza decide if he wanted to talk or not. We walked single file down the narrow path, with me first and neither of us saying anything. I was feeling really nervous, the kind of nervous that makes you feel like you're going to throw up. In fact, I was more nervous than I could ever remember any other time in my whole life. And, that's saying something.

You're likely wondering why I was so nervous, like what's the big deal about going down to the Andre with Kaza? It was something we had done, I bet, hundreds of times.

But this time was different. Really different.

Today was the day I had to tell Kaza we were leaving, that I was moving to the other side of the world the very next day and that, even though we were best friends, we likely wouldn't see each other again—ever—for the rest of our lives. It's hard to describe how I felt. It was this mixture of sadness, anxiety, fear, guilt and excitement. I couldn't imagine not having Kaza as my best friend and hanging out with him every day, lying on our backs looking at clouds, talking about things in the Cave or down at the Andre or sitting in the big tree in front of our place gazing down on the street below without anyone noticing we were there. When I thought about life without Kaza it made me more than just sad and upset. It made me afraid. I don't know why exactly, but maybe it was because just thinking about leaving Kaza made me feel lonely and I've always figured there's nothing worse in life than being lonely. Even though I was going to the New World with my mom and my brother and sisters, the thought of Kaza not being with us made me feel like I would be alone.

The big thing, though, the very worst part, was knowing I was going to hurt Kaza, really bad. Telling him I was leaving would upset him and make him sad. In my whole life Kaza had never hurt me or done anything to make me sad and now I was going to do it to him.

But at the same time, I was excited about what might lie ahead. Going to the New World was going to be this incredible adventure. We would go on the train and eventually on a big boat with hundreds of other people across the ocean and then on a train again. In the New World we would be able to start over. Our family would have enough to eat and there wouldn't be any fighting. Mom said that people would get along and live in peace. When I thought about all that, it made me excited and want to get to the New World as fast as possible.

So I was trapped by a terrible dilemma. I knew I had to go

with my family, knew I had no choice. But I also wanted to go because the thought of a better life for me and my mom and brother and sisters was something that I, even though I was only nine, realized was a good thing.

But to do it, I had to hurt Kaza in a way that made me feel sick to my stomach. The last thing I wanted to do was hurt him, ever, but especially now so soon after his dad got killed and with his mom in such bad shape and knowing how much Kaza loved his mom and worried about her. I knew that when I told Kaza we were leaving it would break his heart and I couldn't stand the thought of it. That's why I hadn't told him long before that we were leaving. I couldn't bear the thought of it. That and because Mom said we had to keep it a secret.

"I brought muh-my marbles," Kaza said as we got close to the Andre. "I dunno, I duh-don't feel like swuh-swimming. Wanna pluh-play muh-marbles?"

"Sure, I guess," I said.

Kaza really got serious about marbles when he was seven. That's because he went to visit his cousin in Saratov who had marbles and showed Kaza how to play ringer, which is when you draw a big circle in the ground and try to knock the marbles out of the circle with your shooter marble. So his mom had Yuri Podnovestov order a bag of marbles from Tiraspol that she and his dad gave them to Kaza for his eighth birthday. It was a really neat bag of marbles, with four different kinds. There was a big fat black one, two shooter marbles—one blue and one red—and 12 target marbles that were clear around the edges but with coloured things—sort of like little leaves or tiny feathers or something—inside them. The big fat black one was the final target marble that you had to try and get out of the ring after you had knocked out all your other smaller target marbles by using your shooter marble.

Kaza was better at marbles than me. It was like he had stronger thumbs or something because he could flick his shooter marbles harder and faster than me. I think maybe I was more accurate with my shooter marble, but the problem was I would need three or four hits on the target marble to get it out of the ring and Kaza could blast them out with just one, or two at the most.

I found a small branch and drew a ring on an open piece of dirt only a couple of metres from the shore of the Andre. We always tried to keep our rings no more than about a half-metre and a bit across. Kaza always gave me my pick of shooter marbles, but he didn't really have to because I always took the blue one because blue is my favourite colour and he always took red, because that was his favourite. Kaza put the big black target marble right in the centre of the ring and then, holding the bag of other, smaller, target marbles above the black one, poured them slowly out and let them roll wherever they wanted in the circle. That way it was fair, because you never knew where the target marbles might go. Sometimes you'd get lucky and maybe two or three of them would roll close to the edge of the ring and make them easier to hit. And other times they'd all stay kind of clumped together in the middle, around the big black one. This time they all stayed pretty much clumped in the middle.

"Darn," I said, because I got first shot. What usually happened when you shot first and the marbles were mostly in the middle was you'd hit one of the target marbles with your first shot but didn't knock it out of the ring and ended up only moving it closer to the edge, which made it easier for your opponent because you took turns shooting. Unless you knocked a target marble out and then you got to shoot again, as kind of a reward for getting the marble out of the ring.

My first shot was a good one. I hit a target marble head on and it rolled, barely, outside the ring. My next one wasn't so good.

Like often happened, I ended up completely missing the one I was shooting at and bumping one of the target marbles out into the open, near the edge for Kaza to shoot at.

Kaza blasted it right out of the ring with one shot.

We played ringer, I bet, for an hour, six games in total. I kept thinking about saying something to Kaza about me going to the New World with my family but just couldn't screw up my nerve. We had all afternoon to hang out so I decided not to say anything and spoil the game of ringer. Besides, as we played, Kaza seemed to feel better, even happy. He laughed and said "yahoo" when I accidently knocked out one of his target marbles, which was one less for him to hit out of the ring before going after the big fat black one at the end of the game. The other thing was Kaza hardly ever stuttered when we played marbles, which I knew meant he wasn't feeling nervous, so I didn't want to ruin that.

After we finished with marbles—Kaza really whipped my butt and won five of six games—we laid back on the grass and looked at clouds. When I think about it now, it was kind of funny how we went from marbles to looking at clouds. Well, maybe funny isn't the right word, more like interesting.

It wasn't as if I said or Kaza said: "Hey, wanna look at clouds?" We just did. It came naturally. We put all the marbles back in the bag and then stretched out on our backs without saying anything.

The July sky was sort of shimmering from the brilliant afternoon sun. It was kind of weird because there were only two clouds in the sky that we could see, off a bit to our left. They were both small cumulus nimbus and looked to be almost the identical size. There was nothing about their shapes that made them particularly interesting. But the fact they were the only two up there in the entire sky, from horizon to horizon, was unusual and so you couldn't help but focus on them.

They moved very slowly together across the sky, from left to right, the small distance between them never changing as they drifted against the panoramic backdrop of a blue infinity. For some reason, we didn't say anything to each other as we silently stared at the two clouds. It was the only time Kaza and me looked at clouds and didn't talk to each other about what we saw.

I don't know for sure what Kaza was thinking at that moment, but to this day deep inside me I believe his mind and mine were one as we looked at those clouds. As I gazed up, with Kaza next to me, I felt as if I was watching the two of us. You might think I'm being all melodramatic by saying that, and maybe I am. But all I know is how I felt at that moment and how that feeling has stayed with me through all these years. There was a serenity to it, and I know Kaza felt it too, because instead of talking we just silently watched those two lonely clouds move together across the sky.

After about 10 minutes, without either of us saying a word, Kaza sat up.

"You know, Anton, having you as muh-my best friend is the best thing thuh-that ever happened to me," Kaza said.

For a moment I didn't know what to say.

So I said, "Me too."

We walked back to town, talking about marbles and, when we saw a hawk soaring far above our heads, wondered what it would be like to fly and how much fun it would be to soar across the sky and look down on people.

"You know, some people can fly. They go in airplanes. That would be neat to fly in an airplane. I hope that someday when I get big I'll be able to fly in an airplane," I said.

"Me too," Kaza said.

We spent the rest of the day in the Cave. It was there that I thought finally I would tell Kaza about my family, about how we were leaving early the next morning on the train from Selz and that I would never see him again, and that I didn't want to hurt him and that I loved him.

But I couldn't do it. I simply couldn't find the courage or the personal fortitude to do it.

So we talked. But mostly he talked and I listened.

"You know, Anton, the best thing is, is you're a guh-good listener. I always feel like I can tell you stuff, be-cuh-cause you're my best friend."

"That's nice of you to say that, Kaza. You can always talk to me and we'll always be best friends," I said.

The moment I said those words I felt guilty and wished I could take them back because it wasn't true, and I knew it. In a day I wouldn't be there ever again for Kaza to talk to. But not only could I not take the words back, but by saying it I seemed to encourage Kaza to talk more openly about his family and how he felt.

"I was asleep, you know, when they came," Kaza said.

"Uh-huh," I said.

"I heard them. I huh-heard them shoot my dad and my muh-mom screaming," Kaza said.

"They hurt my muh-mom too. She had bruises and marks on her face. They made her make sex with them. There was tuh-two of them and they did that to her in the buh-bedroom where they kuh-killed my dad. They did it to muh-my mom when my dad was dead in the bed next to them. Then they went to my sisters' room and did the suh-same. I heard my suh-sisters scream.

"That's why I haven't been able tuh-to do much stuff lately, because my muh-mom isn't the same and I'm afraid to leave her. My sisters are afraid too. It's luh-like they don't want to luh-leave the house because they're afraid something buh-bad might happen and they don't want anyone to see them."

I didn't know what to say, so I just nodded.

"You nuh-know, Anton, I don't un-understand why puh-people are doing things like this. Wuh-why do thuh-they want to hurt people like thuh-that?"

"I dunno, Kaza," was all I could say.

"Why can't they be guh-good like yuh-you are to me? You're my best friend and I don't nuh-know what I wuh-would do if you weren't my buh-best friend. I feel luh-like I have someone to look out for me."

Again I only nodded.

Kaza talked for a long time and mostly I just listened. He talked about how he knew his dad could be mean sometimes, but that he still loved him and that his dad really was a good person who didn't want to be mean but sometimes just couldn't help himself. He said that he was sure that if his dad could, he would apologize to his mom and Kaza and his sisters for the mean things he did before he was killed.

As I listened to Kaza talk, I could tell he regretted that his dad had never apologized, that he had never said he was sorry for what he did and now he was gone and there was no way to mend hurt feelings.

That night as I lay in bed my last night in Fischer-Franzen, I thought about what Kaza said, about how it's important to say you're sorry to people when you hurt them, about how you should never leave hurt feelings unattended because you never know when you'll get another chance to make things better.

Just thinking about it made me feel even more guilty than I already did. I felt like I had betrayed Kaza.

You see, I never did tell Kaza that we were leaving. I didn't have the courage to say the words I knew would hurt him. To this very day I am haunted by the memory of how I abandoned him, how I vanished from his life without having hugged him one last time and telling him that I loved him.

My conscience forced me to get out of bed that night, to go downstairs to the small table near the front door and take a piece of paper and pencil out of the drawer and write a letter in the faint moonlight. This is what I wrote:

To my best friend Kaza,

> *I want you to know that you will always be my best friend. I will never forget you. I'm sorry I didn't tell you. I was afraid to hurt you. I hope someday we will be together again.*

> *Your always best friend,*
> *Anton*

After I wrote the letter, I quietly went out the front door and, in my nightclothes, quickly ran through the darkness and across and down the street to Kaza's house on the "other side." I found a small rock and put it on top of my letter to Kaza. I left it on his front step and ran back to our house.

Before dawn, we left for the New World.

EPILOGUE

THE OLD MAN was almost comically overdressed for what was a particularly mild late November day in Saskatchewan. As the automatic exit doors swung open at the Saskatoon airport, he stepped out into warm, early afternoon sunshine with his parka zipped tight and fur-lined hood pulled over his head, as if he was heading out into a frigid mid-winter Canadian blizzard. He handed his one small, old and beaten black suitcase to the cab driver at the curb, who put it into the open trunk.

Instead of getting into the vacant back seat, the old man opened the passenger side door and sat down next to the driver, who glanced at his ride with curiosity as he climbed behind the wheel. "Where you headed?" he asked.

The old man reached awkwardly into his parka pocket, fumbling before taking out a crumpled piece of paper. He unfolded it and, without a word, handed it to the driver. It read 2225 Preston Street, written in pencil.

They travelled in silence for the time it took to drive from the airport to the address on the piece of paper. The cab driver wondered about his passenger but knew better than to make conversation with the stranger. The one thing he had learned in his 19 years driving cab in Saskatoon was to read the mood of your fare, which meant speaking only when spoken to by the passenger. The old man who sat next to him, parka still tightly done up and hood still over his head, was obviously not the talkative type.

Bundled up the way he was, it was difficult for the cab driver to get a good look at the old guy. Other than a quick glance at his face, slightly grizzled from what looked to be at least two days without shaving, he didn't get a chance to survey the man closely. But judging by the creased and arthritic fingers that had handed him the paper with the address, he guessed the guy had to be well into his eighties. His dark complexion made him think the old man must be from some warm climate, which explained the heavy parka and hood. No doubt, the driver figured, the old guy thought coming to Saskatchewan, Canada in November meant he'd be visiting a deep freeze.

He assumed the old man had arrived on the flight from Denver. The Saskatoon airport wasn't that busy, only 11 arrivals a day, and the Denver flight was the only one that arrived at that time of the afternoon. But the cab driver didn't for a moment think the old man was from Denver. More likely he'd just connected there to catch the flight to Saskatoon. More likely, the cabbie thought, South America or maybe somewhere in Europe—possibly southern Europe—was where the old man had started his journey.

The unseasonably warm afternoon sun radiated through the windows, making it quite warm inside the cab. But the old man didn't so much as attempt to unzip his parka or lower his hood as they drove to the address.

He just sat motionless, staring directly ahead.

The address was for the Extendicare Preston Nursing Home on the south side of Saskatoon. It was a one-storey building with two wings that formed a u and backed onto a small neighbourhood park. A block away, along Preston Street, was a suburban shopping centre.

The driver pulled his car into the small semi-circular driveway, stopping so that the old man would only have a few steps to the front entrance of the nursing home. He couldn't help but feel kind of sad for the old guy, who he assumed had all his worldly belongings in his suitcase and was about to check into the nursing home.

Must have family in these parts, the driver thought to himself.

"That'll be $12.35," he said, nodding at the digital fare metre attached to the front dash.

Feet against the floorboards, the old man stiffly pushed himself back in the seat, lifting his hips so he could reach under the bulky parka to pull out a wallet from his back pocket. It was the oldest leather wallet the driver had ever seen, dark brown, with what looked to be leather stitching around its worn edges. The man opened it and, touching his thumb to his lips, slowly pulled out a wad of bills. The driver didn't recognize the currency, but after a moment the man retrieved a $20 Canadian bill and handed it to him.

The driver made change and handed it to his passenger. Looking at the money that the driver had given him, the man took the 65 cents in coins and handed them back. It was a tip. For a moment their eyes met and the driver thought he detected the slightest smile on the old man's face. The driver smiled back.

He quickly got out of the car to retrieve the suitcase from the trunk and carried it around to the old man, who was slowly getting out of the passenger side.

"Good luck, sir," the driver said, handing him the suitcase.

The old man nodded, turned and shuffled slowly towards the doorway of the nursing home.

Inside the two sets of glass doors at the front entrance was a large board. It had the names of the residents in alphabetical order, their room numbers listed alongside. The man stood in front of it and scanned the list slowly, his head moving up and down.

After a moment, he pulled back the hood on his parka to reveal a full head of closely cropped white hair. Though slightly stooped with age, he was still more than six feet tall. He had the dark skin of someone from the Middle East or southern Europe. Still standing in front of the roster of residents, he finally unzipped his parka and slipped it off, bunching it under his arm. The main hallway off the lobby went left and right. On the wall directly ahead of him were two small signs: one with an arrow that indicated rooms 20-40 were to the left; the other, with numbers 41-60, pointed right. The old man took the hallway to the right.

He walked slowly, deliberately, down the hall until he came to the room with the number 48 above the door. On the wall next to the doorframe was a small, silver-coloured plaque with two names. The first read CHARLES RICHARDSON; the second, TONY SCHERGEVITCH.

The old man stared at the name plaque for almost a minute. Then he stepped into the room's tiny entry, an equally small bathroom visible immediately to the right. The door was slightly open and he could see the bathroom was empty. He set down his suitcase, put his parka on top of it and stepped into the room. The far bed next to the window was empty. In the first bed, its frame slightly curved into an s, was the figure of a small, frail man, asleep under a light cover. On the wall behind him was a cluttered cork board of pictures and drawings. There were photos of young children, teenagers and adults; pictures of what looked to be families together, mothers and fathers with their kids, children with old people who looked like grandparents.

On the bedside table was a photo of an elderly man and woman, maybe in their late 70s, obviously posed by a professional. It was in a cardboard frame with the words PORTRAITS BY SEARS on the edge. The woman was sitting; she wore a dress with a red and blue corsage just below the left shoulder. The elderly man, his thin hair neatly combed, stood next to her in a dark blue suit, smiling, his tie slightly askew and his hand resting on her shoulder. The backdrop behind them read 50TH ANNIVERSARY. Next to the photo was a card, sitting upright and propped open. Inside were childishly handwritten words: "Happy Birthday, Grampa."

As he looked at these tiny shreds of a life on display, the visitor yearned to know more about the sleeping man. He wondered what he had done, where had he worked, who his wife was, if she was she still alive, how many children they had, where they lived. He wondered if Anton ever thought about him. If he even remembered his boyhood friend. How had their experiences together as young boys—the horror of those days—affected him?

Standing silently next to the bed, the old man looked down at the sleeping face of his friend. His head was tilted back, his neck slightly arched, his mouth open, breathing short, laboured gasps.

The old man reached for the chair against the wall and slid it over next to the bed. He sat down. He lifted his arm and placed the palm of his hand on the back of the sleeping man's where it rested on top of the blanket. For a moment he gently stroked the sleeping man's hand.

The old man leaned over slightly so he was close to the sleeping man's ear. He spoke in English, heavily accented.

"Anton, Anton, my dear friend, Anton" he said softly, almost whispering into his ear. "It's me. Kaza. Do you remember me after all these years? Kaza, from when we were young boys in the Old Country, in Fischer-Franzen? I can't believe I have fuh-found you. I've come to tell you that I have never forgotten you, that you have always been my best friend. That I love you."

Anton did not stir. He continued to breathe in gasps of air, the right side of his face dropped by paralysis. Anton's breathing was irregular, sometimes coming in a series of rapid gulps of air, other times many seconds passed before he took another breath.

"I have never forgotten you, Anton. All these years, every day I have thought of you and wuh-wondered; wondered what happened in your life, wondered if you were still alive, wondered if you remembered me, if you ever thought of me.

"All these years, a lifetime, and now I have finally found you, Anton. I have never forgotten you. Every time I luh-look to the sky and see clouds, I think of you and those times we spent together when we were young. I would look at he clouds and I would see you, wonder about you, and pray to God that someday I might see you again. And now here I am, with yuh-you again.

"There is so much to tell you, about my life, what happened to my family. We stayed in Fischer-Franzen for three years after you left then moved to Istanbul in Turkey to be with my mother's family. My mother was very ill and we nuh-needed her family to help care for her. But she never recovered. When I was 15 she took her own life. My sisters were already married and I was sent to live with my uncle and aunt in the city of Ephesus.

"I became a tradesman, a stonecutter and worked in the trade with my uncle for 12 years. I muh-married my wife Cahide and we had six children, four boys and two girls. One of my sons died from the influenza when he was nine. We eventually left Turkey and settled in Palermo, in Sicily, where I worked for a man I met through my uncle, who had a construction company.

"I still live in Palermo. But my wife Cahide—bless her soul—died five years ago and ever since I have wuh-wanted to find you, to see if I could see you one last time before my life ends. And now I have."

Kaza paused to see if Anton would say anything, nod, or open his eyes to acknowledge his presence. But the old man in the bed did not stir, his eyes didn't open. The only sound was his uneven gasps. Kaza gently squeezed Anton's hand.

"There is so much we could talk about, so much I want to tell you and so much I would love to hear from you about your life.

"All my life, Anton, I have thought about you often, wondered if you had grown up and married and had children like me. When Cahide died, I decided that I nuh-needed to find out if you were still alive and, God willing, be with you again one more time before I died. I always remembered the place in Canada where you had gone. I asked my mother if she knew and she spoke with Yuri, the man in the store at Fischer-Franzen, and he told her you had come to Saskatchewan in Canada. I never forgot that.

"Two years ago I wrote a letter to the Canadian embassy in Rome and told them our stuh-story, how we had been friends as young boys in the Kutschurgan and lost touch many, many years ago when your family came to Canada. I said that I hoped to find you someday and visit you again. A man from the embassy wrote back and said that I should contact the government of the province Saskatchewan. He gave me an address for the vital statistics agency and said they should be able to help me. I sent a luh-letter, saying that I was trying to locate Anton Schergevitch, who I believed had come to Canada and this province more than 75 years ago. They said their records showed more than 50 people with the name Schergevitch, including one Anton. They said you lived here in this city of Saskatoon."

For a moment, Anton's eyelids fluttered, like he was trying to open his eyes. Kaza waited, but Anton didn't wake, his eyes remained closed as if he was sleeping. But he seemed agitated, his head swaying from left to right on the pillow, his breathing growing louder and more pronounced.

"I know this sounds silly but I wanted to find you, Anton, because I needed to tell you how I fuh-feel. I needed to find you, to talk to you or else my life would be incomplete; unless I saw you one more time, touched you, my life would have been in vain.

"All my life I have remembered what it was like being your friend, how we played together, how we would lie on our backs and luh-look at clouds, how we talked about how we felt, how you protected me. No one since those days has buh-been a friend like that for me, Anton. The time we spent together has stayed with me, in my memory, for all these years."

Having leaned forward in his chair to speak quietly to his friend, Kaza had not noticed the young woman in the doorway. He became aware of her only when he heard her clear her throat softly to get his attention.

Kaza looked over his shoulder at her.

"Hello," she said.

Kaza got up from his chair and smiled. "Hello," he said. "I am an old friend of Anton's"

The young woman was in her late 20s, perhaps 30 years old. She had dark, reddish brown hair, a round face and wore glasses. She smiled at Kaza, and he felt immediately at ease.

"My name is Theresa. I am Tony's daughter. I don't think we've met before."

"No, we haven't," the old man said. "I have not seen Anton for many years."

Theresa was puzzled by the stranger. He looked out of place, dressed in a heavy woolen shirt and pants with thick leather suspenders. She couldn't imagine a man his age who was a friend of her father's whom she had not met before. But she felt comfortable with him; she could sense the bond between him and her father.

"Do you live in Saskatoon?" she asked.

"No. I have never been here before. This is my first trip to Canada," he said.

At that moment, Theresa intinctively connected the stranger to her father's youth in Russia. "When was the last time you saw Dad?" she asked.

Kaza paused and glanced down at Anton. "It's been 81 years."

"Did you know Dad in Russia?"

"Yes," he said. "We were friends as young boys in Fischer-Franzen."

Theresa's eyes grew wide. "Are you Kaza?" she exclaimed.

Kaza felt faint; the feelings for his best friend, carried with him throughout an entire lifetime, validated in that single moment. To hear Anton's daughter say his name, to know that Anton had not forgotten him, that he had told his children about him, brought an incredible kind of emotional fulfillment. Their bond of friendship from childhood had survived the many decades of their separate lives.

Kaza nodded. "Yes."

"Oh, my God," Theresa said. "My God. You're still alive. You didn't forget my father. Where did you travel from?"

"I live in Palermo, Sicily. I travelled for two days to be here."

Theresa had drawn closer as they talked. Now she reached out to the old man and hugged him. "Thank you, thank you. You have no idea what this means to Dad. He always talked about you. Growing up, we often heard stories about his friend Kaza. He said he wanted to teach us what he had learned from you, to be like you: kind, understanding and loyal."

She pulled up a chair next to her father's bed and they sat down together.

"I need to know about your father. About his life, about him, about his family. I have wondered all these years. What can you tell me, please?"

Theresa didn't know where to begin or what to say. She felt a tremendous obligation to fill the void of their separate lives. But somehow she understood that what Kaza needed to know, more than anything, was what kind of a person her father had grown up to become.

"Dad spent his life as a farmer. We had a farm in the south of the province, near the town of Mankota. He worked hard. I remember as a young girl watching Dad work in the field for hours, baling hay in the hot sun. The image of him that has always stayed with me is at the supper table. Dad would come in, hands dirty, clothes soiled, hair matted in sweat from hours working hard in the sun. He'd wash up at the kitchen sink, sit down with us and say being at the dinner table was the best part of his day. I never, ever remember Dad complaining. He always felt fortunate for his life, no matter what," she said. "He's not an educated man. Because of the Depression, he didn't manage to go to high school but he is still a wise man. My dad was older, 36, when he and Mom were married. I have two brothers and a sister. Mom lives just a few blocks down the street, in the house where my parents retired after we sold the farm. I'm a nurse and live in a small city about 120 miles from here. I come up on the weekends to visit."

Kaza nodded and smiled.

"My dad is kind and gentle. He has a great sense of humour and likes to play practical jokes on people. He has a soft heart and he cries easily when he tells stories that are sad.

"You know, he had a favourite story that he would tell us kids often, even though it made him cry. It was about you and him from when he was a young boy in Russia. He told it to us to teach us about how to treat others.

"He said you used to like to lie on your backs and look at clouds together. That he always remembered those moments with you, the sky and how you would each talk about your thoughts, and how looking at clouds made him feel calm. Kind of at peace, I guess you could say.

347

"One time in particular, he said you were looking at clouds. It was the day after some bullies had been mean to you and beat you. Dad said it was his fault because he had been with you and, even though you were best friends, he didn't stick up for you when the older boys were being mean. Instead he ran away and left you and they hurt you.

"I know Dad always felt guilty about that. But he said the next day, when you were with him looking at clouds, he told you he was sorry and you forgave him. He said that moment taught him the meaning of loyalty and forgiveness, and that us kids should live our lives knowing the importance of those two words. He must have told us that story a hundred times and he'd always finish it with tears in his eyes.

"You know what it's like when you're young—I used to sometimes think 'Enough already, Dad. We know that story, we've heard it a million times and don't need to hear it again.' But for some reason every time I heard it I was glad he'd told me.

"Now I know why."

Theresa looked at Kaza, who had been listening, head bowed.

He raised his head, smiling at her through the tears in his eyes.

"I'll leave you and Dad alone for a few minutes," she said.

KAZA SAT SILENTLY next to the bed for a few moments and looked down at his best friend, listening to his irregular breath, the intermittent gasps for air. He thought about the story, about what Theresa had told him of how Anton had taught his children the meaning of friendship, the importance of loyalty and forgiveness. It felt like the decades he and Anton spent apart had been erased, that their friendship had endured and was as strong today as it was the last time he had seen his friend in 1925.

From somewhere down the hall Kaza noticed an odd, faint sound, a kind of squeaking and rattling. It would stop, then start up again, its tempo even, slowly growing clearer. After a moment, he got up from beside the bed, walked to the doorway and peered down the hallway. A nurse was pushing a small cart. The soles of her white shoes squeaked on the tile floor and the small wheels on the cart, which carried small plastic glasses filled with a pink liquid, rattled slightly as she steered it from one doorway to the next. At each door, she would look at a clipboard, pick up two glasses from the cart and disappear into the room. When she re-emerged, she picked up the clipboard from the cart, took a pen from the side pocket of her blue smock, and marked something on the clipboard.

Kaza returned to Anton's bedside, sat back down and listened to the sound of the nurse doing her rounds grow louder until she stopped outside Anton's room. After a moment, she came in, carrying a small glass and a tiny white envelope. The short, plump woman looked at Kaza and smiled.

"How are you?" she asked him.

"Fine, thank you," he replied.

"You're visiting Tony? Are you a relative?"

"No, just a fruh-friend," Kaza answered.

"That's nice. Don't see many friends coming to visit folks here. Usually just family, and unfortunately for some of our residents, that's not very often. Tony's lucky, though. Either his wife or kids or grandkids come pretty much every day. But since his strokes, I don't think he really recognizes anyone. Do you live in Saskatoon?"

"No," Kaza said.

"Figured not, because don't think I've seen you here before."

Kaza didn't say anything and just nodded slightly. Anton's face had become flushed and there were tiny beads of sweat on his brow. His head kept rolling to the left and right and, even though his eyes remained closed, he seemed upset.

The nurse watched the stranger reach down and caress his

friend's forehead with his palm, as if to calm him. It was a touching gesture, a moment of tenderness between two very old friends.

"Don't worry about Tony. He gets this way every night about this time. This will help him sleep."

She shook three pills from the small envelope into her hand and, with the small plastic glass, walked to the other side of the bed. Reaching behind Anton, she used the crook of her arm to lift and tilt his head forward, then tipped the pills into his mouth.

Anton struggled slightly as she put the glass to his lips.

"Here Tony, time for your drink," she said, pouring the pink liquid past his lips, some of it dribbling down his chin as the old man swallowed in two gulps. "There you go. Sleep tight, honey."

As she walked out of the room, shoes squeaking, the woman looked at Kaza. "You have a good night too, my dear. And thanks for stopping by to visit. I'm sure Tony appreciates you being here."

Kaza smiled and nodded. Alone again with Anton, he sat still, holding his friend's hand.

"Anton, I have something with me, something I have kept close to me all these years, something I have always treasured. I want to show it to you."

Kaza reached into his shirt pocket and pulled out an envelope. He opened it and took out a carefully folded piece of paper. The page was yellowed, the letters faded—in some cases barely visible. But it was still possible to make out the words. Kaza read it aloud.

"'Best friends always,'" he read. "Best friends always."

Anton's hand moved under his. He watched as Anton ever-so-slightly opened his eyes, his breathing less laboured, more even. Slowly, Anton slid his hand from beneath Kaza's. He moved his head and, opening his eyes, looked at his best friend, turned his palm over and gently squeezed Kaza's hand. He tried to speak, but the words would not come.

Best friends to the end.